THE LOOKING-GLASS

BOOKS BY
William March

Company K

Come In at the Door

The Little Wife, and Other Stories

The Tallons

Some Like Them Short

The Looking-Glass

THE
LOOKING-
GLASS

William March

The University of Alabama Press • Tuscaloosa

THE LIBRARY
OF ALABAMA
CLASSICS

The University of Alabama Press
Tuscaloosa, Alabama 35487-0380
uapress.ua.edu

Originally published 1943 by Little, Brown and Company

Manufactured in the United States of America
Cover design: Emma Sovich

∞

The paper on which this book is printed meets the minimum requirements
of American National Standard for Information Sciences—Permanence of Paper
for Printed Library Materials, ANSI Z39.48-1984.

Library of Congress Cataloging-in-Publication Data

March, William, 1893–1954.
The Looking-Glass / William March.
pages cm — (Library of Alabama Classics series)
ISBN 978-0-8173-5812-9 (pbk. : alk. paper) — ISBN 978-0-8173-8836-2 (e-book)
1. City and town life—Fiction. 2. Alabama—Social life and customs—Fiction. I. Title.
PS3505.A53157L66 2014
813'.52—dc23
2014024836

To My Sister

MARGARET CAMPBELL JONES

THE LOOKING-GLASS

‖‖P ROFESSOR ST. JOSEPH, Principal of the Reedyville High School, once said that the milky and yet musty odor which seemed to issue like invisible mist from the walls of the Boutwell house reminded him of nothing so much as the smell of a freshly cut coconut. His comparison was more fanciful than accurate perhaps, but that concerned him little, for he was the town's acknowledged wit, and wits are less interested in the average realities of others than in the deeper, symbolic realities of their own.

It was the kind of remark which, when said against the background of a smile or punctuated by a lifting of the brows, could be made to take on a spurious depth, to achieve a significance beyond the actual meaning of the words themselves, and its implications were so vague, so ambiguous, you could not be sure whether it was meant as a criticism or as a compliment.

Minnie McInnis McMinn, who admired Professor St. Joseph a great deal, accepted the remark at its more significant value, and she recorded it that same day in one of her ledgers, for possible inclusion in a novel about Reedyville which she planned someday to write. Thereafter, when her duties as Society Editress for the *Courier* took her in the direction of the Boutwell house, she would stand outside in the road for a time, her eyes closed so expectantly, her manner so concentrated and patient, that she resembled, at such moments, a rustic maiden awaiting fertilization by a woodland god. But almost at once the spell would be broken, and she would throw her head back even farther, and laugh convulsively, her mouth opened so widely that the slippery, involved geography of her vibrating throat was visible.

"What St. Joseph says is really true," she would murmur. "It's

actually like crushed coconuts — shells and all!" Then, since she
was the adapter of the ideas of others, the expander of the simple
situation, she would have a picture of the Boutwell family sitting
in a semicircle on the floor, smashing one coconut after the other
and eating the meat with famished cries; and at such times she'd
make a mental note to repeat her variation on St. Joseph's original
theme to Robert Porterfield, who was her idea of a truly handsome
man, or to Lucinda Palmiller, her closest friend.

But it is doubtful if Mrs. McMinn could have sustained her
variant phantasy had she passed the Boutwell place on a certain hot
afternoon of September 1916. On that day, the smells which came
through the open front door, and floated across the red, clay road,
were unmistakably those of pork chops, turnip greens and fried
potatoes, with the added aroma of coffee which had boiled out of the
pot and sizzled into brown stains on top of the stove; and as far as
the activities of the Boutwells themselves were concerned, they
were certainly not cracking nuts, for Ada, the mistress of the
household, was standing on her front porch, staring with undivided
attention down the red, dusty road that led to the heart of Reedyville,
and her youngest child, Dover, the only one of her children who now
lived at home, was just behind her in the doorway, his own attitude
anxious and waiting.

The reason for Ada's anxiety was quite understandable, for it was
already late afternoon, and her husband had not returned from
his usual Saturday afternoon's visit to town, and she did not know
what had happened to him. According to custom, he should have
had his supper an hour ago, and he should, at this moment,
if precedent were any guide at all, be stretched out on a pallet
on the back porch, sleeping off the effects of his unimaginative
pleasures.

After a while she sighed and walked to the front gate, spreading
the fingers of her left hand against her cheek, and allowing her chin,
as hard and as knobby as an unripe sandpear, to fit precisely into her
receiving palm. Almost at once she drew her other arm tightly
against her flank, and her hand hung down limply, as if broken at
the wrist. It was a characteristic pose, and Dover knew then that his
mother was really worried. He came onto the porch and sat on the
top step, coughed to let her know that he was there behind her,

and drew up his bony, immature legs so high that his chin rested precisely in the heart-shaped crevice of his knees, while his head, like a balanced oval, swayed mildly from left to right. Then, after a moment, his rocking head came to rest at the instant it was canted a little to the left, as if the mechanism had run down unexpectedly; and without straightening his neck again, he stared upward, seemingly at nothing at all, in an attitude of baffled and waiting patience.

He had his own, individual problem to deal with, and it seemed, at that moment, insoluble to him. Compared with it, his father's tardiness was trivial and rather academic. High school had opened the week before and Dover, through a misunderstanding, had applied for admission to Professor St. Joseph's class in English Construction — having got the strange idea in his head that the course had something to do with cabinet making — and what was even more depressing, from his viewpoint, he had been accepted. It was a special class, intended for talented pupils interested in the arts, a class which St. Joseph had personally organized, and which he taught himself, not because it was one of the requirements of his contract, but because he liked doing it.

The day before, St. Joseph had announced the subject for the first theme of the new class, requesting that it be handed in promptly the following Monday morning. This, of itself, had not seemed too difficult of accomplishment, even for Dover; but St. Joseph, who rarely said what he meant in simple language, had complicated the issue by delivering a lecture just prior to announcing the subject, a lecture which discussed not only writing as an accomplishment in its own right, but one which endeavored to show its affinities with painting, a related form of expression, as well.

And so it happened, as Dover sat in bafflement on the front steps of his home, that he could not be sure whether St. Joseph wanted a literary composition, a drawing, or a combination of some of the elements of both. He lowered his eyes from his lost contemplation of the horizon and examined the pattern in the flat-sawn, pine board below him, shook his head, and picked absently at his callused feet with that rapt, other-worldly concentration of adolescent boys.

Ada, without turning her eyes from the road, spoke over her shoulder, her manner suddenly brisk and demanding: "Haven't you got any idea at all where your father went to after he left the boys

6] [THE LOOKING – GLASS

at Moore's Livery Stable? Didn't he say where he was going to from there?"

Dover bent over and outlined with his index finger the irregular knothole in the step below where he sat. When he had circled it twice with complete concentration, he looked up and said: "No, ma'am. I haven't got any idea where he went to." It was a lie, and he knew quite well that it was, but he saw no point in adding to his mother's burdens; but while he was looking so innocently into her worried face, he was thinking: "Papa's over at Mattress May's house, that's where he's at; but you won't get no information out of me, one way or the other."

Her husband's fidelity was one of the illusions which sustained Ada's faith. When discussing his shortcomings with Mrs. Paul Kenworthy, Professor St. Joseph or the other people of Reedyville for whom she did sewing, or occasional cleaning, she would empha- size this point with insinuating vigor when rebutting their sympathy at the harshness of her lot. Once, while talking with Robert Porter- field, she had said: "Oh, yes, Mr. Robert. I admit it: Wesley Boutwell has got his faults, just like all other men, and I'd be the last person in the world to maintain different." She turned back to her polish- ing and added pointedly: "But at least there's one bad habit Wesley never fell into, and it's this: He don't pinch the backside of every pretty woman that comes along, least of all, other men's wives!"

It happened that Robert Porterfield saw his mistress, Mrs. Palmiller, that same evening, and for her amusement he repeated the conversa- tion. "But, my dear!" said Cindy in a mocking voice. "You've never pinched *my* backside. Not once. Not once in all the time I've known you."

Robert turned slowly and outlined her face with his finger tips, gazing at her with grave, adoring eyes. "Mrs. Boutwell had reference to attractive women — remember?" he said gently.

Cindy turned on her back and stretched her arms high above her head. She pursed out her lips thoughtfully, and when she spoke, her voice was startlingly like the shaky, mincing voice of old Miss Eulalie Newbride, Robert's great-aunt, a woman noted equally for the dullness of her figures of speech and for her dislike of all her kin. "Oh, I see," she said primly. "But that's a horse of a different color!" and added: "Then why didn't you come out aboveboard and say so, instead of beating around the bush, like some damned Porterfield!"

She turned again to her lover, just in time to see his arm sliding innocently under the sheet which covered them. She made an excited, intaken sound and rolled quickly to the far side of the bed, raising her knees and pressing the target of his attack firmly against the flowered wallpaper. "Don't you dare!" she said. "Don't you dare pinch me, Robert Porterfield!"

Robert gazed at her lazily and then, bending over her, he sought some vulnerable spot between her body and the wall. "We Porterfields always try to please, Madam," he said gravely. "We do our best in every social situation." But Cindy shifted her position from side to side with such skill, such vigor, that she managed to keep always just beyond the nip of his menacing thumb and forefinger. "Behave yourself!" she said laughingly. "I'm serious! I really am, this time! And if you dare to pinch me, I'll, I'll—"

"You'll do what, madam?"

"I'll call my husband, that's what!" said Cindy. "I'll scream for my husband just as loud as I can, and when he comes I'll say, 'Robert Porterfield is no gentleman. He always tries to pinch me when we are in bed together, and I want you to tell him to stop this instant!'"

There was a moment's silence in which they both had a clear picture of Mr. Palmiller's entry into the room at that precise moment; then, locked in each other's arms, they laughed until they were exhausted.

But if Cindy Palmiller and her lover got so much innocent enjoyment from her remark, Ada Boutwell had her own peculiar satisfaction in the incident. "Who do you think had the nerve to criticize Wesley the other day?" she asked St. Joseph. Then, not waiting for his answer, she went on: "Why, it wasn't anybody but handsome little Mr. Robert Porterfield! I felt like saying, 'Well, look who's talking! Look who has the nerve to throw stones now!'"

"What did you say in reply, Mrs. Boutwell?"

"First, I looked him right straight in the eye, and so hard that he blushed and turned his head away. Then I said, 'I beg your pardon, Mr. Robert, but Wesley, while having his faults like other men, and not taking care of his family as good as he ought to at times, ain't so bad when you stop and compare him with others I could name. My husband ain't an *adulterer*,' I said, and I said it so pointed that he couldn't help knowing it was *him* I was referring to. 'Wesley has his mind on something else than women,' I said, 'least of all other men's wives, and the mothers of children!' Oh, I shamed him plenty, Professor! I really did, for a fact!"

St. Joseph raised his eyebrows so high above his nose glasses, and furrowed his brow so deeply, that a thin white line, like a long scar, ran across his forehead at the hair line. He turned away so that she could not see his amusement, thinking: "Perhaps she's right, after all. At least I've never heard that Mattress May, or her young lady visitors, were either wives or mothers so far."

But if the whole of Reedyville knew of her husband's attachment to Miss Violet May Wynn and the girls of her establishment, Ada apparently did not. Certainly no such possibility for his lateness occurred to her as she stood looking down the road on the hot September afternoon with which we are presently concerned. Finally she left her position by the gate and came to the steps where Dover was sitting.

She was a tall, strongly built woman with prominent cheekbones, and narrow gray eyes which curved downward at their outer edges. She was approaching her fiftieth year, and her neck and shoulders had already taken on the emaciated, and yet bloated, appearance of old farm animals. Her chest was flat, her arms and legs strong and wiry; but her inappropriate and rounded belly pushed forward in a caricature of desirable plumpness. During the thirty-odd years of her marriage, she had given birth to twelve children, and it almost seemed as if her womb, obeying some natural law of economics, had, in the end, taken on the shape of perpetual pregnancy.

Dover moved a little, making a place for his mother beside him; and he watched, with interest, as she eased herself onto the steps, steadying her protruding belly with her cupped hands, as if it were something fragile and precious which could easily roll off her lap and be broken.

"I'll tell you one thing," said Ada, "and no two ways about it: If your papa's not home in a half hour, I'm going down the road myself and look for him." Dover started to speak, but changed his mind. Instead, he drew up his knees once more and stared stolidly at the western sky. The sun hung balanced now above the horizon, fierce and bloated and seemingly without movement against a sky in which there was neither a cloud to hide it, nor a mist to veil its burning magnificence.

The Boutwells had first appeared on the streets of Reedyville riding in a warped farm wagon drawn by a white mule with thin, flattened ears and a mouth which was at once resigned and sardonic. Significantly enough, it was Ada Boutwell who discovered the old abandoned house at the edge of town and took it for her own purposes. Later on when they were established in their new home, and Ada had come to an arrangement with Mrs. Kenworthy regarding the rent, the family pitched in and built a walk with pieces of broken bricks from the front gate to the doorstep; and they laid out elaborate flower beds, bordered with empty beer bottles driven into the earth, in the patterns of stars, triangles and lancet arches.

While Wesley Boutwell had not welcomed work in those days, at least he had not denied it with the sweeping repudiation of his later years. Even then however he had felt that there was but one career worthy of a man's serious attention, and that career, as he himself phrased it, was "soldiering for the Government." But it would be a mistake to think of him as either a cruel or a bloodthirsty man. On the contrary, he was gentle and kindly, and, paradoxically enough, more quickly moved to compassion by the suffering of others than the average, or non-warlike, person. It was his great regret that his life was to be lived out not in a period of excitement and clanging military glory, but in one of the dull intervals of peace between.

As if to compensate him for the absence of the dramatic from his life, he had many exciting daydreams in which he played an outstanding role; dreams in which he rescued the flag — the flag of the Confederacy, strangely enough — from the hands of a dying comrade, and planted it atop a breastwork so green, so unscarred, that it resembled the Wentworth lawn; or those in which he rallied his men for a desperate charge, and led them to a victory so final that the whole world resounded with his praise.

His emotions, to put the matter in its simplest terms, were those of the twelve-year-old boy. His mind, too, was the eager mind of the adolescent, and this gave his character a boyish and wistful appeal. It was perhaps fortunate that the quality of his mind and the quality of his emotions were so' consonant, since it is from among those whose emotions are juvenile and whose minds are excellent that the dangerous and outstanding people of a generation are recruited.

"Sometimes I wish I'd never married at all," he would say to his wife in a protesting voice. "Sometimes I wish I'd gone to South America, like I said I was going to do before I met up with you."

"Well," said Ada patiently, "you did marry me. And what's more, you've got a houseful of children to prove it. Now you go on to town, and you ask for a job at every place you pass."

And so it happened that Wesley stopped at the Wentworth Compress and Warehouse Company one morning and asked for work. The superintendent looked at him with much professional admiration, thinking that he had never seen a more magnificent physical specimen in his life, not even among the Negroes who had worked for him in the past.

In those days, Wesley's face was dark from the rays of the sun, with high color beneath the skin, and his eyes were dark brown, innocent, and melting. He had a habit when embarrassed of tilting his head to one side, gazing up sideways at the person to whom he was speaking, and laughing nervously — a short, rather high-pitched laugh which was not unlike the flirtatious giggle of a schoolgirl. At such times he showed his large, widely spaced teeth which were strong, solid-looking, and of the grayish cast of cheap crockery.

The superintendent said at once: "We've been looking for a strong hand like you to truck country bales from the receiving shed to the compress. Go see the foreman, and tell him I said put you to work." Wesley stared at him in dismay, a pleading look in his soft, melting eyes, but already the superintendent had dismissed him, had turned back to his work. Being a man lacking in all except military imagination, and seeing no way to extricate himself from the situation, Wesley had stuck to his work for the next few years, hoping that time and chance would somehow combine to solve his problem for him.

Later on he struck up a friendship with the boy who carried drinking water to the truckers and to the workers in the sheds. This child, when Wesley first noticed him, appeared so small and frail that it seemed impossible for him to carry the heavy buckets of water which his work required of him. He wore an old cloth cap whose sides shamelessly advertised a medicine which was guaranteed, if taken faithfully, to lift womankind out of the shadow which the moon had left upon her as a curse. The visor of the cap was of a transparent, verdant substance which resembled the eyeshades once worn by clerks and bookkeepers. Through it, the diffused rays of the sun cast a green, subaqueous shade on the boy's pale face. His paleness was a thing that often puzzled Wesley. Being exposed to the sun all day, a face should have taken on tones of color, as the skins of others did, but this did not seem to happen where the boy was concerned. It was almost as if the skin itself, so long neglected and undernourished, now lacked the power to respond to the stimulus of light, in the same manner that those close to starvation can no longer retain food.

One day Wesley called the child to him and took a long drink of the tepid water. The boy watched with a suspicious, unconvinced look on his face while Wesley's heavy neck thickened even more with the tilting of his head, and his Adam's apple rose and fell in his throat like some lethargic but precise valve; but he watched cautiously and kept beyond reach of the man's arm.

When he had finished, Wesley smacked his lips and threw what remained in the dipper onto the blocks of the runway with a spread, flat sound, like a slap from a fat hand. He wiped his mouth on his denim sleeve and put the dipper back into the bucket noisily. He raised his arms, stretching himself widely; but the boy, at his first movement, took a step backwards and stood like some half-tamed animal who was prepared to leap away, at the first sign of danger, and disappear with incredible speed through one of the dark recesses of the receiving shed.

Then the boy lifted his bucket again, straining upward, under its weight, from the worn soles of his cheap shoes, in an effort which seemed to engage his whole body, to concern itself with every ounce of his strength. He was gradually moving away, his eyes still fixed without trust on the solid back of the man he had just served, when Wesley turned and smiled at him, showing his big, porcelain teeth, and said: —

"I was thinking when you came up that I've been seeing you

around every day for a week, and I still don't know what your name is."

The boy raised his eyes and looked for an instant into the face of the man before him. This was a thing he rarely did. As a rule, he discreetly watched people's hands and feet. Sometimes, when he thought himself unobserved, he would let his eyes lift as high as a man's neck, and fix them there; then, as if turning a forbidden page quickly, his glance would innocently jump upward, with only the quickest look at the face, to a point several inches above the other person's head. But this time, Wesley's brown, melting eyes, which were so free of trickery, so lacking in anger or guile, held his own steadily, and to his astonishment, he smiled too. Then, as if alarmed at his boldness, his face sobered and he said: "My name's Ira Graley." The sound of his voice seemed to startle him, for he turned and looked behind him, to see who had spoken for him, with his voice.

If Wesley was conscious of the boy's odd conduct, he gave no sign of it. His smile was even more disarming this time, and he continued: "My name's Wesley Boutwell. I bet, though, you knew that already. A quick, smart boy like you."

The boy said: "Yes, sir. Yes, sir, I knowed it already." He seemed disturbed and uncertain, as if he wanted to move away and yet found himself unable to do so. From the sheds, one of the workmen came to the runway and called, "Water boy! Water boy!" He beckoned sharply, his arm rising from a point near his knees and making a wide, overhead arc in the air — a gesture which seemed too big, too powerful, for the summoning of anything as small and weak as Ira Graley. Then, as if confident that his summons would be instantly obeyed, he disappeared once more into the duskiness of the receiving shed. The boy was moving away when Wesley spoke again: —

"Got any folks in Reedyville, Ira?"

"No, sir," said Ira. "I haven't." Feeling that his answer was too bare, too unresponsive, he added: "I haven't got folks anywhere. I'm an orphan."

Wesley squatted on the runway, so that his head and the boy's head were at the same level. "In that case, you and me better arrange to hang together, so we can look after each other," he said. "I believe you and me can get along all right together."

The man from the sheds stuck out his head and called, "Water boy! Water boy!" once more. His voice was louder this time and his gesture even more peremptory. The look of fear which had disappeared for a moment from the boy's face came back. He strained at his bucket and moved away sidewise, regretfully, and staring now without hesitation into Wesley's broad, sunburned face. "I got to go now, Mr. Wesley," he said, "before I get into trouble."

Wesley said: "What's the use of being in such a hurry? That fellow won't strangle to death in the next minute or two, will he?" He laughed with appreciation at his fanciful notion, and after a moment Ira laughed nervously with him. Wesley picked up the handles òf his truck, as if preparing to move away, and then said: "I'd say you were about twelve years old, Ira. How far out am I?"

"That's just about right," said the boy. "You hit it just about right the first time."

The man from the sheds came to the door once more, and seeing that the boy had not moved, he came toward him angrily. Wesley put down the handles of his truck and stood quietly, his widely spaced teeth showing, his eyes mild and mellow as if he enjoyed the boy's sudden, paralyzed fright. The boy looked up at him wildly, as if imploring help, but Wesley merely shook his head with an amused tolerance and winked.

The man said: "When I call you, you come!" His face was red with his anger and he was shouting with rage at the affront the boy had given him. "You come when I call you — understand that? You come right away, when I tell you to, or I'll whale the living daylights out of you!"

He took a menacing step toward the boy and kicked angrily at the water bucket, but at that instant Wesley's enormous, iron-like palm crashed against the side of his head with such force that the man staggered backward and sat down in confusion against an empty truck. Then he looked up and sighed, and shook his limp neck from side to side with a dazed, jerking motion, as if there were river water in his ears.

Wesley spoke reprovingly: "I don't like people that act the way you act," he said. He turned his head sideways and laughed his thin, schoolgirl laugh. "I only slapped you that time," he said, "be-

cause I wasn't really mad; but if you keep picking on people that
can't take up for theirselves, I'll hit you one of these days, just as
sure as you're a foot high."

The man got to his feet and went back to the receiving sheds
where he worked. When he had gone, Wesley said: "If people want
to abuse other folks, that's their business; but they'd better not try
to abuse you and me! Ain't that right, son? Ain't I telling the God's
truth this time?"

He shifted the bale of cotton he was trucking, and leaned against
the handles of his truck with his entire weight, pressing with such
a languid, distasteful insistence that the muscles of his back and legs
swelled out like old grapevines against his overalls and his denim
shirt. The boy, overcome with strange emotions which he had never
before known, watched for a moment; then he ran forward and put
his entire weight against one of the handles of the truck, pushing
with all his small strength. He staggered awkwardly, but as if his
clumsiness had its own particular meaning, its definite goal, he
managed to slip under the truck, when Wesley lifted his arms higher,
and press his trembling body against the man's.

Wesley put down the handles of his truck once more, as if he,
rather than a more intelligent man, was able to understand the boy's
emotions at that moment. The child was one of those people whose
need is to give love, rather than to receive it, and as if Wesley somehow knew that, he stood passively against his truck, neither moving
or speaking, while the boy lifted his thin arms and circled his waist.
Then, as if he had forgotten all his caution in this wonderful instant
of his life, Ira slowly flattened his face against the man's live and
breathing ribs, smelling with a delight he had never before known
the blended odors of perspiration, tobacco and tar which seemed
to come, as if filtered through a basket of overripe, musty plums,
from the man's muscular, sweating body.

For a time he clung desperately to his new friend, then, becoming
more sure of himself, he ran his hands over Wesley's back and chest
in wide, affectionate gestures which were at once admiring and
proprietary. Wesley tightened the muscles in his arms and thighs
and the boy tried with his puny fingers to make an indentation in
them, but he could not.

Wesley said: "Big and healthy — ain't I, Ira?"

"Yes, sir," said the boy. He laughed with a sense of wondering delight. "Yes, sir, Mr. Wesley. You sure are." He released the man suddenly, as if his emotions had discharged themselves, raised his small, white face and said: "If your truck gets stuck again, just let me know. You call me whenever you need help, Mr. Wesley."

He watched regretfully as Wesley moved away, his thin nose lifted and smelling again the affectionate, irresistible smell of his friend. His sense of smell was developed to a remarkable degree. Since his existence on earth had always been that of the weak and tormented animal, it was almost as if God, seeing his defenselessness, had at least given him the same protection that animals have against danger.

He was ashamed of this unusual faculty, knowing that it separated him dramatically from others, and he told nobody of it; but the first thing he noticed about another person was his individual smell. His own smell offended him. It was the smell of a washrag whose thin sourness had been warmed at a woodfire. At first he dared not approach others too closely, thinking that they, too, knew what his smell was; and then he realized that others smelled nothing at all, except, perhaps, those ordinary and catalogued smells, which he was conscious of only as backgrounds for more subtle effects.

Afterwards — long after that first meeting had passed — Wesley's odor continued to delight the boy. It was friendly and kind; and even when he was angry, the rich, plumlike smell remained steady and unvarying under the tart acidity of rage. Often he would stand hidden behind the receiving shed, hoping for a chance to talk to his friend, his nose lifted and twitching, like the nose of a hound, so that he would know the exact instant when Wesley turned the corner and approached. Or occasionally he would stand as close to the man as he could manage, and when Wesley's back was turned, he would succeed, as if this were the goal of his unending clumsiness, in touching his friend's hand with his own, or of leaning forward until his head rested, for a second, against Wesley's hot, straining back.

These were the moments that Ira came to look forward to, and for which he lived. Often, at night, when he was alone, he would wake in the darkness and live them over again, remembering, in minute detail, each gesture that Wesley had made, each intonation of his voice. It seems strange that this boy, who had known nothing in his life except abuse, should have so great a capacity for affection; but perhaps he, even more than others, knew that love was not a luxury to be indulged stingily, or bestowed capriciously; that it was something as important as air or light, more necessary, even, than food. He did not ask to be loved in return. He asked only that Wesley tolerate his blind, overwhelming devotion, for that, he felt, was all he could reasonably expect from others.

But there was one thing which troubled him, for he had told his friend a deliberate lie, and the knowledge lay always just below his consciousness. Ira Graley was not, as he had said that first day, an orphan. He was a bastard, and he had every reason to know this well. His mother was alive, and she lived in Reedyville. He knew where she lived, what she did, and who she was, although she did not know him.

The relationship which developed between Wesley and the boy was an ideal arrangement for both of them, for there was no conflict in their natures. Ira was as silent and cautious as Wesley was garrulous and expansive, and he listened attentively to all the things that Wesley said, accepting without question the rules of conduct which the man laid down for his future guidance.

"You want to be careful when the time comes for you to marry," said Wesley. "A marriage can make or break a man. I wouldn't want you to repeat this, Ira, but sometimes I think marriage is something that the womenfolks got together and fixed up amongst themselves so they could really tie a man down good!"

Thus he would talk to the boy, for Wesley had a mind which was uncorrupted by any contact with literature, and he was, in his discontent, having the pleasure of discovering for himself the validity of old, exhausted phrases, of believing that each platitude, when it came to him, was something fresh and profound, and entirely unknown to others.

"Now, tell me this Ira. What makes a man want to work his life away, just to make a lot of money? Ruining his health, like I did, and wasting the little time he has here on earth?" he would ask. "What good does it all do him after he's dead?" He would put down the handles of his truck on the hot, creosoted runway and wipe his face roughly with his denim sleeve. "Did you ever stop and try to figure out such deep things, Ira?"

"No, sir," said the boy. "No, sir, I never did."

It was during those days that conditions in Cuba became acute, and as the situation became more and more an object of American concern, Wesley's interest in the politics of his day, in the actual current of ordinary life about him, as opposed to his former interest in the life of the mind only, became more and more pronounced. He read everything in the newspapers that came his way, and he talked endlessly to Ira regarding the military tactics to be used in the event of actual war, and the advantages of resolute action as against the subtle meanderings of tricky, inconclusive diplomacy.

"You watch what I'm telling you, Ira!" he said, shaking his magnificent head ominously from side to side. "There's going to be trouble, and lots of it, and pretty soon now! There's going to be chances at last for a man to show what he's made out of!"

His mind dwelt on the possibilities of war in the same expectant, excited manner that a child contemplates the approach of Christmas, and when the *Maine* was blown up, he found that he had already made his plans. He said: "Now here's what I aim to do, Ira. They're going to call for volunteers any day now, and when they do, I'm going to take the morning train for Mobile. I'm going to enlist as soon as I get there, if they'll have me, and I'm not going to tell them I'm a married man. That would just mess up things. . . . You follow me so far?"

"Yes, sir," said the boy.

"Now, there's no sense in telling anybody here what I'm aiming to do, either," said Wesley. "That would only cause talk and commotion." He lowered his head, turned his neck to the right and glanced sideways at the horizon, took a letter from the pocket of his overalls and handed it to the boy. "I know I can depend on you, Ira," he said. "Now, what I want you to do for me is this: When you figure I've had time to get to Mobile and sign up, you go tell Ada where I've gone to, and give her the letter."

"Yes, sir," said the boy sadly.

"There's something in the letter about you, too," said Wesley; "and I don't want to hear any arguments out of you, understand that? I want you to do just what the letter says."

The boy said: "I won't give you no arguments. I'll do what you want me to, Mr. Wesley, no matter what it is."

Ada knew the way her husband's mind was working, but she strove to dismiss her doubts as unwarranted; and when he finally left her, she was almost floored. That was in April, and already the Alabama spring was far advanced; already the deciduous trees had taken on a new life of young and reaching green in the precise shade appropriate to that particular tree: green so crisp and fragile that. the new leaves seemed as delicate as gauze against the rays of the mild, touching sun.

"That's all Mr. Wesley told me to tell you," said Ira patiently. "He just said for you not to worry none, and to take care of yourself and the children until he got back safe." He took the note from his pocket and handed it to her. "Mr. Wesley left this letter for you, too," he said. "I been taking care of it since the day he first told me he was going away."

In spite of the elaborateness of his precautions, Wesley's plan had been known almost from the time when he, still wearing his working clothes, had got aboard the train for Mobile; and most of the neighborhood children hurried at once to the Boutwell house, to crowd into the yard, or hang over the fences, gazing with neither self-consciousness nor shame at Ada's weeping face, in the manner that people will stare for hours at the window of a room in which a crime has been committed.

The two Palmiller children, although it would have distressed their father had he known, were there: Clarry, the elder, a girl so blond that she seemed to have escaped being an albino by the merest fraction of chance, and Rance, the brilliant boy who was two years younger than his sister.

Manny Nelloha, the son of the local junkman, was there, too; but — being almost like a member of the Boutwell family, he spent so much of his time with them — he stood on the porch, just behind Ada's rocking chair, fanning her, when he remembered, with that day's issue of the *Courier*.

When she had recovered sufficiently, Ada took the letter from Ira Graley, turned it over twice, and then, in a flood of new emotion at the sight of her husband's untidy, labored writing, she dropped it unopened into her lap. "Did Wesley say how we're going to pay Mrs. Kenworthy her rent, and how we're going to buy some-

thing to eat while he's off having a good time fighting Spaniards?"
she asked.

She raised her right arm and held her fingers splayed in perplexity against her cheek, her other arm, its hand so limp that it
seemed broken at the wrist, hanging over the side of the wicker
chair. "Did he say how we're going to do that?" she insisted. She
was speaking to Ira alone, accusingly, as if he were the reason
for her present grief.

Ira shook his head and looked at the boards of the porch, not
knowing what to say. Fodie, the eldest of the Boutwell children,
came to his rescue. She was tall for her age, and she resembled her
father more than the other children did. His lip was long, and his
teeth somewhat widely spaced and inclined outward, but these
characteristics in his daughter were distressingly exaggerated, for
her lip was even longer than his, and her teeth jutted outward so
insistently that it was only through the exercise of will that she
managed to keep them covered with her lips. She knew that she
was not attractive, and she had got into the habit of smiling
apologetically, pleadingly, as if asking forgiveness for her plainness.
At such times, her teeth, appearing slowly from behind her withdrawing lips, gave one the impression that through the expenditure
of enormous effort, the spread, porcelain fingers of a doll were
being pushed slowly forward through her apologetic, retreating
lips.

"Why don't you just read the letter, and find out what Papa has
to say?" she asked sensibly.

Ada handed the letter back to Ira Graley. "You read it out loud
to us all," she said. "I wouldn't trust myself to read it. Not the
way I feel right now."

Ira stood with the letter in his hands, and then his pale face
turned unexpectedly red with humiliation. "I can't read," he said.
"I can't read a word of writing." A shocked sound came from
the children, but Ira looked at them gravely and said: "I can read
a little print, but not writing."

Rance Palmiller made a whistling sound through his teeth.
"Ira's almost a grown man, and he can't read yet," he said.
"I'm only six years old, and I'm going into high school next
year."

This child was so unusual, so precocious, that he would have been a problem for the wisest of parents. Had he been modest about his gifts, others might have found him bearable. He was a handsome child, large for his age, and unusually strong. He walked with his head in the air, his lips fixed in a smirking, self-satisfied smile, as if he realized his superiority, and wanted to make sure that others realized it too.

Fodie, who detested the precocious Palmiller boy, took the note from her mother's hand and said: "Everybody knows how smart you are, Mr. Clarence Palmiller. You don't have to keep telling about it every time you open your mouth." She started to read the letter herself, but some instinct, born perhaps of her own unattractiveness, told her that she must not do this; that Ira Graley would never in the depths of his mind forgive the person who triumphed over him. She handed the letter with exaggerated carelessness to Manny Nelloha, the junkman's son, and said: "Here, Manny: you read the letter to Mama," adding defensively: "You all make me sick at my stomach. You act like being able to read made any difference one way or the other."

There was nothing unexpected in the letter, except the paragraph which concerned Ira, himself. Wesley, it seemed, had been concerned at the thought of leaving the boy alone and unprotected, and he suggested that his wife take him in and look after him while he was away. If there was not room in the house with the rest of the family, then Wesley suggested that the lumber room above the barn be fitted up for him.

The children, feeling that the peak of the excitement had now passed, moved toward the gate and broke up into individual groups. At once Fodie took charge of things. She turned to Breck, her younger brother, who was exactly the same age as the Palmiller boy, and said: "You come to the barn with me, and help fix up Ira's new room. Mama's got enough to contend with right now, without you bothering her."

She caught the boy by the hand and pulled him forward, but he locked his legs around one of the posts which supported the porch, and held on in silence; then, with the unpredictability of children, he quit struggling and followed his sister. He held up his left hand for Ira to examine, and said: "Look! Look! I got an upside-down thumb, just like a Roman emperor!"

Honey, the second Boutwell daughter, came from behind the house and looked with curiosity at Ira Graley's retreating back. With the air of having settled something in her mind, something which was of little interest to begin with, she made a circle on the ground with her toe, and walked away, swishing her dress from side to side.

"Did Papa say anything to you privately before he left?" asked Fodie. "Was there something else you didn't want to say right out before Mama and all that crowd?"

"Look!" insisted Breck in his shrill, six-year-old voice. "Look, Ira! I really got an upside-down thumb!"

"No," said Ira. "There wasn't nothing else I can think of."

"Papa was always talking about you at home," said Fodie softly, the doll's hand peeping out from behind her withdrawing lips. "He said he never met up with a better-mannered boy in his whole life. He used to say it was a pity his own children wasn't as well-behaved."

Breck pulled at Ira's sleeve, his brown eyes bright and demanding. "Look!" he begged. "Look one time, anyway, and I won't bother you again. I got an upside-down thumb! Look just once, Ira!"

Ira took the boy's hand in his own, examining it thoughtfully, giving the thumb his earnest and complete attention. "You have for a fact," he said at last. "I never saw one like it before."

Fodie said: "Sometimes I wish Mama had never told you what Miss Cordelia Overton said about your old thumb!" She turned, in explanation, to Ira and continued: "When Breck was little, Mama used to do sewing for the Overtons, and she took Breck with her to work sometimes. Miss Cordelia was studying Roman history at the time, and when she saw Breck's thumb she said, 'He's got an inverted thumb, just like the Emperor Elagabalus!' And what's more, she got out her history book and showed it to Mama in cold print; and sure enough, there it was, like she said."

Breck smirked and nodded his head, as if to say: "See, I told you so! I told you I was something special!"

Fodie continued: "Anyway, the Emperor Elagabalus had *two* inverted thumbs, so Miss Cordelia said, and you've got only *one!*" She caught his arm and pulled him forward. "Come on," she said, "and quit talking so much. We've got to fix up a place for Ira to sleep in before it gets plumb dark. . . . Sometimes I think you're even worse than Rance Palmiller when it comes to bragging!"

Ira spoke unexpectedly, as if his illiteracy troubled him: "Because I can't read none, don't mean that I don't want to learn. One of these days, if I get a chance, I'll read as good as anybody. Yes, and what's more, I'll write as good as anybody, too!"

Later that night, when Fodie came into the big room she shared with her younger sister Honey and her brother Breck, her duties for the day accomplished, Honey was standing in front of the cheap, inaccurate mirror, gazing with absorbed interest at the image of her small, gaunt face. "Fodie! Fodie!" said Breck from his cot beside the window. "Make Honey put out the lamp and go to bed. I've told her to, but she won't pay any attention to me."

Fodie spoke in an exasperated voice: "A big girl, almost nine years old, and already so stuck on herself! I'll bet Clarry Palmiller don't even act this way, and she has a right to, because she's pretty."

Honey unbuttoned her dress, and held it draped experimentally around her shoulders, as she strove to catch one last glimpse of herself in the dull, distorting looking-glass. Then, her eyes calm and satisfied, she leaned forward and kissed her own reflection.

Fodie said: "If this is the way you're going to act the first night that Papa's gone, I'm going to write a letter to the President and tell him to send him right back home." She undressed in the dark and got into bed beside her sister, turned on her pillow and sighed deeply. She had a peculiar sense of depression, which was unusual for her, and which she did not understand. It was almost as if some gigantic hand lay heavily upon her immature breast, a hand which she could never shake off, turn and twist about as she would. When she was almost asleep, Honey spoke again, stating what she had learned, in her short life, of the complex relationships which exist between men and women. "If you want a man to treat you good, then you treat him mean," she said.

"They'll never accuse you of treating anybody good," said Fodie. "That's something that won't ever be said about you."

"I'll bet it won't either," said Honey complacently. She turned, pressed her face into her pillow, her thin, scrawny rump thrust into the air, and instantly she was asleep.

The next afternoon, Ada received her first visit from Minnie McInnis McMinn. Mrs. McMinn, a woman of many talents, and with an energy which seemed terrifying at times, not only edited the Society Page of the *Courier,* and regularly wrote feature stories with a strong heart interest for that journal, but found time, as well, to harass the editors of her generation with a stream of poems, sketches and short stories. For a time her contributions were returned with such promptness that she began to suspect that American editors had a Black List, and that she was on it. She became so discouraged that she almost abandoned literature as a career — a stern but just punishment, she felt, for those who would not appreciate her — when she decided to change her material and her style, to work in what was, at least in those times, a fresher field of storytelling.

In short, she decided to write, in dialect, a series of related stories around the eccentricities of Negroes; but since she knew nothing at all about Negroes, and had not the faintest desire to find out, she solved this initial problem by the expedient of writing about white people masquerading in minstrel makeups — people who were more quaint, more humorous and considerably more childlike than their fellow whites who wore no literary blackface at all. Into the mouths of her characters she then put a stylized dialect which was simplified, flexible and whimsical, and one which, up to the time she invented it, had never before been heard by any living ear.

Her success was instantaneous. For a time she sold to the magazines everything she could produce; but in the end, the string of her literary eggs laid itself out. St. Joseph and Robert Porterfield made fun of her characters, her style, and, most of all, her dialect, but she took their joking with that patient tolerance which the successful so easily acquire. On one occasion, Robert said that his mother had read the best known of the McMinn stories, "Sally Johnson's Wedding Dress," out loud to her Negro cook, and that the cook, who had listened in polite amazement to the end, had got the idea in her head that it was a story about Eskimos.

It was then that Minnie pointed out, sensibly enough, that she was not writing her stories for the Negroes of Reedyville, who bought nothing, having nothing to buy with, but for the pleasant, cultured people up North, who apparently had unlimited money, and who certainly owned all the magazines and publishing houses.

The occasion for her call on Ada Boutwell was twofold: The editor of the *Courier* thought there might be a column in Wesley's enlistment; and Minnie, herself, meant to get not only that story, which she could write blindfolded, but much rich, personal material from the lives of the Boutwell family as well.

Mrs. McMinn was a local historian on a grand, if somewhat uncritical, scale. She was a veritable squirrel of a woman, and she recorded in her buckram ledgers each bit of local drama, each item of emotional significance which concerned her townsmen, as if these entries were her insurance against a barren winter, as if they were literary nuts to be disinterred later, and eaten at her leisure. She hoped, someday, that she would be able to shape her accumulating material into stories as polished and gemlike as those of Chekhov. Perhaps some inspiration would enable her, at last, to see her material all of one piece, and the result would be a novel as overwhelming as those by Tolstoy; but she did not permit herself to think of these things often, since, when she did think of them, she ended up petulant and tearful before the meagerness of her own talent.

She was still a young woman, but already she was a celebrity in Reedyville, and Ada, who had long admired her prose style in the *Courier,* was flattered by the visit. She and her guest sat on the front porch in rocking chairs, talking and looking at the landscape before them. A clay road, dusty in dry weather, and almost impassable when it rained, ran in front of the house, paralleling a drainage ditch from whose banks lantana and ironweed grew thickly.

To the right of the house, and perhaps six hundred yards away, was a ramshackle Negro church which had been miraculously put together by its congregation from bits of tin, bricks and old, discarded lumber; and directly in front of the Boutwell house was one of Reedyville's landmarks, the small, almost circular, lake called "Sweethearts' Looking-Glass."

Years before, when Reedyville was only a small village, the pond had been bordered by a grove of oaks and hickories, and there

had been a path under the trees which ran close to the edge of
the water. In those days, the young people in love had taken the
place for their own, and they could be seen at twilight, after their
work for the day was done, walking the path together, with arms
intertwined, while their long, inverted images followed them faithfully in the water. Now, the oaks and the hickories had been cut
down, and where they once stood, there was only a cluster of
cheaply built, unpainted shacks where Negroes lived.

In the dry months, when little rain fell, the springs which fed
the pond were diminished, and as the water drew back from its
banks, a layer of heavy, chocolate mud lay exposed to the hot light
of the sun, mud which dried out, cracked, and turned up crazily
at its edges, like an enormous plate of fudge cut into servings by a
nervous cook. But on the afternoon of Mrs. McMinn's visit, the
April rains were well advanced, and the pond lay full, unrippled
and shining before them.

The shining pond, because of its shallowness, was the perfect
looking-glass for depths greater than its own, and as Ada and her
guest rocked and talked together, they saw an inverted, miniature
sky at their feet, with fleecy clouds reflected, motionless and scaled-
down, in the calm, untroubled water.

"Now, Mrs. Boutwell," said Minnie, "just let your mind wander
gently back to the past, and you'll find you can recall a great many
interesting things."

"Well, then," began Ada, "let me start off by saying that I was
born out in the country, and the first thing I remember real good
is going to Demopolis with Papa. All I remember about that trip,
though, is that I saw a white-faced mare drinking out of a trough,
and then a man came up and jerked her head away before she got
her full." She narrowed her eyes thoughtfully, her gaze fixed on the
image of a chicken hawk flying skillfully among the clouds and
the reeds which lived forever, precise and inverted, in the surface
of the reflecting pond.

"I'm sure, now, it was Demopolis we went to that day, because
it was near the Tombigbee River, and I still remember how yellow the river looked between those high, white banks. I remember
I kept thinking, 'How can a river be so yellow and have banks so
chalk-white?' I spoke to Mama about it when we got home, but

all she said was: 'How can a black man have red blood? How can a brown hen lay a white egg?' And so I never mentioned the subject again."

For a time she talked conscientiously, recalling those small things which only she remembered now, dredging up from the depths of her mind those memories which are so commonplace to others, but are so unbearably sad to the one who recalls them. Mrs. McMinn, although disappointed at the lack of drama in the material, listened politely enough, and made entries in the book which she had brought with her.

She learned at length that Ada's father had farmed for a while after he had come home from fighting Northerners. When he died, her mother had taken the family down to West Florida, to cook in a logcamp for the hands, and it was there that she had met Wesley. She had made up her mind from the start to have him and nobody else, knowing that he was the one man in the world for her, and that's the way it worked out. She had been just seventeen when she married.

"How could you be sure that he was the one man for you, as you say?" asked Mrs. McMinn suspiciously.

Ada looked down at her hands, shook her head and smiled gently. It was none of Mrs. McMinn's affair, she felt, but the truth of the matter was that one Sunday afternoon the loggers had gone down to the river to swim. Hearing them laughing and shouting, she had walked through the woods until she came to a bluff where a live-oak tree was growing. Below her she could see the naked men skylarking and shoving one another off the springboard. Then Wesley Boutwell, a man that she had not noticed particularly before, got up and walked out on the springboard, and in the short space of time when he stood there poised and ready to dive, she had made up her mind.

His skin was such a pretty shade, she had thought. It was just the color of cornshucks which had bleached out in a barn; then, too, the hair on his body was not matted the way it was on the other shouting men. It grew close to his body, and it was flat and silken like the hair of animals that live in the water; then, as he stood on the springboard that Sunday afternoon, for the one important instant in Ada's life, the sun had shifted through the bay trees, and had shone squarely upon him, and to her eyes he seemed to shine all over, as if he were gilded.

For a moment she was tempted to tell these things to her visitor, but she knew dimly that they would not be adequate from Minnie's standpoint. Then, too, the minds of intelligent people were always so dirty in such odd ways, and Mrs. McMinn was sure to read something dark and smirking into the simple situation. For these reasons, she shook her head and remained silent.

Yes, Fodie was her eldest child. Then came Stacy, who was eleven. Honey, the one whose future worried her the most of all, was eight. Breck, the boy with the thumb everybody noticed, was six. Greenie, the baby, was only a year old, and before God, if she'd known Wesley intended to desert them to fight Spaniards, she'd never have had him at all! That made five, didn't it? Well, there had been five others, but they had died in infancy, for one reason or another, before there had even been a chance to anchor their brief lives to the earth with so much as the small reality of a name other than "baby."

Mrs. McMinn had not been taking notes for some time now. She closed her notebook and searched about in her handbag for a peppermint drop.

"It's not what has already happened that's bothering me right now," said Ada. "It's what's going to happen, now that Wesley's off freeing the niggers in Cuba. I been thinking all morning long, and most of last night, too, about how we're going to get along with him gone." She sighed and shook her head. "Of course, there's a boy named Ira Graley that's come to live with us. Wesley sent him. I didn't expect him to pay anything for his keep, but he said he wouldn't stay unless he paid what he could, and that'll help out some." She stopped and spread the fingers of one hand against her cheek.

"I been getting a little work now and then from old Mrs. Overton," she continued, "but it's not enough for us all to live on." She sighed again and turned to Mrs. McMinn, and instantly that overpowering and kindly woman became completely alert.

"Don't worry about that!" she said. "Leave that to me! I'll see that you get all the work you can do! I'll see that you get good pay for doing it!" She opened her notebook again and wrote: "Arrange for Ada Boutwell to get work she needs," her t-bars crossed so firmly that the paper curled back and broke under the pressure of her pencil. She tapped her teeth in concentration and then added the words: —

> Possible sources of work for A. Boutwell: —
> Cindy Palmiller. She can't refuse anybody anything.
> St. Joseph. Can wrap him around my finger, any time.
> Myself. Naturally.
> Millicent Kenworthy. Flatter her, but in words of one syllable.
> Old Mrs. Porterfield. Tell her how wonderful Robert is.

"Fodie could help me," said Ada. "Fodie's only twelve, but she's more reliable than lots of grown women. Only I wouldn't want to take her out of school when she's getting along so well."

"We are not to consider that possibility, I assure you," said Mrs. McMinn. "There are few enough girls as it is who are interested in developing their minds, without which woman can hardly expect to modify a world planned by man for his own selfish pleasure, or to lift the hand of patronage which rests so harshly on us!" Unconsciously she had risen from her rocker. She was no longer conversing. She was now making a speech. She raised a stern forefinger, touched her nose thoughtfully and continued: "As I see the matter, the thing to do for the present is to concentrate on — "

She broke off, seeing that she no longer had Mrs. Boutwell's attention, turned and looked in the direction of Ada's fixed stare. At once she understood Ada's inattentiveness, for around the old path which lovers had once taken, on the far side of the unruffled, reflecting pond, there walked the strangest character which Reedyville had ever produced. She walked slowly, as if one of her legs were broken, her reflection in the water moving forward with her jerking, and yet gliding, stride.

Years before, somebody who had understood her, and the vocation she had set for herself, had called her "The Goodwife of Death," and that name, with its variants, had clung to her since. But the original was a little too long, and a little too poetic in its implications, for most people, and she was now spoken of usually as "Death's Wife," or, more often, as "The Goodwife."

When the old woman had circled the pond, she hesitated at the place where the lovers' path once joined the Reedyville Road; then, having come to a decision, she approached the Boutwell house, stopped at the gate and examined Ada and Mrs. McMinn with her passionate, burning eyes.

"Won't you come in and sit awhile, Goodwife?" asked Ada. Her words were perfunctory, and there was no real invitation in them. The Goodwife shook her head reprovingly, as if astounded at the ineptness of the invitation. "There's no work for me to do here," she said. "You have no need for me."

"Who was it this time?" asked Mrs. McMinn, shaping her words precisely, as if talking to someone whose vocabulary was limited to the essentials of language. "Was it that old Aunt Zorah who worked so long for the Porterfield family?"

The Goodwife said: "I'd like a glass of water, if it's entirely convenient." She spoke grudgingly, only when necessity compelled her to speak, but when she did, her voice came as a surprise to her listeners. You expected it to be harsh and creaking, as rusty, perhaps, as the old black draperies she wore, but instead it was soft and beautifully modulated: the gracious voice of a great lady. At last, as if Mrs. McMinn's question had only then sunk into her mind, she said: "It was a Negro man. I'm sure you didn't know him."

When The Goodwife had finished her drink, she bowed elaborately and continued on her way. Mrs. McMinn got up almost at once and moved toward the gate. When she reached it, she turned and said: "Don't worry any more about how you're going to get along. Everything will work out all right. Leave everything to me."

She was correct in her predictions, and when Wesley came back to his family the next year, Ada was well established, and her patrons were steady and predictable. This was fortunate for at least two reasons: In the first place, Wesley returned to Reedyville as a sergeant and a hero, and it was plain that work as a common laborer, the only work he was capable of doing, was now beneath his dignity; then, too, he had lost his left arm below the elbow, and hard labor was no longer practicable for him, even if he had wanted to do it.

And so it happened, during the years following his return, that he spent much of his time on the bench in front of Rowley's Pool Parlors, or in the back room of Moore's Livery Stable, talking about his adventures. It soon became evident that he had been more efficient in his destruction of Spaniards than the medieval God had been in His annihilation of heretics who would not affirm His mercy, His gentleness or His love.

Gracefully he settled down to the life of the hero in retirement. His ability as a narrator improved as he reworked his material into more flexible forms, and his material, itself, grew as surely as multiplying yeast after he had read old copies of newspapers in the public library, and had found out, from the foreign correspondents of his day, precisely what he had experienced.

Occasionally he took a party on a fishing trip to Pearl River, or drove a crowd of picnickers to James' Lake. For a time he worked at Rowley's, and for a time he acted as a deputy sheriff. But no matter what the nature of his work was, it was always temporary, and each Saturday, after he had eaten his twelve o'clock lunch, he shaved, put on a clean, denim shirt and went to town for an afternoon of relaxation. And this particular Saturday in September 1916 had been no exception. The only difference was that in the past he had always returned home promptly in time for his supper, and this time, inexplicably, he had not.

Ada came into the house after a while and put a new stick of wood on the embers in the firebox. Critically she examined her husband's supper, now dried out on the back of the stove. "Dover? You Dover?" she said sharply. "I'm worried about your father, and there's no use trying to hide it. Something's happened to him in town. I know it."

She raked the embers around the piece of wood she had just put in and the stick burst into flames, revealing her face in all its leathery harshness. She reached for another stick, but her motion was never completed, for suddenly she straightened and tilted her head to one side, as if somebody outside had called her name. "I can't stand waiting any longer," she said. "I'm going down the road and look for him."

Dover followed his mother through the breezeway of the house, his cap twisted in his palms, but when they reached the porch again, they stood still and stared at the western sky, their mouths opened in wonder.

All day long the yellow, the red and the lavender particles of dust had stirred and trembled and lifted beneath the feet of the passer-by; and they had risen in fragile clouds, like dry vapor, from the bed of the road, to drift outward languidly, in ever-widening arcs, toward the horizon. The multicolored, drifting particles of dust had seemed of no importance in themselves: trivial and unseen in the burning light of day; but now, when the sun had withdrawn its power into concentrated light in the west, the drifting dust had caught fire, and had broken at last into flames, so that it seemed now, at the close of day, as if the whole world were burning up in a mystic, unquenchable fire.

The last light of the sun lay as evenly as water on the surface of the dried-out pond, and brought such a rich color to it that its caked, fudgelike bottom, cracked so crazily into squares and angles, gleamed as richly as old, much loved wood; but at the center of the pond, where there was still water above the springs, the color cast by the rays of the sun was the dark red of clotted blood. The color of the stagnant water in the ditches beside the road was the color of blood as well, and the lantana and ironweed grew from it red and unreal and withered, as if rooted in carnage too rich, too strong for their lacy roots to digest.

Ada looked at the sky, shading her gray, sloping eyes with her hand, and then she spoke: "I seen a sunset like that when I was a little girl and lived near Demopolis, but I seen it that time across the Tombigbee River." She sighed and became silent, knowing how inadequate her words were. A moment later she half-turned and stared at the crazily built church to the right of the pond. The place had taken on an odd and individual color, and it seemed not only to repeat shallowly the dying light of the sun, but to emit from its haphazard surfaces an unreal and shimmering light of its own creation.

Already the congregation had gathered for their Saturday night's service, and she saw that they stood humbly before their church, their faces lifted upward and uncertain. Then, as she watched, a lamp was lit in the church itself, but the worshipper who had done this, as if abashed at his presumptuousness, blew it out again, came in front of the building, and lifted his face with his brothers.

Ada said: "It looks like something was burning up in the distance, don't it? A whole world, maybe!"

At that moment, as if the watching Negroes had only awaited their cue, they began to sing with passionate and earthly beauty a song which their parents in slavery had sung before them: —

> "The world gwiner end with a burnin' in the sky,
> With a burnin' in the sky, a big burnin' in the sky;
> Oh, the world gwiner end with a burnin' in the sky:
> Prideful brother, you better trimble and hide!
> Trimble, trimble, trimble and hide!
> Trimble, trimble, trimble and hide!"

And as Ada stood there, watching the sunset and hearing the song, a feeling that she was overwhelmed, and left alone, in a world which she had, of necessity, accepted, but which she did not understand, came over her. You must take the world and its strangeness for granted, she knew. You must neither ask too much, nor pry too deeply into its mysteries, for there was not wisdom at the end of that path, but only mumbling and madness. Then, as if to deny the sense of fainting strangeness which had come over her, she shoved the shoulder of her son vigorously, and said: "What are we wasting time for? What are we standing here waiting for?"

She slammed the gate behind her with a creaking of its leather hinges, and a clanging of the iron scrap which weighted its chain, and kept it closed; and without so much as a backward glance, to see if her son followed her, she hurried down the footpath that paralleled the road, her chest bent forward a little, her hands laced beneath her protuberant, rounded belly.

Dover, being barefoot, walked in the center of the road, and let the red dust come in spurts through his wide-spaced, primitive toes. The soles of his feet knew each inch of this road: There were stretches, like the present one, where the coating of red dust above the roadbed was as voluptuous and as yielding, against his flesh, as velvet — giving him a sense of flattering softness, but with the knowledge of hardness beneath. Farther ahead, there was the bed of an old washout, and here the velvety dust had settled loosely, so that when you went there, your feet sank downward without hindrance, as if you walked upon feathers.

Beyond the culvert, which they were now approaching, there was a stretch where the surface dust had blown away, and had left the naked, gritty spine of the roadbed exposed. The feeling here against your feet was the tickling contact of prickly burlap. You shivered and hugged your flanks, as you walked here, and laughed nervously, as if you were in the grip of some mild and stimulating pain; and you curled your toes under, in excitement, and hopped from side to side, as you sought to escape the wedge-shaped, temporary scars which the sharpened surface of the roadbed imprinted, like hieroglyphs, against the soles of your mincing, withdrawing feet.

Dover said: "There's no sense in worrying about Papa. He'll come home, when he gets ready to." He looked back over his shoulder, in the direction of the pond, the church and the burning sky. The sunset was waxing in power, and as the color grew stronger, the voices of the singers became more passionate, more pleading. There were still stragglers coming to the meeting, and even before they turned off from the path, and approached the church, they began to sing with their brothers, walking toward the church with their eyes fearful and raised upward, their hands held forward before them, as if they felt that the sense of sight was no longer enough.

When he turned his head again, Dover saw that his mother had stopped just beyond the culvert, her whole body concentrated and listening, as if she awaited the repetition of some small sound. He came closer to her side, but she shook her head warningly, and made a downward, slapping motion with her hand; and then the throttled and gasping noise which she had heard, but had not been entirely sure of, was repeated.

At once she went down the embankment, pressing aside in her haste the rank and withered weeds which grew on the side of the slope, in the shallow ditch, and even across the abandoned fields beyond; and there, hidden where the weeds were thickest, to the right of the drainage ditch, lay her husband.

Looking upward from where she stood, it was not difficult to understand what had happened. Apparently he had staggered too closely to the side of the road, lost his balance and had fallen headlong down the embankment. In his fall he had struck the side of a drainage pipe, bruising his forehead and cutting his cheek a little. He must have lain undiscovered in the weeds for a long time, for already his blood had dried out on his face and crisped to dark maroon; already it was flaking at its edges like cheap paint on water pipes.

Ada unbuttoned her husband's shirt and massaged his neck, calling his name, "Wesley! Wesley! Wesley!" Then she and her son put their arms about his enormous chest and tried to carry him up the embankment, but the task was beyond them. In their effort, they had stirred up the sediment at the bottom of the drainage ditch, and had broken the weeds beneath their feet, so that the odor which came to them as they rested and looked about helplessly was that of an overbaked fruitcake, which had burned from the smell of spice and citron melons to the soured tang of cypress butts.

Ada raised her eyes to the road once more, seeking help from that source, and she saw three Negroes, two men and a woman, watching her. They had been on their way to church, and they stood uneasily now, ready to help if they were called upon, or at the first sign their presence was not wanted, to turn and walk away, pretending they had seen nothing.

Before Ada could speak, one of the men came down the embankment toward her. "It's me, Miss Ada," he said. "It's me, Jesse — Mr. Palmiller's yardman." He spoke with that uncertain, desperate dignity which Negroes so often assume in their dealings with white people. "That's Lula, my wife, standing on the bank," he said. "You know Lula, too, don't you? And that's her brother from Meridian, standing there beside her. His name is Amos. He's a good singer, and his church sent him to Reedyville, to find out how good we can do."

Amos said: "I won the banner for my church. They named me the best singer in Mississippi."

Jesse knelt and examined Wesley's body, to determine if there were any broken bones. He was a tall man, with gray eyes and reddish, crisping hair. His face was a pale, dry brown, almost the shade of sycamore leaves in autumn, and splattered across his nose and cheeks, were minute freckles, like fly specks on butcher's paper. He called to his companions, when he had finished his examination, and they joined him beside the body.

Ada said: "If you'll help Dover and me get him home, I'll take it as a true kindness, and one I won't forget soon."

"Don't you worry, Miss Ada," said the woman. "Don't you go and worry none."

Amos said: "When's those niggers gwiner quit mumbling around? When they gwiner start singing?"

The two men lifted Wesley's inert body and walked easily up the embankment with him, and the weeds, which they had trampled, rose upward slowly, the white, cottony spittle of insects still clinging to the twigs and crotches where they had first been placed. They readjusted their grips when they came to the road, turned and continued in the direction of the Boutwell house — Jesse, the redheaded man, walking backwards and supporting his shoulders, while Amos bore his feet.

Lula had picked up Wesley's hat, and she carried it now in her hand: "Tote him easy, Amos!" she said warningly. "You, too, Jesse! Tote him easy!" She fanned Wesley's face with his own hat and went on: "You can't ever tell for sure about anybody that's had a fall. I knew a man that got hit on the head once, and it looked to everybody like he was all right afterwards, like nothing had happened to him."

"We don't have to take him far," said Ada to the men. "It's only a little piece further down the road." Then, collecting her thoughts, she spoke to her son. "Run, Dover! Run as fast as you can, and get Dr. Kent. Tell him Wesley's been hurt bad, and ask him to come as quick as he can!"

"This man I'm talking about, the one that got hit on the head," continued Lula, "*said* he was feeling all right, and he didn't want nobody to go to no trouble over him. Well, sir, he *acted* all right, and it didn't look like there was anything the matter with him at all, but the next morning when he bent down to tie his shoes, he fell over dead on the floor, right amongst his children."

She paused, to let the point of her story sink in, and in the silence, Jesse said: "There's no use in sending for Dr. Kent, because he can't go nowheres right now. Miss Clarry's sick, like you know already, and Dr. Kent's been over at our house since about eleven o'clock this morning."

Lula said: "Why don't you send for Dr. Snowfield? He might come, if he ain't got nothing better to do."

Ada walked a few steps in silence, turning this unexpected complication over in her mind. "I don't know anything about Dr. Snowfield," she said with sudden petulance. "I never even met him so far. Is he a good doctor, Jesse?"

"Yes, ma'am," said Jesse. "Dr. Snowfield's a mighty good doctor."

"Go get him, then!" said Ada. "Go quick, Dover! Run every step of the way!"

Then Dover, who had been trotting anxiously beside his father's swaying body, listening to his strained breathing and watching with fascination the odd, almost humorous twitching about his lips, turned and ran in the direction of Court House Square, where Dr. Snowfield had his office, his feet kicking up clouds of the dry, powdery dust from the bed of the road.

"I knowed another gentleman that got hit on the head," said Lula. "He didn't die, though," she added reassuringly. "He got all right in no time at all, and the only thing the matter with him afterwards was he had fits. It looked like he blamed his po' wife for what happened, 'cause afterwards he was always chopping at her head with a hatchet."

Amos, who had come to Reedyville to exhibit his voice, and not to act as a stretcher bearer for people he did not even know, kept turning his neck in the direction of the church, taking a step or two sideways in his effort to see. Unconsciously he adjusted his stride to the rhythm of the song which the congregation continued to sing; then, as if he could no longer contain himself, he began to hum with them, his voice tentative and apologetic.

Lula said: "Go on, Amos! Go on to the church and sing! You ain't got your mind on what you're doing! . . . Here, give me Mr. Wesley's legs. . . . Go on!" she continued. "Go on and tell the folks that me and Jesse'll be there directly!"

As if glad to be freed of his burden, Amos walked away rapidly, and before he had even reached the footpath, he began to sing: "My God's gwiner light a big burnin' in the sky," he sang. "Prideful sinner, you better trimble and hide!" His voice lifted powerfully above the voices of the other singers, and as he walked toward them, still singing passionately, they were silent at first, and then they began to hum an accompaniment to his bountiful voice, adjusting their smaller voices to his, as if they were only a chorus, and knew it, and a great soloist had appeared miraculously in their midst.

The sunset had reached its greatest power and color washed upward to the high poles of space. Long clouds, like islands, had now drifted to the place where the sun had set. They were purple and opaque, and their rims smouldered, as if washed in translucent and burning gilt. The sun itself had disappeared from sight, but somewhere its strength was not diminished, and its powerful rays, shooting upward from below the edge of the world, were caught against the backs of the opaque clouds, as if they were mirrors, and were reflected upward again in searching beams of steady light, reaching so high into distance that the mild, limited eye could not follow.

〰〰〰〰〰〰〰〰〰〰〰〰〰〰〰〰〰〰〰〰〰〰〰〰〰〰〰〰〰〰〰〰〰〰

Chapter 2

〰〰〰〰〰〰〰〰〰〰〰〰〰〰〰〰〰〰〰〰〰〰〰〰〰〰〰〰M RS. BOUTWELL was in error, when she said so positively that she had not met Dr. Snowfield; and she would have been astounded had she known that he was none other than Manny Nelloha, now grown to manhood and masquerading under a false name. Little Manny, of all people! Little Manny Nelloha, who had lived in Reedyville so long!

He had been the peculiar child of peculiar parents, and the family had settled in Reedyville from nowhere, it seemed, with no background, and apparently with no past. You thought of the elder Nellohas less as husband and wife, than as brother and sister: not because, separately, they resembled each other, but because, collectively, they resembled nobody else.

Manny, the son, was the same age as Fodie Boutwell, and they had been classmates. More often than not, he had come home with her from school, and had played fiercely with the Boutwell children until it was time for him to go home to his supper, delaying his departure with such transparent excuses that Ada would often say: "I declare, Fodie, it looks like your little friend don't *want* to go home, now don't it? If he had his way, I believe to my soul he'd get his clothes, and come live with us." Then she would laugh and shake her head, wondering what reasons lay behind the boy's odd behavior.

The truth of the matter was quite simple, and it was this: Manny was so ashamed of his parents that he often succeeded, through an involved series of subterfuges, in dismissing their existence from his mind, until that final, desperate moment came when he had to face, once more, the reality of their being.

The Nellohas ran a secondhand store, and junkyard, not far from the railroad station; and Joe, the husband, drove a brown mare, hitched to a canvas-covered wagon, through the streets. There was a cowbell fastened to the arch above the driver's seat, which he rang, for it was thus he told the townspeople he was approaching, and ready to buy from them those nondescript, worthless things which accumulate everywhere.

Sometimes, as if he were a wounded bird, whose one desire was to communicate its pain to mankind, he supplemented the ringing of his bell with an anguished cry of his own. Apparently the cry consisted of several words, although not one of them could be separated from its context, and understood; but since excellence of diction is only of the slightest importance in the junk trade, those who had old bottles, old metals or old clothes to dispose of knew easily enough what it was he wanted of them.

While her husband was away with the horse and wagon, Mrs. Nelloha served their customers at the store. These were mostly Negroes from the outlying farm country, or the wives of workmen looking for a bargain. Nobody knew how much English Joe or his wife could actually understand. In the store they would hold an object before a customer's eyes and state its price, sighing and lifting their brows upward in a gentle, supplicating manner. If the customer, in turn, asked a price lower than the one the Nellohas had fixed upon, they would look at each other in blank dismay, sigh, and confer with a muffled, chirping intensity. Then, having arrived at a decision, they would meet their customer's counter-offer, or restate, even more timidly this time, their original asking price.

They lived entirely to themselves, but isolation from their fellows seemed no hardship to them, and they appeared satisfied with the unexciting routine of their lives. The townspeople, if they had considered the matter at all, would have dismissed their oddities with a shrug, as they dismissed the oddities of all who had not been born in Reedyville, content to let the matter rest there.

Only St. Joseph, one of the most curious of men, tried to find an explanation for the baffling, almost eerie, impression they gave you of being rootless, abandoned, and the last of their kind. Once on seeing them chirping at each other in their native language and fluttering excitedly about their littered store, he said that they made him think of the last two specimens of a doomed species of bird, and he always felt at such times that some collector would momentarily rise from behind a counter and shoot them, with a cry of triumph, for preservation in his particular museum.

Manny spoke Spanish with his parents, when he found speaking with them unavoidable; or at least he had believed that what he spoke was Spanish, until he entered high school. He had thought that Spanish, since it was the language that he had first known, would be simple for him; but he soon discovered, at first to his puzzled astonishment, and later to his shame, that the dialect he had learned from his parents bore only a slight relationship to the classic Spanish taught in schools. This knowledge depressed him beyond all proportion to its importance, and for some days he was not able to go to school at all. He remained at home, in his room, during this period, and when his mother brought him food, he would not eat it. "We can't even speak Spanish, as I thought," he would say. "Not even that." He twisted his thin hands together, as if he wrung out a dishcloth, and said: "This is shameful! This is shameful!"

In those days, shame was the core around which his tangled thoughts and his tangled emotions shaped themselves endlessly. Some of his shame was grounded in the remediable fact that his suits and caps and overcoats were the recognizable castoffs of others which his father had bargained for on the streets of the town, and had bought after so much sighing, so much rolling of the eyes. Often he was conscious, as was everybody else in the school, that he was wearing a coat or a pair of pants which one of the boys in his class had discarded, as worthless, some months before.

When, in his desperation, he pointed this out to his parents, they rolled their eyes even more dramatically, and wondered from what source their son had inherited his peculiar notions. The clothes in question, they pointed out, had been washed and mended, and they were almost as good as new. They were warm and substantial. What else could anyone expect? It was not that they were poor, or even that they were stingy: it was merely that they lacked the capacity to understand humiliation, and to their way of thinking, no problem existed, outside their son's unpredictable mind.

It was this feeling of shame which bound Manny to the Boutwells, for they had no standards at all, and with them he need not make those comparisons between himself and others with which his mind was so often busy. He had been at the Boutwells on the day Wesley enlisted, and he was the boy who had stood behind Ada's rocking chair, and had read the note which Ira Graley confessed himself unable to read.

When he had finished, he stood there holding the note in his hand, not quite knowing what to do with it, while Ada rocked back and forth in her chair, and her tears, stifled successfully for a time, broke through afresh. "I declare," she said. "It looks to me like somebody's always trying to free colored people from something. First it was the Northerners that jumped on us, because they didn't have colored people of their *own,* and wanted to free ours so they could take them back North to work for *them.* My own papa fought the Northerners for four solid years. I remember him telling all about how it happened when I was a little girl."

Rance Palmiller, the precocious child, made his characteristic whistling sound of derision. He turned to the congregated children and winked, jerking his head backwards, in Ada's direction, as if to say: "Watch me! Watch me make a fool out of her!" Then he smiled in his maddening, superior manner and said: "If that's what your father told you, obviously he was too ignorant to know what he was talking about."

Clarry, his sister, said gently: "Rance! How many times has Papa told you not to dispute grown people, whether what they say is true or not? You ought to be ashamed of yourself, always disputing what people say."

But Ada, long adjusted to this obnoxious child, chose to ignore him. "First it was the Northerners freeing the colored people down here; now it's Wesley freeing the colored people in Cuba." She held her arms outward in a wide, dramatic gesture and continued: "Tell me now, what business is it of his? I say let the Cubans stay slaves! Little good freeing the colored people right here in Alabama has done!"

Rance Palmiller spoke naturally, forgetting for a moment the annoying mannerisms he affected: "Cubans aren't Negroes! How did you get that idea in your head?" He raised his eyebrows in a gesture which he had copied from St. Joseph, and shook his head, as if to repudiate any responsibility for the stupidities of those less gifted than himself.

Ada turned on him triumphantly, as if she had patiently waited her opportunity. "Now, Mr. Clarence Palmiller, this is the time I got *you!*" she said. She rocked more vigorously and continued: "How about that married couple who live on the far side of Sweethearts' Looking-Glass? They're from Cuba, ain't they? They're colored, ain't they? . . . Then how about old Cuban Annie that cooks for Miss Emmaline Maybanks and talks so funny you can't understand more than half of what she says? If Cuban Annie ain't black, may I never see black again!"

Rance lifted his handsome, plump face, so oddly mature, so oddly unlike the face of a boy of six, and said: "Of course there are Negroes in Cuba, but that doesn't make everybody there black. There are Negroes in Reedyville, too, but that doesn't make you one, does it?" He seemed bored, all at once, with the whole matter. He buttoned his coat, turned toward the gate and said reasonably: "Manny's people came from Cuba, or somewhere in that part of the world, I imagine; but that doesn't make *them* Negroes, does it?"

Clarry spoke patiently: "Rance," she said. "Rance, if you don't stop being rude to grown people, I'm going to tell Papa how you behave. I really will this time."

It was at that instant that Manny dropped the note he had just read, turned and walked down the steps. At the gate he stopped and looked back, knowing, somehow, that this was the last time he was to come to the Boutwell house during the days of his childhood.

There was something working in his mind which had not, as yet, become as definite as knowledge, and as he walked along on the footpath beside the red road, he held his nervous hands against his temples, as if to force back to its source a dreadful doubt, which, if permitted to enter his consciousness, must of necessity destroy him. But no matter how desperately he pressed with his hands, he remembered that he, too, had lived on an island somewhere, as Rance had thought possible; and on that particular island there had been no white people at all, if his memory could be trusted.

He sat down beside the road, but he could no longer control the flood of his thoughts. . . . There had been various shades of people on the island: pure black, yellow, brown, light brown — and, of course, themselves. If the other people were not white, what reason had he for assuming that they, the Nellohas, were white? For a moment it seemed as if his breath had stopped forever. He put his hands over his mouth and said: "No! No!" Then he got up and walked more rapidly down the road, glancing over his shoulder, as if he were being followed.

From that time onward, his shame, which at least had been built on realities, became lost in the wider and more flexible possibilities of doubt. It was not the doubt of the average man, which can be reconciled with reality, and dissipated with reason. It was a more massive thing, and its roots were so deeply hid in his mind that there was no possibility either of seeing where they originated, or of destroying them at their source.

He got into the habit of looking at himself in mirrors, seeking his salvation in the formation of his features. "If I really were a Negro," he would say to himself, "it isn't likely that I would have gray eyes and straight brown hair. My lips would be thick, and my nose would be flattened at the tip, instead of the way it is."

He would turn from the mirror, reassured for a moment, and at peace; and then his doubts would come over him once more, and he would hurry back to the looking-glass. "No," he would say. "No. The way I look means little. I never thought of myself as a full-blood Negro. I was never that silly. . . . But it isn't necessary for me to be a full-blood Negro. The slightest taint is all that's necessary!" And at once the maddening cycle of doubt would begin again.

Like all people of his kind, he projected his subtleties upon the outside world, and in the simplest responses of others, he now read the most abstruse and sinister meanings. He read these hidden meanings everywhere. If his teacher asked him to clean the blackboards, or to act as monitor for the day, a feeling of despair would come over him, a feeling so deep and so painful that he felt he could no longer bear to live. "You see?" he would think. "I'm fooling nobody. Everybody in town knows. They all know what we are."

It was some months later that he first considered the idea of changing his name to something so unmistakably white that there never could be another doubt, in his own mind, or in the minds of others, regarding his color; but here, again, uncertainty hindered him. Should he, for example (later on, of course, when he was far from Reedyville and his own master), take a name for himself whose sound was white, or should it be a name which was white through its associations?

He guardedly discussed this question with St. Joseph one day, leading up to his problem so indirectly, by such devious stages, that his intention could not easily be suspected. St. Joseph had had no suspicions at all, and he was delighted with the imagination of his clever, eccentric pupil. He raised his brows very high, and moved his hands about, as he always did when interested, and for a time he talked of the phenomenon of color-hearing, and the fascinating, incidental possibilities which such a faculty carried with it. He wondered if the boy himself were a color-hearer, but to his disappointment, this was not true.

He concluded, at length, that there were probably no light and no dark sounds in their own right; certainly not insofar as normal hearers were concerned; and it seemed to him, even in those authenticated case-histories where there appeared to be a tendency to see color through a joint functioning of the ears and the eyes, that the real answer was association as well, if all the baffling facts could be understood.

This intellectual preoccupation with his doubt was to come later to Manny, after his problem had become so acute, so all-embracing, and at first such abstractions did not concern him at all. On the day at the Boutwells' when doubt first came into his mind, the problem itself had instantly suggested its own solution: His mother would know whether or not they were Negroes, and he would ask her the question at once, with no waste of words.

He visualized the scene with crystal, unwavering clarity. At that hour his mother would be standing beside the stove cooking one of the dishes of rice, pork and tomato paste on which they lived, and he would walk up to her and say: "Are we white people or not? If we aren't, what part of us is Negro?"

At that moment something seemed to draw him up sharply from where he sat beside the clay road, and he walked rapidly away, his hands twisting and squeezing the moisture from each other, for in the reassuring dream which he had been seeing in his mind's eye, his mother had put down the chipped, blue platter she was holding and had said: "Certainly we are white people! Where do you get these strange ideas from?"

But suppose she did not say this? Suppose, instead, she sighed and answered: "We tried to keep it from you. How did you find out the truth?" Then, perhaps, she would come fluttering toward him, making her birdlike gestures, and saying: "We are not all Negro, of course. There's white blood in us, too. I don't know what the proportions are. I don't suppose it really matters."

It was then that anxiety almost intolerable in its intensity came over him, and he turned quickly from the road and went through the weeds and the young, second-growth pine, in the direction of the pond. Was it better, he wondered, to learn the truth from his mother, and thus forever settle the matter, or was it better to remain silent, never to ask the question, never to know the final answer?

He stood there among the young, knee-high weeds and looked at the countryside which flowed so serenely around him in its spring dress of new, untouched green. The sky above him was blue and beautiful, and its color was as even and as lustrous as bright enamel on a bowl. It seemed clean and new, as if polished that day by an industrious hand; and as the boy stood there in his agony, seeing the sky and the green earth with some level of his mind quite separate from the part concerned with his problem, a wet wind blew through the weeds, rippling them precisely and then releasing them, touching his flesh, and leaving an imprint of dampness against his hands and his cheeks, like drawn-out, clumsy kisses.

Then he dropped to his knees among the young, bitter weeds and wept bitterly, knowing at that instant how cruelly, and how wholly, the net had caught him. He cried with an intensity which left him breathless and drained of emotion, and in that first moment of exhaustion, when he uncovered his eyes and looked upward once more at the blue, complacent sky, it seemed to him that the sum of life was too harsh and too perplexing to be endured, and that was a sad conclusion for a boy of twelve to make.

A period of still quietness came over him then, a calmness so deep, and waiting, and sure that it seemed to him as if his mind were lit from within by an intense, cold light of its own making. He closed his eyes with a sense of overwhelming tiredness, feeling at that instant that the core of the world was wordless horror, and that he touched it, at last, with his wet, twisting hands.

He was to know many of these periods in the future, and in them he moved with certainty, his brain acting with such rapidity, such uncalculating surety, that nothing seemed beyond his grasp, no task too difficult for him to accomplish. Sometimes these clear, and yet dreamlike, periods were to last for an hour only, sometimes for days at a stretch. Much later, when it became necessary for him to make some compromise between the hidden world of his compulsions and the world of everyday reality in which he must also live, he found that he could, when necessity demanded it, summon or banish these periods of arrogant, trancelike suffering at will.

Later, he got up from where he lay in the weeds and went away, saying over and over: "I'll ask my mother the question at once. What have I got to be afraid of now? I'll ask her today, as soon as I get home, and settle the matter forever!" But he did not, neither that day nor that year.

The obsessed obey laws different, in the economies of their application, from those more normal people know; but on their own terms, they are rational, and they accord completely with the uncertainties which forced them into operation. And so it happened, not long after Wesley Boutwell returned mutilated, but in triumph, to his family, that Manny's mind made an enormous effort to discipline the obsessiveness of his thinking. This time his compulsions chose to work through the medium of another human being, a little girl some years younger than himself. Her name was Clarine Palmiller, although only her father called her by that somewhat pretentious name. To her mother, her teachers and the other people of Reedyville, she was simply Clarry.

Manny had known her for a long time, but he had not really been conscious of her until the time came for her to play her part in the sick drama of his mind. Her importance to him lay in her almost albino whiteness, and through some unconscious transposing of symbols, he became gradually convinced that as long as she remained immaculately white, it was impossible for him to be black. Since this was the way his mind was now to go, he could not have found a human being more suited to his need than Clarry Palmiller.

Her skin was of milky whiteness, with no hint of the yellowish-pink tint called flesh in it. Her hair was not yellow, nor even flaxen, as might reasonably have been expected. It was that silvery shade which was, years later, to be known as platinum. Even her eyes were as close to whiteness as it was possible for eyes to be: they were of the palest possible shade of blue, and they were as unexpressive and as substantial as moonstones in her calm, plump face.

It was, as Mrs. Palmiller soon discovered, a problem to find colors becoming to a type as unusual as that of her daughter. She solved the matter by enhancing the child's whiteness, rather than by attempting to modify it. Even the child's shoes and stockings were white, and she dressed her in the sheerest and whitest of frocks, with white satin hair ribbons and sashes.

She was a sweet, unimaginative child, the delight of grown people, and she submitted to their adulation with patient composure. Cindy, her mother, was afraid that her child would be made unbearably vain by so much praise, but she concerned herself without reason, for Clarry was stolid and practical by nature, and she took the admiration which she received everywhere as something to be accepted quietly, if the feelings of others were not to be hurt.

But if she put only the slightest value on the moist, clacking approval of adults, she found the intense, almost religious, adoration which she got from Manny exciting and sweetly disturbing. Soon she looked forward to seeing him after school, and if she did not find him waiting for her at their customary place, beneath the big sycamore tree in front of the Kenworthy house, she was disappointed, and as close to petulance as it was possible for her to be.

They were alike in at least one respect, for neither of them found any pleasure in speech, although their silences sprang from different causes. With Clarry, silence originated in a sense of proportion remarkable in a child, for already she had appraised her possibilities, and she knew that nothing she would ever say or think would be of the slightest importance. With Manny, the situation was entirely different, and he repressed speech as he repressed everything else, fearing that if once he let himself go, he would shout out his hatred against the world until people came, tied him, and took him away.

Clarry's birthday came in January, and each year her parents gave her a party. These celebrations had always been ambitious affairs in bad taste but the birthday party for 1900 was planned to be even more elaborate than the others, since as Mr. Palmiller pointed out so vigorously, it was both Clarry's tenth anniversary of life, an important enough milestone in itself, and the first month of a new century too. These were two things, two reasons for a party surpassing the others in lavishness. The third, the unstated reason, was the fact that, during the previous summer, the Palmillers had bought the old Wentworth home on Reedy Avenue, and it was proper that the first party in the new place should be on the same scale of magnificence as the house which was to be its background; for the Wentworth Place (as it was always to be called, no matter who happened to live in it) was the special pride of Reedyville people.

It had gone down in the twilight of the Wentworth grandeur, but with a man as rich as Mr. Palmiller for its new master, it was taking on much of its old splendor again. With its grounds, it occupied an entire block, and it was surrounded both by an iron fence and a privet hedge. By standing tiptoe and stretching your neck a little, if you were tall, or by stooping even lower, and peeping through gaps in the hedge, if you were not, you could see the smooth Wentworth lawns, populated with the iron images of stags, retrievers and rabbits, and studded with clumps of boxwood which had been cut back to resemble armchairs and sofas, with the addition of a few scattered tables and footstools.

The armchairs and the sofas were traditional, but the footstools and the occasional tables were the inspiration of the artist himself, as if, in the end, he had been taken in by his own cleverness, and had added the incidental comforts of civilization in order that when Mr. Palmiller's disembodied guests sat on the unreal sofas and chairs, they would have a resting place for their unreal feet and their unreal small belongings.

And so it happened that Mr. Palmiller wanted something special for his much loved little daughter, something more distinctive than imported caterers, or an orchestra from Mobile. He talked the matter over with Cindy, who, in turn, dumped the problem into the capable lap of Minnie McInnis McMinn. Mrs. McMinn saw the answer immediately.

"Why not," she began excitedly, "why not have a New Century Party? Why not ask the children to come dressed as the ideal of their dreams?" She stopped and tapped her lips, her eyes narrowed. "I mean by that," she continued, "since it's being given for children, and since it's the beginning of a new century, why not have the little guests fix themselves up to represent what they expect to become in the twentieth century?"

Cindy was pleased with the idea, and so were the two Palmiller children. At first she was not sure how her husband would react to such a frivolous and unscientific idea, but he fell into it at once. Nothing, he felt, could be too unique, too wonderful for his child, for Mr. Palmiller, so cold in his dealings with others, was humble and blindly adoring where Clarry was concerned. She had always known this, and the sense of fairness which had always individualized her told her that she must neither exploit the power she had over him, nor use his love as a lever to gain her own ends.

Manny Nelloha was the first child to hear about the coming celebration. That first day, when the children were marching into school, Clarry signaled to him, with mysterious smiles and nods, that he was to wait for her without fail when school was over; and as they walked home together that afternoon, she said: "You are the very first person I've invited. I wanted you to be the first to know about it, Manny. Before the other children knew, I mean."

"Why?"

"I won't tell you why, if you don't know already," she said. She took her books from him and stood at the gate which led through the carriage house to her home. "You're conceited enough as it is, and you know it!"

There was a silence and then Manny said: "I know what you must dress as. You must dress like a big lily." He squeezed his hands together and turned his head away nervously.

"What sort of a lily?" asked Clarry. She knew precisely what he meant, but she wanted the pleasure of hearing him say it. "There are lots of different kinds of lilies: There are rain lilies that come up around the house every spring, and there are tiger lilies that leave yellow soot on your fingers if you touch inside them. Then there are those little pink lilies that grow wild in the woods and smell terrible." She straightened the white satin bow which bound her long, flowing hair and looked innocently at him. "You mean you want me to dress as a bad-smelling pink lily, Manny?" she asked in a hurt voice.

"I mean an Easter lily," said Manny. "I mean a white, pure Easter lily." He came closer, and for the first time in his life he touched her face and her hair with his thin, twisting fingers. "You are so white," he said, as if the confession were wrung from him under torture. "You are so white and beautiful." Then, as if alarmed at his boldness, he wheeled and ran away, not turning his head again, not pausing to look back again, or to see Clarry standing there beside the carriage house gate, watching him with an approving, gentle smile on her lips.

When she could no longer see him, she went sedately up the long walk which led to the house. Her hands were thrust into her white wool coat, and her white serge skirt swished from side to side. Cindy met her at the door, and went with her to her bedroom. "Who was the boy you were talking to at the gate?" she asked. "He has such a disturbed face, hasn't he? Such an interesting, disturbed face!"

"That was only Manny Nelloha," said Clarry calmly, and added: "He's head over heels in love with me." She slipped from the white wool coat, and stood obediently while her mother brushed out her albino-like, unrippling hair, which hung limp and silken to her knees. "I asked Manny to come to my party," said Clarry when her mother paused and put the brush back on the dresser. "He thinks I'm the whitest, the purest and the most beautiful thing in all the world."

"How sweet of him to say it," said Cindy. She got down on her knees and held her daughter at arm's length, inspecting her with a new curiosity. "So soon?" she asked. "Oh, my dear — so soon?" Her cheeks were flushed a little, and her brown, leaf-colored eyes twinkled with amusement. "Of course you and Mr. Nelloha plan to be married one of these days," she added gaily. "I hope all the tiresome details have been arranged."

Clarry calmly ignored the question. At times she felt much older, much more settled than her mother. Since she was only ten, it wasn't likely that she'd be thinking seriously of marriage for some years, and that was a thing her mother should have realized, if she had stopped to think. To change the subject, she said: "I decided today what I want to be at the party. I want to be a white Easter lily."

Cindy said: "Dear! Dear! Never let a gentleman know how much power he has over you!" She hugged her daughter and laughed, and Clarry waited calmly until her mother released her. Then she said with curiosity: "How did you know *Manny* wanted me to go that way, Mama? Did I tell you that?"

The family was enthusiastic at her choice, and Mattie Tatum said she could make the costume. She took her crayons and a pad of paper, and made the right sketch at once. The cup of the lily began above the child's waist and ended just below her arms. The skirt of the costume was to be of white satin, and around it there was to be sewn a strip of green material which indicated the green of a lily stalk. There was another and a smaller lily to be worn on the child's head, and from beneath it, Clarry's hair was to flow white and silken and unimpeded.

As Clarry examined the sketch, she was reminded that everyone she had invited to her party, except Manny, had said instantly that they would come. He had neither refused nor accepted, but when she mentioned the matter to her mother, Cindy laughed, pretended to pinch her daughter's nose and said: "Manny is coming, my dear. If I know anything at all about boys, I know nothing in the world can keep him away. He's just trying to seem remote and bored. It's a well-known pose among males. You'll find out what I mean, after you've made your debut."

But Cindy, who had so much instinctive knowledge, was wrong where Manny was concerned; for to him the party became, at once, less a birthday celebration than a testing ground for his doubts. The problem of a costume, so difficult for many of the other guests, was simple enough for him, for he had the entire stock of his parents' haphazard odds and ends to choose from.

He wanted more than anything to go to the party, and if he did, he knew precisely how he would dress: He would represent a doctor in a frock coat and silk hat, who carried a medicine case. To make the illusion complete, he would wear a false mustache, and stick a Vandyke to his immature cheeks and jaws.

At first, he thought that it would be possible for him to go, but as he pondered the matter, the possibilities of disaster for him became more and more plausible. Suppose, for example, that Clarry had not told her parents she had invited him; and suppose, at the party, Mr. Palmiller should ask him to leave in a calm voice which would be more terrible, even, than shouts and curses?

He saw the entire scene with sickening clarity. "I'm sorry," said Mr. Palmiller in his nasal, Eastern voice, which had always seemed so strange and affected to the people of Reedyville. "I'm sorry my daughter was so thoughtless as to ask you here. Mrs. Palmiller and I ask your pardon for her mistake, but naturally we can't permit a Negro to come into our house as a guest."

Then he could see himself taken to the door, and hear it close behind him, while the last sound in his ears was the mirth of the children, who had held back their laughter as long as they could. At that instant, Manny jumped up and pushed back his schoolbooks. Sweat covered his face and hands, and his throat was so dry that he wondered if it would be possible for him to swallow again. His birdlike features twisted in pain, and his hands made a horrified, shoving gesture against the air; but when he had completed the senseless cycle of his agony, he became calmer, and he ridiculed himself and the foolishness of his doubts. With resolution, he washed his face and hands, and said: "I'll ask my mother now! I'm going to settle the question once and for all!"

Under the force of his new decision, he took three steps toward the door, only to stop there. Suppose his mother said: "Yes, son, I am white. It's your father who has the Negro blood." Or, "Your father is as white as anybody alive. I only wish I could say the same thing for myself." He stood with his mouth opened and twitching, his hand on the doorknob that led to his parents' room, caught up in new doubts, which he had not before anticipated.

In the past, in his speculations, he had considered no answer except a simple yes or no, an answer which included them all, without distinction. His new doubts tapped potentialities more subtle in their implications, for if one of his parents were white, and the other were not, then the injustice — or so it seemed to him — was enormous indeed. The adjustments he would have to force upon himself in such a situation! The compromises he would have to make!

He moved away from the door and lay face downward on his bed. "No! No!" he said aloud. "It's better not to ask at all! It's better never to know the truth!" Then, instinctively, as it always did when he was caught up in anxieties which were almost unbearable, his mind turned in a last desperate hope to Clarry Palmiller, and her unchanging whiteness. Without thought, and without understanding the implication of his words, he spoke from the muddied depths of his driven mind: "Clarry! Clarry!" he said. "Don't ever change. . . . If you change, I'll die."

And so this sick, pitiful child lived during the days preceding the New Century Party. In one of his trancelike stages, he assembled the costume he had planned. He was nearing fifteen, and he had almost got his full height, so the old Prince Albert coat from his father's shop did not fit him too badly. The striped trousers were somewhat large at the waist, but he fastened them with safety pins at the back, and at least they were adequate. The only opera hat in his father's store — it had once belonged to old Colonel Wentworth, and the Paris label was still readable — was too large, but he made it fit him after a fashion by padding the sweatband with pieces of paper cut into strips. Then, with much patience, he fashioned the mustache and the Vandyke, which seemed so important to him, and fixed them to his face with spirit gum.

The effect, as he looked at himself in the mirror, was astonishing. He stared back at his image, fascinated by the changes he had been able to make in himself. Then, in a flash, he thought of the one thing his outfit needed: It was a pair of nose glasses, with gold rims and a black ribbon dangling from one end of the frames, and his father had had it in stock for a long time. He got the glasses and slipped the cord around his neck. He held the glasses to his eyes, first as one holds lorgnettes, but he found that he could see nothing through them; and very carefully, very delicately, he took out the lenses and set the vacant gold frames onto his nose. He took a slow breath, stepped forward and stretched out his hand to the unfamiliar figure. "How do you do, Dr. ——" he began, and stopped in bafflement, for the name he was eventually to take for his own, had not, at that time, occurred to him.

This had been on one of his calm mornings, when he moved with surety in the frozen, crystal clarity of his individual world, when he could see himself with some objectivity, and even ridicule the monstrous thing he had built up for his own destruction; but before the day was over, he had slipped back into his old uncertainties, his old doubts. It was thus that things went until the day of the party. On that afternoon, he dressed himself twice, and twice he took off his costume and distributed its parts to their original places in his father's stock. At last he sat on the edge of his bed, trembled with exhaustion, his thin face held in his hands. "I can't do it!" he said. "It's too much to ask of me! It's too much to expect!"

Since he had made up his mind at last, a small feeling of peace came over him, and he thought that if he dared not risk being driven from the Palmiller house, he could, at least, compromise by slipping unseen into the Palmiller yard, which he knew well, and looking at the guests through one of the drawing room windows. It would be enough, he felt, if he could see Clarry dressed as a lily, in all her whiteness, all her purity. That would be enough. It would have to suffice.

January was always an uncertain month, and the Palmillers could not decide whether to hold the party on the lawn, or inside, in the big, double parlors. As a matter of precaution, it was decided to hold it indoors, but as it turned out, it could have been held outside as easily, for the day of Clarry's party was remarkably mild and springlike.

It was one of those still, bright days of winter, when the sun shines with clear, impersonal brilliance, but with little heat, as if its rays were filtered through cool water. There was no wind that day, and the intricate, lacelike silhouettes of trees stood flat and brittle against the washed horizon — unbending, toylike, and fixed beneath the spread dome of the shining, crystal sky.

Cindy Palmiller had invited a few of her women friends for the afternoon, but it was understood that they were neither to participate in the party for the children (after the various costumes had been admired) nor interfere with their pleasures. Later on, Mr. Paul Kenworthy, the photographer, was to come with his camera and take pictures, and as the ladies sat in the Palmiller library, talking together, or playing cards, they touched their hair and straightened their clothes at each strange sound from the hall, thinking that already Mr. Kenworthy had come.

Mrs. McMinn put down her cup of tea, broke off a bit of angel cake and popped it into her mouth. "I'm thinking of giving up fiction," she said in answer to Miss Emmaline Maybanks' question. "It seems to me I've already exhausted the possibilities of that form."

She went on to explain that at the moment she was toying with the idea of doing a scientific book, to prove that the progenitors of the human race had not been male and female, as was popularly supposed, but female alone: a self-sufficient female, capable of her own fertilization. Those lost days had been the ideal days, the Golden Age of the sexual relation, but tragically enough, with the passing of time, certain biological sports had appeared — decadent females in whom the fertilization factor had been disproportionately great. Then, gradually, other attributes which the primal female stock had possessed disappeared, until the offshoot type became so limited, so specialized in its one trivial function, that apparently a second sex, the masculine, had appeared to beset and disrupt the world.

It was thus plain that there was no such thing, historically speaking, as a man. There was only that true to type ancestress of us all, woman, and the degenerate offspring which she had inappropriately produced.

Miss Emmaline Maybanks covered her ears with her black-lace-mitted hands. "I think what you say is horrible, Minnie!" she exclaimed. "How does a respectable woman like yourself learn such things?"

"If you think that's shocking," said Minnie cheerfully, "just listen to the life story of the Bonellia, one of the marine annelids. *There's* something that will make you sit up!" She raised her eyebrows patiently. "To my mind," she continued, "the Bonellia is the most fascinating of all living creatures. The size of the male, as compared with the female, is about the size of an English pea compared to a haystack, as nearly as I can estimate from the measurements I read about; but even at that, the grown female Bonellia is no bigger than a pigeon's egg, so you can imagine what the male of the species must be!"

She paused, letting the full force of her words sink in, and then went on dramatically. "If the female Bonellia comes across the larva of her kind, while it is swimming about in the ocean, she catches it up and pops it into her mouth. There the larva, quite sexless so far, undergoes certain changes, and develops into a complete male."

"Good heavens, Minnie!" said Mrs. Kenworthy. "Are you telling the truth, or is it something you made up in your own mind?"

"Every word is true," said Minnie. "We have the assurances of scientists that it is. I read about the Bonellia in a book the other night. . . . Why, of course it's true!" she added indignantly. "It's common knowledge! It's a thing which educated people everywhere know about, and discuss when they get together!"

She had a feeling of triumph, seeing her respectable friends so impressed. "Now, listen to this part," she went on, "and deny, if you can, that my theory is wrong: After the Bonellia is fully developed into a male, he fixes himself to his wife's body like a parasite, and there he stays for the rest of his life."

Old Mrs. Wentworth put down her cup and leaned forward in her chair, her eyes starting from her head. "Minnie McInnis!" she thundered in her baritone voice. "How can you sit there and say such indelicate things! You, a college woman from a good family!" She reached up and eased with her ringed fingers the wide, jet collar which supported her crumbling neck. "Why, I knew your poor mother!" she went on in a horrified voice. "I actually knew your mother, young woman!"

"*I* don't say indelicate things!" said Minnie indignantly. "*Science* says indelicate things!" She turned to old Mrs. Porterfield, but the latter would not let their eyes meet. Then she shrugged her shoulders, straightened her skirt defiantly, and continued: "There's one other thing about the Bonellia which I think you ladies ought to know, having heard as much as you have, and it's this: If the young of the species fails to come in contact with a female, for modification, it grows up on its own account, and it grows up invariably as a *female!*"

She lifted the silver locket which she wore on a long chain and raised her hands outward in triumph. "So you see?" she said. "Universal femaleness is obviously the natural state of the Bonellia, and the male, from the evidence I've given, is pretty plainly a degenerated female with a specialized function to perform."

Cindy Palmiller leaned back in her chair and laughed, shaking her head from side to side, her brown eyes dancing with merriment. "Perhaps you ladies would prefer to hear about the sexual oddities of the snail?" said Mrs. McMinn. "Or even about the praying mantis, or the Louisiana heron."

"Young woman," said old Mrs. Wentworth, bringing both feet solidly down upon the carpet, as if she had reached the limit of human tolerance, "young woman, don't you dare!"

It was at this moment that Cassie, the Palmiller cook, came to the library door and asked to speak in private with her mistress. Cindy followed her into the kitchen, and when they were alone, with the door discreetly closed, Cassie spoke slowly, as if weighing her words. The problem was a delicate one, since it concerned white people, but it seemed that Jesse, the yardman, had seen a white boy sneaking through the yard and behaving in such a manner that he wondered if he weren't a thief. So he had kept out of sight behind the big boxwood sofa on the lawn, and watched while the boy approached the house, and hid behind the sweetshrub bushes. Then Jesse had come up and he had caught the boy red-handed, at the moment when he was trying to work loose one of the shutters.

"Was it a child, you say?"

"It was a half-growed boy," said Cassie, and added: "Jesse keep saying to him, 'What you doin' around our house, white boy? You better go on and tell me like I asks. You better tell me.' But the boy, he don't say nothing, and so Jesse locked him up in the woodshed, until he could ask you what to do." Then, seeing the disapproving look on her mistress's face, Cassie's voice went an octave higher, as if thus she established her own innocence, and she said: "I told Jesse not to lock that boy up! I told him: 'How that white boy gwiner tell what he been up to? That boy so scared, he can't tell nobody nothing!' "

"Do you know who the boy is?"

"Yassum," said Cassie wryly, as if his existence were an affront to her. "Yassum, I knows who he is; but don't worry none about *that,* cause it ain't nobody we'd ever be likely to know." She dusted her hands with distaste, and continued: "Hit's that old junkman's son, that's who it is." But before she stopped speaking, Cindy was already hurrying down the walk, in the direction of the shed; and when she came inside, she saw Manny sitting on a bench, while Jesse stood blocking the door, shaking his red, kinky head and saying: "Don't you move offen that bench, white boy! Don't you try and run away again, befo' we see what you stole out of the house!"

As Cindy hurried down the long walk, she had not been certain what she should say, what course she should take, and she whispered with exasperation: "Really, Clarry must be more careful. Perhaps her father and I have shielded her too much. She must learn to use better judgment in selecting her friends."

At that time, the reasons behind Manny's behavior had not occurred to her, but when she saw him dressed in his shabby, everyday clothes, his face still set, as if frozen, in the agonized expression it had worn when he realized that the thing he had sought to avoid with such care had happened to him, after all, she understood, or at least she fancied she did, the reasons which forced him to refuse the invitation to the party, and yet made it imperative for him to creep up, like a thief, and look at the guests from the outside. "Poor child," she thought indignantly. "He had nothing to wear like the others! How could he possibly show himself inside?"

Her manner changed at once and she came to him with her hand outstretched in welcome, as if she always received her more distinguished guests here in the woodshed. "How nice of you to come, Manny!" she said gaily. "We've been expecting you. Clarry kept asking if you'd come. She particularly wanted you to see her in her new dress!"

Manny neither turned his head nor lowered his eyes from his stunned contemplation of the woodpile in front of him; and Cindy, knowing her first approach had failed, sat beside him on the bench. "I know precisely how you feel," she said. "Your pride is hurt. . . . Oh, I know all about hurt pride. Mine has been hurt often enough, you may be sure. Now, here's what I suggest: Nobody knows about this except the three of us, and we'll all swear not to tell, if you want us to. So let's do this: Let's you and I go up the back stairs, and I'll fix you up in a costume which will look perfectly fine on you."

The boy seemed not to have heard her, and she turned to the two servants, who were watching the scene from the doorway. "Before you go back to your work, I want you two to promise you'll never say one word about this to anyone. It's a mistake, and I don't want anybody to know what's happened."

The two Negroes looked at each other and then spoke at once: "Yassum! Yassum!" they said, their voices hesitant and unconvinced. They turned from the door, and Cindy was alone with the boy. She took his limp, icy hands in her own and spoke in a coaxing, eager voice: "There's a perfectly fine uniform which my brother wore in military school. I know just where it is, and if you'll agree, we can have you dressed up in it in no time at all. Shall we do that, Manny? Shall I make a dramatic entrance on your arm down the big front stairs?"

She paused and regarded the child more carefully, turning his frozen, unresisting face toward her own. She looked earnestly into his luminous, birdlike eyes, and he lowered his lashes, took a deep breath and shuddered weakly, as if bringing himself back to reality with a force so tremendous that it left him drained of all energy.

"I'd like to go home," he said.

A sense of pity, so deep that it made her twist her head from side to side helplessly, came over Cindy. "Manny! Manny!" she said desperately. "You must not let this bother you so. I know how you feel, my dear. But you'll forget all about it, in no time at all. It's of no importance. Please be sure of that." Then she tried another way: "I know how you feel, so well, because things like this have always happened to me. Yes, they have! From my childhood! They used to call me Fuddlehead Cindy at home. All my friends did. . . . Why, once when I was just about your age, I was visiting my mother's people in Natchez, and one afternoon my aunt had some of her friends in to four-o'clock tea. She was showing me off, you see, and I was nervous, and I didn't know what to do with my hands and feet. Then my aunt took me by the hand and led me over to an old lady and said: 'Mrs. Nettletown, I want you to meet my young niece, Lucinda Lankester. She's from Reedyville, Alabama, and she's visiting us for a few weeks.' "

Cindy lowered her eyes, collecting her thoughts. When she looked up, she saw that Manny had turned his face away from her, and again his agonized, frozen gaze was fixed on the wall before him. She shook her head with disbelief, as if amazed at what she was going to tell him, and touched his arm gently. "When my aunt finished the introduction, I didn't know what to say, so I just blurted out the first thing that came into my mind — I was so

clumsy and foolish, you see — and this is what it was: 'Nettletown?'
I repeated. 'That's an unusual name, isn't it?' 'Yes,' said the old
lady, 'yes, it is, my dear.' Then I said, 'I've only heard that name
once before in my life: Back home, some people were talking about
a Mr. Nettletown. It seemed that he took a lot of money from the
bank where he worked, and when they were about to catch up with
him, he put a pistol in his mouth, and blew his brains out, right
there before everybody.'

"By this time," continued Cindy, "the whole room was listening,
but I couldn't stop! Oh, no, not me! . . . 'Was he a relative of
yours?' I asked. And then the old lady took my hand and said
quietly: 'Yes, my child. He was my dearly loved son.' "

Cindy shuddered and laughed at the same time. "So you see,
Manny? I do know how you feel, in a way! . . . I stood there
while the old lady held my hand, and thought: 'Dear God! Dear
God! — Open up the earth, and let me fall in!' And when the people
here in Reedyville heard what I'd done, they simply roared with
laughter and said, 'Well, isn't it what you'd expect from old Fuddlehead Cindy Lankester?' "

Cindy raised her hands and held them over her face. When she
took them away, she saw that the boy had got up and was walking
down the path that led to the gate. He held his neck rigidly, as
if he had lost the power to turn it, and he moved his feet with
such a jerky, shambling motion that it seemed as if contact between
his body and his brain had been broken. She walked to the door
of the shed and watched him. She had expected him to turn back,
for a last look, but he neither moved his head nor varied his pace.

He had been engaged with his own thoughts while Cindy had
talked to him, and he had heard nothing of what she had said;
for he was living, at that interval, in what he had come to call
his White World; and in it, this child who had never so much as
seen snow stood on the crest of a hill and watched the white flakes
falling and covering the earth. The snow dropped softly down, in
his dream, and as he walked down the side of the hill, and into the
frozen world, the flakes fell coldly on his hands and his upturned
face.

Already his world was white and frozen and soundless when
he walked away from the Palmiller house. Its harsh outlines were

gone, lost under a satin quilt of white and stinging snow; and when
he reached the gate, and passed through it, he heard, at last, the
sound of the pure, silver bell, which rang, at such moments, in
the sick cave of his mind.

Cindy watched as he passed through the gate, thinking: "Poor
child! Poor, pitiful child!"

She never saw him again, and not long afterwards, his parents
sold their store and disappeared. It was said later on that they had
gone to Pensacola, but nobody seemed to be sure; and years later,
when he came back to Reedyville, not as himself, but as Dr. Albert
Snowfield, and rented offices in the Howard Block, he had long
since been forgotten. At that time, his parents were dead, and he
had been practising medicine for about four years.

Nobody recognized him upon his return, and this was not strange,
for the changes in his appearance were startling. He had not grown
very tall, but his body and his thin, birdlike face had filled out
somewhat. His limp, straight hair was now brushed back in the
flat pompadour so popular at that time, instead of falling into his
eyes, as it had in the past. Then, too, he was wearing a mustache,
and his neat, carefully trimmed beard hid his chin, and added at
least ten years to his age.

It is difficult to believe that eyes can, at once, be cold and disinterested, and yet suggest the most feverish eagerness, but that was
the effect which the long, gray eyes of Dr. Snowfield had on others.
Perhaps too much study had weakened them, for he now wore
gold-rimmed pince-nez, with a black ribbon attached. He was something of a dandy in his dress, and since the death of his father had
made him a well-to-do man, he wore beautifully tailored morning
coats, and expensive, striped trousers.

For a week or two Reedyville asked itself why a man so cos-
mopolitan, so gifted, and obviously so prosperous, should pick a
town like theirs to settle in, and then it forgot him again. Dr. Snowfield could have told them quickly enough, had he cared to, that
his return to Reedyville was a thing over which he had no control;
that the force which had brought him back was Clarry Palmiller
and her whiteness.

Following her party, he had gone through a period of violence.
He told his parents that they must leave Reedyville at once, and

when they made their liquid, conciliatory protests, he went into
rages, in which he cursed them and called them Negroes. At night
he walked about the store muttering furiously to himself, eaten up
with a rage so intense that he felt he must be demented.

His hatred of his parents, when they would not meet his demands,
grew so much that they were afraid of him. At night, they locked
themselves in their room, and huddled together, trembling. At last
they gave in, sold their business, and moved away.

It was then that Manny entered upon a new phase of his sickness,
a period of furious mildness. In it, he decided to dedicate his life
to relieving the oppressions of the poor, to righting the injustices
of the world, and to destroying the barriers which mankind has
erected between its classes; provided, of course, that he be the arbiter
of what was oppressive and what was not, the judge of what con-
stituted injustice, and what did not. Had he lived in other times,
he would have fitted his obsessions into other movements with equal
ease; for the great distinction of his particular type is its ability to
adjust its drives to the ideas of its day, and so, while the impulse
and the power remain constant throughout all generations, the
goal of the drive is a variable one.

During this period, after his graduation, when Clarry came back
to play her role in his mind once more, he daily wrote her a letter
which he did not send, a letter in which he poured out his un-
happiness and despair. These letters, some of which have been
preserved, were much alike, and a quotation from one of them
will give the flavor of them all. He wrote: —

My thoughts have been turning toward you again, my darling — my
pure, incorruptible darling — now that I am a doctor and ready to
start my life's work of curing the sick, and of comforting those who are
even more unhappy than I — if such people really live! I have changed
much; I have learned much; I have gone far, my white one! I understand myself now, in a small degree, and I could even tell you, in
general terms, what besets me. I am like a diagnostician who can
describe his illness, but must remain helpless with his knowledge, being
able neither to relieve his pain, nor to cure his sickness.

Are you angry with me because I forgot you for so many years?
You must not be, my lily, my white one! I implore you not to be angry
with me! You would not be, if you knew that I was not able to forget
you, after all; that you have come back to me again in all your power,

and that I stand ready, at this moment, to serve you forever with my hand and my heart — with my life, too, if you want that of me!

I do not want you in any physical sense, my beloved. I have been through all that. I have had my full, ugly share of experiences. Oh, no, that isn't what I want of you, and I implore your pardon for even thinking of you, at the moment that these other things are in my mind.

I do not even ask to take part in the realities of your life. It will be enough for me to know that you are alive and white and immaculate! . . . Does that make you laugh? You must not laugh at me! You must not! If you could see me now, you would not. Your sweet, untouched heart would be torn with pity for me, instead!

Do not betray me, my love! Do not destroy my last hope! Remain forever the one pure, incorruptible thing in this hideous world!

Each night and each morning, for a time, he said a curious, meaningless prayer, whispering her name at the end as if it were a mystic amen. He imagined, in so doing, that he compelled her to think of him at the same instant. And at last, when he could no longer bear being away from her, he returned to Reedyville. He returned more complex, more baffling even, than he had been when he went away, for with the passing of time, and the maturing of his mind, the factors of guilt and innocence, sin and atonement, had been added to the less elaborate structure of his original black and white.

The offices he took were not quite what he wanted insofar as space and comforts were concerned, but their windows faced the Palmiller State Bank, across the square, and that was the important thing; for he had learned that each afternoon at precisely one o'clock Clarry came to take her father home to lunch, in the automobile which he refused to drive; and from his desk by the window, Dr. Snowfield could plainly see her as she sat and waited. This was his one contact with her, but it was all that he asked.

He had told himself before his return that she had probably become fat and unattractive, or that she had married one of the local boys long ago, and at the age of twenty-six, she was no doubt the mother of several whining, sniffling children. In his heart he believed none of these things, and when he saw her for the first time after his return, it seemed to him that she was more beautiful, more perfect, according to his standards, than he had remembered her as being.

He looked forward with greater and greater eagerness for the hour when she drove up in front of the bank and waited for her father. At such times he would gaze steadily at her from behind his blinds, his eyes fixed and unblinking, his hands resting as quietly against the shutters as if they were dead. If she failed to appear on any particular day, he was depressed and unhappy until he was able to assure himself once more of her existence.

Sometimes when this feeling was very strong, he would pass her house or go to one of the places where she was likely to be, for he soon became a specialist in her habits. He never looked at her openly, but often he was conscious that she was examining him with impersonal, well-bred curiosity, and at such times he wondered how it was possible that she had forgotten him so completely, forgetting, for the moment, the elaborate pains he had gone to in order to insure her not recognizing him.

And then, one afternoon, after his last patient had gone and he was alone in his office, the thing which he had not taken into account in his plans actually occurred. From behind his blinds, where he had been watching her as she walked down the street, he saw her look about her in a manner which was almost furtive, and then glance directly at his window. It was almost as if her eyes had met his own, as if she had seen him there watching her, and he stepped back instinctively.

At once he realized that it was not possible for her to have seen him, and he went cautiously to his post again, and adjusted the slats of the blinds so that he could follow her movements across the square. When he saw her cross the street and turn into the courtyard which led to his offices, he abandoned all caution, and leaned through his opened blinds, to follow her as far as he could. Then quickly he closed his blinds again and stood beside his window, caught up in one of those panics which he had not experienced since childhood, his hands beating back and forth against the air.

Instantly he closed his eyes and summoned all the power of will that he could command. In a moment he knew that he was safe, that one of his efficient, frozen intervals of calmness was taking possession of him; and when Clarry came into his office, he seemed entirely self-possessed, entirely the master of himself.

He did not speak at once, but sat behind his desk, surveying her

with unhurried, professional interest. She had changed little with
the years. Her hair had darkened somewhat. It was now a pale
yellow, but somehow the deepening of its color enhanced, rather
than lessened, the pure, incredible whiteness of her flesh. She was a
tall woman, taller than Dr. Snowfield himself, and her bust and
hips were of the heroic mold once so greatly admired. She spoke
after a while: —

"I've come to consult you professionally, Dr. Snowfield."

"Yes?"

"I am Miss Palmiller. Perhaps you know who we are?"

"Yes," said Dr. Snowfield. "Yes, I know."

Clarry frowned, lowered her eyes and played nervously with the
handles of her pocketbook. Dr. Snowfield spoke first: "Dr. Kent
is your family doctor, isn't he? Then why did you come to me for
advice?"

Clarry spoke without raising her eyes. "I came to you because I
need help, Dr. Snowfield. I'm desperate, and I need help very badly.
When I've explained, you'll see why I couldn't go to Dr. Kent;
why it's easier for me to talk to somebody I don't know."

She bit her lip and looked at the wall beyond him, and for a
moment Dr. Snowfield thought that she was going to cry. When she
recovered, and was able to look at him once more, he said: —

"You are pregnant, of course."

"I'm so ashamed!" she said. "I'm so ashamed!"

Then, collecting herself, she looked at him steadily and told him
the story with practical directness, which was the quality he remembered in her so well. When she had finished, he said: "Why don't
you simplify matters by marrying the man? That would be the
easiest way out."

She seemed alarmed at the suggestion, and quite prepared for it,
as if it were a thing she had debated in her mind for a long time.
"No! No!" she said at once. "That would never do. In the
first place, he wouldn't marry me, I'm sure. Then, too, I wouldn't
want it either. Oh, no, Dr. Snowfield — that's not to be considered!"

Dr. Snowfield closed his eyes, and his brain raced furiously. He
remembered all the men he had seen her with, all of those whose
names had been linked with hers in the *Courier*, since his return to

Reedyville — trying, in his desperation, to fix upon the one responsible for her plight. He could not, and so he said: —

"You haven't told me who the man is, Miss Palmiller?"

She seemed greatly perturbed at that. She shook her head and said at once: "No. No, I can't do that! There's no reason why he should be dragged into this! No, I won't tell you that!" Then, feeling that she had been too vehement, she added apologetically: "I'm willing to take all the responsibility. The man knows nothing about it, at all. I don't want him to know."

"He betrayed you, didn't he?" asked Dr. Snowfield gently. "It seems to me that he should be held responsible now."

Clarry spoke slowly, as if measuring each word. "No, he did not betray me," she said. "Perhaps he thought he did, but really he did not. I knew quite well what I was doing. I went into this thing with my eyes wide open. . . . No," she continued, "he must not be held responsible. It wasn't his fault." As she sat there looking helplessly at her hands and shaking her head in stubborn denial, she would have been surprised to have been told that she was a woman of great moral character, but that is what she was.

She spoke again soon afterwards: "If it's a question of your fee, that can be arranged. I have some money of my own. I can afford to pay you generously, if you'll help me."

Dr. Snowfield got up from his desk, as if the interview were over. "My fee," he said distinctly, "is three dollars a visit — that is, when I bother to collect any fee at all." He walked to the window and looked through the blinds. "I'll do what you want," he said at last. "Come here again tomorrow morning, before my regular office hours start, and we can arrange the details."

She nodded, and he went on quickly: "Of course there's always a risk in these operations. I have my professional reputation to consider. Now, I want you to bring with you a letter, written in your own hand, saying that you'd attempted the operation yourself. Or better still, that some old woman, whom you refuse to identify, tried to help you, and failed. Then you must say that only afterwards, only after the operation had been done, did you call me in."

Clarry said: "I'm quite willing to do that. It's only fair to you."

She collected her belongings and went away, and it was, he felt, just in time, for the control which he had maintained with such an enormous effort was now leaving him. When he saw her crossing the square once more, he went to his bedroom and lay on his couch, staring with fixed, unblinking eyes at the ceiling above him.

This meeting between Clarry Palmiller and Dr. Snowfield had taken place a few days before Wesley Boutwell fell down the embankment and hurt his head; and when Dover, almost out of breath, ran up the doctor's steps and rang the bell on that particular night in September, there was no immediate answer. He rang again, but still nobody came. Then, seeing that the door was on the latch, and that a light was burning inside, he went in, whistling loudly, so that those inside would not mistake him for a thief.

Dr. Snowfield sat in front of his desk, at his post beside the window, examining his spread hands as if he had never seen them before. At first he gave no sign that he knew the boy was there, and then he looked up and spoke. "Well, what do you want with me?" he asked. His voice was blurred and without expression, as if he spoke from a dead world to dead people.

"Papa fell off the culvert and got hurt," said Dover. "Mama says, please sir come as quick as you can."

There was a silence, and then Dr. Snowfield said: "You're one of the Boutwells, aren't you? Which one? Stacy?"

"No, sir," said Dover in surprise. "Stacy is a grown man about thirty years old. He's a brakeman on the L & N. Stacy's married and lives in Atlanta, Georgia, now."

"Are you Breck?"

"No, sir. Breck's the one with the turned-back thumb. He runs Rowley's Pool Parlors. He's a grown man too."

Dr. Snowfield sighed and got up, reaching, from habit, for his medicine case which was packed and on the table to his right. "Of course," he said. "I'd forgotten how time passes. . . . Of course, you couldn't be either Stacy or Breck; I see that now." He went into his bedroom and washed his face and hands. Through the door he said: "You must be the baby of the family, Grennie."

Dover was on the point of explaining that Grennie was nineteen years old, and had left home the summer before to sail on a schooner out of New Orleans; but before he could speak, Dr. Snowfield came out of his bedroom, wiping his face on a towel. He seemed to have lost all interest in the Boutwells and their particular histories. He said, leaning for support against the door: "My price is three dollars a visit. Three dollars in advance. Put the money on my desk, please."

"I haven't got any money with me," said Dover quickly. "Mama didn't say anything about paying you. She just said for you to come as quick as you could."

Dr. Snowfield stood by the door, as if undecided whether or not to make this professional call; then, heavily, he sat again in the chair at his desk, shook his head and stared once more at his spread fingers, as if he read a revealing sentence there. Dover watched him uneasily, undecided what to do next; and then he ran down the steps, in the direction of his home. His mother would know what to do in this unexpected emergency, and he sped toward her as fast as he could.

The sunset was diminishing, and some of its color had gone from the sky. Now, there were more delicate shades of color to be seen: there was pink and lavender and pearl against the horizon, smoothed out unevenly, and spread thick, like luster. The insects and the small animals which had been silent while the sun flamed so brilliantly, so dangerously, above them, now, as if reassured, made their particular noises once more; and from the withering reeds at the lip of Sweethearts' Looking-Glass, there came the harsh and patient cries of frogs, imploring rain. A line of sparrows, settling for the night on the telephone lines, ruffled out their brown feathers and made a drowsy sound; and in front of the Boutwell house itself, two martins, flying precisely, turned and dipped for the same insect, the last, broken rays of light caught, and held for an instant, in the depths of their falling, purple wings.

When he came into the house, his mother and the two Negroes had put Wesley to bed, and were standing beside him, watching him. Ada had washed the dried blood from his face, and had combed his hair. With the aid of the woman, she had put a clean, blue shirt on him, so that he would be decent when the doctor came. Dover told the story quickly, and Ada said, almost before the last words were out of his mouth: —

"I never heard tell of anything like that in my whole life! A

doctor's a public servant! He don't have no say about who he's
going to treat, and who he ain't!"

Lula spoke in a high, indignant voice: "That don't sound like
Dr. Snowfield, to me!" she said. "It just don't *sound* like him!
Why, he's been treating me and Jesse ever since he come to town,
and he ain't never asked us for money so far!" She shook her head,
saddened at the depravity of humans. "But if this the way Dr.
Snowfield gwiner act from now *on*," she added ominously, "always
going around asking people for *money,* then I'm gwiner start right
back with Dr. Kent."

Ada was not listening to these trivial things, for already she was
turning over in her mind the sources from which she could reasonably expect to get three dollars. "I do wish Professor St. Joseph and
Mr. Robert Porterfield had stayed here in town, instead of going
on that fishing trip together," she said in exasperation. "Either one
of them would let me have the money in a minute."

Lula said: "Yes, ma'am. Yes, ma'am, that's the truth."

"Mrs. Palmiller owes me four dollars and fifty cents," said Ada
reflectively. "I didn't stop by to get it today because I knew Clarry
was so sick, and I thought they might all be upset." She spoke
more vigorously to Dover: "Son, maybe Mr. Palmiller is still at
the bank. Now, you run there as fast as you can and collect the
money. Tell him what it's for, and he'll pay you."

Dover moved away, but she stopped him. "Wait a minute," she
added briskly. "Wait now." She spread her hands flat against her
cheeks and inclined her head to one side. "If Mr. Palmiller's gone
home to be with Clarry, then go see Mrs. Kenworthy, and ask her
to advance you the money against next week's work that I promised to do."

"Yes, ma'am," said Dover.

"If Mrs. Kenworthy is over at the Palmillers' too, then you go
see if you can get the money from your sister Fodie. Don't tell her
what it's for, if you can help it. Just say I sent you and that I need
it bad." She turned in explanation to Lula and added: "If there's
a tighter woman in this town than my daughter, I haven't met up
with her yet."

Dover moved more closely to the door. "Wait, now!" said his
mother. "Don't be so fast! If Fodie can't let you have the money,

then go see Minnie McInnis McMinn. I don't like to worry her while she's working so hard on the moving picture story, but if I have to, I have to."

Dover stood half in and half out of the door, and his mother continued: "You ought to have the three dollars long before now, but if you haven't, then maybe you can borrow it from your brother Breck at the poolroom. But don't ask him except as a last resort."

She sighed and rearranged her stringy hair, and Dover bounded through the gate, in the direction of the Palmiller State Bank. When he had gone, Jesse went to the church to join the singers, but Lula said she'd wait with Ada until the doctor came. The two went to the front porch where it was cooler, and Ada rocked back and forth in her chair, while Lula sat on the steps below her.

"I knowed one more man that got hit on the head," she began. "He was a Mr. Whitesides, from Florala, and he — "

Ada said: "Don't tell me about him, Lula. I feel right now like I couldn't stand anything else."

"Yassum," said Lula regretfully. "Yassum."

There was a silence, and then Amos' voice rolled magnificently against the hot, September sky. At once Lula raised a warning finger. "That's the song he sung when he won the banner," she said. "They named him the best singer afterwards, like he said."

The two women leaned forward a little, listening to the fervent richness of Amos' voice: —

> "My back so tired and easy bendin';
> My back so tired and easy bendin';
> Oh, my back so tired and easy bendin';
> Please God don't lay no more on me!
> Please God don't lay no more on me!
> On me, on me.
> Please God, don't lay no more on me!"

"Tell Him not to lay no more on me, either!" said Ada suddenly. "Tell him for me, too, Amos!" Unexpectedly both women began to cry. Lula said: "Ever'body got to tote a heavy load, Miss Ada. *Ever'body!*" Then, feeling that her statement was too sweeping, perhaps, she added: "Leastways, ever'body I knows totes one!"

Chapter 3

||||||||||||||||||||||||||||||||||||||||||||||||||||||||||||||||||||||||||||||||||||

|||||||||||||||||||||||||||||||||||||||||||||||||||||||||||||||||||||||||||| T HE manner in which this
story will be told is now plain. It is one which Professor St. Joseph
called "the basting-thread technique," shaking his head with such
regret, and twisting his mouth, at such times, with so great a distaste, that we, the pupils of his special class, would look at one another guiltily, as if responsible for the failings of clumsy writers.

Being one of those people who find it impossible to discard anything with which they were once concerned, he kept all his old
lectures, notebooks and school papers filed away, on the principle
that, at the appropriate time, everything is of value; and when he
was an old man, long, long after the events with which this book
is concerned had been forgotten, and he had been pensioned by
the School Board, he would read them over with much amusement.

In the end they served a most interesting purpose, for his pro-
nouncements to his pupils, during the long years of his teaching,
revealed to him, with the accuracy of growth-rings around the heart
of a tree, his steady, if erratic maturing as a man.

He particularly admired one of the old lectures, and he reread it
oftener than the others. He had used it in his classes following his
first trip to the Continent. On that trip he had become interested
in early portraiture, and he was convinced that there was a closer
connection between painting and writing than was generally understood.

To illustrate my point [he had written], you need only examine those
portraits which early artists painted of their patrons. There, smirking,
frowning, condescending, or even praying — with their best angles
turned to the painter, and their pleats and ruffles elaborate and precise —
but always solidly planted in the foreground, are the sitters. They
are wearing all their lace, fur and jewels for the occasion, and often, as
if they demanded the last square inch of value from the artist, they have

dragged into the picture their pets, and even their assorted, inanimate possessions.

The people seem quaint and slightly ridiculous to us now, although we may be sure they seemed neither quaint nor ridiculous to themselves; and if we have any interest in them at all, as human beings, it is only to wonder, looking through the reducing telescope of four hundred years or more, what uses they found for those objects of wood and bone and metal which they seem to have prized so highly.

But if the sitters, as once living people, have lost their importance to all but historians, the painting, itself, is often prized for reasons quite different from those which made it precious to its original owners; for to our impersonal eyes the excellence of likeness is quite unimportant, and the thing we now value is not how the people looked, but the individual flavor which the painter added to the portrait from his own, unique imagination.

At this point, St. Joseph moved to his west window, where the light was better, and sat in his favorite chair. He put the old lecture on the table beside him and continued to read as he fumbled among his papers for a cigarette. It had seemed to him, when he wrote the lecture, that the artist himself had had some intimation of the impermanence of his dull, vain sitters; and as if to give a wider significance to his work, and make it more understandable to other times, he had often left a window open in the background behind them.

Through this window, he had painted glimpses of the sky, the autumn woods or a waving field of young grain. Sometimes the window framed a little hill with snow still on its summit, sometimes a glimpse of the sea. If this had really been the intention of the artist, St. Joseph felt that he had been wise in anchoring his work against eternal, recognizable things; for no matter how strange the sitters might seem to other generations, the imperishable things, seen through the window, would be familiar and sure forever, being changeless.

He lit his cigarette, his eyes still fixed on the lecture which he had written almost forty years before, and went on, this time reading aloud, his ear on the alert for clumsy phrases: —

Perhaps the lesson which the painter learned should be learned, as well, by those writers who are concerned too greatly in reproducing each wrinkle, each mole, each tiny shadow on the faces of his characters: who strive to copy too faithfully the intonation of voices, or to create a background with too literal an excellence; for if worthy, precise realism is all a writer has in his work in the beginning, in a day of other tastes he will have nothing.

Some of you in this class will strive to become artists yourselves. To those of you who have such aspirations, let me give my first piece of tedious advice for this term: Try always to leave a small window open in your poems, your stories or your novels, for then the unchanging things may be glimpsed against the decay which must inevitably overtake your characters, and though they may seem a little less than flesh and blood to another time, they will be lighted forever, in some measure, by the lamps of Truth and Beauty.

When he had finished, St. Joseph said: "It's not bad. Really, it's not too bad. . . . Overblown and dated, of course, but still — " He raised his eyes and stared guiltily at the Picasso which Minnie McInnis McMinn had given him on his seventieth birthday. It showed a red and green woman, engaged either in plucking a fowl or playing a guitar, who, being unable to decide in which direction to turn her head, had turned it in all directions at once. With his eyes still fixed on the painting, he refolded the old lecture and slipped it in its envelope. "I know! I know!" he said apologetically, and then added: "But don't judge me too hastily. Wait and see what happens to you, too, Madam!"

I had made an appointment with him for that afternoon, and it was at this point that I rang his bell. He let me in and asked me to sit down. "I'm Richard Mellen," I said. "I hope you understood me over the telephone. I was in one of your classes, years ago."

"I remember you," he said. "I remember you very well indeed, Richard. I understand you're writing a book about Reedyville. Well, if I can help, call on me." He lifted his bushy, gray eyebrows and laughed suddenly. "Will Minnie McMinn be burned up when she hears about this!" he said. "You know, Minnie always said that *she* was going to write the Reedyville book."

He went to the filing cabinet and put the lecture away. Over his shoulder he asked, "What class were you in, anyway? Were you with the little Parker girl who always seemed to have a cold?"

"I came a little later on," I said. "I was in the class with the Barron twins and Dover Boutwell."

St. Joseph sat down and lifted his chin, his eyes narrowed intently, as if he sought to recall something, his hands raised an inch above the arms of his chair, as if he knew somewhere in his mind that he must get up again immediately. For a moment he held this intense, contemplative pose, and then the thing which he sought to remember came into his consciousness.

It was the first theme which Dover Boutwell had written in the English Construction class, and now that he remembered what it was he wanted, he knew precisely where to put his hand on it. He got it from his files and gave it to me to read. He had once considered it the perfect example of incomprehensible stupidity, but now, with the lecture on the literary window fresh in his mind, as it must have been fresh in Dover's mind when he wrote the composition, he understood at last both the boy's purpose and the reason for his confusion.

He had given his class of beginners that year the shopworn subject, "What I See From My Window," and Dover, with the pathetic effort to be agreeable which the dull so often make, had painstakingly drawn a frame which represented his bedroom window at home. Inside the frame he had written: "The canning factory, a string of box cars and a clump of oaks back a piece from the road," and nothing else; but at the bottom of his canvas, where an artist signs his name, he had added: "Yours very truly, Dover Leander Boutwell."

When I read this part out loud, St. Joseph laughed and shook his head from side to side. "Now, tell me about your book," he said suddenly. "I hope you're using me as one of your characters."

"I'm afraid I am."

"How about Minnie McMinn? Or do you consider Minnie too unbelievable for the retail trade?"

"Do you think she'd mind?"

"Of course she wouldn't mind my boy! She'll be very hurt if you don't."

But his mind was on other things, and in a moment he laughed again and said confidentially: "You know, Richard, I believe Dover Boutwell was the stupidest little boy I ever met, not to have been an institutional case, of course."

St. Joseph remembered much about Dover and his unique application of the framed-scene-open-window theory of art; but one thing he did not recall was that the composition had been written the day following his father's fall from the culvert. To Dover, the preparation of the composition had seemed as unreasonable as one of the labors of Hercules. All that afternoon while his mother waited and watched the road, he had thought about it; and the need for its accomplishment lay in the back of his mind even as he ran in the direction of the Palmiller State Bank.

When he reached the first houses of Reedyville, he slowed his pace to a walk. His most direct route was through the alley in front of him, and he entered it, keeping on the alert for broken glass; but before he had gone far, he pulled himself up sharply, dug his tough heels into the dirt and stopped with the abrupt, clumsy efficiency of a puppy. Then he tiptoed, as if his bare feet could be heard, behind the walnut tree which grew at the Porterfields' back gate; for there, outside the iron fence of the Kenworthy house, blocking his path, was The Goodwife of Death herself, waiting patiently.

In the twilight, her face was like creamy, antique ivory which had yellowed slowly in a cathedral. Her head was as undecorated and as austerely oval as an egg. Over it, she wore only a sateen veil, which she had adjusted, like a smooth stocking cap, to the nudity of her shaven head, a veil which she permitted to flow downward in a neat drapery below her ankles; and there on the ground, beside her flat, nunlike shoes, was the black bag which held the horrid necessities of her calling.

It was growing duskier, and over the Gulf of Mexico to the south there were ballooning clouds against the sky; but there was no wind as yet, and the parched leaves of the trees exhaled the vinegary sweet smell of sunburned flesh.

The Goodwife lifted her draped head and looked passionately at the clouds. Thinking herself alone in the twilight, she spoke aloud: "Rain!" she said. "Rain! We need it badly, and I think we're going to get some before morning!" She took a few steps in the direction of the walnut tree, and her face, in the last, wan light from the sky, seemed as unreal as a discarded carnival mask in a deserted street.

It was possible to believe anything about The Goodwife of Death, except that she had once been beautiful; and yet old Mrs.

Wentworth and others who had known her since girlhood insisted that she had. Her hair, they said, had once been dark, silky and abundant; her skin soft and smooth; her eyes dark and velvety, and with a melancholy, melting light in them which people had considered irresistible.

Mrs. Wentworth said these things all over again to Mrs. McMinn when the latter called upon her, ostensibly to gather social items, as a representative of the *Courier,* but in reality to learn about The Goodwife for her ledger.

"And please stop calling her The Goodwife!" said old Mrs. Wentworth in her baritone, aggressive voice. "She's got a name like you and me and everybody else! For your information, her name is Virginia Dunwoody Owen. Please call her that! Call her Miss Virginia, if you want to! Call her Miss Owen, if that pleases you better! But stop calling her by that sickening name which the people of this town have tied to her!"

Then, in a more conciliatory voice, she continued: "I've got an old picture of Virginia in my album, taken when we were girls together. Wait a minute, and I'll show it to you. You'll see then what I mean."

The photograph was of four girls grouped together. Three of them were standing with their arms around one another's waists. The fourth was sitting in a chair which had been draped with a photographer's shawl. Mrs. Wentworth said: "I'm one of the girls standing up: the one on the left. It's a miserable photograph, isn't it? It makes me look as if I had a mustache."

Minnie examined the photograph and glanced again at her hostess. She smiled noncommittally and shook her head, but to herself she said: "But you *have* got a mustache, old girl! You've got as nice a little mustache as there is in Reedyville!"

"The two girls standing with me," continued Mrs. Wentworth, "are Anne May Kimbrough, who later married Ralph Porterfield, and became the mother of the peerless Robert that you admire so much, and a girl from Montgomery, who was visiting the Kimbroughs at the time. Her name was Effie something-or-other. Silly-looking, isn't she? Anyway, she made a good marriage, I understand. He was very rich, and they went about everywhere; but he

was a Northerner, from New York, so of course nobody expected
him to be quite a gentleman."

She shrugged and went on: "Oh, yes! That's Virginia Owen sitting in the chair. You didn't recognize her, did you? You had your
mind set for something that resembled an old, moulting buzzard,
didn't you, my dear?"

Minnie examined the old photograph more carefully. The girls
who were standing gazed hopefully above the head of the unseen
photographer, their mouths fixed in coy and unconvincing smiles,
their faces struggling to register, at his insistence, that sparkling
gaiety which he felt was expected of them, as handsome young
ladies of quality; but Virginia's face, in its frame of silken ringlets,
was resigned and melancholy. Her beautiful hands lay languidly in
her lap, and her eyes looked outward into space with a concentrated
intensity.

"Well, Minnie!" thundered old Mrs. Wentworth. "What do you
think of her now? Are you satisfied? Was she a beautiful girl,
as I said, or was she not?"

Minnie learned much that afternoon, enough to fill many pages
in her current ledger. The Goodwife, it seemed, had been born,
not in Reedyville, as was commonly thought, but in Mobile, on
Conception Street — a name which had always struck Mrs. Wentworth as being in the worst possible taste — in one of the old, red
brick houses there: a dark red house with balconies and slender,
iron pillars, and webbed lavishly with intricate, lacy grillwork.

She had been the only child of General John Overman Owen and
his first wife, who, in turn, had been Florence Dunwoody before
her marriage. The bride had not wanted to leave Reedyville, so to
make the transplantation easier, her father had given her two of the
Dunwoody house slaves of whom she had been particularly fond,
one of them being Judy, her old nurse, to take with her, as part
of her dowry. She had tried her best, but she had never felt at home
with General Owen, a man older than her own father, and after
the birth of her daughter, she had become what was called, in those
days, a "semi-invalid."

She died when Virginia was two years old, and shortly thereafter General Owen married again, this time a woman whose sta-

tion in life was much below his own, in Mrs. Wentworth's opinion, and one whose standards were far below the standards of his first wife.

"He married his wife's *night* nurse, my dear!" said Mrs. Wentworth in a shocked voice, giving the impression somehow that night nurses were a little more depraved, a little more lecherous, than their sisters who worked in the day. "A woman named Maybelle something-or-other. Such a difficult name for anybody, with ambition to be a lady, to carry off, don't you think? But it was one quite suited, I dare say, to her own temperament and mode of living. She came from impossible people, I'm told. They operated a small fish stall at the Big Market. The whole Dunwoody family was furious."

Virginia's life had been a sad one, burdened almost from its beginning with death and the talk of death. Her stepmother had developed no affection for her, and in her lighthearted, shallow nature, there was no capacity for understanding the peculiarities of the child, even if she had cared to make the attempt, for the odd strain of morbidity which was to be so overwhelming in her later life was apparent in Virginia from the first.

Judy, the house slave brought from Reedyville, who automatically became the child's nurse, was the one person in the Owen household who showed any interest in Virginia's future. She had been brought up in the unbending tradition of the Dunwoody gentility, and she had at her finger tips all the niceties of deportment, all the rules of etiquette, which, in her belief, distinguished the lady from her less fortunate sisters.

She disliked General Owen's second wife as much as she had loved his first; and so complete was this slave's identification with the family who once owned her, that she, even more than the Dunwoodys themselves, felt the humiliation of the widower's second marriage. It was, she felt, as if thus he publicly showed his contempt for them, and repudiated, in this manner, all that they stood for.

But there was one thing she had determined upon, and she meant to see it through, no matter what humiliations she had to endure to achieve her goal, and it was this: She meant for the child of the Dunwoodys, for whom she felt more than ever responsible now, to grow up to be a great lady, one who would take her rightful place, at length, in a society so distinguished that it made the social worlds of Mobile and New Orleans seem inconsequential by comparison.

Patiently she worked with the child from the time she could toddle about, teaching her to hold her head high, to use her hands charmingly, and how to veil her eyes, at the right moments, with a fan. The greatest bar to her plans was not Maybelle's interference, as she had feared, but Virginia's own unconquerable sadness.

But Judy did not despair. She worked each day with her charge, and for hours the little girl would perform, with a touching, automatic excellence, the beguiling tricks she had been taught.

Sometimes in the afternoon Maybelle's friends came to see her, and as if Virginia were a part of her marriage portion, an asset like the carpets and the chandeliers, Mrs. Owen would instruct Judy to dress the child in one of her best frocks, and bring her in for inspection and handling. The guests exclaimed at once over the child's solemn prettiness, and at such times Maybelle would say doubtfully: "Oh, really? Do you really think so?"

She was not a cruel woman, and it did not even occur to her that she was an unkind one at times. She was merely an unimaginative and a limited woman, and she was not nearly so happy in her marriage as she had expected to be. She felt her uncertain position as the second Mrs. Owen more deeply than others realized, knowing that the very slaves she owned looked down on her, and that they ridiculed her among themselves — a knowledge which at once angered her, and left her feeling particularly helpless.

The slave said: "Yassum, she's mighty pretty, ain't she? She gwiner be the prettiest of all the Dunwoody ladies, I expect, and that'll be something, because the Dunwoodys are a race of beauties!" She spoke with just the right note of childishness, so that Maybelle could not easily suspect her purpose. In reality she could speak English as well as any one of the great ladies she admired so much, and theirs was the speech she so patiently taught Virginia; but for purposes other than the education of her charge, she used the dialect of Negroes, feeling that anything else for her, a slave, would be pretentious and vulgar.

"Little Virginia gwiner make herself a great match, when she grow up," she continued with giggling simplicity. "She gwiner make a great, brilliant match. I tell her fortune over and over, and that's the way it come out ever' time."

Maybelle spoke excitedly. "Can you tell fortunes, Judy? Tell mine for me now."

Judy turned to the other guests and spoke humbly: "Mistress like to make fun of me befo' fine ladies. Mistress know as well as you all do, that quality folks don't take stock in nigger talk." She had once again insulted Mrs. Owen, but so indirectly that nobody could accuse her of anything except fumbling stupidity, and that quality she freely admitted in herself.

One of the guests, seeing Maybelle's sudden embarrassment, said: "Who's the little girl going to marry, Judy? Another famous man, like General Owen, perhaps?"

"Higher than that, ma'am. Way higher."

"Maybe she's going to marry a prince," said Maybelle angrily. "A pretty prince out of a storybook, maybe. Or a king."

"Maybe so, Mistress," said Judy, bowing her head with spurious humility. "Maybe so, but my teacup says higher."

Maybelle spoke in a bored voice: "Take the child to her room, Judy! We're all tired of her now." And as the slave took Virginia's hand, she added: "I suppose she's pretty enough to suit most people. It's too bad she's such a little storyteller, isn't it?" She looked sternly at the small girl, and Virginia stared back at her with fixed, solemn attention.

The slave said: "Come on, honey. Come on now. Let you and me go cut out paper dolls."

Maybelle nodded significantly at the departing child and said: "I think she's going to be as bad as her mother." She laughed her gay, loud laugh, and rolled her eyes, and when the nurse and the child were out of the room, she said: "Virginia told me the other day, with a perfectly straight face, mind you, that she remembered her mother very well. Now, that's an untruth, and you know it is. So you see?"

In this she did her stepdaughter an injustice, for an unfocused memory of the flavor of her mother's long sickness and death was fixed in the child's mind in the same way that the mood of a book, read years before, remains constant after the characters and the situations which comprised it have been lost to recollection. But aside from this generalized feeling of wordless horror which she had when she thought of her mother afterwards, Virginia had kept three pictures of actual happenings from that period, pictures which, though apparently of little importance, accorded well with both her morbid temperament and the balanced structure of her prehistoric mind.

The clearest of these pictures was one concerning her mother lying in bed. She seemed to be both terrified and exhausted, and her eyes were enormous in her sunken face. Then Judy had lifted Virginia up, and the first Mrs. Owen wearily raised her arm as if to touch the child's head in blessing; but at that moment her wedding ring slipped from her wasted finger and rolled across the carpet. She lay back against her pillow at once and wept bitterly at the loss, seeing an omen in her rolling marriage ring, a sign that her life was drawing to its end. "Take Virginia back to her room, Judy," she said. "It's better for her not to remember me at all, than to remember me this way." Perversely, that picture, which her mother wanted her to forget, was the one which became fixed forever in the child's brain.

The second memory was shorter. Her mother had just died and some old lady was offering her father food in his study upstairs. When he refused it, she said: "But you must eat, General Owen. You need to eat more than ever now."

The third and last memory was concerned with her mother's burial. In life, Mrs. Owen's favorite flower had been the red camellia, and when they were in bloom, she wore them, like an emblem which she had taken for her own, in her hair or on her shoulder. She died when camellias were in bloom, and her friends, remembering what her flower had been, sent great wreaths and sprays of them to the funeral. As if the undertaker knew this too, he had separated the camellias from the other flowers and had arranged them in an oval formation around the raw, new grave.

Judy took the child to the funeral, and held her high in her arms so that she could see; and as Virginia watched while her mother's coffin was lowered slowly through the oval of fleshy camellias, it seemed to her that the grave was like an unnatural mouth with minstrel lips, which swallowed her mother at its ease with a measured, gulping pleasure.

Afterwards she would sit beneath the azalea bushes which grew in the Owen back yard and try to understand the enormous things which troubled her. Gradually she was able to piece a small part of it together: She had seen pictures of skeletons in books, and Judy had told her that this was the way people looked after they had been buried for a long time. The child nodded solemnly, remembering these things: It was the way her mother looked at this moment, too: cold, fleshless and grinning; all whiteness and length, all hard, unfeeling bone.

She shuddered, and at once the carcass of a turkey which the slaves had picked clean in the kitchen that day appeared to her; and it was thus that the second link between eating and death came to her mind. It was the measure of her primitiveness that she was concerned eternally with these matters, and before she had learned to read, she had created a cosmogony of her own.

Since the earth stripped everything of its soft, edible flesh, and left only indigestible bone, she thought of the earth afterwards as a stomach which must be eternally fed; and the graves which men dug for the earth's convenience were the mouths through which it took its food. To die, then, as her mother had died a few years before, was only to be eaten and digested by the earth, as her mother, in her own lifetime, had eaten the flesh of countless living things.

When the child reached this point, she got up, walked to the intricate, iron gate and stood there trembling. Then, without warning, she made a shrill, wavering noise and ran into the house. Judy tried to comfort her, to find out what had frightened her so badly, but she would not answer, for she felt her knowledge was so overwhelming in its importance that she could not speak of it to another.

Suddenly she pulled away from Judy's arms and threw herself in soundless terror on the floor, for at that moment she saw, in her mind's eye, the carcasses of cattle which hung in long, precise rows at the Big Market, where she and her nurse sometimes went shopping together. They hung with the cut veins of their circular necks stretched toward the people who passed; and their stiff legs were held forward pleadingly, as if they had died while they asked mercy. There was something lost and horrible in the skinned, dead carcasses, and yet their proud stubs of neck, their jutting breasts and their stiff, unbending legs somehow gave the impression of arrogance, as if they were proud, in some ways, of the shocking thing which had happened to them.

After that, flesh became so repugnant to the child that she would no longer eat it, and when Maybelle insisted that she must do so, Virginia would turn white, shudder and shake her head with such a gesture of despair that the slave would say: "Don't ask her to eat it, Mistress. Please ma'am, don't do that. She ain't like other chillun."

"That's ridiculous," said Maybelle petulantly. "Meat is very nourishing. You can't live without eating meat. . . . Now, Virginia, we're all tired of fooling with you. You eat this nice little chicken leg, or I shan't let you go out walking with Judy until you do."

The child spoke in horror: "No! No! No!" she said, her voice becoming increasingly louder. "No! No!" she continued steadily, shaking her head from side to side. "No!"

Then Maybelle, exasperated beyond her endurance, tried to force open the child's mouth, but Virginia pushed back her chair, fell to the floor and vomited upon the carpet. That time the doctor was sent for to quiet her, and Maybelle, confessing herself beaten, said to the slave: "I don't want to see her from now on, Judy. You take charge of her, since you think you understand her so well. But keep her out of my sight, do you hear? There's something horrible about the little monster! . . . Just keep her out of my sight, that's all I ask from now on!"

Her father, feeling that his little daughter's life was too lonely, asked her one day if she didn't want a pet of some kind, a dog or a cat to play with. Virginia wanted none of these. What she did want was a pigeon. Her father drove with her to one of the farms near by, and she selected the bird herself. It was a young hen, pure white except for a few small tan markings on its wings and throat. She seemed happier after that, and she cared for her pet with fierce devotion.

Maybelle said to her husband not long afterwards: "I don't understand your daughter, General Owen. Any normal child would

have asked for a rabbit or a little dog, but not her! Not that one!
Oh, no! She must have nothing except a mourning dove that cries
all day long and drives you distracted!" She shook her head in
amazement, and thoughtfully set her hairpins more securely. "I'm
astonished at your daughter!" she continued. "I feel free to say to
you, General Owen, that your daughter continues to astonish me
day by day!"

She was to be astonished even more at Virginia's conduct, for
a few weeks later, the dove, betrayed into a false security by the very
love which had been lavished upon it, permitted a wandering cat to
crush its tender neck. The cat dropped the dove at once when
Virginia moaned and ran forward, but already it was too late.

The child did not cry, as might have been expected, at the loss
of her much-loved pet. She picked up the bird and went back onto
the porch where she had been playing with it only a moment before.
She turned it over and over in her hands, a lost, horrified expression
on her face. Later, she went to her bedroom, and when Maybelle
found her, she still had not given way to her grief, but her face
was so distorted, her hands so cold and rigid, that Mrs. Owen herself was alarmed. She tried to loosen her stepdaughter's grip on the
bird, but the child shook her head stubbornly and would not give
it up.

"The little bird is dead," said Maybelle coaxingly. "You must let
me have it now. We'll ask Judy to dig a nice little grave, and we'll
bury it in a pretty box under the fig trees. . . . Come, Virginia! Let
me have it now! Don't you understand that you can't keep the
pigeon any longer?"

But Virginia only shook her head and held the bird more stubbornly to her breast, having, at that moment, a clear picture of the
insatiable, pitiless earth which ate everything that she loved: her
mother first, and now her bird; and with some strange prescience,
she knew, then, that the earth would always be her enemy. The
earth was stronger than she was, and already she knew that well;
but nevertheless it should not triumph over her again. Of that she
was certain.

She closed her eyes and shuddered, and when she opened them
again she had made an enormous decision, for she had decided to
fight her enemy the earth with its own particular weapon.

"I'm going to eat it," she said. "I'm going to eat the dove."

Maybelle said: "You are disgusting! You are a completely disgusting little girl! How can you possibly want to eat anything you're fond of? You claim to love the pigeon, don't you? . . . And yet you can say a thing of that sort!"

She tried to take the pigeon from the child's hands, but Virginia stood up suddenly and stared at her, her eyes blazing with such unconcealed hatred that Maybelle drew her arm back, as if she had been struck. "I must," said the child desperately. "I must eat it!"

Even her father was disturbed this time, and when he came home that night, he too tried to argue with the child, to persuade her to give up the dove. He wondered how she, of all people, who would not even eat impersonal meat, could yet devour the thing she loved the most. The child could not answer his logic, nor could she tell him that eating the pet bird was far more dreadful for her than it would have been for him, who ate meat as a matter of course. She could only say over and over: "I must eat it! I must eat it!"

She had her way at last, and the cook prepared the bird for her. When she had eaten the last morsel, she wept bitterly for a long time, but she felt that she was now the equal of the dreaded earth. General Owen spoke quietly to his wife: "Perhaps it's a good thing, after all. Possibly she'll eat meat like others from now on." He was too optimistic, for the eating of the pet pigeon was the last time that flesh was ever to pass the lips of The Goodwife of Death.

Afterwards, a period of religion set in. The family were Episcopalians, and when Virginia began to attend the Catholic cathedral on Dauphin Street, they were perturbed. She went each time that she could escape her stepmother's or Judy's eye; and when she was found, she was usually inside the church, staring upward at the crucifixes and the gilded altars with a terrified and transported expression on her face.

The priests, seeing her there so frequently, nodded and smiled indulgently, believing she had a vocation. They were correct, but as it turned out, it was not the more conventional vocation they had in mind.

When Virginia was six, the event which was to shape her life into its final form took place. Her father died unexpectedly that summer of a heart attack, although his daughter was not told of it until after he had been prepared for burial. Maybelle had long since been reduced to sobs, smelling salts and cups of strong tea. She dreaded having to cope with the child, but to her surprise, Virginia had looked into her father's waxen face with apparently no emotion whatever.

Then Judy had lifted her up to the bier, in order that she might give him the conventional good-by kiss, and the little girl, as if she had waited this opportunity, leaned forward and put her arms about his neck. She clung to her father so fiercely, and kissed his dead face with such passionate abandon, that Maybelle said hoarsely: "Take that child away from him! Take her away this instant, Judy!"

Later, she said hysterically to her friends: "I can't begin to tell you the queer feeling that child gives me! She makes my blood run cold, just to watch her! She's a little monster, that's what she is, and I've said it from the very first! . . . There was the same expression on her face when she kissed her father as there was when she ate her pigeon last year!" She covered her tear-stained face with her hands, and said: "Oh, my God, don't let me think such terrible things!"

Later that day, the child watched while the men lowered her father into his grave. She was dressed in black, in the mourning costume which Judy had hurriedly made for her, and she wore a long black veil over her hat, as if she, too, were a widow. Since General Owen had been such an important man in life, his funeral was a big, impressive one, and there were many strangers there, people the family did not know.

The child stood inside the family group, next to her stepmother, but quite apart from her, and as she waited for the services to begin, two old women, who seemed to be sisters, came up and spoke to her with a breathless, startling abruptness.

"You poor child!" said one of them in a hoarse whisper, rolling her eyes and looking furtively over her shoulder. "Death has robbed you today of the most precious thing in your life!" Then the other old woman, like an imperfect echo, said sadly: "Yes. Yes indeed, my poor child! Death robbed you cruelly when it took General Owen in the prime of life." Almost at once, the women passed on and began a whispered conversation with Maybelle, with whom they seemed well acquainted.

The contact was momentary only, but it was enough to reveal to the little girl what she, at least, considered the last piece in the involved picture puzzle of living and dying.

If the earth was a stomach which must be eternally refilled with flesh, and if graves were the mouths through which it took food, then Death, of whom people spoke so often, and who seemed always to be present on such occasions, was plainly the earth's butler. His part in the cycle of eating and digesting and eating again was to go about the world and select for that stomach those tidbits of human flesh which would both stimulate its sated appetite, and nourish it for another day.

She thought, then, of her father, whom Death had selected, and who had been prepared, by those who loved him, so beautifully for the earth's appetite, and a nervous horror impelled her to disengage her hand from Judy's, who was now busy talking with the two old women, and to move quickly away from the graveside.

Instinctively she ran toward the cemetery gate, her face twisted soundlessly, but before she reached it, she saw a tall, bearded man standing squarely in the graveled path, blocking her way. He was no member of the family, and he was nobody she had ever seen before. Then, instantly, she knew: This tall stranger, with his sad, drooping eyes, was powerful Death himself, who killed what pleased him, when it pleased him to do so.

In her desire to placate Death, to win his friendship and secure her own immunity, she became aware, for the first time, of the usefulness of her prettiness, and her infantile charms, which were so admired by adults. Now, those things which had seemed so enormously important to Judy were important to her as well, and she approached the stranger and took his hand in her own, rubbing it provocatively against her soft cheek. She made him a low curtsy, and said, "How do you do, sir?," rolling her dark eyes roguishly at him. Then she tapped his arm with an imaginary fan and stepped backwards, allowing her lids to drop seductively; but almost at once she was gay again, and as she walked away, she laughed and looked at him through her curls. She went through the entire ritual of coquettishness, which Judy had taught her, using, in her terror, all her baby charms.

The stranger, who had seemed astonished at first, smiled finally and put his hand on the little girl's trembling head. Then, bending a little, he picked her up in his arms and said: "What a fascinating little beauty you are! What is your name?"

But the child would not tell him. She shook her head playfully and drew her mourning veil flirtatiously across her mouth. She hid her face coyly against the lapels of his coat, and then she raised her hands and stroked his face with her prettiest gestures.

Judy came up at that moment and spoke, as if the stranger were only a man, like any other. "She's General Owen's little girl, sir. She ran away from me when I wasn't noticing." She held her arms out to the child. "Come, Virginia," she said. "Come, now, baby!"

The man said: "Then she doesn't know? She doesn't realize?"

"No, sir," said Judy. "She's too young yet to understand about such things."

The stranger bent down and touched the child's forehead with his lips. "Would you like to be my little girl?" he asked. "I have none of my own, you know. Would you like to come live with me, and be my little sweetheart?"

But the little girl pulled away from him, staring at him with her enormous, dark eyes. Then slowly she nodded her head and said yes, but so faintly that nobody but herself and the stranger heard. Judy took her, then, and walked with her to the cemetery gate, and let the child cry out her terror and despair against her breast. Later, she carried her back to the graveside, and when they arrived, the services were just beginning.

It was The Goodwife of Death's great misfortune to be born long after her proper age had passed, for in reality she belonged back at the beginning of time, in the dawn of the human mind, when man first tried to discipline his fears, and to find reasons for them. She was of the lost age of personification, when the myths of the world were being made, and in her proper setting, she would not have seemed strange at all. Her true era might reasonably have deified her, had she lived in that age and not her own, and she might have come down to us from the edges of antiquity as an obscene earth goddess, to delight the mythologist.

After her father's death, the Dunwoody family took her to Reedyville to live with them, and when the Civil War commenced, she was already a young lady. She had been habitually languid in those days, and she spent her afternoons in a barrel-hammock on the lawn, reading the sad romances of her day while a slave sat beside her and fanned her with a turkey-wing fan. The superficial facets of her type fitted well with the ideal of her day, and many young men from Reedyville, and the near-by plantations, came to court her. Of them, there was only one she liked at all. His name was Bruce Howard, and had she married him as she once planned, her life might have been different from what it later became. As it happened, he died at Gettysburg, and Virginia was free to go on with her ordained career.

Her oddities grew so gradually, so inconspicuously, that it was impossible to say, "Here eccentricity ended; here madness began!" It was almost as if she, having made her own shaky, individual compromise with the outer world of others, repudiated it when she found it not appropriate for her, and retreated slowly through the layers of her mind, and the minds of her ancestors, as an archeologist works through the diverse cultural levels of civilizations occupying a single site, until she reached at length the savage bedrock of time, where she belonged.

At first she was content with a scrapbook of obituary notices, and the accounts of funerals, which she clipped from papers. Later she felt it her duty to personally care for the neglected graves in Magnolia Cemetery.

She began to wear black as a matter of course, and as the meaning of her life became clearer to her, her dress was more standardized, more like a uniform whose purpose was to separate her from others.

It was at this period of her life that she thought again of her father's funeral and of the stranger she had met there. The scene came back to her in its entirety, but modified somewhat by her own desires, for instead of the stranger saying, "Would you like to come live with me, and be my little sweetheart?" he now said, more honorably, "Will you be my wife, and keep my house proper and clean?" Then, at the instant Judy had taken her from him, he had looked at her with an overwhelming passion, and had slipped a ring on her finger. The ring was still there, she knew, although she could not see it: it was there on her finger nonetheless, an eternal reminder of both her promise and her duty to her lord.

Had she been the bride of God rather than the bride of Death, her problem would have been a simpler one, for then she would have had long ages of precedent to guide her. As it was, she was alone in her field of worship, and she had to feel her way with care, experimenting, discarding and perfecting her individual ritual, her rules of devotion.

But she had been reared in the tradition of the great lady, and a great lady she remained even after she was left a pauper, and a charge on Miss Clemence, the last of the Dunwoodys of her mother's generation. When Miss Clemence died, the Reedys wanted to buy the old house for their daughter Millicent, who had recently married Paul Kenworthy. They planned their lavish gesture as a surprise, after the couple had come back from their long honeymoon in Europe, but they felt unwilling to dispossess Miss Virginia, and the Dunwoody heirs themselves refused to sell unless some arrangement satisfactory to her could be worked out.

The Goodwife solved the matter at once. "I suggest that the Reedys fix up that old outdoor kitchen for me," she said sensibly, "and I'll move out there. There's an entrance through the alley, and it's so far away from the house, Millicent and her husband won't see any more of me than they would if I lived in another part of town."

The Reedys were agreeable, and The Goodwife settled in her new quarters not long afterwards. Once she had left the old house, she thought she would have no further interest in it, but on the night the honeymooners were expected home, she wanted to see it again, knowing this would be the last chance she would ever have. She had expected to examine what the workmen had done, and still have time to get back to her quarters before the bride and groom took possession; but as she started down the stairs, she knew that she had lingered too long, for already she could hear the Reedys and their friends talking excitedly on the front porch.

Old Mrs. Reedy came in first. She opened the front door wide to the others and said dramatically: "You always wanted the old Dunwoody house, Millicent! Now it's yours! Your father and I bought it for you, and we've modernized it throughout, and furnished it the way you said you wanted it."

The bride was an ungainly, clumsy girl, so pink that you suspected her of having a rash. It would seem that so many generations of such careful breeding should have produced a less peasant-like daughter, but apparently the ankles of the Reedys thickened as their blood thinned. Milly's face was the color of a tea rose from the mere effort of climbing the long front steps, and when she came into her new home she was panting a little. She walked behind her parents and her relatives, admiring everything, loving everything; and commenting again and again on the thoughtfulness, the tenderness, which had prompted this unexpected, generous surprise.

Everything was perfect, and she said so over and over; and long before the last room in the imposing house had been seen and exclaimed over, Millicent found that she had exhausted both her vocabulary and her gratitude. She could only incline her pink, multiple-chinned throat and repeat hollowly, like a parrot: "It's just too wonderful to take in all at one time, Papa!" Or, "It's really marvelous, Mama! It's just too wonderfully, marvelously perfect for one girl to have for her own!"

She looked over her plump shoulder and located her groom. He was even more subdued than usual, against the overpowering generosity of the Reedys, and she went to him and took his arm, squeezing it against her hot side. She was not very tall, but already she weighed a hundred and eighty pounds, and it was plain that she would unfold, in time, into an imposing maturity.

The kitchen was the last room to be examined, and as the beaming family stood aside, to let the couple pass in ahead of them, they waited for Millicent's final explosion of gratitude. They had saved this room for the last, because, in its way, it represented the ultimate in thoughtfulness, and it was stocked completely with groceries, vegetables and fruits. A fire had been lighted in the big range, and beside it, as if she had always been there, was Mattie, the Reedys' old cook, whom they had willed to their daughter, as the final test of their unselfishness.

Mattie got up when the bride entered and said with that casual artistry which all Negroes seem to possess: "I declare, Miz Kenworthy, I done forgot what you said cook for supper! But iffen you express yo' wish again, I'll fix it, 'cause we got ever'thing in the house you can think of!"

There came a burst of applause from the family, and Millicent embraced her parents again, but hesitantly this time, as if all the spontaneity had gone out of her, as if thoughtfulness had been stretched too thin. She turned uneasily, and again she went and stood by her husband.

Mattie continued after a moment: "What I just said ain't entirely true! I got to take back a little of it, because there's one thing we done overlook, and that's *salt!* There ain't a speck of salt nowhere in the whole house!"

Mrs. Reedy said: "Oh, of course! I knew there was something we'd left out! . . . But salt! Salt of all things to forget!" She laughed mildly and turned to her daughter, but at that moment Millicent sat down heavily in one of the kitchen chairs and cried convulsively.

"It looks like you might, at least, have thought of salt," she said. "It seems to me that's the least you could have done! It only costs five cents for a big box, you know."

Her mother came to her soothingly, suggesting that her daughter was being a little unreasonable, but Millicent pulled away and said: "I don't think I'm being unreasonable in asking for anything as small as a box of salt. It seems to me that's little enough to ask for."

"We forgot it, Milly," said her mother. "We just overlooked it! All of us did. I don't know how it happened, dear!"

Millicent cried more loudly. "I know you did!" she said. "That's the whole point of my story! That's what I'm trying so hard to make plain! . . . But it seems to me you could have thought of salt. That's all I can say."

Old Mr. Reedy lost his temper and began to shout. "There's a barrelful of salt at home," he said. "I'll go right now and get you enough to last you all winter! I'll get you enough to fill your bathtub with!"

Millie drew herself up. "Thank you very much!" she said with quivering dignity. "It's most kind of you, I'm sure; but as it happens, I don't need your salt! I wouldn't take your salt now as a gift!" She got up from the chair and stood solidly beside her groom. "My husband will buy me all the salt I need, thank you!"

Mr. Kenworthy, still awed by his superior relatives, spoke for the first time since entering his new home. "Milly's tired and upset," he said. "Maybe you'd better see her in the morning, or do you think so?"

Millicent lifted her swollen face, and her tears broke out afresh. "Just a little salt," she said through her sobs. "Just a plain little five-cent package of salt! . . . It looks like anybody would have been willing to do that, doesn't it?"

In the excitement, The Goodwife slipped down the stairs and went to her own quarters, knowing she was never to enter her old home again until circumstances made a professional call necessary. The last link with her past was broken, and she was free to go on with her tasks in earnest. She soon became a figure of mystery in the town, and her name was a threat used by housewives in the management of their children.

Ada Boutwell had blackmailed her children into maturity under one broad, covering threat to call The Goodwife to her assistance, when all other efforts to shame, threaten or bludgeon them into conventional respectability had failed. For example, her daughter Honey would be outside near the gate, making suggestive, rolling motions with her stomach and singing one of the songs she had learned from the Negro women on Lower Lee Street — perhaps the particular song that shocked her elder sister Fodie the most, a local favorite called "Throw It Up Crow."

At such times, Honey, with an exaggerated shaking of her small, applelike buttocks, would lift her eyes to the topmost branch of the red-gum tree which grew in the Boutwell yard, pretending that she could actually see the bird she addressed, and sing in her hoarse, powerful voice: —

> "Tell me the truth, ol' Mister Crow,
> How come you love yo' black wife so?
> Her feathers done about fell out
> And her feets can't scratch up worms no mo'!
> How come you love yo' old black wife
> That's always pecking at other folks' corn?
> That goes round pecking round other folks' corn?
> Whoopcat! Hotman! What yo' woman do?"

Fodie summoned her mother from the kitchen at once. "Mama!" she said nervously. "Come quick! Honey's at the gate singing dirty songs again. Some farmers have even stopped their wagons to listen, and half the niggers in town are outside laughing and clapping their hands." Her eyes burned with her depressed anger, and her reaching teeth were naked and exposed for all to see. "It looks like Honey could at least keep her mouth shut. People look down on us enough as it is, without her dragging us all further in the dirt."

Honey glanced briefly at her mother and her elder sister, then she turned back to her audience and sang the chorus for them. At that moment Ada got her broom from the corner and said: "Honey! Honey Boutwell! Come in the house this minute! You better mind me now!"

Honey tossed her small stomach about even more wildly and went on with the interminable song, but she glanced now and then over her shoulder to see if her mother really contemplated an attack with her broom. Since Ada stood there impotently, shaking her head in sadness, Honey began the second verse triumphantly. In it, the old crow appeared quite willing to go into the precise, anatomical details of what made his wife, despite the loss of her pretty feathers and her waning ability to scratch his food for him, so much more charming than all other crows.

"Honey!" shouted Ada, shaking her broom in helpless fury. "Ain't you ashamed of yourself, shaming Fodie and all of us this way! When your papa comes home tonight, I'm going to tell him how you act when he ain't here. I'm going to tell him to whup you so hard that you can't sit down for a whole week!"

Honey did not take these threats seriously, for she knew her father would do nothing of the sort. The punishment of his children was one of the things he had decided ideas about. "Lord knows I got beat on enough when I was just a little fellow," he had often said. "It's a wonder that I'm bright. I'm not going to do it to my children, and if they turn out bad because I didn't, like everybody says they will, then they'll just have to turn out bad. Now, Ada, just look at the Ewing boys back in Florida where your ma worked. They got a beating every day of their lives. Well sir, if what people said was true, the Ewing boys would have turned out to be preachers. But did they do that? You know well enough they didn't, Ada! They was all hung, one after the other, as *highwaymen.* . . . All except the youngest one, Ab, and they hung him for *rape.*"

Honey, knowing her father's opinions so well, went on singing, her voice getting louder and louder. A fat, coal-black woman, with a horseshoe scar on one cheek, doubled up with mirth and groaned:

"What old Mr. Crow keep saying afterwards? What he keep on saying to that white man?"

Honey obligingly repeated the chorus, raising her voice so much that it carried almost as far as the canning factory: —

> "Captain Whiteman Boss, gwiner tell you true:
> My wife do something you *sho'* can't do!"

Nappy Ida, a small Negress with a head shaped like a croquet mallet, leaned against the fence for support and beat her black hands together in ecstasy. "I speck Mr. Crow was telling the truth, too," she said, "I speck he knowed what he was talking about right along." Then Honey, like a true artist, sang directly to this, the most appreciative member of her audience: —

> "My wife knows tricks that you don't know.
> Throw it up to me, Mama! Throw it up crow!
> Done told you, done told you,
> Done told you to throw it up crow!"

In her ecstasy, Nappy Ida fell to her knees beside the gate and rocked back and forth, her mallet head tapping the palings as if she were driving in nails. "Better lissen while yo' man talking to you, Miz Crow!" she shouted. "I'm telling you, better do like he say do!"

Honey spoke to the delighted Negroes with false humility: "Too bad I ain't got a little nigger blood in me. Maybe I could sing real good if I did."

"You don't need nigger blood," said Nappy Ida generously. "You sing as good as ever I heerd right now!"

One of the snickering white farmers spoke from his wagon. "Sing 'Stay Out from Under My Lava Lava,' next, Honey. That's one I haven't heard in Lord knows when."

At this point, Ada changed her tactics. "All right," she said ominously. "Sing it for the gentleman, like he asks, if you're as anxious as all that for The Goodwife to catch you! But don't say later on I didn't warn you!" She stretched her eyes wide, and started back in simulated fright. "Ain't that The Goodwife coming round the bend now, Fodie?" she asked. "Ain't that her coming as fast as she can to catch Honey for being dirty-mouthed, and to lock her up in a little cold grave?"

There was no need for her to proceed further, for Honey had become silent at last, and her audience, which had been so amused a moment ago, was now moving sheepishly away.

Once The Goodwife passed the Reedyville school when the children were going home. She stopped at the sidewalk and waited for them to pass, but they went back through the gate and shut it behind them. They had been talking about her the instant before she came into view, and her appearance gave them a startled feeling, as if she had heard what they had been saying.

Rance Palmiller had just said that in his opinion The Goodwife was no different from any other old woman in Reedyville, and he saw no reason to be afraid of her. He was an unusually gifted child, and already he was in high school, in classes with pupils twice his age. His teachers found him completely unbearable. That same afternoon, Miss Doremus, the mathematics instructor, having reached the limit of her endurance, had told him to report to the principal for further discipline.

The boy came into St. Joseph's office not defiantly, as might have been expected, but composed and inclined toward tolerance, and with an air of bland, wronged innocence. He sat down opposite St. Joseph and glanced about him with the patience of a martyr; and in a moment Miss Doremus followed him through the door. She was still furious, and when she tried to speak, her voice was so tremulous, so unnatural, that her words came tensely through her lips, with small whistles blowing somewhere behind them. "I won't stand this boy's insolence any longer!" she said. "Something must be done about him, and done now!"

St. Joseph fastened his glasses onto his nose and spoke mildly: "What have you done to Miss Doremus this time, Rance?"

Rance turned his head back from a bored contemplation of the blackboard and answered: "Nothing. Nothing at all. I only said that I wasn't impressed too much with the law of gravitation. That's all. I said there was still much to be explained. Then Miss Doremus asked me if I considered myself more intelligent than Sir Isaac Newton, and I said, yes, as a matter of fact I did."

Miss Doremus could no longer contain herself. "He said that!" she murmured in a shocked voice. "It seems incredible, but he really said it! Can you imagine such egotism in anybody, particularly a seven-year-old boy?" She shook her shoulders angrily and plucked at the lobe of her ear.

Rance waited until she had finished and then went on: "Miss Doremus said she believed every word that the great scientists had ever uttered. I thought that a little naïve of her, since a lot of the things scientists have said contradict each other, and I asked her if she didn't think so too. I believe that's about all."

Miss Doremus said: "That isn't all! It isn't all by a long shot! His exact words were, 'Well, isn't that what you'd expect a well-educated mediocrity to think?' He called me a mediocrity before my entire class! How can you expect me to keep discipline or have the respect of my pupils if — " Her voice broke all at once, and it was plain she was not far from hysteria.

Rance spoke in his thin, immature voice: "Do you know the meaning of the word mediocrity, Miss Doremus?"

"Certainly I know!" she said. "You needn't try to insult me any more than you have already. It means fool! You called me a fool before my entire class!"

"That isn't the way the dictionary defines the word," said Rance. He lifted his plump, smug face and looked at St. Joseph, smiling with good-natured patience. "The dictionary defines mediocrity as a thing of moderate excellence. In other words, the average person is a mediocrity." He turned to her with false humility and went on: "I see now where I made my mistake, because apparently you consider yourself far above the average, well-educated person."

"I never had such pretensions!" said Miss Doremus angrily. "I'm not that vain! I'm not that egotistical! You're the one who pretends to be so much cleverer than others, not I!"

"But if you *agree* with what I said, why are you so upset?" asked Rance patiently. He turned to St. Joseph and winked knowingly behind his hand, at the moment Miss Doremus buried her face in her handkerchief. St. Joseph lost his balance and tilted back in his chair, feeling in his shocked surprise as if the boy had actually pushed him. There was an unexpected anger rising in him, and as he righted himself, he thought: "Nothing would give me more pleasure at this moment than to take a razor strop to you, my fat, insufferable little friend!" But above his anger was the insistent thought: "Just the same, the boy is right. Ella's a well-educated mediocrity, and nothing else."

He had always prided himself on his fairness, and he thought of school children as being particularly defenseless in their relationships with their teachers, so that now, in his effort to control his anger, to be entirely just to the boy, he kept thinking: "Perhaps Archimedes, when he was Rance's age, had the same opinion of his instructors, and with as much reason. Perhaps Rance sees Ella and me in the same light that we see old Miss Maybanks, who believes it's sinful to teach physiology, since man's body is the province of God." That idea made him wince, and he looked at Rance with a new forbearance, a new respect.

Later, he suggested that Miss Doremus leave the matter in his hands. "Rance will apologize to you before your class, I'm sure," he said. "Will that be satisfactory?"

She hesitated and then said, "I suppose it will have to be." She had expected some larger, more dramatic satisfaction, but she knew an apology was all she could reasonably count on. When she had gone, St. Joseph spoke seriously to the boy: "You may think what you please about Miss Doremus, or me either, for that matter, but in future, try to keep your opinions to yourself. That's all I'm going to say to you now."

The boy looked at the wall above St. Joseph's head and smiled, as if he found the lithograph of George Washington, which hung there, mildly amusing. "If you continue to be so conceited," said St. Joseph, "you'll end up with everybody disliking you. I don't think you'll find that very pleasant, Rance."

"They do already," said Rance. "Everybody dislikes me now."

"Do you enjoy it?"

Rance thought a moment. "Yes, I suppose I do," he said brightly. "When people dislike me, I know it's only because I'm superior to them, and they know it too. So you see, when people dislike me, they really pay me a compliment." He got up and went to the window, bored with the conversation. His well-fleshed thighs, in their tight-fitting serge trousers, rubbed together as he walked and made a thin, fanning sound, like the whinnying of pigeonwings.

St. Joseph joined the tips of his fingers together and sighed. Mathematics was not one of the things that interested him, but languages were, and he had always prided himself on the excellence of his French. Recently he had introduced a French course in the high school, having got a Frenchwoman from New Orleans to teach it. He had met her in the hall only a few days before, and she had said enthusiastically: "That little boy! That little Rance Palmiller is wonderful! He has learned to speak French as if it were his native language. The boy is remarkable! He learns without effort! He is marvelous! He is a delight to teach!" She lifted her arms excitedly and continued: "But those others you sent me — those little mental defectives . . . !" And finding no words for what she wanted to say, she merely lifted her eyes upward and sighed.

St. Joseph got up and joined the boy at the window. Seeing a group of children waiting beside the steps, he said: "You may go now and join your friends, but in future try to remember that the mind isn't the only factor that makes a person superior." He opened his window and watched while the boy joined the waiting children, and for a time he could catch scraps of the conversation, hearing his name repeated over and over; then, somehow, the conversation veered without warning, and the children were discussing The Goodwife of Death, and her powers, instead. They moved from the steps toward the gate, and their voices were lost; and it was at this instant that The Goodwife herself appeared, and stopped beside the wall, when she saw the approaching children.

"If you're so brave, and stood up to Miss Doremus and Professor St. Joseph like you say, why don't you tell The Goodwife to go about her business and let us pass?" said Fodie Boutwell. "You're the one that's always talking so big!"

Rance turned quickly and looked at her, as if a new way of demonstrating his superiority to others had just occurred to him. "Would you like me to go home with her and have tea?" he asked. Then, before the effect of his words on the startled children could wear off, he went up to the old woman and spoke in his most ingratiating manner. The Goodwife seemed a little surprised at his proposal, but she inclined her head graciously, and they walked away together.

There was about the old woman a not unpleasant smell which seemed compounded of limewater and decaying floral pieces at the moment they reached their highest odor, the odor they had for a

short time before they become objectionable. She came through
the alley with her guest and opened the door. Everything was neat,
clean and cared for. A fire was burning on the hearth, and The
Goodwife filled the teakettle and fastened it to its hook above the
flames.

When Rance was seated comfortably, he looked around and said:
"Are the things they say about you really true? Do you believe
you're married to Death, or is it something people made up?"

The Goodwife looked thoughtfully at the child and raised her
bony fingers to her temples, as if debating her answer. She got out
her teapot and her gold china and put them on a serving table
beside the fire. Only after she had done these things, did she answer.
"Yes," she said. "It's quite true."

"But how can you be sure?" the boy insisted. "How can you
speak so positively?" Characteristically, he glanced over his shoulder and winked, but to his disappointment there was no audience
to admire his cleverness this time.

The Goodwife got out a cloth and laid the table. "I know," she
said. "I know very well indeed."

Rance waited a moment, but as she did not continue, he repeated: "But how? How do you know whether you're the wife
of Death, or not?"

The Goodwife sighed and turned to him. "It's quite simple," she
said. "Really, there's no mystery about it." Then she told him of her
father's funeral, and the stranger she had met there; she spoke
of Bruce Howard, and how she had been the innocent cause of
his death. "You see," she continued, "although I had forgotten my
early marriage, my husband had not." She deliberated a moment,
nodded and went on: "My husband has a quick, impulsive temper.
He was furious when he learned about Bruce, and he took him
at Gettysburg, before his time. Oh, he acted the role of the jealous
but devoted husband to perfection! . . . Afterwards, I knew there
was no other way for me, that I was his wife forever. We had a
talk that night, my husband and I, and he told me what my
duties were to be. He made everything so clear, and he was so
sweet to me after we had promised to love only each other, that
I didn't fear him any more."

Rance, who had been having difficulty in controlling his mirth,

laughed derisively at this point, and said: "Do you believe that?
Do you *actually?*"

The Goodwife looked at him strangely, but she did not answer
at once. Behind her, on its hook, the silhouette of the kettle was
like one of those decorative, footless birds which penmen used to
draw as an exercise in facility with one stroke of their writing
instruments: in this instance a bird poised above a nest of fiery
coals the instant before it settles to rest.

"Naturally, I believe it," said The Goodwife. "How could I
believe otherwise? . . . My husband still visits me, although not
so often as he did when I was younger and more attractive to men.
He sits where you're sitting now, and we have long talks together.
Of course I believe it. I'd be insane not to believe the evidence of
my senses, wouldn't I, my child?"

The bird-shaped kettle at that moment began a song built on three
liquid notes, all a little flattened, a little off key. The Goodwife
moved the kettle from the flames, and its metal lid, like a spent
coin, settled down noisily with a clapping motion, vibration dying
from its core outward.

Rance shook his head with tolerant disbelief and said in his
superior, maddening manner: "Don't you think it's peculiar that
Death selected you for his wife, instead of somebody else? Don't
you think you're being a little vain, when you say that?"

"Not in the least!" she said quickly. "It was my destiny to marry
one of the great people of the earth! Then, too, you must bear in
mind that my father was a famous military man, as were my grandfather and great-grandfather. I was in the royal line you see, like
a princess."

Rance was not dominating the situation as he had intended, and
that knowledge made him uneasy. He looked straight at the old
woman, laughed sneeringly and said in a voice which was too
loud: "Now, show me the coffin you sleep in!" And added, "Don't
tell me you haven't *got* one! I think that's the least you could do
for people!"

The Goodwife had started to pour the tea, but she stopped and
put down the pot, mopping up a drop of water which had fallen
on her rosewood table. She mopped it slowly, thoughtfully, as if
her mind were engaged with more important matters; and when

she lifted her head and looked into the boy's face, her eyes had an amazed, appraising look.

"Why, you're strange too!" she said. "How nice! How delightful! — Not in the way I am, of course, but strange too! . . . Oh, yes, my dear — quite strange! You and I aren't like other people at all, and we've always known it. It's the reason we're afraid of things which others don't concern themselves about."

To the boy it seemed as if she were looking through his eyes and far beyond, where the hidden parts of his mind were. He took the cup of tea she offered him, bowed with exaggerated politeness and laughed again. He was beginning to enjoy his visit, since he was now the subject of the conversation. He stirred his tea slowly, feeling at that moment vastly superior to the draped, demented old woman who sat so close to him that her knees almost touched his own.

"Oh, yes," she continued. "There's no doubt of it. . . . But in your own way, naturally! People know it about you, too, because you can't really fool people about such things, no matter how stupid they are. They know when another person is strange, even if they can't tell you what it is they know."

The Goodwife poured herself more tea, and went on: "What do people like us do when others know we're queer? For my part, I pretended I didn't hear what they said, and after a time I really didn't hear them." She stirred the fire, laughed excitedly, and spoke again from beside the hearth: "You have another way, haven't you? And I'm sure it suits your nature very well." She broke off, and added contritely: "I'm not being a very good hostess, am I? Let's talk of less personal things."

When Rance spoke this time there was a note of respect in his voice. "Please go on," he said. "I want to hear the rest. What was it you started to say?"

"It wasn't anything really," said the old woman in a hesitant voice. "I was merely going to remark that arrogance is as necessary for you as what I do is for *me*."

"Yes," he said. "What else?"

"I'm sure I'm being very rude," she said, "so let me apologize in advance. But it seems to me that as long as you say over and over that you are strong and clever, and others aren't, then you needn't be so afraid of the people you despise." She looked at the boy with unconcealed admiration and added enthusiastically: "And you do it so superbly! You don't know how greatly I admire you!"

Rance sipped his tea thoughtfully, wondering if what The Goodwife said was true or not. It was an idea which had not occurred to him, and he found it interesting, as all things concerning himself were interesting. "Do you think I should change?" he asked after a long silence. "Is that what you hesitated to tell me?"

The Goodwife seemed alarmed. "Oh, no, no!" she said quickly. She raised her bony hands and pressed against her forehead with her spread fingers. "Oh, no! You must never lose your protection! Never!"

She seemed anxious to change the conversation, and before the boy could answer, she said quickly: "Let's draw our chairs closer to the fire. It's more cozy that way." When they had done so, she spoke again: "Tell me about yourself!" she said. "Tell me about the things you're interested in, and what studies you like best in school." She picked up the piece of embroidery she was working on and began to sew. She laughed apologetically and added: "I've talked about myself so much this afternoon that really I'm quite ashamed."

To his surprise Rance found himself talking earnestly to this crazed old woman, while she listened, sewed, and nodded her head. He talked of things she knew nothing about, and that gave her a sense of familiar security, for in her day ladies were not supposed to understand the conversation of men. Their purpose was only to listen, encourage and smile gently at the proper intervals.

"And so you see?" said Rance, after he had talked a long time. "The great scientific discoveries of the future must come through a knowledge of the laws which govern light and time. . . . And they will come, too! They will come, you may be sure of that!"

"Light and time," repeated the old woman vaguely. "Light and time. How nice."

Rance had long since forgotten all his mannerisms, all his arrogant poses, and he talked enthusiastically now, his voice trembling with excitement. "There's another thing I'd like to tell you about, but it isn't clear enough in my mind. I can feel it well enough, and I know its basic principles must be true, but I can't put it into words. It's the most tremendous thing of all! It's the most — "

The old woman put down her sewing and turned to him suddenly, as if she had caught some of his excitement. "What is it?" she whispered. "What is the other thing?"

"It's the law of the decay and renewal of space," said the boy. "That's as closely as I can define it now. It's where the last truths will be found hiding." He pulled his chair closer to his hostess. His eyes had lost their clever, suspicious expression; they were luminous and passionate now, and they were both daring and a little frightened. "Isn't it exciting?" he asked. "Just think, at this very moment, while we sit here talking, somebody may be making the great discoveries! Perhaps somewhere, somebody already knows!"

"Would you like to know what I've learned from my work?" asked The Goodwife of Death. "You're clever, and possibly you'll understand it, although I don't. Anyway, it's simply this: The more a person hates life, the more he fears death . . . That's odd, isn't it? It seems as if it should be the other way round."

Afterwards there came a knock at the door, and when The Goodwife opened it, Cindy Palmiller stood there. She explained that Clarry had told her what the boy had done, and where he had gone, and she wanted to apologize, knowing that he had made a nuisance of himself. The Goodwife said: "Not at all. I've enjoyed the visit. The little boy is entirely charming, and I hope you'll let him come again soon."

"Of course," said Cindy gaily. "Of course he may." But he never did, and afterwards when he and The Goodwife saw each other, they pretended that they had never met.

Seventeen years later, Dover Boutwell, from his hiding place behind the walnut tree, watched The Goodwife anxiously. He wanted to ask in what direction she intended going, but he did not dare. Then, unexpectedly, she walked away from her gate and saw him. Neither spoke at once, and then Dover blurted out his question: "Who is it going to be tonight? Will it be Miss Clarry Palmiller?"

The Goodwife said gently: "Really, I don't know, my child. I have no idea at all."

But Dover did not believe her. He closed his eyes, twisted his foot in the dirt and said: "Will it be Wesley Boutwell? Is he the one you're waiting for tonight?" He pressed his sweating hands together, fearful of what her answer might be; but she only said: "Wait. If you'll wait, you'll know as soon as I know."

She stared at the anguished boy for a moment, then she raised her bony, dead white hands and pressed them against her temples, as if she suffered an unendurable headache. She turned almost instantly and went back to her gate, adjusting her veil as she walked, her arms akimbo under their floating, black draperies; and as she moved in the twilight with her gliding, yet limping stride, she resembled nothing so much as an enormous, wrinkled bird, who, when her feet were tired of touching the earth, would flap her draperies and fly laboriously above the trees and the house-tops.

It was then Dover remembered an incident he had witnessed some years before at Court House Square. Several workmen from the sawmill at Hodgetown were on the streets that day. They had been drinking too much, and, since they were strangers, they did not know who The Goodwife was. When she passed them in her grotesque, flowing robes, they took hold of her draperies and held them taut behind her, as if she were a bride and they were her trainbearers, laughing boisterously among themselves at both their imagination and their wit. Old Mrs. Wentworth had been sitting in her carriage outside Shepherd's Department Store, and when she saw what was happening, she stood up in fury and shook her cane at the men. "You scum!" she said in her baritone voice. "You presumptuous scum! Don't you recognize your betters when you see them?"

The men stopped sheepishly and looked up at the angry old woman, sobered all at once. Mrs. Wentworth stared back at them with a hostility as great as their own. "You do a thing of that sort again," she said, "you annoy her again, and I'll have my coachman lash your insolent backs!" She sat down angrily, her pearl choker vibrating, and said: "She is the last of the great ladies, you clowns! But of course you don't know what I'm talking about!"

Dover did not know what Mrs. Wentworth was talking about either, for the unreal age to which she and The Goodwife belonged, and remembered so well, with such regret, was over and forgotten before he was born. He stood for a moment longer under the walnut tree, but when The Goodwife went into her house and shut the door behind her, he ran down the alley again, but faster this time, to make up for the minutes he had lost.

Color had faded from the sky, and it was now a dark, velvet blue, with only a diffused edging of smoky silver at the horizon. Then the evening star came out and shone purely with cold, dispassionate light, hanging like a lamp set in the window of an unknown world. Light appeared in houses which a moment before had been dusky, and there was sudden activity in Reedyville with the approach of darkness. There was a shutting of doors, a sound of rocking chairs and a tinkling of dishes being washed and put away until the morrow came. In the trees, locusts made their changeless, patient noises; and far away, in the part of town where his sister Fodie lived with her husband, a dog barked with measured dignity, deeply, ponderously. Hearing his unhurried voice, you knew that he was concerned with something large: that a dog of such unbending dignity did not believe in the existence of anything smaller than a horse.

||||||||||||||||||||||||||||||||||||||||||||||||||||||||||||||||||||||||||||||||||||||

||||||||||||||||||||||||||||||||||||||||||||||||||||||||||||| T HE most important thing
that Clarence Lankester acquired from his four years at the University of Alabama was his friend Hubert Palmiller, and he brought him home, like a particularly imposing sheepskin, to show to his family during the Christmas vacation preceding his graduation. His parents, and especially his young sister Lucinda, were prepared in advance for Mr. Palmiller, since Clarence had been writing them accounts of the accomplishments of this remarkable young man for some time.

He came from a wealthy New York family, it seemed, and his name — a name which Clarence hoped his family would not consider amusing — was an Anglicized variant of a more difficult North European original. His family had intended him for one of the big, Eastern universities, but Hubert had democratically chosen a Southern school instead. Clarence once wrote his sister: —

Hubert Palmiller is the most remarkable man I ever met, or ever expect to meet, even though he believes neither in God, nor in the existence of the soul. In fact, there is only one altar at which he is a supplicant, and that is the Altar of Science. He hates religion more than anything, I think. No, I'm wrong there. The things he hates the most are weakness and abnormality of any kind. In talking with him the other day, he said to me: "You asked me what *positive* things I believe in. Here they are: I believe in the impersonal justice of science. I believe that men are not the children of God, but are the test tubes of nature."

Do you wonder, my dear little sister, how it is that a man like myself, to whom the spirit is everything, and one who means to dedicate his life to the service of God, and a man like Hubert Palmiller, to whom the soul is nothing, could be roommates and excellent friends? I have wondered about it myself often enough, but the fact remains that we are. But do not be alarmed, for I don't agree with his views, although I admit I find them interesting. Each night and morning I pray for the salvation of the splendid soul which he denies possessing, and I'd like for you to do the same. Perhaps God would more quickly heed a prayer from your sweet, attractive lips than from my own.

Lucinda put the letter down thoughtfully. It had not occurred to her that God's decision might be swayed by a pretty face, but the idea was an interesting one, and, since man was created in God's own image, it was not nearly so implausible as it appeared at first glance. She decided she'd better take out these pages before reading the letter to her mother later on. All at once she laughd and said: "He sounds dangerous! Possibly Clarence shouldn't have anything to do with him!" But her thoughts had veered again, and she was now thinking not of God, but of Hubert Palmiller. A moment later she picked up the letter and went on: —

You would imagine that a man of ideas would hardly be a man of action as well, but Hubert is an outstanding athlete. There is no sport at which he is not an adept.

"Goodness me!" said Cindy. "Mind and body both! . . . I wonder if he's good-looking too." She skimmed until she came to the part of the letter which answered her question: —

Hubert is a great advocate of physical culture, having developed his body from childhood, and you may believe me, my dear sister, when I tell you that in face as well as in figure he could have been the model for a statue by Praxiteles. I often wonder why a man like himself chose our state university instead of going to . . .

With regard to Hubert's choice of a school, which seemed to have bothered Clarence so greatly, there was one thing he did not know, for a sense of delicacy (entirely nonscientific) had prevented Hubert Palmiller from saying outright that he had come to Alabama because he considered the South the ideal place for his research work, since it was such a rich field, as everybody in his intellectual set back home knew, for the study of stupidity and degeneracy; a place so lacking in culture, or in the new scientific approach, that he expected to accomplish much of a missionary nature there.

A burning wish to rescue, to reclaim, was the intangible cement which held the two, very different, young men together, although Clarence was the gentler, more passive partner in their fierce mar-

riage of the spirit. Both knew in their hearts that man must be
redeemed, and both had faith in his ultimate salvation: Clarence
through an intensification of his religious impulses and a more rigid
application of the moral code; Hubert through a dispassionate understanding of the laws of science.

He would often say, nodding his handsome head slowly for
greater emphasis: "If we give evolution a chance, Clarence, she
will reward us with a superior race. Perhaps you and I won't live
to see it, but it will come. In the new world of the future there
will be no place for the weakling." Then he would glance up and
examine himself thoughtfully in the mirror, wondering if nature
could do better than to take his own, precise perfection of mind and
feature as a pattern; wondering, indeed, if the new race had not
already begun to evolve, and if he, like a more proportionate Adam,
were not actually its first man.

Clarence looked up and smiled absently. This was the fourth
year of their friendship. He had heard all these things many times
before, and of late Hubert was beginning to bore him. He repressed the thought as disloyal to his friend, and said: "I'm glad
you're going home with me for the holidays. I hope you like the
people of Reedyville. They're all prepared to like you." He got up,
went to his bureau and brushed his thinning, curly hair. "I got a
letter from my sister Lucinda this morning. She says you must be
wonderful. You see, Hubert, I've told her so much about you in
my letters."

Hubert smiled and examined his nails thoughtfully. All at once
he frowned, his eyes lifted upward in an intense, brooding pose
which was quite characteristic of him. He hoped that the young,
romantic girl had not fallen in love with her brother's descriptions
of him, and that if she had, she would not make too great a
nuisance of herself. He expected to marry someday, since it was the
first duty of his superior man of the future to reproduce his own
kind: children as healthy, wholesome and normal as himself. . . .
But Southern women, he felt, were vapid, shallow and avaricious,
and already he wondered if behind the invitation there lurked a
plot to get his money, for the Lankesters, as he knew, had been
impoverished since the Civil War.

When he met Cindy that Christmas he was forced to modify his doubts a little, to admit that her undisguised admiration was for himself alone. She was very pretty and very charming, he thought. She had many admirable qualities. The one thing he found objectionable in her was a gay, light-hearted levity, and unlike her brother, who listened in silence and in respect to all he said, Cindy would often go off into peals of laughter while he was in the midst of one of his most interesting scientific observations. Cindy herself had no reservations about him at all. She was in love with him from the start, and as she told her friend Millicent Reedy, he made her think of the engraving of Sir Galahad which hung, stained and bleak, in the gutted Lankester parlor.

She saw at once that her brother had not exaggerated Hubert's good looks. In reality, he was an outstandingly handsome man. His body was so perfect in its development that it barely escaped being monstrous. His hair was flaxen, and he brushed it back from his forehead, allowing it to settle loosely in clusters of thick curls, in the manner of Greek athletes. His eyes were a bright, criticizing blue, his lips full-fleshed and sensual, his features proportioned in a chiseled perfection. The effect produced by his ascetic, disapproving eyes, and his sensual mouth, was a most peculiar one, and you thought of him afterwards as a young voluptuary, with every vice at his finger tips, who had become a monk after all.

Cindy was with him as often as she could manage, and they took walks together, or sat before the fire talking. He explained his views to her, and Cindy said quickly: "But isn't that a little narrow-minded? Don't you think you're being *intolerant?*"

He looked up gravely. "That's a very unjust thing to say," he began in a stiff voice. "Most assuredly I'm *not* intolerant. Nobody stands for the freedom of the individual more positively than I. Without freedom of the individual, there can be no advance in science. . . . But the fact remains, Miss Lankester, from a cool, scientific viewpoint, that there is a way to do things, according to the laws of nature, and a way not to do them. The abnormal must be crushed without sentiment and without false pity, not because it is sinful, as Clarence believes, but because the scientific approach demonstrates that the unnatural, like a weed in a flower garden, chokes the growth of the good, the normal and the true."

Cindy laughed happily, the deep dimples, which ran through the

Lankester family like a provocative mark of identification, appearing suddenly in her cheeks. Her mother came into the room at that moment, and listened to the conversation, but a little later, Hubert made his apologies and went upstairs to dress. Mrs. Lankester took up the book she was reading, found her place, and said: "I declare, Cindy, I don't know how you and your brother manage to understand what Mr. Palmiller says. I never realized it before, and I don't mean to be unkind when I say it, but Northerners talk exactly like Negroes, don't they my dear?" She waited a moment, looked anxiously at her daughter, and added: "What do you and Clarence see in him, for heaven's sake? Tell me. I'd really like to know."

"Mr. Palmiller has very original and advanced ideas," said Cindy defensively. "I like a man of that sort." She had almost added: "I know what you mean, Mama, and I don't like it in him either, but those things will disappear when he falls in love with me, and asks me to be his wife." Like many women before her, she attributed a curative quality to marriage, not understanding that love is the origin of oddities, not their solution.

The two young men went back to college for their graduation, but by that time it was plain to Hubert that Clarence was passing from under his control. The idea distressed him, and he did not understand what was happening between them, what was becoming of the friendship which had lasted so long. To his dismay, after their graduation Clarence announced, with an aggressive certainty which seemed out of place for him, that he had never abandoned his original idea of becoming a missionary, and he meant to go on with it.

Hubert tried to dissuade him, to convince him that religion belonged to the unscientific past, but Clarence could not be swayed. The next year he went to Africa, and died at once of fever. But before the end came, he managed to write a letter to his estranged friend, regretting their rupture, and imploring Hubert's pardon for the sorrows he had caused him. In this letter he told Hubert that Cindy was in love with him, and he hoped, as a dying wish, that Hubert could find it possible in his heart to return her affection, and make her happy.

This part of the letter came as a surprise to Hubert, but upon reflection, he could understand how he had made such a lasting impression on the young lady, and why Clarence felt that only a man like himself would be worthy of her. The more he thought of the idea, the more logical it became. Cindy had her faults, but then what woman did not? At least she was healthy, attractive and could, no doubt, be trained easily enough to become the sort of wife he wanted. Then, too — and he considered this bordering on the miraculous for the South — her family had that genteel, unimaginative placidity which, to his mind, was synonymous with wholesomeness. In the end he wrote Cindy and asked her to marry him. With almost indecent haste she said she would.

After the wedding, Cindy went about in a haze of delight. She was prepared to go North with her husband to live, but she felt an enormous sense of relief and gratitude when Mr. Palmiller decided that his business future lay in Reedyville.

Before the marriage was six months old, she knew she had made a serious error of judgment, one which she could not easily adjust now, for already she was pregnant with her first child. Her disillusionment, when it came, came quickly, and it seemed to her that she had passed, with no period of transition, from the romantic tradition in which she had been brought up, a tradition which she knew, now, nobody had ever really believed in, to a world of hardness and actuality. She looked over her life, trying to retrace the steps which had led her to her stupid marriage, but she could not. Millicent Reedy had recently married Paul Kenworthy, and the two young matrons were often together. Once Mrs. Kenworthy said: "When will your baby be born, Cindy? You know, you forgot to tell me, when we were talking the other day."

Cindy moved from the sofa and sat beside the window, the late sunlight touching her finely spun hair and high-lighting it with liquid amber. "The baby will be born when Hubert decides it's time for it to be born," she said. "Not one minute before." She laughed with a nervous exasperation, her head tilted forward, the amber lights spreading and breaking like water with the movement of her head. "I know that sounds terrible, Milly," she continued, "but it does seem as if a woman could have her own baby in peace, doesn't it? But, oh, no! If she's married to Hubert Palmiller she can't! He has to supervise every little thing I do. This isn't scientific! That isn't in accord with the laws of dear Mother Nature! . . . He's even given me a set of bending exercises to do, and he stands right there beside me, to see that I do them, too! Sometimes I feel like saying: 'If you know so much about it, why don't you have the baby yourself?'" She played with the tassels of the velvet curtains and added: "I never have said it, though, and I never shall, because, before God in heaven, I really believe he'd only say, 'Very well, my dear!' in that quick, alert way he has, and really do it!" She came back to the sofa, beside her friend, and said: "So you see, Milly? Don't ask me when the baby will be born. Ask Mr. Palmiller. He'll know."

Actually, the Palmiller baby was born in January of 1890, and it was a girl. Hubert wanted to name her for her dead uncle, but since he could not very well call a girl Clarence, he did the next best thing, and announced to his wife that the child's name was to be Clarencia. Cindy objected with such vigor that he wished again that her nature was more like the gentle, obedient nature of her brother.

"No child of mine will ever be called Clarencia!" she said. "So you may as well get that notion out of your head at once! Why, it's an old maid's name! It's something you'd expect your mother's maiden aunt to be named! Imagine a girl named Clarencia Palmiller making a debut! People would stick their heads out of the window and say, 'Just listen to the guns at Fort Sumter! Aren't they loud tonight!' . . . Why, it would be enough to frighten away all the eligible young men! No, no! I'm willing to consider any reasonable suggestions, but Clarencia I will not put up with!"

The result was a compromise, and the child, as we now know, was christened Clarine. Two years later Mrs. Palmiller gave birth to her second child, a boy this time. This child was called Clarence without argument, but being unable to pronounce the name when he first began to talk, he called himself Rance, and that was the name others called him too.

Rance looked a great deal like the uncle for whom he had been named, and it would seem as if that circumstance alone should have endeared him to his father. Oddly, it did not work out that way. Hubert loved his firstborn, the little blond girl whose hair was the texture and color of cotton — the child who looked so astonishingly like himself. To her he gave all his love. His duty he reserved for his son.

He would rock the little girl for hours on end when she was small, singing to her and gazing with fascination into her face, as if it were a reducing mirror in which his own image was reflected, tender, precise and softened with babyhood. A new existence seemed to open for him with the birth of his daughter: a rich life of the emotions of which he had had no conception before. She absorbed all his thoughts, all his desires, and she was the core around which his whole life centered.

Sometimes, when he realized how unimportant others had now become to him, he felt a sense of blustering guilt, and almost at once he would say to himself, as if defending his position: "But how is it possible for me to feel affection for anybody else? A man has only a certain amount of love to give, and Clarry takes all mine. It isn't my fault that I have none left over — not even for my wife and son."

He was a man whose complexities had found not one, but many, channels for drainage to the outside world; and it was thus that a truth and its denial could exist in his mind without conflict. He was like one of those exercises in cancellation which teachers used to give their pupils in the fourth grade, the essence of the intricate problem being the necessity, before the answer can be determined, of many divisors going into one another and canceling themselves out. No doubt an answer to Mr. Palmiller's inconsistencies could be found through a similar technique, but the method is tedious, and perhaps the result would not justify the effort, for there is always the possibility, as every schoolboy knows, that after long minutes of squirming application, the end result of the imposing sum is not determinable value, but zero.

One of his more obvious contradictions was his attitude toward his son. It would seem that a man who laid such importance upon the evolution of a superior race of beings would have been pleased with a superior child of his own, but Hubert dismissed this problem by denying its existence, by not admitting that the boy was in any way out of the ordinary. No matter what the opinion of others might be, Mr. Palmiller considered his son stubborn, timid and unnatural, and nothing more: the precise opposite of his ideal.

He had never clearly defined his superman of the future, but as
nearly as one could judge, the mind was no essential part of his
equipment. He appeared to be merely something posed and overpowering, an operatic creature with the physique of a discus
thrower and the nobility of an obedient collie.

The true motives in his attitude toward his son were those hidden
from his consciousness. He would have denied them with a shake
of his handsome head, had he been confronted with them, but the
fact was, if Clarry was the mirror in which he saw his own essential
image reflected, Rance was a mirror reflecting a likeness of the
uncle for whom he was named. This was unfortunate for the boy,
for Hubert, who forgot no disloyalty, forgave no slight, had never
recovered from the wound of his friend's repudiation of him.

It was almost as if his son were Clarence Lankester reincarnated
from his hot, African grave; and when Hubert treated the child
with such stiff-necked coldness, he was really saying to the boy's
namesake: "You showed once that I meant very little to you. I'll
show you now that two can play at that game. You repudiated
me for religion, although you knew religion was the thing I detested the most. Very well, then: I repudiate you, too! You mean
nothing to me at all!" But he was unaware of the deeper motiva-
tion of his attitude, and his stern treatment of the boy, as he told
his wife so often, was intended as a checkrein for the child's
obviously depraved nature.

He subjected his son almost from birth to a strict athletic discipline, and when the boy could walk, he could also balance himself on his father's outstretched arms. Then Hubert, stripped to
his undershirt and trousers, and giving off the lemon tang of
well-washed sweat, which seems so essential a part of wholesomeness, would lock his son's small fingers in his own, and resting on
his back, he would rise from the floor and lift the child so high
above his head, that the boy's legs — rigid and strong, not in confidence, but in terror — almost touched the ceiling.

One Sunday when Rance was about three, Hubert took his
family to James' Lake for a day's outing. He had a theory that
swimming was as instinctive to the human race as it was to animals,
and to prove this, he carried the frightened boy to the end of the
wharf and dropped him into the deep water. The child made a ter-

rified, strangling sound, beat at the water with his hands and sank. Hubert watched with exasperation, but when he was certain that his son would drown, that he would not turn and swim ashore with the instinctive skill of an otter, he dived from the wharf and rescued him.

Cindy, hearing the sound, came running toward them, her eyes angry and tearful. Her husband handed her the half-drowned child and explained carefully what had happened. He did these things, he said, to condition the child against fear, to develop a greater sense of self-reliance in him and to inure him to discomfort: in other words, to make a man out of him. "He was in no danger, I assure you," said Mr. Palmiller smilingly. "I was watching him all the time." He shook the water from his yellow, curly hair and added: "Do you think I'd endanger the life of my own child? If you do, you're a peculiar woman, indeed."

It was then that Clarry came skipping down to the beach. When she saw her father, she said: "What happened? Did Rance fall in the water?" Hubert's eyes softened at once and he said good-naturedly: "Yes, my angel." He got down on his knees and put his arms about the child's shoulders. "How is my darling?" he asked. "How is my little sweetheart?" He picked her up and tilted her head backwards so that her hair hung like a waterfall over his arm. His face seemed released now into one joyous, begging smile. He kissed her neck and added in the whimsical, unnatural voice he reserved for his daughter alone: "My little sweetheart gets prettier and prettier every day, doesn't she?"

"You shouldn't do those things to Rance," said Cindy angrily. "He hates them. It might be all right for another child, but not for him, and I want you to stop it."

Clarry, as if realizing at last what had happened, said: "Put me down, Papa. Please put me down, now." When he had done so, she straightened the strap of her bathing suit, glanced at her brother and smiled mildly, as if to say: "It isn't my fault that he loves me so much more than he does you. I don't even encourage him." But Rance stared back at her with cold, implacable hatred, turned to his mother and shivered.

"What makes you think the boy dislikes the way I handle him?" asked Mr. Palmiller. "Why is it you consider yourself so much

wiser than others where Rance is concerned? Do you think I'm
not as interested in his future as you are?"

When Rance was older, his father determined to teach him
baseball, not as children learn it among themselves, but scientifically,
thoroughly; but long before that, the boy had discovered his amaz-
ing mental gifts, and his whole character, his whole attitude toward
the world about him, had changed. He made the discovery by accident. His sister, being six years old at that time, was going to
school in the fall. Cindy, in preparation for the event, thought it
wise to teach the child her letters, and Rance sat listening as she
explained, illustrating what she said on the nursery blackboard.
He had a familiar feeling as he listened to his sister's first lesson,
for it seemed to him that the things his mother was saying were
only things he had known somewhere before, but had forgotten.

Clarry mastered the alphabet and learned to count up to forty
under her mother's teaching, but long before that, the boy had
finished the first grade. With this start, the acquisition of knowledge became a passionate necessity for him. There were many old
schoolbooks in the attic, and he found them and took them for his
own. He worked through them with a rapid, unswerving attention: with such confidence, such surety in himself, that his purpose often seemed less a desire to learn than to verify the fact
that others also knew what he did. Afterwards he read with insatiable eagerness everything in the Palmiller library, fiercely,
nervously; and when he was six himself, and it was time for him
to go to school, he was ready for the eighth grade.

He was no longer afraid of his father. It was almost as if the
contemptuous ridicule which Hubert had given his son was now
returned to its source, for Rance took great delight in disputing
everything his father said. He criticized his speech, sneered at his
scientific theories and laughed derisively at what Hubert considered
his profoundest remarks. But despite this change in his son's character, this new sense of overwhelming superiority he had developed,
Hubert held to his own position, and he was stubbornly determined
to go on with the boy's athletic education whether Rance liked it
or not.

He hoped that baseball would prove the antidote for his son's
unwholesome studiousness. The game, he maintained, taught a

person to act for himself, to think quickly and to co-ordinate brain and muscle as no other activity did. At this point Rance drew down his lips, stared above his father's head and smiled with the air of patronizing patience which Hubert found so irritating.

"If you'd show me the respect due me as your father," he said stiffly, "and not sneer at everything I try to teach you, perhaps you'd get something out of the game. You needn't be so contemptuous. There are many famous men in baseball. I was an outstanding player myself. Doesn't that make you want to be a great baseball player yourself?"

"Not in the least," said the boy, drawing his words out with languid affectation. "No, not at all."

Ada Boutwell was at the Palmillers that afternoon to do some sewing. She had brought her son Breck with her, as she wanted him to run a few errands for her, after she had collected the money Mrs. Palmiller owed for last week's work. While he waited, Breck sat on the back steps and watched Hubert hit pop flies to his son, but when he could stand his inactivity no longer, he got up and said excitedly: "Knock some grounders to me, Mr. Palmiller! Let me show you what a good fielder I am!"

In appearance, Breck fitted in somewhere between his father and his sister Honey. He had the broad face, the bright eyes and the facial structure of the alert yet relaxed animals. His eyes were black and sharp, and they were never quite still in his face. The tip of his tongue was usually thrust out and touching his upper lip, not in concentration but in eagerness, and when he rolled his eyes at you, and tilted his head to one side, you felt as if you were participating against your will in some lewd conspiracy. He shook his black hair out of his eyes, ran to the back fence and said: "Come on! Come on, Mr. Palmiller! Knock me some ground balls! I'll show Rance how to field a ball right!"

Rance tossed his glove to the boy and stood against the gate. For a time Hubert knocked ground balls to the visitor, and Breck ran excitedly about, scooping them off the top of the grass with one hand, pivoting, and returning the ball as if his individual life and the fate of the world depended on the accuracy of his throwing arm. He ran across the yard with the quick assurance of a water beetle darting over the surface of a pond, his face flushed with pleasure, his eyes bright and dancing. He made the simplest plays seem enormously complicated, scooping up the ball with one hand at the moment it seemed inevitable that he had lost it, falling forward, rolling over, and recovering himself in time to make a play. To his regret, his mother called him just when he and Mr. Palmiller were really beginning to enjoy themselves.

Hubert watched thoughtfully as Breck went away, wishing his own son were more like the Boutwell child in temperament. A little later he came and stood beside Rance at the gate. Since his son was interested in ideas, rather than in athletics, he decided to use another means of gaining his interest. "Baseball is a game which also develops the most superior qualities of the mind," he began after a moment's thought. "I'll give you an illustration of what I mean. It was a play once made by Mike Kelly, and for quick thinking you'll have to go a long way to equal it."

Rance sighed and stared at the second button on his father's shirt. He struck the glove twice with his fist, but languidly, with so little force that he knew his father would be irritated. Mr. Palmiller refused to lose his temper this time, and after a moment he went on: —

"His name is really Mike Kelly, but everybody calls him 'King' Kelly, and you'll see the reason for that very soon. In 1889 he was captain of the Boston Beaneaters, and one day while Charlie Ganzel was catching for Boston, 'King' Kelly was sitting on the bench watching his team. Boston was playing Cincinnati that afternoon. And so one of the Cincinnati men hit a slow foul behind the third base line. Ganzel ran for the ball, but he couldn't get it." Mr. Palmiller paused and then made his voice more clipped, more energetic than it was normally: —

"At this point," he went on, "the quickness of thought which baseball had developed in Mike Kelly became apparent to all, and he saw that while Ganzel didn't have a chance to catch the foul and make the out, he, Mike Kelly, did, because it was coming straight toward the bench where he was sitting — almost into his hands. Instantly he got up and shouted: 'Ganzel taken out of the game! Kelly now catching for Boston!' And he stood there for a second grinning back at the crowd; then, just at the right moment, he turned, reached up and caught the ball. . . . Now what do you think of that, Rance? Wasn't that an example of wonderfully quick thinking?"

Rance, who had not even listened very closely, said: "I wonder why somebody doesn't invent a mechanical umpire? You know, they're always having arguments with the umpire. . . . Well, if it could be fixed so that balls and strikes register themselves on a machine back of the plate, some of that could be avoided." He looked thoughtfully at the ground, and added: "I believe it can be done, too! I believe somebody could think it out."

"Go to your room," said Mr. Palmiller coldly. "Go to your room, and stay there until I tell you you may come out."

The child turned without a word to obey, but he stopped at the back door to look at his father, vague emotions tearing at him. Apparently the purpose of his waking life was to prove over and over, to himself and to others, that his father was a fool, and yet, in reality, that was the thing he wanted the least to prove. When he remembered his father and Breck Boutwell playing together on such terms of pleasant equality, a feeling of angry jealousy came over him. To himself he said: "I don't care. What difference does it make? He's always liked everybody else better than he did me. I ought to be used to it by this time!" Nevertheless, the feeling of jealousy persisted, no matter how much he strove to convince himself that what his father thought or did was of no importance whatever. To reassure himself, to establish his right to an identity of his own, he counted over his remarkable accomplishments, his obvious superiority to others. He did these things with a desperate, heartbreaking earnestness, and yet he remained frightened at the thought of alienating his father entirely, of losing the little he had.

Afterwards he showed a greater willingness to conform to Hubert's wishes, to adjust his own temperament more closely to his father's idea of what a son should be, and when the New Century Party became a certainty, he decided, as a gesture of conciliation, to go as Willie Keeler, since he was the baseball player Mr. Palmiller admired above all others. "Willie Keeler," he had once said, "is the greatest player baseball has ever developed, and I'm not forgetting A. G. Spalding of the old Forest City team, Ted Breitenstein, Matt Kilroy, or even a promising youngster like Hans Wagner, when I say it." After Rance made his decision, he

clipped a picture of Willie Keeler in uniform from a sports maga-
zine, and from this photograph, a smaller uniform, precise in every
detail, was to be made for him by Ada Boutwell.

Clarry's party seemed to occupy the attention of many people in
Reedyville for a week or two, and Ada suddenly had more sewing
than she could easily take care of. Between her other duties, she
made the costumes for her own children. Only Honey, who was
Clarry's age, and in her class at school, had actually been invited,
but the other Boutwells considered this the most trivial technicality,
and all accepted. Fodie had decided to represent a housewife, and
one of Mrs. McMinn's dresses, padded with cotton batting to ape
the contours of ripe, stimulating womanhood, was all that was
required. Stacy was to be a railroad engineer, and while his outfit was not out of the question, it was a little more difficult. His
mother decided at the last minute that it would be a clever touch
of realism to soak oil into his hands, since all the engineers she
had known were outstanding in her memory because of their dirty
nails, but when she called Stacy to her, and took his grimy hands
in her own, she saw that this was the one detail of his costume which
he had been able to arrange without outside assistance.

It was from her daughter Honey that she expected difficulties.
Her expectations were entirely justified. Honey wanted to go to the
party as Little Egypt, but Ada wouldn't listen to it. Finally Honey
had to consent to wear the Red Cross uniform which Ada had
made for her, or stay at home. It was perhaps the most inappropriate
costume which could have been thought of for Honey Boutwell,
for of all the things she wanted from the new century, the unselfish
nursing of the sick was the most remote from her plans.

This, then, took care of all the Boutwell children except Breck,
but since the Emperor Elagabalus and himself had the same sort
of thumb, Breck knew that he must go as a Roman emperor, and
nothing else. Ada confided this particular problem to Minnie
McInnis McMinn, and the latter said: "Well, why not, if he wants
to?" She added a moment later: "Purple was the color of the
emperors. Imperial purple. I know just what we want. It's that
silk undershirt of old Emmaline Maybanks'. She's been wearing it
for years, to my personal knowledge, and I'll figure out some
way of getting it off her." She closed her eyes and laughed boister-

ously in anticipation of the scene she was to have with Miss Maybanks, and went on: —

"There ought to be enough material in it for a toga and skirt.
That's what the Roman emperors wore, you know. But if there
isn't, we'll piece it out, somehow." She turned back to her desk,
wrote a few lines and then said: "I'll go to the library this afternoon and find out how to make it. Somebody there will be sure
to know."

As it turned out, the Roman costume had been simple enough, but
after it was finished, a new problem arose. Ada tried the dress
on her son and stood back critically to examine the effect. Its scanti-
ness alarmed her. She spread her fingers against her cheek, sighed
and said in a worried voice: "Emperors sure must of wore something *under* it. They just couldn't of gone around that-a-way. Why,
they'd of got arrested, sure!" All the material had not been used
up. She glanced at it, nodded with sudden decision and added:
"Son, I'm going to make you a little pair of purple drawers to go
under it. Won't that be nice, now?"

"No," said Breck. He scowled ferociously and walked up and
down the room. "No! I won't wear nothing under it, Mama! The
Emperor Elagabalus didn't wear nothing under *his,* and I'm not
going to either!"

Ada sighed deeply and raised her hands outward in a gesture
of mock despair. She wanted her son to be historically accurate, but
she also wanted to preserve the common decencies. Then, having
made up her mind, she got up with sudden decision and said
firmly: "I don't care what Elagabalus wore! You're going to wear
a little pair of drawers, too, or you ain't stirring one step out of
this house!" She put away her workbasket and went to the kitchen
to start supper. From the kitchen she continued: "If Roman emperors didn't wear no more than what you got on now, it was
because they were all well-mannered and had good characters. They
wasn't like you, young man. You could trust one of them not to
pull his clothes up when he was around little girls, and make
them cry and run home the way you do."

The Boutwells prepared for the approaching party with such
wholehearted enthusiasm, and talked about it so continuously to
others, that a stranger would have got the impression that they,

instead of the Palmillers, were giving it. Ada worked as fast as she could, but when the day of the party finally arrived, Rance's baseball suit was still not complete. She put everything aside for a time and with Fodie's help she finished it quickly. She folded it into its box, thinking: "If anybody had to get left out, I'd rather it'd be Rance than one of the others." She tied the string vigorously, as if his neck were beneath it, and said aloud: "That uppity boy! That stuck-up, uppity boy!"

Fodie left a half hour earlier than the other children in order to deliver the package to the Palmillers. She was the oldest guest who would be present as a child, and when she reached the door, she felt a sense of self-conscious inappropriateness. Cindy was waiting in the hall for her, and as Fodie handed her the uniform, she noticed that she was a full three inches taller than her hostess. Cindy said: "So your mother got it finished after all? I'm so glad. . . . Make yourself at home until the others come!" She started up the stairs, turned and said: "The suit is to be a surprise for Mr. Palmiller. Rance seems to think it's most important for some reason and he's been fuming all afternoon about it." She walked a few steps in silence, but when she reached the bend in the stairs she stopped and added: "You know, I didn't recognize you at first in long skirts and with your hair up. How old are you now?"

"I'm fourteen," said Fodie. "Mama says she hopes I've already got my full growth."

The folding doors between the double parlors had been thrown wide. Most of the furniture had been taken out for the occasion, and the walls were banked with vines and potted plants. The band had already come, and the musicians sat in one corner of the room on the platform built for them, looking bored and dejected. Occasionally one of them sounded a note on his particular instrument and sighed, as if the wonderful events of others were only bitter tasks for them. A juggler, a magician and a contortionist had also been engaged, but they were out of sight in one of the back rooms where they waited for the time to come when they were to appear, smile and perform.

But despite the occasional note from one of the musicians and the muted conversation of the performers in the back room, the house had a hushed, waiting feeling as Fodie walked from place to place, admiring its magnificence. Occasionally, as if overpowered by such cumulative splendor, she would stretch her long neck forward and upward in the gesture a hen makes when drinking water, as if she endeavored to swallow something too large for her throat to take easily. Slowly a sense of injustice came over her. "Why should the Palmillers have all this?" she thought angrily. "What makes them have so much, when we got so little?" She wondered, now, how it had been possible for her to have come to the party at all. She felt shamed and conspicuous, and she knew that nothing could induce her to stay. She turned and went hurriedly into the hall. She spoke imperiously to Jesse, the yardman, who was acting as butler that day: "Tell Mrs. Palmiller I decided not to stay. Tell her I got too much work to do at home to waste my time."

She went down the steps and walked across the lawn, thinking: "They needn't be so smart about it. Someday I'll have just as much as they do. . . . I don't know how I'll manage it right now, but I'll have it, all right!" She glanced back angrily at the house and added: "I'll have it! I'll have it! You just watch and see!"

At once she thought of Ira Graley, and in thinking of him, she saw his face plainly — and as plainly she heard his deep, cautious voice. There was no longer any point in hiding the truth, and she admitted to herself that she had known for a long time that he must be the means of her escape from the existence she had always known, to a higher existence of respectability and importance; knowing, as well, that the things she desired came to a woman through her relationship to a particular man, and in no other way.

She nodded her head as she came down the Palmillers' walk, well satisfied with the choice she had made, for in him, beneath his shy, halting uncertainty, she had from the first recognized a quality which others had missed, and that was a passionate, itching ambition. The fact that she could neither understand the motive behind his ambition, nor comprehend its specialized aim, which had nothing in common with her own more obvious aspirations, was hardly to be charged against her as a fault.

He would be free from work early this afternoon, since it was a Saturday, and this was the angry excuse she gave herself for leaving the Palmiller party. She shut the gate and walked rapidly away, thinking again of herself and Ira. He had stayed with the family even after Wesley came back from the army, and he was now like one of them. He ate his meals with them, of course, but on that first morning when he came to them, Fodie cooked his breakfast and took it to him in the room above the barn. She wanted to see him alone, to discuss matters with him which concerned them both. She put the food on the table and spoke, trying to keep her voice casual and disinterested: "You said yesterday evening you wanted to learn how to read and write. If you meant it, and wasn't just talking, I'll teach you as much as I know. I'm smart in school, so everybody says."

Ira lifted his thin face and said with earnest surprise: "Will you? Will you really?" He was so overcome with emotion that he could not eat the food she had brought. He looked up at last and said: "I'll do my best to learn. I'll study all the time and do my best."

Afterwards, when her work was done at night, she came to his room and methodically heard his lessons. She considered the relationship between them a romantic one, resembling a situation in books, and she had taken for granted the fact that her teaching would uncover a mind of rare brilliance. This was not to be. Ira did not learn quickly, although he learned much. It almost seemed as if everything he was to get in life was to be toiled for, sweated over, and won with courage only after an exhausting struggle.

Later, when it was spring, they would go on Sundays beyond the fields, and the grove of pines which lay to the east of the Boutwell house, to where a stream ran between a row of trailing willows; and there, under the tree which they had taken for their own, they would sit in the shade, as if they rested beneath an umbrella. It was cool under the trailing streamers of the willow, and the world was shut away at such times and of little importance to them. Then, when the last lesson was done, they would talk about the things that interested them in their own small world, or sit in silence and watch the stream flow evenly at their feet.

Once, as they sat side by side breaking up dry twigs and tossing them into the slowly moving water, Ira was tempted to speak of his life before he came to Reedyville, but he could not bring himself to do it. He had told nobody of these things, but he was the bastard son of Violet May Wynn — known locally, to her public, as Mattress May. The very fact that he breathed air through his lungs, that blood flowed in his veins, affirmed eternally his mother's disgrace, and in passing on to him the puny, gasping life which had once been his, she had destroyed a life of her own. He sighed and put his face in his hands, remembering these things; but they were things he must never reveal, and already he knew this well.

He was fifteen at the time the Palmillers gave their party, and already his voice had settled to its final level. It was astonishingly deep. His nose was thin and somewhat long, and its fleshy, triangular tip resembled man's first effort to shape an arrow. His hair and eyes were almost the same shade of average brown, and he looked at people with a solemn, intense gaze, as if he calculated the weight of the simplest statement before accepting it. He was not dull; he was slow. It was not the slowness of stupidity, it was a deeper, a more involved slowness, and one which Fodie did not understand at all.

She had hoped to get home and change to her ordinary clothes before he came back from work, but as she hurried up the path which led to the rear of the house, she saw him standing at the back gate watching her. She went to him at once and said: "I'm not going to the party after all. I figured I'd rather stay home and help you." She laughed, seeing the disapproving look on his face, the doll's hand appearing slowly as she raised her neck outward and swallowed. "Don't worry," she added reassuringly. "I told them I had work to do at home, and that's the truth, too. I told them I didn't have time for parties and such truck."

From where they were standing they could see the other Boutwell children, who had been held in check by their mother until a decent time for departure came, setting out with restrained haste. Honey, in her Red Cross uniform, was leading; but almost shoulder to shoulder with her was Breck and his Roman toga. As he trotted along at his sister's side, he kept reaching down to tug at the purple drawers, which broke just below his knees, but each time he did it, Honey, remembering her mother's final instructions, slapped warningly at his hand.

The Boutwell contingent was the first to arrive. They were all

a little out of breath, but they had thriftily reserved enough energy
for a final spurt up the long, flag-paved walk which ran from the
front gate to the steps. They had been talking excitedly together
as they came up the walk, but when the door opened in front of
them, before they even knocked, they became so silent with embarrassment that one would have thought them unable to talk at all.

Clarry, dressed in her lily costume, stood beside her mother
greeting the guests. Her cottony hair had been shampooed that
morning, and it hung like white floss below her knees. When she
turned from one person to the next, the electricity in the winter
air fanned its silken, fine-spun strands apart, lifting them outward and upward in a gesture so curved, so effortless, that one
thought somehow of the relaxed yawn of a cat. She was very self-
assured in the midst of the admiring people, very anxious to please;
and she turned obediently when her elders told her to, so that every
angle of her person, every detail of her dress, could be seen and
appreciated.

The Boutwells had been the first to arrive, but they had been
first by the slenderest of margins. The invitations had been for
three o'clock. At five minutes past the hour all of the children
were there. With widened eyes and expressionless faces they walked
in a subdued single-file to the double parlors. Noticing nothing
there, they went at once to the windows and looked at the Chapman
house across the street with fixed intensity. Cindy came to the
door at once and made them a speech. She wanted this to be a real
party for children, she said, with no restraining hand of an adult
in it. She was leaving them to their own devices, but if anything else
were needed, she could be found in the library. When she had
finished, the orchestra began to play; and when the music started,
a torrent of sound broke from the children. The party was well
started when Rance came down the stairs. He went first to the
library and listened at the door, but not hearing his father's quick,
nasal voice, he continued on to the room where the children were.
The band was resting for a moment, but the guests were playing
games so shrilly, and shouting at one another with such vigor, that
it is doubtful if it could have been heard, anyway.

Above every other voice was the loud, insistent voice of Honey
Boutwell. She was not happy anywhere unless she was the focal

point of the occasion, and her method for achieving her wish was as simple as it was exhausting. She would join a group of children, and without listening to what they were saying, she would talk more rapidly, more loudly, than they did, until, at length, they were forced into silence by the sheer weight of her aggressiveness. She had never sung with a band, but she had heard of such things, and she meant to do it now. "Listen!" she shouted above the din. "Listen to me! Listen, I'm going to sing with the band!"

She moved from one part of the room to another, shouting: "Listen! Listen to me, I tell you!" Her voice was so intense, her manner so demanding, that one by one the children obeyed her. When she had the attention she wanted, she spoke to the band leader: "Play for me, while I sing!" She licked her lips, rolled her black eyes and swayed her hips from side to side with a snapping motion. "You colored boys know a song called 'Mamie's Melon' don't you?" she asked.

The leader looked at her quickly and then averted his eyes. "We can't play no song like dat," he said. "Miz Palmiller ain't gwiner leave folks play songs like dat." The trumpet player laughed with a sneezing sound, showed his stubs of teeth and added in explanation: "Dat's a Basin Street song, only we calls it 'Run, Little Mamie, Run,' 'stead of what all you said."

"Play it, nigger!" said Honey. "Play it like I say, and don't give me no back talk!" Then, seeing that the leader was weakening, she added: "What you so scared of? You play it soft, and I'll sing it soft." She added, more practically: "Nobody's going to care, unless it's Mr. Palmiller, and he ain't even here yet." She turned to Breck and continued: "Stand by the window and watch. If you see him coming in the gate, say so."

The Negroes still glanced doubtfully at one another, but Honey, as if knowing they would do what she said, lifted her skirt above her knees and snapped her neck back the way the women at the Tonk did, singing as softly as it was possible for her to sing: —

"Mr. Blue, put down yo' knife.
Little Mamie's melon still ain't ripe.
Mean man, mean man, go away now.
Won't be no cuttin' in my house tonight.
Go on away, you cuttin' man: you cuttin', mean man, you!"

The members of the band laughed softly, and one by one they began to pat their feet and nod their heads in time to the beat of the song. The trumpet player was the first to pick up his instrument. He was playing it before Honey had reached the third line of the song. He looked at her from above his puffed-out jaws, and with respect, for Honey was adding something of her own innate vulgarity to the song.

When she came to the chorus, the whole band was playing with a muted abandon. All kept time with their feet and heads, and those of them who did not need their mouths for their music, sighed and made low, moaning noises. Honey, feeling her triumph, swayed her hips, clapped her hands and sang: —

> "Run, Mamie, run! Run, Mamie, run!
> All clappin' for you, stompin' for you,
> Run, Mamie, run!"

At this point, the clarinetist got up from his chair and made a lost, wailing sound on his instrument. The trumpet player took it up, and the pianist said over his shoulder: "Don't ketch Mamie, Mr. Blue! Go on 'bout yo' business, now, and let po' Mamie be! We's all beggin' you now! All beggin', please sir, don't ketch Mamie!"

Honey continued, speaking this time: "Lord God! Lord God! Make Mr. Blue's legs stumble and fall!" She made a low, wailing sound, and instantly the piano player took it up and elaborated it into a new theme. He ended his improvisation with a crash of his hands against the keys and then lifted them, palms outward, in a gesture of despair. The other players cried out: "Mr. Blue caught her! Mr. Blue caught little Mamie!" There was a hush, and then the clarinet player picked up the original air, and Honey continued: —

> "Mr. Blue, you thumpin' man,
> Don't thump Mamie with yo' horny han'.
> Mean man, mean man, go away now.
> Go thump at the melons on other folks lan'.
> Go on away, you thumpin' man — you thumpin', mean man you!"

When Honey first stated her intention of singing with the band, Rance left the room he had recently entered, for nobody in the world annoyed him as much as Honey Boutwell did. He went to the steps and sat there out of sight, behind the banisters, waiting for his father. Almost at once the front door opened. He got up, straightened his Willie Keeler suit, and turned expectantly; but when he saw it was only Mr. Kenworthy, the photographer, he sat down again. Mr. Kenworthy stopped at the sound of the singing, concealed himself behind the curtains and peeped in at the children. Honey, seeing his eyes staring at her with such hot disapproval, moved in the direction of the curtains, singing hoarsely: —

> "Hide, Mamie, hide. Hide, Mamie, hide!
> All clappin' for you, stompin' for you,
> Hide, Mamie, hide!"

When she was so close she could hear his excited breathing, she licked her lips and closed her eyes in a gesture of meek surrender. Then, when he least expected such a thing, she put her hands behind her neck, agitated her hips and threw her stomach up so violently, that instinctively he stepped backward. Then, adjusting his tie nervously, he turned and walked away. His legs, from knee to thigh, seemed both too short and too massive. They bulged outward, above the frail base of his knees, in clumsy arcs, like the jointless, stuffed thighs of dwarfs. Since his marriage to the rich Millicent Reedy, he had had his clothes made by the best tailors, but he could not get a proper fit, and as he went toward the library, his trousers at the back puckered and pulled up in odd ways, at unexpected places.

"A child like that!" he thought indignantly. "A child not a day more than ten years old! If she was mine, I'd break her of her bad habits quick enough! . . . Either that, or I'd break her little neck!" But almost at once he had another and a gentler thought, and it was this: "My wife is a little girl that's too big, but this little girl is a woman that's too small."

Hardly had he entered the library before the music changed abruptly from Mamie and her pursuer, Mr. Blue, to a slow, unstimulating waltz; and Rance knew that his father was now coming up the walk. He got up with nervous haste and straightened his uniform. He had made a great effort to please his father, and he hoped that the flattering inference of the Willie Keeler costume would mean the beginning of a better understanding between them. He felt that the sensible thing for him to do, since he had determined to make these concessions, was to treat his father with the same relaxed affection which Clarry showed him, and when Hubert came into the hall and took off his hat and coat, he said to himself: "I'll run up to him, take his hand and dance up and down the way she does. That's what he likes. That's the best way to do it."

With his new determination fixed firmly in his mind, he ran down the stairs toward his father. Mr. Palmiller turned and looked questioningly at him, and against his will, in complete repudiation of the new resolves he had made, Rance found himself speaking in his old sneering, superior manner: "This is the surprise I had for you. I'm dressed like Willie Keeler — the one you like so much. Everything is correct." Then, to his astonishment, his lips drew down contemptuously of their own accord, and his eyebrows went up in amusement, managing thus to make it plain that his childishness was only a concession to Hubert's juvenile dreams, and not an indication of his own tastes.

Mr. Palmiller glanced at the child and said coldly: "That's very nice, I'm sure. I'm glad to know you managed to get something right, for once in your life." He looked in the hall mirror and smoothed back his thinning curls, adding: "Where is your mother? I want to speak to her alone." At that moment all the boy's old resentments returned, and he knew that he would rather die than say the things he had planned. He swaggered, laughed insolently and turned back toward the stairs. "She's hiding behind the japonica bush, so she can jump out at people when they come up the walk and say 'Boo!' . . . Isn't that where she told you this morning she'd be?"

Hubert closed his eyes, determining to keep his temper. He started to speak, changed his mind and went to the library where his wife had previously arranged to meet him. When he came out again, Rance had not moved from his post by the steps. He felt lost and depressed, knowing that he had failed in his purpose. He regretted his insolence, and he wanted desperately to repudiate it, to make one more effort at reconciliation before it was too late for both of them.

"Look, Father!" he said in a placating voice. "I got the uniform

because I thought you'd like it. Please look at it. I've been waiting
a long time for you. I wanted you to say it's all right."

Had Mr. Palmiller turned and touched his son's outstretched
hand at that moment, the boy would have cried; but he was offended
now, and he walked past as if the child did not exist. He went to
the room where the other children were, but he stopped when he
saw Clarry, all his anger vanishing. He seemed to forget everything at that moment, except the fact that she existed, and his face
lit up with wondering disbelief. She came to him happily, and he
got down on his knees and put his arms about her.

Of late, Hubert had found it necessary to wear glasses. He put
them on now, closing the metal case with the abrupt, snapping
sound of hungry jaws. Clarry stood back, so that he could see her
better, and he said: "Why, you look perfectly beautiful, my darling!
How did you manage to think of such a wonderful costume?"
Rance came up at this moment, his heavy knees, in their uniform,
rubbing together and making a scratching, intimate sound. He
walked slowly around his sister, looked humorously at the other
children, and laughed his loud, derisive laugh. Mr. Palmiller could
no longer ignore his son's conduct. "Rance!" he said angrily. "If
you can't behave like a gentleman, I'm going to send you upstairs and have Jesse put you to bed!" Rance stopped laughing at
once. He shrugged his shoulders with exaggerated disdain and
walked to the window, playing absently with the curtain tassels.

When nobody was looking, he turned hurriedly and went upstairs. In his room, he took off his uniform and lay on his bed, but
he was restless, and he got up almost at once and went into the
hall, not quite knowing what he intended doing next. Then a new
idea came to him: He would go to the party again — not as Willie
Keeler, this time, but as his own sister. He went at once to her
room and opened her wardrobe. Her lacy party dress was hanging
there, wrapped in tissue paper. He examined it critically, put it
on and buttoned it before the long mirror. The effect pleased him,
but he felt it was incomplete, and a moment later he put on a
pair of her white stockings and shoes. He walked up and down
in front of the mirror, rehearsing his sister's gestures and mannerisms until he felt he had them down perfectly; but all at once he
shook his head and sat on a footstool to think, for no impersonation

of Clarry, he felt, would be adequate without her long, cottony hair. Then he got up excitedly, knowing what it was he wanted.

In his parents' room, in the big closet, were stored the holiday decorations, so lately in use. Around the base of the Christmas tree that year, there had been wrapped a decorative fringe of silver paper, a fringe cut so finely that it resembled silken thread. He found what he wanted at once, and pinned the long fringe securely to Clarry's white, rabbit-fur hat. The result amused him enormously, and he came down the stairs again well pleased with his cleverness. At first the children merely looked at him with their mouths open, but when they understood his intention, they doubled up with laughter at the joke.

The boy walked up and down and said: "Do you like my pretty dress, Papa? Do you really?" For the first time in his life, his contemporaries approved of what he did. It brought him down to their own level of humor, and it made him more understandable to them.

Rance was not enjoying himself, although everyone else seemed to be. There was a sick, angry feeling inside him, but he tried to ignore it. He lifted his finger to his lips, simpered, whirled his skirts, and said in a piping voice which he fancied resembled his sister's: "Don't come too near me! You'll get me all dirty!" He swirled again, the paper hair floating outward. "And don't you touch my pretty hair, no matter what you do!" he said; "because I'll tell my Papa on you, and he'll be mad."

Then he looked out of the corners of his eyes, to see how his sister was taking this burlesque. To his astonishment, she seemed to have no resentment at all. She was standing beside Harry Piggott and Breck Boutwell, and all of them were laughing, as if the thing he was doing was of priceless wit. "I don't talk that way!" said Clarry good-naturedly, when she was able to control her laughter. "I don't talk that way at all, and you know I don't, Rance!"

Suddenly Rance saw the laughter disappear from the faces of his audience. They turned away and began talking among themselves. For a moment the boy wondered what had happened, and without moving his body, he glanced over his shoulder. Mr. Palmiller was standing in the door watching with a strange, intent expression on his handsome face. "Go upstairs!" he said furiously to his son.

"Go upstairs at once!" Clarry came to him and took his hand. "Don't punish him, Papa!" she said. "He wasn't doing anything! We were just having a little fun!" But Mr. Palmiller was too angry this time to be influenced by his daughter. He pulled his hand back and said: "Go upstairs! Go into my study at once!"

When they were alone in the study, Hubert shut the door and looked searchingly at his son. Suddenly he lost control of himself, as if his patience had reached its end at last, and he struck the boy across his sneering, superior face. Rance neither cried out nor drew back. He stared back at his father more contemptuously than ever and said: "That's what people always do, when they're too stupid to do anything else, isn't it?"

Mr. Palmiller closed his eyes and shook his head from side to side, as if the situation had got beyond his power to control it. It was the first time he had struck the child because of his own anger, and he felt a little ashamed of himself. At that moment he almost doubted the merits of his individual system for handling children. If you were firm with children, he had always said, and showed them at once that you were their master, not because of your superior physical strength, but because of your greater maturity, greater mentality and experience, the child would automatically become a happy, contented little citizen. . . . Only it had not worked out that way with his son, and he wondered how he had gone astray.

He spoke after a moment: "I've tried to bring you up to be a healthy, happy boy, with a wholesome boy's desires and instincts. It seems that I've failed. Perhaps the fault is mine. Perhaps I'm being punished by Nature for something I've done, some error I've committed."

"Don't be absurd, too, Father," said the boy.

"How would you like it if people ridiculed you?" asked Mr. Palmiller suddenly. "It wouldn't be so funny, would it, if the shoe was on the other foot?" He looked thoughtfully at the wall with narrowed eyes, as if an appropriate punishment for the boy's conduct had just occurred to him.

Rance started to speak, to remind his father that everyone, and particularly Hubert himself, had ridiculed him from the time he could remember, but instead he said coldly: "Haven't you got

even ordinary sense, Father?" He sighed, shook his head in astonishment and sat down.

At that instant Mr. Palmiller decided definitely to go through
with the unusual punishment he had in mind for his son. He got up
and said: "I'm going to teach you a lesson you'll never forget as
long as you live! I'm going to take you downtown dressed the
way you are now and let everybody have a look at you. Maybe
that'll knock some of the conceit out of you! Maybe that'll teach
you not to ridicule others!"

Had the boy cried, or even begged his forgiveness, Mr. Palmiller
would have been content to abandon his plan, but Rance said
superciliously: "Do you really imagine it makes any difference to
me one way or the other what people think about me, Father?"
Hubert buttoned his coat and pulled his cuffs down. "We'll see
about that!" he said angrily. "We'll see, young man! . . . And
remember you brought this on yourself, with your own conceit!"

Since it was a Saturday afternoon, Court House Square was
more crowded than usual with shoppers. Mr. Palmiller stopped in
front of his own bank, tied his horse to the iron ring there, and
ordered Rance onto the sidewalk beside him. A crowd gathered
about them, and Hubert explained conscientiously what the boy
had done, and why it was necessary to punish him in this particular way.

Joe Tyler, manager of McAndrew's Shoe Store, was the first to
speak. "You make a right sweet-looking little girl, Rance," he said
waggishly. Then he doubled up with mirth and pointed his forefinger at the ridiculous little boy. When he could control himself
once more, he continued gaspingly, weak from laughter: "You
know, it wouldn't surprise me any if you turned out to be even
prettier than your sister Clarry!" Everybody laughed again and
wiped the tears from their eyes, but Rance lifted his head and said
scornfully: "Did it ever occur to you yokels that you look even
sillier to me than I do to you?"

Everybody laughed more than ever at that, and Rance, for their
greater amusement, took a few exaggerated, mincing steps across
the sidewalk. He raised his arms and whirled on his toes so rapidly
that his long silver-paper hair floated out stiffly behind him. He had
recovered his self-assurance now, his habitual, contemptuous poise,

and when he had finished his clownlike antics, he stood again beside his father at the edge of the sidewalk and stared back at his audience with an amusement as great as their own. He started to speak again, but Hubert jerked at his arm, and they moved away together. Mr. Palmiller had confidently expected his son to draw back long before they reached the Square, and beg to be taken home again, but to his amazement Rance seemed to be enjoying the experience. He swaggered insolently as they walked along, replying cuttingly to everything said to him, speaking sometimes in English, which the people understood, and sometimes in French, which they did not.

They passed the Empire Drug Company a little later, and George McMasters, the prescription clerk, came outside to enjoy the fun. His skin was the dingy tan of a cornstalk which had stood alone all winter in a field. He was so thin, lifeless, and dried out that when a wind blew against him, you were astonished that he did not lean forward stiffly and rustle. He cleared his throat and spoke in his strained, whispering voice: "Maybe you can tell me something I always wanted to know, Sonny: How does it feel to be a little girl?"

Rance stopped and narrowed his eyes, as if deeply pondering the question. A moment later he said with false humility: "I'll tell you, if you'll answer a question for me, too. It's very simple for a chemist to answer, and I know you can tell me right away: What is the basic difference between a univalent and a bivalent element?"

Mr. Palmiller pulled quickly at his son's arm, but the boy would not move this time. One of the crowd standing in front of the drugstore said: "Looks like he done got you that time, George! Looks like he done got you sure!"

Rance spoke again in the silence, this time in French: "Stop scratching your head, and close your mouth, you ignorant fool, because you haven't any idea what I'm talking about. I always knew you were a fool, and now everybody else knows it too." He shrugged his shoulders and moved away with his father, adding: "I'm glad this is happening to me, because when I'm a famous man, known the world over, my biographers will write this scene with much pleasure. Perhaps it will be referred to forever as the perfect example of the persecution of genius by the stupid."

Mr. Palmiller, whose French was not nearly so fluent as his son's, had not understood all Rance had said, but he had understood enough. There was a strange, baffled expression on his face as they walked along together, and his son seemed more incomprehensible to him at that instant than ever before. He did not know how it had happened, but he realized that Rance had managed somehow to change this experience, intended as a humiliating object lesson, into an amusing, personal triumph. He frowned and closed his eyes, knowing, then, that it was not Rance but himself who was being made ridiculous.

Rowley's poolroom was on the far side of the Square, and Wesley Boutwell sat on the bench outside talking with some of his friends. His back was to the street, and although he had heard the progressive laughter behind him, he had paid little attention to it, being entangled at the moment in an involved account of how Commodore Dewey and himself had defeated Admiral Montojo, and destroyed the Spanish fleet, at Manila Bay. He had been out of the army for some months, but he still wore his uniform. He had been drinking a little, and as he talked, he waved his left arm, still powerful despite its missing hand, for emphasis; but so vigorously, with such involved precision, that it almost seemed as if the mutilated bone repeated, in a more primitive alphabet, the things his lips were saying. Then his sleeve fell away from his forearm and showed his severed wrist. The wound had healed long ago and had puckered into a bulging knob of bone and flesh, with a small, dusky crater in its center, like a scar within a greater scar, and resembling in its irregularity of line the last, thrifty biscuit which housewives hurriedly press together and bake from the remnants of their leftover dough.

When Mr. Palmiller and Rance turned the corner and approached, Wesley got up in astonishment and stood beside the bench. His jaws dropped at the strange sight, and instinctively he tilted his head to one side and looked upward, as if he were going to laugh his high, thin laugh; but before any sound of mirth came from his lips, he felt a sense of depression so profound and so sudden that he could hardly catch his breath. Perhaps what he saw released something lost and deep in his own mind, perhaps the drinks he had had battered down his self-consciousness, for instead of laughing at the grotesque sight, as others had, and as he had meant to do, he turned, pressed his face against the post which supported the bench, and wept with deep, tearing pity. He stood blocking the path when Hubert and his son came abreast of him and said pleadingly: "Don't shame the afflicted little boy no more! Please don't do that!"

Mr. Palmiller stopped and looked at Wesley coldly, his eyes resentful and drawn upward. "I think I know what's best for my own son," he said in his rapid, nasal voice. He shoved at the man's enormous chest, but Wesley shook his head mildly and would not move. "I ain't saying you don't," he said. "I wouldn't try to argue nothing like that with you, Mr. Palmiller. . . . I'm just asking you to take the poor little boy home now, and not to shame him no more."

He patted Rance's shoulder with his remaining hand and smiled reassuringly at him, as if to say: "Don't be afraid, because I won't let folks hurt you no more. You just sit back and leave everything to me." Rance looked with curiosity into the man's brown, compassionate eyes, as liquid, and as vacant of thought, as the weeping eyes of a spaniel. Their melting gaze disturbed him, and he tried to laugh his loud, protective laugh, but something had gone wrong with his old systems, and he could not. He pulled away and stood beside his father, anxiously opening and shutting his hands.

Wesley pushed back his hat from his forehead and said: "Some folks can stand one thing, some another. . . . But me, I can't stand to see children treated sorry. When I was a boy myself, they beat on me with everything they could lay their hands on, and I didn't even know what for, half the time. That's how I know so good how Rance feels right now; that's the reason — "

Mr. Palmiller interrupted him. "We're not interested in your life history," he said. "I'm telling you for the last time to get out of the way, and mind your own business. If you don't, I'm going to have you locked up on a charge of public drunkenness."

Wesley sighed and looked helplessly at the crowd, knowing that Mr. Palmiller could easily do what he threatened. He sat on the bench again, as if defeated, but he held the child's unwilling hand in his own, and drew him forward a little. "I wouldn't try to interfere this way," he said in a more placating voice, "if he was an ordinary boy, able to take care of himself like I was; but everybody knows this poor little fellow ain't right in the head. He's not bright, like other children, Mr. Palmiller! He needs to have somebody look out for him!"

Rance, hearing these things, trembled a little. Something strange was happening inside him, something which threatened the foundations of his security. He glanced pleadingly at Wesley, as if begging him not to go on, but Wesley drew the boy closer to him, and put his mutilated arm about his waist. "To show you what I mean," he continued, "I was listening to the little fellow trying to talk, when you two turned the corner a minute ago and came up, and the first thing I thought was this: 'Why, the poor afflicted boy! As big as that, and can't even talk plain enough for folks to figure out what he's saying!' "

There was a long, waiting silence. In it, it seemed to the child that the last shred of his old protection was taken from him. If the stupid hated him because they recognized his superiority to themselves, that was one thing. It was a situation he was familiar with, and one that he could handle well. . . . But if the stupid pitied him because he was not as slow-witted as they were, then he was lost indeed, and there was no security left him anywhere.

In a sudden, sickly panic, he moved from his place beside his father, a look of horror on his face. He shook his head slowly from side to side, as if to repudiate a shocking and an inescapable truth. A moment later he turned and ran down the street, while Hubert stood on the pavement in front of the poolroom and called: "Rance! Rance! Stop this minute. . . . Rance, come back here!"

Once he looked back over his shoulder, and in doing so, he lost his balance, tripped, and fell on his face, while the white fur hat with its ridiculous fringe of paper hair came loose and fell to the sidewalk. At once he got up and ran again, as if pursued by forces of which he was, as yet, only partially aware. At that instant he wanted only the safety of his own room, and when he reached it, he lay on his bed, rigid and staring upward at the ceiling. Downstairs, the magician was doing his act, and dimly, as if from another existence, he could hear the children laughing and applauding in delight. He tried to remember Clarry's party, to bring its details into his mind, but he only frowned and shook his head, finding it difficult to recall such distant things from such a remote past.

Cindy came to his room when she heard what had happened. She undressed him in silence and sat beside him, holding his hand and singing to him as she used to do when he was small. When her husband came into the room, she stood up and stared at him silently. He had never seen her so angry before, and he lost some of his bland self-assurance before her silent wrath. She asked no explanation, but he said after a moment: "It was necessary to teach him a lesson! It was a lesson he won't forget very soon, either!" Her lips moved in speechless fury, and he went on: "Do you think I got any pleasure out of the experience? Do you think I liked confessing to people that I'd failed in my efforts to make my son a happy, wholesome little citizen?"

He bent above the child, and Rance looked at him stupidly. "Have you learned your lesson?" he asked. "Are you ready to apologize to your sister?" Rance answered in a nervous, anguished voice: "Yes, sir!" he said. "Yes, sir! Yes, sir!" Then he turned on his side and looked again at the wall. Mr. Palmiller nodded cheerfully: "That was a fine, manly thing to do!" He picked up his son's limp hand and shook its boneless length. He said: "I believe we understand each other now!"

That night Cindy had her things moved into another room. When her husband asked the reason for her dramatic conduct, she said furiously: "I'll never forgive you for what you've done to your own child! Never as long as I live! And if you ever come near me again, I'll cheerfully kill you!" Mr. Palmiller said: "You sound like something out of a very bad play, my dear!" He paused at the door and added: "I've done the boy a great service. He'll thank me for it one of these days."

From that time onward Rance was so changed that no part of his old personality seemed to have survived. In school he was now abjectly quiet until a teacher asked him a question; then he would lower his eyes, shake his head foolishly and mumble something which could not be understood. In the past he had been a strong, aggressive child — a boy both able and eager to defend himself against the attacks of others. From the beginning, he had established the certainty in the minds of other children that he would take no insult from them, would permit no interference with his person. Even the older boys had been somewhat afraid of him, and had left him alone; but now, seeing the change in him, his schoolmates had their opportunity at last to satisfy their old, accumulated resentments. They twisted his passive arms in their sockets until he cried out in pain; in class, they kicked his shins beneath his desk so consistently that he was forced to sit with his legs folded under him; they shoved him about at recess and tripped him in corridors when no adult was watching. He seemed not to resent these things, and he complained neither to his parents nor his teachers.

When school was over, he would remain alone in the deserted room until he thought his enemies had tired of waiting for him, and had gone about their own affairs; then, breathlessly, he would run home as fast as he could; and when he got there, he would sit alone in his room, staring, as if stunned, out of his window.

There was no longer any conflict between Mr. Palmiller and his son, for Rance now obeyed him with a tense, depressed eagerness which was almost too painful to witness. Hubert considered the change a favorable prognosis of his son's future happiness. "Rance is learning some sense at last," he said cheerfully. "He's having the conceit knocked out of him by stern experience. Right now, he's mastering one of Nature's hardest and most valuable lessons!"

But perhaps I concern myself too much with this gifted, unhappy little boy, who could never determine what his individual relationship was to the world about him, for when he was twelve years old, he got out of bed one night, put on his best suit and drowned himself in Sweethearts' Looking-Glass. The water was no more than four feet deep at its center, and Rance did not go very far into the pond. He stopped at the inner rim of the reeds, and there he lay flat upon his foreshortened shadow, clutching the reeds in his hands and pressed his face into the mud, as if the problem of life was too great for him to solve, and he wanted, now, to go back to the earth from whence he came.

The Goodwife of Death, returning from a call in the Negro quarters, was faced with another and a more unexpected task as she walked the old lovers' path on her way home. In the clear, early light of morning, she saw the dead boy lying quietly among the reeds, the rays of the lifting sun gilding his hair and tinting pink the water in which he lay. Dew had fallen that morning, and The Goodwife, as she moved along, held her draperies above her clumsy, vocational shoes, prim and balanced, and so high that they cleared evenly the dripping dampnes of the grass. She stood in perplexity when she saw the child, moved closer to the pond and peered through the thin, sparse reeds, while small mists, as delicate as smoke, lifted from the surface of the water, rolled forward and vanished under the mounting power of the sun. "Little boy!" she said reprovingly. "Little boy, whoever you are! You're getting your clothes wet!"

She made no effort to go to him, for her mission was not to rescue the living, but to bury the dead. There was no sign of life, as yet, in the still sleeping town, and she stood quietly for a time, deciding what to do. Then she turned abruptly and moved toward the Boutwell house for help. When she reached the gate, she called out in her low, beautifully modulated voice: "There's a child drowned in the pond. You must help me. You must really help me, now." Before she had explained her visit, the entire Boutwell family was awake. Half-dressed, they followed the old woman around the pond until she stopped and showed them the place where the boy was lying.

Ira Graley ran as quickly as he could through the splashing water. He lost his footing on the bottom, fell, and got up again, calling out at the same moment: "Wait! Wait a minute! I'm coming now!" as if Rance could hear him, or hearing him, would care. A little later he lifted the boy in his arms and walked ashore with him, stumbling under his weight; then, seeing that the child had been dead for a long time, he carried him to the Boutwell house and put him on the cot which Fodie had prepared. The boy's drenched clothing adhered to his body, and water ran down and made a pool beneath him. His face was blackened with mud, and mud was caked in his ears and nose, but his light, tan-colored eyes were wide open, glassy and staring.

The Goodwife, being on familiar ground now, washed his face and hands and straightened his clothing, knowing that his parents would soon be there. When they came, the crowd stood back, and Cindy looked into the drowned, white face of her son. All at once she dropped to her knees beside him and pressed her clenched knuckles against her quivering mouth. "Thank God!" she said. "Thank God for this great mercy!" Only The Goodwife knew what she meant, and she did not explain, but in death, the cringing, sickly look had gone from the boy's face forever. His lips curled downward now with their old insolence, and his eyes stared back at the world once more with amused, haughty contempt.

The Goodwife closed the child's lids with her smooth, practised thumbs, and Cindy, knowing that she understood, spoke directly to her: "God knows it was little enough!" she said in anguish. "It was little enough, but it was all he ever had!" Then she cried harshly and without restraint, not alone for her son, but for the lost and bitter people everywhere — people she would never know, never understand. Wesley and his wife lifted her from the floor and laid her on the bed they had so recently slept in. Ada, not knowing what else to do, sat beside her, held her hand and said, with no conviction in her voice at all: "Don't take it so hard, Mrs. Palmiller. Try not to take it so hard."

The funeral was private and afterwards Hubert had a slab put over the grave with these words: —

CLARENCE LANKESTER PALMILLER
BORN APRIL 15TH 1892
DIED MAY 8TH 1904

Then, since truth had always been a passion with him, and he wanted nobody misled, he had the stonecutter add the words: *"By His Own Hand."* Afterwards, when people expressed their sympathy, tears came to his eyes and he turned away to hide his emotion. "It's probably better this way for the boy," he would often say. "It's a sad thought indeed, but the child was plainly one of those unsuccessful experiments which Nature sometimes makes."

But if Hubert bore the death of his son with such fortitude, the illness of his daughter, some years later, left him weak and terrified. On that particular night in September of 1916, when Dover reached the Palmiller State Bank, he knocked loudly, and a watchman came to see what he wanted. The watchman said: "Mr. Palmiller's done gone home. He left two hours ago." His own words seemed to exasperate him, and he added angrily: "They pay me to watch a bank, not to answer the fool questions boys ask! Ask me something about watching a bank and I'll tell you."

Dover went to the horse trough at the curb and washed his face and hands. There was nothing left for him to do except call on Mrs. Kenworthy, but he sat down first on the curb to rest a moment. Then, seeing that he was not observed, he went back to the trough, sat on its side and rested his feet against the slippery bottom. The thick, green mold felt cool and delightful against his skin. He spread his primitive toes even wider and let his feet sink voluptuously down until he felt, at last, the solid unyielding wood against his flesh.

He was the twelfth and last of the Boutwell children. He had had a sister two years older than himself named Santiago. She had been born in 1900, precisely nine months to the night after his father came back to his family, and her existence had been proof of Ada's almost instantaneous forgiveness of her husband for having so dramatically preferred the pleasures of war to the pleasures of marriage. But she had died in childhood, and Dover hardly remembered her any more.

Being the baby, he had always been his father's favorite among the children, and he acknowledged this fact with a deep, unchanging devotion of his own. At that moment he had a clear picture of Wesley lying in bed at home, hurt and abandoned, possibly breathing his last. He had a sudden feeling of anger against Dr. Snowfield for his incomprehensible conduct, and as he moved away from the trough, he raised his eyes and looked across the square. There, above the tops of the small trees, he saw a light burning steadily in the doctor's office. He frowned and said sullenly: "All right! I'll get you the three dollars! Don't worry, I'll get you your money!" Then he straightened his clothes and hurried away across town, in the direction of the Kenworthy residence.

Chapter 5

PEOPLE were surprised when an obscure photographer, a little nobody as unprepossessing as Paul Kenworthy, married the town's heiress and blue blood, Miss Millicent Wentworth Reedy. He was twenty years older than his bride, and his courtship had been methodical, persistent and uninspired. In the end Millicent accepted him, to the chagrin of her family and the astonishment of her friends; but even the town's expression of dismay carried with it both an explanation of the inappropriate union, and a recapitulation of Millicent's attractiveness. Perhaps old Mrs. Wentworth explained everything when she said defensively in Shepherd's Department Store a few days after the engagement had been announced: "I don't see why my niece had to be so hasty. After all, she's only twenty-one, and I'm sure she would have had other admirers, possibly, if she'd waited!"

Mr. Kenworthy at the time of his marriage was becoming stout, and his stomach pushed forward with the minor, rounded arrogance of small men. His curves were all in front, for his buttocks were depressed and frostbitten, as if his belly had taken all the nourishment from them, and they hung inside his deflated trousers like two large, wrinkled V's. He was an absurd man, even in his own eyes. Comedy was what his townsmen expected from him, and he had not betrayed them when he married Millicent Reedy. She had never been a success socially, despite her advantages, but she tenaciously attended all the teas, dinner parties and dances; and she had made an elaborate bow to society when she was eighteen, at a huge ball in New Orleans — a ball at which every man present had danced with her precisely once.

She was always expensively, elaborately dressed, and her costumes accorded with the two basic illusions of the stout woman: One of them was that velvet was the weavers' blessing to the fat; the other was that if shoulders were bulky enough, with no indication of a bone structure beneath, they were beautiful. Her soft, babylike skin was pink and yielding. You could feel its quality beneath the plating of whalebone, rubber and steel which compressed her waist and thighs, and forced her mauled belly up so cruelly that even as a debutante she had had the topheavy, tottering look of an old contralto.

Seeing her flesh so braced, so corseted, so artfully restrained, you wondered what she was like in the nude, as she stood beside her bed in the privacy of her own room, at the moment she lifted her arms and slipped her nightgown over her shoulders. St. Joseph once discussed this precise point with Minnie McInnis McMinn. "With all those supports taken away," he had said, "and her flesh sliding back where it belongs once more, I'm sure she must look like a big saucerful of melting peach ice cream." Then he had sighed regretfully and added: "It's a sight I'd dearly love to see, Minnie!"

St. Joseph did not know it at the time, but he was later to have an opportunity, at least in part, of witnessing what he desired. It was the summer following Milly's honeymoon, and she and her husband had been invited to a bathing party at James' Lake. Milly, without her corsets and her rubber garments, but dressed modestly enough in a brown bathing suit whose skirt came far below her knees, was the first to sidle out of the women's dressing room and go toward the water. Others might speculate about her appearance, but she knew precisely how she looked, and that was why she had determined to be in the lake before the remainder of the party came out of the old boathouse.

On her way to the beach, she spoke to her husband through the door of the men's dressing room, telling him he would find her in the water when he came out. She hurried away, glad that her ruse had worked so successfully, but before she had gone far, she broke one of her garters and had to go back to mend it. This was a thing her husband did not know, and at a moment when she was still busy with her needle and thread, he came out of the boathouse and went toward the lake to look for her.

He had left his glasses with his clothes, and as he picked his

way gingerly down the path, he peered with a shortsighted, hostile
look at the ground, keeping on the alert for pebbles which might
bruise his blue-veined, tender feet — feet which still bore on their
dead-white, doughlike surfaces the ridged and fluted designs of the
socks he had so recently taken off. When he reached the edge of
the water, he squinted and looked about for his wife, but she was
nowhere in sight. He thought this somewhat odd, and he called
to her twice in a low, earnest voice, but there was no answer.
Suddenly he became panicky and began to call: "Milly! Milly!
Where are you? Why don't you answer me?"

He thrust his neck forward as far as it would go and peered
anxiously across the lake. It seemed to him at that moment as if
his heart had stopped beating, for there, in the middle of the water,
he saw what he thought was the rounded behind of his wife bob-
bing seductively up and down. Robert Porterfield and Johnnie
Worthington came out of the boathouse together, and when Mr.
Kenworthy saw them, he began to wring his hands and make a
tragic, moaning noise. Then he ran a little way into the water
and returned, like a terrier who wants to fetch something, but
knows the task is beyond him.

The men stopped in surprise and then hurried to him, asking
what the matter was. "It's Milly!" he said in an anguished voice.
"She's drowned sure!" He pointed to the brown, circular object
and added: "She got beyond her depth and the current took her
out! She's drowned sure! Milly's drowned, and I know it!"

But long before he had reached this point, Robert Porterfield
and his companion were swimming toward the drifting object.
Hearing the excitement, the other guests hurried at once to the
beach, and Mr. Kenworthy told his story again, while he peered
forward and watched the rescue. The last person to arrive on the
scene was Millicent herself. Her arrival at that particular moment
was most unfortunate, for just then the men returned to the
beach, towing the object which Mr. Kenworthy had identified so
unequivocally as his bride. It proved to be one of those enormous,
rounded baskets which cotton pickers used in the fields, and beneath it, some worker had tacked a trailing burlap sack for the
protection of his neck and shoulders after he had balanced the
basket on his head.

Mr. Kenworthy, when he saw the basket and its dangling length of brown burlap, laughed with nervous relief and said apologetically to the men who had made the rescue: "I thought it was Milly. I really did. I wasn't trying to play a joke on you!"

Johnnie Worthington, whose sight was perfect, had seen Millicent trying to conceal herself at the back of the crowd. He looked warningly at Paul and made a silencing sound with his lips, but Mr. Kenworthy, thinking his motives were being doubted, began to explain all over how easy it was for him to have made the mistake he had. "You may not know it," he said confidentially to the crowd, "but to nearsighted people like me, everything looks bigger than it is, when you got your glasses off; and so from where I was standing, that basket looked like Milly."

St. Joseph put his finger to his lips, shook his head violently and said: "Come on! Who wants to help me build an oven for the steaks?"

But Paul was not to be silenced so easily. He lifted the basket and set it on the wharf which ran a short distance into the water. Then conscientiously he draped the burlap over the curved surface of the basket and added: "It does look like Milly! I don't care what you people think, it looks just like Milly does when she leans over to tie her shoes!"

He was aware, at that moment, that his wife stood in front of him, perfectly safe, perfectly dry. "You're impossible!" she said. "You are a completely impossible little man!" She made a sound which was somewhere between a groan and a sniffle, turned and hurried back to the boathouse. Paul followed her and stood outside the door, listening to her sobs. "Milly! Milly!" he said. "I didn't mean anything, dear! . . . I was just worried about you, that's all!" At his words, Millicent cried all the louder and said: "Go away! Go away and leave me alone!"

Later on Mrs. McMinn came to the door and took charge of the situation. "Why don't you join the others, Paul?" she asked. "I'll straighten your wife out!" She went into the dressing room and stood over the damp, heaving woman. "Stop it, Milly!" she said firmly. "Stop it at once! You're behaving like a baby!"

She opened the handbags of some of the women she knew, to see if anybody had remembered to bring smelling salts, but before she had gone very far, she paused and looked at her patient with a new interest, remembering a remark which Mattie Tatum had once made to her. She was a dressmaker of exceptional ability, and she had been commissioned by the Reedy family to design a part of their daughter's equipment for her debutante year. Minnie dropped in one afternoon while Miss Tatum was still working on her assignment, and Mattie had put down her crayons, clutched her head in despair and said: "There's no use trying any more! There's only one thing that will look right on her, and that's a christening robe!"

At last Mrs. McMinn understood what Mattie Tatum had really meant, for there was something unchangingly infantile about Milly's soft, unboned features: her tender, button-shaped nose, her fine-spun, dainty hair which curled in soft tendrils at the back of her neck. Even her fine downy skin was the too-delicate, the too-pink skin of the well-cared-for baby, and as she found the smelling salts and bent above the woman, saying: "Here, Milly! For heaven's sake smell this!" it seemed to her that the infantile line of Milly's body itself had changed in no important particular since she had lain in her crib. Others developed painfully into their maturity, but Milly, it appeared, had achieved the same result through simple expansion.

Millicent said: "I've never been so insulted by anybody in my whole life! Who does he think he is to say such things? To hurt my feelings in public? . . . A ridiculous little man like him, too!"

Later, Mr. Kenworthy took his wife home. They were both completely silent during the drive back to town, and the mistake at the lake was the beginning of a quarrel which was never to be settled between them. At first Millicent was mildly perturbed at the rupture. She tried for a time to salvage what remained of her marriage, and then she gave up the effort as too fatiguing. At last she admitted to herself that the new arrangement was entirely satisfactory to her, and that she had always found her husband's warm, incessant advances repugnant, even on their honeymoon; for no matter how unromantic his exterior might be, inside, he was a small volcano of passion.

And so Millicent sat on her front porch, read love stories about handsome, ideally mated couples, ate three large, rich meals a day, and rocked ten years of marriage into nothingness. It was her greatest regret that she remained childless. She thought often of this, and sometimes she cried when she was alone and hidden behind the coral vine, anticipating the loneliness of old age. The bawdier element of Reedyville, who frequented the back room at Moore's Livery Stable, or sat on the bench in front of Rowley's Pool Parlors, was also interested in the fact that the Kenworthy-Reedy union had produced no heir, but professed no surprise at all, even though it did not know that the couple had reached the point where they now occupied separate rooms. They offered one another many ingenious explanations, but even the mildest of their theories can have no place in a book which hopes to have a general circulation.

The winter of 1899 had been a dull one for Milly, and she was excited when Cindy invited her to the New Century Party, to help with the refreshments. In her gratitude, she suggested that her husband come in with his camera and take a few photographs for souvenirs. Paul did not look forward to the party with pleasure, but since his wife had committed him, he went. Except for the fact that he heard Honey Boutwell singing one of her songs, he would have taken his pictures, paid his respects to Cindy, and returned as quickly as possible to his studios.

But now he could get neither Honey's face nor her song out of his mind, and as he sat in the library and listened to the chatter there, he was thinking: "The little devil is depraved! I'll bet there's nothing she don't know about already! . . . She could tell me things I never even heard of!" The rising swell of talk disturbed his thoughts and he went to the window, staring fixedly at the Palmillers' double protection of iron fence and high hedge, wondering if she could be considered pretty.

At ten, there was little in Honey's face to predict the voluptuous beauty for which she was to become famous later on. She was thin and sallow in those days. Her mouth was large and flexible, and her upper lip rather too short, so that her primitive nostrils cast a perpetual shadow on her lips and gave her a spurious quality of complexity which she did not, in reality, possess.

He decided after a time that she was not at all pretty — in the way that Clarry Palmiller, for instance, was pretty — but pretty or not, he could not banish her from his mind, and as he stood there at the window, he had a sense of anger at himself. "What am I thinking about?" he kept asking himself. "What's happened to me all of a sudden?" Then he realized that he did not even know the child's name. He knew at once that he must know, and he moved toward Mrs. McMinn, sat on the edge of her chair and said: "Who is the little girl in the Red Cross uniform? She was singing a song when I came through the hall, and you know, she's got a real pretty little voice."

To himself his words carried no conviction at all, but Minnie said gaily: "That was Honey Boutwell, and I hope for the sake of your reputation you didn't listen to what she was singing. I don't know what it was, but I know it wasn't fit for your respectable ears." To his surprise, he found that Minnie's words annoyed him, and he bowed and moved away. Suddenly he wheeled about, went to his wife and kissed the astonished woman squarely on her lips, for already, in the depths of his mind, he was formulating his plans for the child's capture. Now that Minnie had told him her name, he remembered much about the Boutwells. In a way, they were retainers of his, for they not only lived in one of the houses his wife owned, but the mother did cleaning and sewing for them as well.

On Monday, while developing the photographs he had taken at the party, he remembered another fact about the Boutwells, and it was this: Millicent had once told him that Mrs. Boutwell sometimes brought her daughter to help her work, and today, he thought, was the day Mrs. Boutwell came. He was not sure on this latter point, but he was so anxious to see Honey again that he went home in the middle of the afternoon on the chance that she might be there. To his disappointment, Mrs. Boutwell's helper was not Honey, but Fodie. He was so taken aback that he sidled out of the room without speaking, wiping his damp forehead with his handkerchief. On the whole, he was glad the child was not Honey, for the role of a mother's capable assistant would have taken away from her some of the sensual, abandoned quality which he found so shocking and so irresistible in one so young.

His wife spoke to him at the moment he entered his bedroom, asking if he was sick. "No!" he said. "No, I'm not sick, thank you!" He opened his bureau drawer and added over his shoulder: "Can't I even come home for a clean handkerchief without having to go through a big dramatic scene with you?"

She glanced suspiciously at his flushed face and followed him down the long hall. A decade of marriage had broadened her physically, at least. Fat had accumulated in such corrugated ridges on her back and shoulders that in profile she seemed a little humpbacked. She breathed noisily as she lumbered down the hall, trying to keep abreast of her husband, and fat from her ankles dripped downward over her insteps and almost hid the straps of her slippers. When Paul opened the front door and stood on the porch, she spoke again: "Are you sure you're feeling all right? You look to me like you had a fever." Paul shook his head and hurried to the gate, but to himself he said bitterly: "I've got an *inward* fever, if you must know! I've always had an inward fever that you didn't understand!" He looked back at her from the gate, wondering if she had guessed his intentions; but at once he thought reassuringly: "What are my intentions? What do I expect to be the end of all this?" Then he sighed and shook his head, for he did not himself know.

His mind continued to work in this direction as he went back to his studio. Certainly he was not interested in the child in a crude, sexual sense. Of this he was positive, for it was unthinkable that a man of his character and standing would be physically attracted to a little girl. This certainty that his feelings were, of necessity, only the noblest, the most dispassionate, reassured him, and he entered his studio with some of his depressed, nervous anxiety taken away. He sat down and took stock of himself, reasonably examining both the reward and the punishment which would logically come from his unhappy passion, if he left it uncontrolled. Finally he determined not to think of Honey again, and in the weeks that followed, he was often successful in his resolve for hours at a time.

He was less successful with his thoughts at night, and in that horrid interval before sleep comes, when the reality of the world becomes confused under its own complexity and gives up its small assurance, her face would appear before him in the darkness, gaunt, animal-like, and inviting; and her lips at such times whispered such depravities to him, that he would turn on his light and sit up in bed, staring with shocked unbelief at the vacant air where she had so recently been. He would go to sleep at last from exhaustion, and then, with the barrier of his will taken away, the things he had seen in his half-waking state would return to him, cryptic, elaborated and softened in tone.

One of these dreams occurred to him over and over. In it, he was a blind man whose skin had turned blue from cold. He carried a beggar's cup in his shaking hands, and as he passed down the street, he wailed to all who would listen: "I'm old and poor! What can I expect now? Give me your charity for the love of God!" When he reached the Beehive Store, he saw Honey Boutwell standing in front of the glass, her arrowlike tongue darting out, her eyes fainting with desire — not for him, but for a passerby. There were many objects in the window for sale, and everything had its price plainly attached. He saw this with a sickening clarity, but being blind he could understand nothing. Honey was fashionably dressed, with a feather boa that fell to her knees, and when he saw her, he came up and said: "Give me alms for the love of God." And Honey, not understanding what it was he wanted from her, held out her arm at his bidding. At once he grasped her wrist and pulled, and to his horror, her arm came off at the shoulder joint. Blood flowed from the wound, and when he looked up, he saw that people were muttering and staring at him with a hostile look. He shoved the child angrily, but she would not move, saying: "Run little Mamie, run! Run little Mamie, run! Do you want to ruin me? Run you little fool!" At this point in his dream he would usually wake up, sick with fear and drenched with sweat, but trembling, too, with a voluptuous excitement which left him weak and breathless.

He fell into the habit of looking for her on the street, and he would often stand at his window and watch while children passed, hoping she would be among them. Thus he managed to see her occasionally, and once, when she passed his window alone, he went out and spoke to her. It was a situation which he had prepared for, and he had rehearsed his lines until he considered himself letter perfect. That was two years after the Palmillers' party, and Honey had grown a great deal; but she was still thin and gangling, and her olive skin, with its individual, almost grayish cast, seemed more stretched than ever over her gaunt face.

He knew that he must speak to her, that he must somehow impress on her mind the fact that he existed, and as he stood facing her on the sidewalk, he pretended that she was a child named Maudie Winslow, whose entirely fictitious parents had recently moved to Reedyville to live. He had prepared an elaborate story, and in it, Maudie's mother had been in to have some photographs made to send back to their relatives in Beaumont, Texas. He had meant to be terse and businesslike, with just the right touch of professional patronage beneath his words, but when he tried to talk, he found that his lips were set in such a painful, nervous smile that his words seemed thin and artificial.

His story would have misled nobody, certainly not a person whose wits were as sharp as Honey's, but he realized this for the first time only when he heard the words coming from his lips with such eager, quaking energy. He had expected the child to listen in surprise, shake her head, and say at once that he was mistaken, since her name was not Maudie Winslow, but Honey Boutwell. What happened from that point on remained speculative, but he had planned to laugh heartily, apologize for his mistake, and then, perhaps, if things went well, offer to buy her an ice-cream soda as compensation for the embarrassment he had caused. But Honey did not respond as he had thought she would. She merely stopped and looked at him with an amused, amorous stare until he finished his unconvincing story.

Mr. Kenworthy pulled nervously at his lapels, wiped his glasses and said with false joviality, as if prompting her in her lines: "I haven't made a mistake, by any chance, have I? You are Maudie Winslow, of course."

Honey said: "Oh, sure. I'm Maudie, all right; and I was just coming in to see you when you stopped me, because Mama says she ain't going to take the pictures after all!"

Mr. Kenworthy caught his breath in surprise. "What a little liar she is!" he thought. "A child so young, and already such an accomplished liar!" He licked his dry lips and added in a hurt voice: "What's the matter with the photographs, please? Your mother said positively she was going to take them. Don't you think it's pretty late in the day for her to be changing her mind like this?"

Honey slid her tongue slowly across her lips and stared up at him in silence. She said finally, "They were light-struck. Mama said she wouldn't think of sending work like that back to Beaumont, where they have some real good photographers." Then she shrugged in a languid, affected way and continued down the street; but as if certain that he would watch her until she was out of sight, she swayed her small hips from side to side enticingly. All at once she became interested in the tin buckets, mops and garden hose displayed in the show window of the Central Hardware Company, and without bothering to turn her head again, to verify the fact that he still watched her, she snapped her stomach upward with such inviting finesse that Mr. Kenworthy was appalled. He went back into his studio, but he could not work for a long time. "Why, the little streetwalker!" he kept thinking. "The shameless little streetwalker!" He strode angrily up and down the room saying: "She ought to be run out of this town! . . . They shouldn't let her run loose in the streets with respectable people!"

With determination, he went back to his work, but he could not concentrate on it; and then, at last, as if some pocket of his mind had burst into consciousness, he knew that he was in love with Honey, and that there was no longer any hope of concealing the knowledge from himself. Afterwards, he went into his dark room and stood among his plates and developing fluids, aghast at what was happening to him, seeing his ruin so clearly. He kept thinking as he walked up and down and touched the familiar objects in the room: "How is it possible that such a thing happened to me? . . . The superintendent of a Sunday school! A man who has always been so upright and moral in all his dealings!"

He came back into his reception room and watched his ceiling fan wheezing and turning endlessly above his desk, feeling, at that instant, a sense of doom so strongly that he shook his head in despair, as if he could thus prevent what awaited him, and said, "No! No! It can't be!"

Afterwards, he forced his mind into oblique and devious channels, trying to find a way in which he could logically see the child, and yet arouse no suspicions in others. The sensible thing to do was to arrange a simple situation in which he would be in some unnoticed, yet close relationship to her, but each plan he worked out defeated itself through its protective complexity. Later on he put into action the only one of these schemes which seemed at all feasible. It was not ideal, but it was the best he could do, and he had to be satisfied.

His wife owned several houses in Reedyville which had been managed for her in the past by the Home Realty and Rental Company; and now, as a matter of economy, he suggested that he handle her property himself, in his spare time. He was interested only in the Boutwell house, of course, but he took on the other obligations as a matter of precaution, a small smoke screen of endeavor which he hoped would hide his real intent. Afterwards he called in person each month to collect the rent, and Ada thought that she had never met a more agreeable landlord, one more willing to make the repairs she suggested, more tolerant when the rent money was not ready.

He made his business calls at an hour when he knew Honey would be at home, and at such times, although she rarely spoke, she would follow each move he made with her black, knowing eyes. Once, at the door, with a trembling, elaborate carelessness, Paul put his hand on her head, in what he hoped was the impersonal, patronizing gesture of an adult toward a child. He took his hand away at once, for it seemed to him that his perspiring palm, as if it were a magnet, had pulled up a long, desperate sigh from the little girl's body. When he dared look at her he saw the fainting, depraved look on her face which always shocked him so much. She shook her head warningly and turned to see if her mother was watching; then, seeing that they were unobserved, she lowered her lashes and her lips shaped a shocking sentence. He could not be positive, for with a teasing sense of timing she moved away at the very moment when he would have been sure, but the words he thought he had read on her lips were: "How much will you pay me?"

And so he waited while the child grew up, hoping that his unhealthy desire would wear itself out, and yet knowing that it would not. From the beginning he had known that he could have what he wanted from her if he were only willing to pay for such possession; that while she had no regard for him at all, not even friendship, she would not repulse him.

A chance to see her oftener, to make more intimate the waiting, nervous relationship between them, came unexpectedly, when Honey was fourteen. He had called to collect the rent as usual, and Ada had said: "Mr. Kenworthy, I just don't know what I'm going to do with Honey! I'm really at the end of my rope, this time! I been crying all day long, but I guess you noticed that right away when you come in — how red my eyes are, I mean."

Paul spoke in sudden alarm: "Why, what's the matter with her? What's she been doing to upset you so?"

"She's been in the sixth grade two years already, and she didn't pass this year either!" said Ada bitterly. "It's not that she ain't bright; it's just that she won't interest herself in her books any more. I'm always telling her, 'Why don't you apply yourself more? Why don't you study hard and try to make something out of yourself the way your sister Fodie does?'"

Mr. Kenworthy glanced uncertainly at Honey. At fourteen, she considered herself a grown woman, and she had fixed her hair that day in a high, elaborate pompadour. Oddly enough, her new maturity made her seem younger than he had ever seen her before. She touched her hair languidly and said: "I don't want to go to school no more. What's the use in doing that? I want to take me some singing lessons from Professor Inman. I want to learn how to sing real good." She went out and sat on the front porch, gazing stubbornly at Sweethearts' Looking-Glass. At once she shaded her eyes with her curved palm, for under the force of the high, steady sun, the pond vibrated and reflected a brilliance too strong for the eye to endure. Then a breeze blew languidly from the direction of the Negro shacks, ruffling the surface of the water and bending the reeds, bringing with it, as it stirred up the red dust of the road, the cool, wet smell of freshly killed flesh. Honey turned her neck and spoke to her mother: "I'm not going to school next year. How many times have I got to tell you that? I made up my mind already, and that's final."

To his dismay, Mr. Kenworthy heard himself saying briskly, in a detached, businesslike manner: "Then why don't you let her come work for me, Mrs. Boutwell? There's no sense in sending her to school if she's not going to learn. I've been thinking about getting somebody to help around the studio for a long time now, and Honey can sure make herself useful, if she wants to. I'll pay her for her work, of course, and what's more, I'll teach her to be a real good photographer, too. It's a good steady profession, and it's something that might come in handy for her to know later on."

An instant before the words were said, he had had not the remotest idea of making any such offer; and when he stopped speaking, he felt an impulse to grab up his hat and say apologetically: "Please forget what I said. I'm sorry, and I don't know what made me do it"; for his conscience accused him so strongly that it seemed as if everybody else must know the actual motives behind his generosity. He waited humbly for Ada to order him out of the house, but instead she answered: "Maybe you don't really know what you're getting into, Mr. Kenworthy. You better think it over, because Honey's lazy, except when it comes to doing the things she likes to do." She spread her fingers against her cheek and continued: "No. No, Mr. Kenworthy. We all think too much of you, after the fine way you treated us, to let you get chawed this way! No, sir. I thank you for your kind offer, but we'll just have to figger something else out."

But the more vigorously his plan was opposed, the more logical it seemed to him, and he began at once to defend it with spirit, to prove that the experience gained as a photographer's helper became, later on, the decisive factor in the domestication of headstrong girls. At last Ada sighed and said: "Well, I sure do thank you for your offer. I'll talk it over tonight with Wesley and see what he has to say. If he don't object, I'll give my consent too!" Then Paul went down the brick-paved walk and opened the creaking gate, jubilant and yet frightened a little, for he knew that Honey was in his grasp at last.

As it turned out, Fodie was the only member of the Boutwell family who seriously opposed the plan. She was eighteen years old, and for a long time she had managed the household, thus giving Ada more time for her outside duties. She was like her mother in many ways, and she was at once more ingenuous and more shrewd. With maturity, a strain of watchful bitterness, which had been present in her character from the beginning, had developed strongly — a pathetic, untrusting bitterness which ridiculed affection and laughed at sentiment, as if she had examined the world about her and had found it too hateful for approval. She resented everything about her family's existence: the way they lived, the place they occupied in the town; and, most of all, she resented her own unalterable homeliness. When she spoke, there was a thin, exasperated sourness in her voice, and everything she said sounded as if she had memorized it backwards from one of the inspirational calendars so popular in her day.

"Don't you see through Honey at all?" she asked her mother when they were fixing supper together. "All she wants to do is get away from home as quick as she can, so she can lead a bad life. I'm surprised that she can fool you and Mr. Kenworthy so easy. He's always acted like such a little gentleman, that I hate to see him imposed on, that's all! . . . The way she behaved at school with the older boys was scandalous. It's a wonder to me she wasn't expelled long ago, and she would have been, too, if the principal had been anybody but Professor St. Joseph who don't even know what good morals are, it seems to me half the time."

Ada said: "Shut your jealous mouth, Miss! And watch them biscuits so they don't burn. I'm going out on the front gallery and finish some hemstitching for old Mrs. Porterfield before it gets so dark I can't see good."

Ira Graley came back from work not long afterwards, and while he washed at the basin on the back porch, Fodie told him with an elaborate wealth of detail about Honey's failure at school and Mr. Kenworthy's offer. "You know what Honey is, as well as I do, Ira!" she said sourly. "I hate to say such a thing about my own sister, but she's just a common little streetwalker, and half the people in town know it already. Mama's going to let her do just what she wants to, like she always does, and so will Papa; but mark my words: Honey's going to end up bad!" She turned back to the stove and rattled the pots angrily; then she came to the door again and lifted her neck in a forward and upward drinking motion and said: "I'd rather see Honey in her coffin than see a sister of mine turn out to be a common woman that men run after and talk about amongst themselves."

Her words brought back painful memories to Ira Graley, for

they sounded so much like the words he had heard in his childhood, the words his grandparents had used when they spoke of
his own mother, for his mother's trivial biography was a thing
he had been familiar with from his earliest years. She had begun
life as Katie McCorley on a farm in the eastern part of the State,
near the Georgia border. The Violet May Wynn of her business
career was a poetic invention, as if she strove through suggestion
to impute to herself both the sweet modesty of a flower, and the
explosive, fresh promise of spring.

Her parents, old Dan McCorley and his wife Hannah, had been
as bleak as the land they worked with so small an expectation, and
when Katie was old enough to decide her own destiny, she left
home, her parents' sour prophecies ringing in her ears, and went
to Atlanta, feeling that any life, no matter how hateful, would be
preferable to the one she knew at home. She got work finally as
a waitress at a railroad lunch counter, and being young and un-
deformed, she had many chances to go out at night with the
strangers she served. One night she made a date with a man she
knew only as Eddie. Since he had not asked her last name, she
considered it impolite to ask his.

He took her to dinner, to the theater and to his hotel room, in
that precise order. It seems astonishing that a new, complex human
life could come from a contact so casual, so hurried and so un-
satisfactory, but that is the way it happened. At last, having exhausted her savings, and having no other place to go, Katie went
home, and there she had her puny, nervous baby. It was a boy, and
she wanted to call him Cyril, knowing that all she could ever
do for her child would be to give him a pretty name; but her
father called the boy Ira, instead, thinking the name had something
to do with the wrath of God.

At best, what the child was to be called seemed a matter of
relative unimportance, for nobody, not even his mother, expected
him to live long enough to recognize a name when he heard it,
or hearing, respond to it; but the frail child clung to existence with
a tenacity which was astounding. He should have died a dozen
times over, but he would not, and each time when they thought
him dead (and a good thing it would have been, too, if his grandmother's opinion can be believed) he would give one final shudder,

close his weak, desperate eyes and suck air into his lungs once more with a shrill, rattling sound. "It's the devil in him that keeps him alive," said old Hannah angrily. "It's the devil a-looking out for his own! A baby born in decent wedlock would have done been dead and buried long ago!"

When the boy was a few months old, his mother left him with her parents and went away again. Believing herself ruined beyond all hope of salvation, she methodically entered the trade open to her, and each month thereafter she sent a part of the money she earned with her sweating, unselective flesh to her parents for the support of her child, although this was the one detail of his mother's shameful life which the boy never knew about.

Old Dan and Hannah McCorley were furious when the first money order came, and the old man swore he'd never touch one penny of a whore's earnings — that they'd all starve to death in righteousness before they'd demean themselves in such a way. He cashed the money order promptly the next morning when the post office in the village opened, and after a few years, he and his wife quit trying to work their farm at all. Sustained by the justness of their anger, they lived entirely on the money their daughter sent them, and their denunciations of her mode of life increased with their dependence upon her. Each time a money order came, the old woman would go into one of her blind, terrifying rages. "That whore!" she would shout to her frightened grandson. "That whore — your mother! Leading a life of luxury in the lap of sin. Eating off of the fat of the land! Drinking and dancing and wearing silk and lace from her filthy skin out! That's her! That's that whore a-ministering to the lust of rich men!"

She was a stocky, powerful woman whose features seemed too closely set in the center of her broad, bony face. When she was angry, she had a habit of lowering her head and shaking her neck loosely from side to side, in the stupid manner of an enraged cow. Her upper teeth had been pulled long ago, and she spoke now with a quaint, juvenile lisp, which somehow made her rage even more terrifying to others. "That whore that dares to call herself a mother!" she would continue to the boy. "That one! Living in luxury, with servants to wait on her hand and foot, when I ain't even got me no uppers to chew meat with!"

During these scenes, the boy's grandfather would stand by in silence, scratching himself or chewing thoughtfully on a sliver of pine. He was an unhappy man whose only hope for the future was the promised destruction of the world by fire. It was a thing he did not want to miss, and each night he prayed that it would come in his time. His cheeks and chin were covered with a graying sprout of tough beard, and the leathery, loose flesh about his throat fell downward, folded together and formed a shallow, triangular cave, like the crude, yet ingenious, traps of insects. He walked with an individual stride, his feet kicking forward, lifting, and coming down squarely at last, as if he crushed somebody's sin with each step he took. His attitude toward his grandson was one of aloof contempt, and he left the actual disciplining of the child to his wife. "Hannah knows how to raise that boy without no foolishness," he would sometimes say. "Me — I just leave that part of it up to her. If she can't beat his mother's sinful nature out of him, then nobody can, I say!"

Hannah, hearing his words, nodded her head with considerable satisfaction, trying not to seem too pleased at his flattery. "I don't aim to spoil him, and that's a *fact!*" she said. "But the punishment I mete out to him ain't nothing at all to the punishment *God's* going to mete out to him, because don't it say plain enough in Holy Writ that no bastard can enter into the congregation of the blest?"

Her justification for the way she treated her grandson was easily arrived at: Since he would be excluded from that heaven which her own life of personal purity and good works entitled her to enter, then plainly he had no soul; and having no soul, he must of necessity be on the same spiritual plane as an animal, with an animal's inability to distinguish between moral values, and its acknowledged insensitivity to pain.

When he was older, she would often tie his hands to the bedpost and lash him with the stump of a buggy whip until his thin, cheap shirt was stained with his own watery blood. The child under the fury of her blows would scream with pain, fall to his weak, uncertain knees and cry out imploringly: "Please don't! Please don't! Please don't!" She was an adept at knowing how much her grandson could stand, and she always stopped short of murder. She would calmly fix her loosened hair when the beating was over, and as deliberately she would untie his limp arms, so that he slid down from the bedpost and onto the floor. Then, seeing her still standing above him with the stained whip in her hands, he would crawl toward her, his belly flat to the floor like a dog's, and say desperately: "I'll be good! I'll be good!"

Had old Hannah treated the most dangerous criminal as cruelly as she treated the child left in her care, she would have been locked up at once on a charge of atrocious assault, but, as everybody knows, what is bad for an adult is good for a boy, and the neighbors passing down the road and hearing the child's lost, pitiful screams would smile, nod wisely and say: "Old Hannah sure is giving Ira a good one this time, ain't she? Well, I guess he must need it! Guess she was too easy on that no-count daughter of hers, and that's why she disgraced them all like she done!" Had they stopped, come closer and listened, they could have often heard the old woman shouting in her furious, lisping voice: "That one! That whoring mother of yours! Living a life of ease while I have to struggle and scrabble for enough to eat! I'll show her! . . . Wearing jewels and gems, when I ain't even got me no uppers to chew with!"

Remembering these old things with such pain, Ira turned from the basin and took the towel from its hook. He sighed and wiped his face and hands thoughtfully, but he remained silent. Fodie came to the kitchen door and said: "Why don't you answer when I talk to you, Ira? Sometimes I think you don't pay attention to half the things I say to you." She drew her lips back sourly and shook her head. "I've been trying to tell you all about Honey and the job Mr. Kenworthy wants to give her," she added. "I'm going to talk to Papa and tell him to put his foot down this time sure. Did you hear anything at all I just said?"

"I heard you," said Ira. "I heard you well enough."

But despite Fodie's objections, the following Monday morning, in June of 1904, Honey Boutwell entered the intricate world of business. A new assurance had come over her, and at the end of the first week, when Mr. Kenworthy paid her the wages he had promised, it seemed as if she had reached her final, individual maturity; that her temperament and her character settled into their permanent forms with the settling of the four silver dollars against her palm.

Her strength lay in the happy fact that she had no understanding of sin, no capacity to feel guilt, and no ability whatever to comprehend the perverse complexities of goodness. For these reasons she could be nobody's victim, since, to be victimized, you must concur in your own sacrifice, and find it both just and appropriate.

She mistrusted those who thought there was a reason for everything, who, through the medium of the mind, endeavored to muddle an experience as simple as life. She had no misgivings at all concerning the new situation she found herself in. The arrangement with Mr. Kenworthy was entirely satisfactory to her. It was plain she had something he wanted and was willing to pay for, and while the idea of repudiating her end of the bargain would have seemed unethical to her, she meant to get the most she could for what she had to sell. The in-between aspects of the affair troubled her not at all, and she settled down to her new duties with triumphant assurance, waiting for her patron to come to the point at last and state the plans he had made for them both.

Since he had been so determined to have her, so consistently clever — at least from her uncritical standards — in his unresting pursuit, she was vaguely concerned over the circumstances that he did not make his advances at once, now that what he wanted could be so quickly had. The truth was that the seducer, himself, felt none of his victim's matter-of-fact assurance. He quaked inwardly a dozen times a day, and he doubted with sick anxiety the wisdom of what he had done, seeing so clearly the dangers inherent in the arrangement; but he was in love more than ever with the young girl, and to be in love is to lose touch with most of those everyday yardsticks of reality which are the concern of practical people, and so it happened that while he could anticipate every pitfall which lay ahead, and dramatize with such an elaboration of detail the ruin which a girl below the legal age of consent, and one who in the ingenuous eyes of jurists still kept her primal innocence, since that was the way the law plainly read, could bring to him if she cared to, he could still feel jubilation in his possession, and congratulate himself on the finesse he had shown in shaping his fortune so boldly, for nobody, not even his wife, seemed to see anything out of the ordinary in the situation. They accepted the fact that he needed an assistant around the studio, as he said, and had hired one cheaply,

with an almost suspicious lack of interest, thus making the elaborate
excuses he had prepared unnecessary in the end. He would have been
hurt had he known that it was not his delicate handling of the affair
which protected him from gossip, as he so trustingly believed, but
his signal lack of personal attractiveness, for people have always considered that only those capable of arousing passion in others are able
to feel passion themselves.

He felt more assurance after the first week had passed and he
had still received no anonymous letters of warning from angry
Reedyville citizens, no visit from a representative of Mr. Palmiller's
Society for the Fostering of Temperance and the Eradication of
Vice; but he limited the expression of his affections to a delicate
squeezing of Honey's arm when they were alone, to a brisk stroking
of her cheek, which he hoped would appear impersonal and fatherly,
or, at the most, to pressing his nervous hand heavily against her knee.
At such times she would look at him expectantly, sigh, and tighten
her muscles in encouragement, but after a moment he would take
his hand away, glance about him guiltily and turn back to his work.

Once he remarked in a voice which he hoped was lighthearted
and casual: "Sometimes I wonder what you think about sitting there
so quiet by the window. I never realized it before, but when you're
not singing a song or entertaining people, you don't talk much,
do you?"

"Maybe it's because I ain't got nothing much to say," said Honey.
She twisted her lips, lowered her eyes professionally and turned away.
It was the truth, although none of the men who loved her was ever
to believe it, for she was destined to attract only complex, imaginative
men, who, having projected their own brilliance upon her, were
precluded from seeing that, away from her couch, she had always
been something of a bore. It was not that she was stupid, for she was
far from that. It was merely that she was one of those frightening
people who, while shrewd enough at their own levels, are so lacking
in imagination that they are never able to see beyond the immediacy
of the current hour.

From the first Mr. Kenworthy had attributed subtleties to her
which she did not possess, and which she could not have understood
had he attempted to explain them to her. Once he came up behind
her, pressed his body against her own and kissed her on the neck.

She turned and looked questioningly at him, and Paul said hurriedly, his words tumbling over each other in his eagerness to make his position clear: "I want you to know that I understand what you're thinking right now! I realize you aren't able to care anything about me, and I've known that from the first! I just want you to know that I don't blame you in the least! I must seem old and repulsive to a young girl like yourself! I understand that, my dear, as well as you do!"

Honey stared at him in complete surprise, wondering what difference personal charm or the lack of that quality had to do with their arrangement. A grocer would hardly refuse to sell his merchandise to a person merely because he didn't like him; a singer didn't ask that her audience be only those she found personally pleasing. "Why, what's that got to do with it?" she asked in surprise. "I don't believe I know what you're driving at." She waited a moment, but Paul went back to his work, glancing over his shoulder at her and sighing deeply. He spoke again after a moment: "I made arrangements with Mr. Inman for you to start taking lessons from him at once. I thought I'd fix it all up and then tell you as a surprise. . . . He was the one you wanted to take lessons from, wasn't he?"

She started her voice lessons the following Wednesday, and almost at once she made friends with one of Mr. Inman's piano pupils, a woman in her late thirties, who was destined to play a small part in Honey's career, and who was known in Reedyville as Mrs. Bessie Jowder. She had come to town about three years before, and she lived alone, with great discretion, in a cottage on Oak Street. She told the renting agent that she was a widow, that her husband had been a traveling salesman, and that his insurance had left her modestly independent for life.

When she first arrived, her nearest neighbor had called to welcome her to Reedyville, bringing with her a chocolate layer cake which she had baked. "I'm Mrs. Henry L. Poutney," she said cheerfully, "but don't mix us up with the Poutneys on Millwall Street. They're a different breed entirely, I can assure you. We're the Poutneys who live next door, and if any of us can help you to get settled down, just let us know." She extended the cake triumphantly, but Mrs. Jowder pretended that she did not see it. She stood defensively blocking the entrance to her front door, staring above her neighbor's head in complete silence. A moment later she said with a passionate ambiguity: "I'm a widow, so I'm sure you'll understand why it is I can receive only my late husband's dearest friends."

Mrs. Poutney, with a vacant look on her face, backed slowly down the front steps, trying to conceal the cake behind her. She laughed nervously and said: "Of course! That's entirely natural, isn't it? Of course I understand!" But she did not, and neither did anyone else in Reedyville.

The life Mrs. Jowder led was so circumspect, so apart from the rest of the street, that she hardly left her house at all, except to do her shopping, and, of late, to take her music lesson three times a week. Nobody knew anything against her definitely, but everybody regarded her with a certain suspicion. As Mrs. Poutney said darkly up and down the street: "I wish I'd known what I do *now* when I called on her and she said she didn't receive anybody except her husband's friends! If I had, I could have come right back at her and said, 'But of course, my dear Mrs. Jowder! That's a full-time job for any woman, isn't it? I'm sure your husband must have been the most dearly loved drummer on the road!'" Mrs. Jowder's callers were all traveling men. They were all middle-aged, and they looked so much alike that it was almost impossible for poor Mrs. Poutney, from her post behind her shutters, to tell them apart.

Of late Mrs. Jowder was beginning to find her life of isolation a little tiresome. She longed for the companionship of a person of her own sex, someone with whom she could talk freely, and she went out of her way to be pleasant to Honey Boutwell. She explained at their first meeting that she was taking piano lessons not because she thought she had any talent, nor even because she particularly liked music: the simple truth of the matter was that her husband's friends, when they dropped in to see her, liked nothing so much as to gather around a piano with their cheese sandwiches and glasses of beer and sing the old sentimental songs. She had played fairly well when she was a young girl, she said, and much of it was coming back to her now.

The two women had understood each other at once, so well, in fact, that from the beginning neither tried to deceive the other. Some days later, as they walked toward Mrs. Jowder's cottage,

Honey told her friend about Mr. Kenworthy and his peculiar conduct. "He chased after me hard enough," she said. "He wouldn't let me have any rest, he was so anxious to get me to work for him, so he could give me voice lessons. . . . But now, he acts like I was poison or something! Like I was — "

Mrs. Jowder smiled tolerantly and nodded her head, as if this was the one situation in human affairs that she knew the most about. "Just let him have his own way, my dear. Elderly gentlemen have rules and regulations all their own. They are often a little temperamental, if you know what I mean." She shook her head and continued in a tragic voice: "Your friend apparently belongs to the old school, and God alone knows how well I realize what *that* means! . . . They're as bad as the others — worse, if anybody wants my opinion — but they've got to convince themselves first, while a young man just takes things more for granted."

Honey's lesson followed Mrs. Jowder's, and the older woman fell into the habit of waiting until her friend was free. More often than not, Honey would then go to the house on Oak Street for a visit, although this was something she did not tell Mr. Kenworthy when she returned late to the studio. It was from Mrs. Jowder that she learned the substantial framework of her trade, and for a while she admired the woman enormously. She continued her friendship on even a more intimate basis after she left Mr. Inman, for her career as a voice student did not last very long.

Her teacher, having decided that her voice was "more of a contralto than anything else," gave her, as her first piece, the hackneyed aria from Saint-Saëns' "Samson and Delilah," since this was his usual testing piece for voices of her type. He listened critically while she sang, frowning and shaking his head with an almost imperceptible motion. There was something in the girl's voice which irritated everything he stood for. It was difficult to say just what it was, but it seemed to him that she somehow managed to make the respectable old aria obscene. When she came to the end, he stared for a moment unhappily at the piano keys. "No! No!" he said at length. "Not that way! Not that way at all!" He got up from the piano, walked to the window and looked down at the street. He turned after a moment and said: "You have no conception of the part at all. Whoever taught you to interpret Delilah that way?"

He came back to the piano and sat on the stool. "Now, let me show you how a real singer would interpret the part — an operatic star who has devoted years of her life to an understanding of the role!" He tightened the muscles of his diaphragm and relaxed his jaws, then, accompanying himself with one hand and using the other to gesture with, as if he drew each note against the air as he sung it, he went through the worn-out old aria in his thin, tremulous voice.

"You see!" he said triumphantly. "That's the way it should be sung! You put something in it which the composer never meant at all! I can assure you Delilah would never have sung it the way you do!"

Honey glanced across the room at her friend, but Mrs. Jowder, determined to take no part in the argument, lowered her eyes and examined the needlepoint of her elaborate handbag. There was a silence while Honey stood sullenly beside the piano, digesting what she had just been told. She spoke after a moment: "This Delilah you're talking about right now: is she the one they talk about in the Bible? The one we learned about in Sunday school that cut off Samson's hair and treated him so sorry?"

"Yes, of course it is," said Mr. Inman impatiently. "Who else did you think it could be? . . . Come now, try it again! And sing it correctly this time!"

Of all the rules Honey had been told regarding the way a lady behaves, she had heeded only one, and that was that the genteel and the well-bred never use their hands to gesture with. Perhaps she took this particular rule for her own since it was one which would hardly concern her in any event, for she had always found her large, flexible mouth capable of expressing her most sweeping emotions. She lifted her lips now and held them level and half-parted while she made up her mind; then, unexpectedly, she pushed them forward and downward in a puckered gesture which was as conclusive as a slap. She walked away from the piano and pinned on her hat with elaborate disdain. "I don't believe you know nothing about giving singing lessons," she said. She swung her hips insolently from side to side, and added: "I don't believe you know nothing about nothing! Me, I'm going to get a good singing teacher, so don't expect me back in this dump!"

Mr. Inman got up, trembling with anger. He struck the piano

keys with his open palm and said: "You dare criticize me! You dare tell me how to teach voice! I, who have sung in the world's principal cities! I, who am considered one of the most important oratorio tenors America has yet developed!" Overcome with his own astonishment, he sat down on the stool again and shook his head. "This is really too much," he continued bleakly. "This is really an experience for one's memoirs!"

Honey had waited for him to exhaust himself, to catch his breath. When he did, she twisted her flexible mouth into one contemptuous, undulating line and made a suggestion which was at once so obscene and so difficult that he jumped up in a new rage and banged the lid of the piano up and down. He stamped his foot on the floor and his eyes blinked, as if he were a child, and he expected to cry at any moment. Mrs. Jowder, who prided herself on her ability to handle unpleasant situations, came over to him and squeezed his arm reassuringly. "She's terrible," she whispered in his ear. "I was never so embarrassed in my life. I'm not accustomed to such language, from ladies." She turned away to follow Honey down the stairs, but came back to say: "Don't feel bad about it! You're well rid of her, I say!"

She caught up with Honey at the pavement, took hold of her shoulders and laughed until tears came into her eyes. "Somebody should of told him what to do years ago, and now you have," she said. She linked her arm intimately in Honey's and continued: "I could hardly keep my face straight, he looked so put-out and funny."

Honey's anger was dying down, and she began to feel a little sorry — not for Mr. Inman, who meant nothing to her, but for herself. It seemed to her sometimes that the world had conspired from the beginning to make her unhappy, to frustrate her modest and innocent desires. She refused Mrs. Jowder's invitation to come in for a chat and a bottle of beer with a sullen shake of her head. At that moment she wanted only to get back to the studio, there to pour out her troubles, to recite her list of the world's injustices, to Mr. Kenworthy. She wanted him to comfort her, to take her side as he always did and tell her how right she was and how wrong Mr. Inman had been to criticize her singing. But most of all she wanted to see the cautious, lustful look in his eyes once more, to reassure herself regarding the power of her personal charms, since she had lost faith, for the time being, in her voice. She parted from Mrs. Jowder at the corner, saying: "No, not today, Bessie. I got to see Mr. Kenworthy right away. There's something I got to settle with him now or never at all."

Mr. Kenworthy's studio was at street level and it consisted of three rooms. The first, which opened onto the street, was furnished in traditional golden oak, and its walls were covered with specimens of Mr. Kenworthy's most creative work. The middle room contained his cameras, his backgrounds and his artificial lighting devices. The room in the rear was where he kept his chemicals and where he did his developing. It was here, too, that he spent most of his leisure, lying stretched-out on an old sofa which was too shabby and too out-of-date for the reception room.

With the connecting doors open, he had a view of his entire establishment and he saw Honey at once when she entered the reception room, took off her hat and sat down in one of the big, red leather chairs. She pushed her pompadour even higher and stared in perplexity at her nails. It was plain to him that she was concerned with some desperate problem, and her effort to solve it was so apparent that you could almost see Thought laboriously entering her mind. He raised himself upward on one arm and craned his neck, in order to see her better, and at that precise moment she reached her decision, got up and walked straight in his direction. A moment afterwards she came into the back room and shut the door impatiently with her foot.

She went at once to the couch and sat beside him. "Are you really crazy about me, like you say, or not?" she asked. "I can't figure you out. You're getting me so nervous I don't know what I'm doing half the time." She bent over and kissed him on the lips. "Why can't you make up your mind? Why can't you decide what you want to do?" she asked. When he sat up, his hands were trembling and his eyes had a lost desperate look in them. "You know I love you," he said. "I can't live without you any more. I can't even bear to think what things would be like with you away from me."

"Then what are you waiting for?" she asked. "What makes you waste so much time?" More practically she added, before he could answer her questions: "Don't worry about anybody coming in un-expectedly. I locked the front door and thumb-bolted it, too."

He took hold of her arms and sighed, gazing at her with both passion and mistrust. He wanted to say: "I'm in love with you, but I haven't any faith in you. That's what makes me hesitate this way. Common sense tells me that I'd have to pay too much for what I want." Instead, he shook his head and said weakly: "There are a lot of things about me that you don't know. I have reasons which you wouldn't understand."

"I know what you want, don't I? All right, you can have it."

He got up in sudden panic and began walking up and down the room, torn between reason and lust. "It looks like the laws of this state were made just to spite me," he said tragically. "I've looked them up, and they're all against me, all in your favor." He went to the cooler and drew himself a drink, but his hand shook so that he had to put the glass down again. Honey walked to the door, opened it, and stood with her back pressed against the paneling. Mr. Kenworthy came to her and said earnestly: "Do you know what they could do to me if you decided to tell on me? All right, I'll tell you what they could do: They could put me in prison for rape. I'd be completely at your mercy from then on. You could ruin me afterwards, if you wanted to."

He turned away from her and sat again on the couch. "No, no!" he said stubbornly. "It's too much to expect! It's too much to ask!" Then, since she did not speak, he added fiercely: "Now do you understand? Now do you see my side?"

Honey said: "I don't care one way or the other. You ain't the only man in the world that likes me." She went into the reception room and unlocked the street door. He followed her humbly, already regretting that he had stated his position so clearly. He held her hand and talked desperately in an effort to convince her, babbling equally of his devotion and of the injustice of laws. "You must try to understand my position!" he said. "You must make an effort to do that!"

Honey did not even bother to listen to him. She went about the room collecting her personal belongings, and when she had them all, she went out of the door. "Send the money you owe me over to Bessie Jowder's," she said. "That's where I'm going now. That's where I'm going to stay from now on." In a way, she was glad that things had turned out as they had. She bore him no malice, and she was not offended at all, as he feared. In fact she was rather grateful to him for having pointed out to her the law's jealous concern for her chastity. It was a nice thing to know, and some day it might come in handy.

He stood in the doorway watching her as she walked insolently across the square, swaying her small hips from side to side professionally. For some months he never saw her again, but he knew precisely what she was doing, since her conduct after she left him quickly became the town's chief scandal. She had established herself as Mrs. Jowder's permanent guest, and from that base she operated without deliberation and without caution.

A stock company was playing at the opera house that summer, and Honey got a job singing a specialty number. No matter what opinion Mr. Inman might have of her singing, the common, uncritical people of Reedyville obviously liked it, and at one performance, when she sang "Who's Gwiner Holp You Smoke Your Shoat?" between the second and third acts of "Faust," she took ten curtain calls. After that, she felt that she was an actress and a woman of the world. One of the players gave her an old make-up box, and she painted her face so alarmingly that one would have thought her afflicted with one of the rarer eczemas. Dressed in Mrs. Jowder's hats and dresses, she paraded around Court House Square, or picketed the Magnolia Hotel, waiting for one of the drummers to pick her up.

It is doubtful if she ever thought of Mr. Kenworthy after she left him, although his thoughts were concerned eternally with her. He told himself over and over that his unhealthy interest in the young girl could have had no other ending. He had acted sensibly, and he congratulated himself on his strength of character in refusing to give way to his passions, to involve himself more deeply with her; but the certainty that he had been wise did not bring him comfort. He went at once into a period of massive depression. He considered his life finished, and he thought constantly of suicide. It was not a sickness of the spirit alone, an unwillingness to find the bigger world outside himself of the least importance; it was physical as well, as tormenting as unremitting pain. The very clothes he wore seemed too oppressive for his flesh to endure. He felt despair each morning when he woke and knew that he must face the world once more, for the day which did not bring him Honey again, brought him nothing. Sometimes when his pain, his sense of weariness with the world, was more than he could endure in silence, he would press his face into his pillow, roll his head from side to side and make a choked, moaning noise. "I'm an old man," he would whisper. "What can I expect from the future now? What happiness can I possibly know?"

When this acute period of his depression had abated somewhat, he returned to his office and tried to interest himself in his work once more. On the surface things seemed much as they had been before, except that now he did not even have hope to sustain him. He tried with all his strength to put Honey out of his mind, to return to that period of his life, which seemed so happy in retrospect, before he had known she existed; but this was not possible for him, and he spent much of his time stretched out on the old sofa in the back room of his establishment, going over and over the events of that day when she had left him forever.

He was lying thus one afternoon in late October when he heard his front door open. He got up and went into his reception room, and there he found Fodie Boutwell waiting for him. When she said at once that she had come to talk to him about her sister, he became animated for the first times in months. It seemed that Fodie considered herself personally responsible for Honey's conduct and she believed it to be her duty to rescue her from the fate which so plainly awaited her. She had come now to enlist his assistance, to ask him to go to see Honey at once, since he had always had such influence with her, and plead with her to abandon the life she was leading and return to her family, who still loved her. She talked earnestly and for a long time. When she had finished, Paul said: "But what can I do? Do you think she'd pay any attention to me? If you do, you're entirely wrong, because I'm the last person she'd listen to now."

She went away at last, stiff-necked, virtuous and angular, and hardly had she crossed the street and disappeared from sight before Mr. Kenworthy had another visitor. This time it was Breck Boutwell, and he came into the reception room and sat down in the chair which his sister had so lately vacated. He and Honey looked more alike than the other Boutwell children. They were something alike in temperament, too, but the boy was more imaginative and more friendly, and he possessed a sense of the ridiculous which his sister did not have and would not have understood. He laughed all the time, at everything that happened, his hair slipping downward under the force of his mirth and falling over his dark, sparkling eyes, his tongue placed knowingly in one corner of his mouth. He was not laughing this time, however. He was entirely serious, and he said with much earnestness: "I watched Fodie, and followed her to see where she was going. She's going to make a lot of trouble if somebody don't stop her."

Paul said: "Maybe not. Maybe she won't. . . . But if she does, how can I stop her? What can I do?"

"Nothing, I reckon," said Breck. He sighed and pulled at his inverted thumb, adding: "You know what she's figgering on doing? All right then, I'll tell you: She's going to turn Honey over to Mr. Palmiller's vice committee. That's what! She's been threatening all week to do it if Honey ain't home before the end of the month. She says it's her duty and she's doing it for Honey's own good. She says that when she tells the committee what she's found out, they'll send her off to reform school, where she'll be made to behave."

"I think she's just talking big, Breck. I don't believe she'll really do anything like that."

Breck waved his thumb back and forth and laughed mockingly. "That shows how little you know about Fodie," he said. "Fodie'll do anything, if she thinks it's her duty." He got up and went to the door. "I just thought I'd tell you," he added. "I don't reckon it'll do any good, though."

When the boy had gone, Paul sat thinking for a long time. The possibility of Fodie's appearing before Mr. Palmiller's committee alarmed him, and he wondered anxiously how much she suspected of his own relationship with her sister. He decided, at length, that she probably knew nothing, since she had come to him for assistance; lit a cigarette and went back to his work considerably reassured; but two weeks later, when the Executive Committee of the Society for the Fostering of Temperance and the Eradication of Vice held its monthly meeting, she appeared before it voluntarily, and stated her case. It was plain that she had not been making idle threats, for she had gathered a staggering amount of evidence against her sister.

As usual, the committee met in the directors' room of the Palmiller State Bank, a paneled, rectangular space on the ground floor, whose barred windows looked upon a brick-paved courtyard. Fodie arrived early and sat in the most uncomfortable chair she could find, thinking with satisfaction of the commendable thing she was about to do, her face proud and contented, as she waited for the meeting to begin.

The greatest arrogance of which the furious human mind is capable is the assumption, which many have, that they are the agents of God, and that their mission is to restrict, to define — to formulate the precise conditions under which others may indulge their sexuality. It is not strange that such types should exist in a world as rich and as varied as our own; the unbelievable thing is that their normal brothers, against the evidence of their own senses, so willingly accept the restrictions laid upon them. Perhaps only the primal guilts, which lie like a foundation of quicksilver at the bottom of man's mind, could make such craven compliance possible. Conceivably, there are people so wise and so experienced that they are qualified to draw up codes broad enough for the conduct of all, but these are the ones least interested in such matters, and thus the ability to mind one's own affairs is the surest indication of emotional maturity.

Shall we examine superficially the Reedyville vice committee and see what special qualifications they have for performing the duties they have assumed with such certainty? Shall we glance first at old Miss Emmaline Maybanks, since she is the first to arrive?

She had built her life around a motto, which seemed effective if repeated often enough, but which was, in reality, entirely without meaning. "The body of man is the temple of God!" she would say in a hushed voice, raising her forefinger warningly and shaking her head from side to side. "The body of man is the temple of God, and there's no way to escape that fact, my friends!" Since she believed this literally, it was plain that when man departed from those rules of personal purity which this virgin, naïve old lady had worked out for him, he profaned not only himself, but the dwelling place of his creator as well. Her particular deity was both imbecilic and hysterical, and since he was not himself capable of making the distinctions between right and wrong which he demanded of his worshipers, he blindly punished all for the offense of one. Thus when Honey Boutwell did the things she did in the rooms above the Deerhorn Café, or in one of the assignation houses on New April Avenue, she put the entire town in jeopardy; and since Miss Maybanks did not relish the prospect of being smitten with lightning, or drowned in a freshet, after her inflexible years of purity and good deeds, there was stupid logic in her persecution of those who endangered her security.

She paused at the door, glanced around expectantly, and then seated herself at the table. She took off her gloves, turned her neck and stared at Fodie with suspicion. Almost at once Mr. Baker Rice came in and took his usual place beside her. The old lady spoke to him in her meek, almost inaudible voice. "Who is she anyway?" she whispered. "What's she doing here at the meeting?"

Mr. Rice said: "She has information of interest for us all, I understand." He was a tall, freckled man with a mauve-colored wen pushing upward, like a tiny balloon, from beneath his mustache and pouting his upper lip. He was more of a specialist than Miss Maybanks. He regarded with indifference the things men did: his hatred was reserved exclusively for women. No doubt he would have been both astounded and indignant had he been told that he hated women because he, himself, was not one, and yet that was the simple key to the riddle of his furious life. An interesting sidelight on his character was the fact that his wife was as unattractive as it is possible for a woman to be, and that he kept her perpetually pregnant. He liked Miss Maybanks even less than he did women in general, and to avoid her eye, he took out a pencil and sharpened it nicely. When he looked up again, all the members of the committee had arrived and had taken their seats.

At the proper time, after Mr. Palmiller had explained matters, Fodie got up and began her story. She addressed all her remarks to Hubert, since he was the one member with whom she was well acquainted. "Some people might think hard of me for what I've got to do now," she began humbly; "but I've examined my conscience, and I believe it's my duty. It'll be for my sister's good in the long run too." She raised her downcast eyes and smiled placatingly, her teeth protruding nakedly to their full length. "I blame that Mrs. Bessie Jowder for her downfall as much as anybody," she said. "She's been a bad influence on her."

Miss Prescott interrupted her. "Is it that Mrs. Jowder who lives in a gray cottage on Oak Street?" she asked. When Fodie said that it was, she folded her arms and smiled tightly, as if to say: "I can tell the committee a few things about her myself!" Of all the members present, her attitude was the most logical, the easiest to understand. She had been denied those pleasures of the flesh which others delighted in, for no man, in her entire life, had even so much as tried to kiss her, and she was determined, in her grim middle age, that others should not have them either. She coughed and looked significantly at Mrs. Daniel O'Leary, and the latter narrowed her eyes and nodded twice — once for herself, once for her husband.

They both served on the committee, and neither had ever missed a meeting. Their union was a close one, but it had its differences, like all marriages: points of theory which they argued endlessly when they were alone together. Mr. O'Leary, for instance, believed that sexual union was quite permissible for a married couple as moral as themselves, if its aim was not pleasure but the creation of a soul for the glory of God. His wife was less abandoned: she partially concurred with her husband's views, but believed further that the embrace must be entirely without interest for either participant — preferably they should find it repellent. Despite all the limitations which they had placed upon themselves, they had produced six children in eight years. This circumstance alone seems almost to prove the correctness of Mr. Palmiller's concept of sly, undefeatable Nature.

Fodie was now talking more specifically regarding her sister's conduct. She recited a long list of immoralities, with names and dates noted in a blankbook. Her most sensational piece of evidence came out a moment later, and it was this: A group of local men had given a stag party at the Magnolia Hotel, for one of their friends who was going to New Orleans to live, and they had hired Honey to come in later and sing a few of her songs for them. Later, somebody offered her ten dollars if she'd take off her clothes and dance naked. It seems she had done this at once.

Howard Carraway, a lawyer, and the last member of the committee, came to life quickly. "Dancing naked!" he said in a shocked voice. "Inciting men to commit crimes!" He was the most dangerous of them all. He particularly disliked nudity. Once, when the Home Hand Laundry showed a reproduction of Botticelli's "The Birth of Venus" in its window, he had had the proprietor arrested and brought into court on a charge of impairing the morals of the community. The sight of the naked female body, he said, inflamed men so greatly that they were in danger of raping, killing, or tearing asunder with their hands. The jury who listened to these ravings had never felt any of the things he described, but they looked at the painting with a new interest, feeling that they were somehow lacking in a proper spirit of morality. Three years from the date of Honey's trial, he tried to cut a young farm-woman's throat. They put him in an insane asylum — many years too late.

These, then, were the people who found Honey Boutwell's grubby immoralities so appalling. They decided unanimously that Mr. Palmiller swear out a warrant for her arrest the next morning, and they pledged themselves, as a society, to see that she was prosecuted and put away in some prison school, where Reedyville would be protected from her. They reached their verdict with straight faces, nobody seeing how amusing it was. Hubert was pleased with the decision. "We must make an example of her!" he said coldly. "A depraved girl of that sort isn't fit to breathe in the same air that a pure girl like my own daughter breathes!"

One thing which neither Fodie nor the committee knew was that at least one outsider heard their proceedings that night. It was Breck Boutwell himself, and he hid behind a barrel in the courtyard, seeing everything, hearing all. The committee had hardly reached its decision before he was off to warn Honey of what awaited her. She was contemptuous at first, but Mrs. Jowder, being more experienced, said: "You don't know what people like them can do! You got to get out of town tonight before they get their hands on you!" She walked up and down nervously, grateful that the committee had taken no action regarding herself.

"Where'll I go to?" asked Honey. "Who's going to help me?"

Mrs. Jowder turned triumphantly. "That little Mr. Kenworthy is the one to help you now! Why didn't I think of him right away! You telephone him and tell him the trouble you're in. Ask him to meet you here as soon as he can, and tell him to bring all the money he can spare."

What happened afterwards, and what did not, is difficult to determine, for Minnie McInnis McMinn used much of Honey's career in *Shattered Roses,* her first successful novel. People even now insist that the vice committee attempted to tar-and-feather Honey, since that had been their decision regarding the McMinn heroine, and that they had dragged her, proud and silent, from the protecting arms of her widowed mother. The actual facts were less dramatic: Mr. Kenworthy had come at once. He said there was but one thing to do, and that was for him to drive Honey to Morgantown, where she could board the midnight train for Memphis. Dressed in Mrs. Jowder's best suit and hat, Honey got into Mr. Kenworthy's buggy and was driven off, while Breck and Bessie stood at the gate and waved good-by. They had expected Mr. Kenworthy to come back that same night and tell them what had happened. They waited up for him until daybreak, but the town never saw him again.

He, himself, had expected to return, but at the last minute, as the train was pulling out of the station, Honey said: "What you want to go back for? There's nothing in that town you want, is there?" Then he had run forward blindly, and Honey, from the vestibule of her car, had braced herself and pulled him, limp and panting, on board.

But all this had happened so far in the past that Dover remembered nothing at all of his sister's flight. He knew only that he had had a sister named Honey, and that she had done something shameful; but if he remembered nothing, his brother Breck remembered everything with angry clarity. His sister's disgrace had had a great effect in shaping his character, and illogically he attributed her downfall solely to Mr. Palmiller, feeling that he, and he alone, was responsible. Afterwards, he never passed the Palmiller house without a sense of rage, and he would stop on the pavement outside, contort his face and spit violently. "You wait!" he'd say. "All the cards ain't on the table yet! You wait and see!"

Mrs. Kenworthy continued to live in the old Dunwoody house even after her husband had deserted her. She would never have admitted such a thing to others, but in reality she felt an enormous sense of relief, now that he had gone. She had an irrational sense of power in being the mistress of an elaborate house which had no master, and she entertained her friends a great deal during the years she was alone. She had gone to bed early on the particular night in September with which we are now concerned, but she felt a sense of guilt, even though her sick headache was quite genuine, thinking it was her duty to get up and go to the Palmillers', and ask if there was anything she could do for Clarry.

The house was completely dark as Dover approached it, but to the east a moon was rising — hot, bloated and giving off the red, steady glow of metal fresh from a forge. It rested evenly atop a green horizon of pines, as if moored there, and when the trees rippled mildly and moved forward under the wind, the moon, itself, seemed to lift upward with them, as if straining at ropes, as if, although of unbelievable heaviness, it had no weight. Dover found the old-fashioned bell cord and pulled it, and far away he heard a small, icy tinkle. Mrs. Kenworthy from her bedroom, which faced the side porch downstairs, said petulantly: "Who is it? Who is it please?"

Dover explained his mission, and Millicent said, trying to hide the exasperation in her voice at being waked up at the moment she was about to drift off into sleep: "I can't talk to you now. Tell your mother to come see me tomorrow. I'll discuss the matter with her then."

Dover went regretfully down the steps, wondering what to do next. It seemed that he had been only a moment on the Kenworthy porch, but in that interval the moon had freed itself of the trees and was rising now up the sky, shrinking in size, paling in color, as it ascended. He turned and walked away in the direction of his sister's house, watching the moon as he walked.

Chapter 6

W HEN Ira Graley was an older man, and had with both the gentle muscle of the heart and the bitter muscle of the mind expelled his secret and unforgotten past, it seemed to him that his formative years had moved, not with the calm, almost imperceptible, rhythm of happy people, but with veering, small explosions of change, as if the chance events themselves had been minor springboards to bounce him from one phase of his existence to another. The first of these well-defined turning points in his life had been the events which gave him courage enough to escape from the brutality of his guardians.

That day he had gone to Mr. Kingman's store at the crossroads to buy meal and molasses for his grandmother. When he got there, he saw that the proprietor was sitting at his desk in the rear, laboriously checking an order blank. A well-dressed drummer stood on the other side of the counter drinking a bottle of rootbeer, and Ira, too timid to speak, moved toward the side wall of the store and stood there patiently, not daring to make his presence known. His eyelids fluttered upward and then closed, so that sight would not modify his pleasure in the quivering, rich and fruity smells which lived in the air about him. Then, to his surprise, the stranger said: "Come here! Come here a minute, Sonny!" Ira looked up quickly, to see if the drummer was speaking to him; as quickly he lowered his eyes again and moved closer to the wall. The man started to laugh at the boy's rustic embarrassment, but yawned instead, patting his mouth with his white, manicured hand. "I was going to buy you a bag of candy," he said, "but if you don't want it, stay where you are."

Ira moved his feet back and forth nervously, but he did not answer. Life had taught him to be suspicious, and already he knew that the only hope the weak have lies in their silence. The drummer sat on the counter and kicked his heels idly against the unpainted wood of the partition. "What's the matter?" he asked. "Can't you talk?"

The boy shook his head with a gesture which was both humble and final. He moved a foot or two toward the door, then, losing his balance, he sat down on a sack of potatoes. As if this was the thing he had meant to do all the time, he stared fixedly through the door, watching the roadway shimmering in the hot, afternoon light of August. It was vacant of all life except for an ancient, rheumatic Negro man who sighed and limped and carried a bundle tied up in a faded, blue bandanna, his free hand slapping patiently at gnats.

The stranger pulled in his plump belly, removed his straw hat and carefully blew the dust from its band. "What's your name?" he asked. "Tell me what your name is, and maybe I'll tell you mine."

There was still no answer and Mr. Kingman, interrupted in his calculations, turned and looked over his shoulder, to see who it was that the drummer was talking to. He laughed at once with a sharp, clattering sound: "You done asked that boy something he can't answer, Mr. Graley," he said. "You done asked him something he'd mighty well like to know hisself."

Seeing the arch, sidling expression on the proprietor's face, the drummer asked: "How does it happen he doesn't know his own name? I thought that was something everybody knew."

Mr. Kingman laughed with explosive pleasure. "This one don't, and you can take my word for it. This one's a little bastard that never knew who his pa was." He raised his spectacles, to lengthen his range of vision, and added: "Ain't that right, Ira? Correct me if I've made a mistake."

Ira held his head even lower, but he neither answered nor looked up as Mr. Kingman continued his personal history: "That's why he ain't got any name except Ira. Of course he might call himself after his grandpa, but the old gentleman says if he ever catches him using that name he'll beat the living daylights out of him."

Ira, with that peculiar leaning quality which some animals possess, lengthened his body without moving from his tracks. His nostrils closed for an instant and then opened widely as he en-

deavored to pick up the drummer's basic scent and to separate it
from the rich, musty odors of the store. He was successful almost
at once, and he was surprised at its pleasantness. The man's smell
was that of a washed hairbrush left in the sunlight to dry. This
knowledge reassured him, and he permitted himself a quick look
into the man's face. It was ordinary, unassertive and mild.

The stranger got down from the counter and said: "Thanks for
such a good order. I'll see to it that everything comes like you want
it." He seemed badly in need of sleep, for he yawned again widely
behind his plump, white hand. "It looks like I've still got time to
make the 2:20 for Chattanooga," he said. "I'll be sure to see you
when I come through again in October." He picked up his sample
case and moved toward the door, but, as if changing his mind,
he came to Ira, put his forefinger under the boy's reluctant chin
and tried to raise his head. The child got up, sighed and turned
away; but the drummer, taking hold of his hand, pressed a fifty-cent
piece against his palm. "Don't let people worry you," he said. "What
you are is no fault of yours. A lot of great men have been in the
same fix and it didn't hold them down. . . . So hand it right back
to people. Say to them, 'Wait twenty years from now and then see
who's got a right to laugh at who.' "

He picked up his case and went out of the store, while Ira gazed
stupidly at the money in his hand. Mr. Kingman said: "Hasn't
old Hannah beat no manners into you yet? Can't you thank Mr.
Graley for his nice present?" Later on in the afternoon he told the
story to several of his customers.

"You know Ben Graley, don't you? No? Well, Ben travels a line
of candies and fancy notions out of Chattanooga, and there ain't a
better-dressed or a better-liked man on the road than Ben is. Well,
sir, he ups and gives old Hannah McCorley's grandson a four-bit
piece, and the boy just stood there looking down at the floor like
he didn't have good sense. Just stood there with his head hanging
between his legs and not saying anything; and leaning forward and
stretching his neck out, when Ben went down the steps, like a hound
puppy does when spareribs are a-cooking in the kitchen. If I didn't
know better, I'd swear to God Ira was trying to smell the man!"
Then he laughed, scratched his back guardedly and delivered his
punch line: "Well, maybe it ain't so funny after all. You know

what they call his ma, don't you? . . . Well, sir, I guess it's only natural for the son of a bitch to act like a dog, too!" He leaned back against his shelves and laughed so heartily that the canned goods above him vibrated with borrowed mirth.

What he did not know was that the boy had been too overcome to speak. He turned his neck slowly and watched through the window as Ben Graley crossed the porch and stepped onto the ground, leaving the impression of his shoes in the dust at the store's foundations. Perhaps he thanked his patron in a manner more conclusive than words, for after he had made his purchases, he went to the place where the man had stepped down and stood in the tracks he had made. He had a sense of anxious, waiting unrest as he stood there, for there was something important coming into his mind and he did not, as yet, know precisely what it was. Then, lengthening his stride, he followed the tracks until he came to the place where the drummer had tied the rig he had hired in the village. For a time the boy stood there too, wrinkling his brow in puzzlement, shielding his eyes with the peak of his cap as he stared down the vacant, shimmering road; and then the certainty which had been trying to break through the barriers of his mind came clearly into consciousness. He raised his head, put down the supplies he was carrying, and said, as if answering the question the stranger had asked him in the store: "My name's Graley. Ira Graley."

Mr. Kingman's story about Ira and the drummer came at last to the ears of Hannah herself. She tried to make the boy give her the fifty cents, but he lied clumsily, saying that he had lost the money on the road. "I don't aim to take it away from you," said the old woman gently. "I just want to put it up for you, so you'll know where it is when you want it." She went back to her work, pretending that she had lost interest in the matter. "I know you didn't lose it on the road," she said mildly. "You never lost anything in your life. I know you're lying just as well as you do."

"I lost it!" said the boy desperately. "I lost it!"

The old woman looked at him over her glasses, making her voice soft and winning. "Don't you trust me?" she asked innocently. "Don't you trust me when I promise not to lay a hand on you if you'll only tell me where you hid it?"

The boy stood in perplexity, not knowing what to do; then, since his need to believe in the goodness of others was so overwhelming he said rapidly: "I put it in a tobacco can and hid it under the back steps. I'll go get it now." Hannah watched with interest as her grandson recovered the coin and brought it to her. When the money was safely in her hand, she sailed it edgewise into the tangled underbrush of weeds and vines which grew behind the house. "That'll teach you!" she shouted. "That'll teach you to have more pride! . . . Taking money from people like a beggar!"

The beating that time was the worst the boy had ever received, and his lost, pitiful pleas for mercy rang out plainly in the still, afternoon air. In her rages, Hannah's face seemed relaxed rather than drawn, soft rather than unforgiving. Her eyes were moist and widely stretched, with a shocking quality of childlike innocence behind their fury, while her mouth, at such times, puckered provocatively, as if, despite the absence of uppers, she considered the possibility of whistling a tune.

When he could stand no more, the boy fainted. His grandmother stood above him, prodding him with her foot and saying: "You ain't fooling me none! Get up offen that floor and go wash!" But since he did not answer, and since his body seemed impervious now to her blows, she became somewhat alarmed. She drew a bucket of cold water and threw it over him, repeating: "Get up! You ain't fooling me none by trying to play possum!" Slowly he opened his eyes, turned, looked at her and shuddered.

Later, when she went into the kitchen to start supper, the boy dragged himself through the weeds and began patiently to search for the lost coin. He searched without rest, inch by inch, parting the weeds and the briers with quiet precision, peering under leaves and beneath dead branches, seeking with his entire being, his long, thin nose ranging close to the ground. It was not the coin that he sought to regain, but the things the coin stood for in his mind. It was, he felt dimly, the emblem of his right to a name of his own, a name which, while limiting, defining and separating him from all others, yet merged his anonymous existence into the vast, fluid current of life as well. Without this tangible symbol, the episode at the store, which had been so important for him, took on a dream-like, imaginary quality: a wish, rather than the fulfillment of a wish; and so he searched patiently, each time that he could escape his grandmother's childlike, wide-stretched eyes. At the end of the fourth day he found the coin, and with it clutched once more in his pale hand, he could again hear the drummer saying: "What you are is no fault of yours. A lot of great men have been in the same fix, and it didn't hold them down."

He made a little bag for the coin and hung it about his neck on a leather thong; and that night when his grandparents were asleep, he went to the village and waited below the water tower until a freight train going south slowed down for the crossing; then, looking desperately about him, he climbed into an empty boxcar, hoping that it would take him in the direction of Reedyville, for that town, as he well knew from his grandmother's furious words, was where his mother ran her establishment.

For a long time afterwards he thought of this separation from his early ties, this knowledge that he was a being in his own right, as the most important moment in his life. Later, when he was more experienced, he knew that it was not — that Wesley's defense of him that hot day at the compress had a far deeper effect, a far wider implication. Before that memorable event occurred, it is true that he had been a person with a name of his own, an individual with a right to live and to seek a particular salvation, as others sought theirs; but he had found little comfort, little benefit, in the bare acquisition of identity, for he realized more and more that he was a being having no permissible contact with any of the patterns of existence: one denied even the average, unremarked affection which others knew.

He lived, during those first months in Reedyville, in a room at the rear of the Deerhorn Café. This room, with his supper added, was given him in return for his services about the place. Even after he got his job as water boy, he continued to live at the café, washing the accumulated dishes after he returned from the compress, and, later on, after the last patron had gone home, scrubbing the tables, the floor and the woodwork. When he was finished at last, he would go back to his bare room, having spoken to nobody all that day, and lie on his pallet in exhaustion, staring with hopeless anger at the brown, rain-soaked walls, wondering if his life was always to be so barren, so apart from the lives of others.

He would sigh and move nervously on his pallet, and with the things which concerned his everyday life put aside at last, his thoughts would turn once more to his mother. He had left old Dan and Hannah with no hatred against them, no desire for revenge; and once beyond their power to hurt him, he had forgotten them with quick efficiency, as one forgets the unbearable pain of an illness. His attitude toward them was inconsistent perhaps, but he had accepted their valuations of himself and his mother so completely that he regarded them now, not as human beings in the sense that others were, but as the impersonal agents of justice — a pair appointed by God to inflict upon him punishment for his share in his mother's shame.

His hatred was reserved for his mother, for he was convinced that she, and she alone, was responsible for his separation from others, his life of expiation and suffering; and since he was, as yet, without experience of his own with which to measure the reality of others, he had accepted the imprecations of old Hannah as true, and he pictured his mother as living in a world of unending luxury, her every desire granted by her sweethearts. Sometimes he wondered what precious thing she gave her lovers in return for all she took from them, what factor in her mode of life, what unique quality in herself, made her so much more desirable, so much more precious than a faithful wife would ever be to them; then he would sigh and close his eyes, knowing that an understanding of such matters was still beyond him.

Often, when he reached this baffling point in his thoughts, he would get up and go to his mother's establishment, standing outside in the dark and listening to the sound of merriment which came to his ears, his thorough, implacable mind turning over and over the few facts that he knew; but he made no effort to have her acknowledge him as her son, nor did he wish to speak to her, or even to see her as yet. These things were reserved in his mind for a later date, for an occasion of special importance to him. Already the details of that meeting were shaping themselves; already he knew what he would say to his mother when they met at last, in accordance with his plans, and what she must, of necessity, say to him in return.

If some of these situations have a familiar ring, it is only because Ira himself used so much of his own life in his monumental book,

The Structure and Development of the Ego, a book which was, later on, to become one of the great turning points in man's perverse but persistent struggle to understand his nature. In the disguised and edited account of his own early years, which he called simply, "Case History of an Illegitimate Boy," he said in his summation: —

No boy can grow into manhood unaided, and thus the appearance of Mr. W. B. to play his role of protector and father so opportunely, undoubtedly saved the illegitimate child from those antisocial and abnormal trends which, as we have seen, were developing so strongly in him. It is unimportant, for our purpose, that when Mr. W. B. came back from the Spanish American War, the boy had outgrown his protector both mentally and emotionally. The man had appeared, almost miraculously, at the exact moment the boy had needed him the most. His work was done. He had served his purpose conscientiously and well — although he had had no conception of the important role he had played — and he had left the child with the power to move forward from him toward other and more adult goals.

As he wrote these words, Ira remembered a day in summer when he and Fodie rested under their willow tree beside the stream which flowed so quietly within its lush, emerald banks. They had been silent for a long time, and then Fodie said: "I believe you think more of Papa than anybody else in the world. Sometimes I stop and say to myself, 'Ira really thinks more of Papa than anybody. He really does.'" She waited for him to answer, but since he did not do so at once, she added with false humility: "I'm not criticizing you for it. I'm just saying what I think is the truth."

"I do think a lot of him," said Ira cautiously. "I've got a right to think a lot of him, it seems to me."

When Fodie spoke again, there was badly concealed jealousy in her voice. She had expected Ira to repudiate his affection for her father at once, to say that she, and she alone, was the person he loved, but he had not. She had taken the boy for her own long ago, and she knew precisely what she wanted both from him and from the future. Her ambition was none the less fierce for being limited in its aim, and the most important factor in its fulfillment was her future marriage to Ira himself. She was convinced that she loved him deeply, but she did not; for she wanted from him only those material things which a successful, respectable man — a man such as he must inevitably become in time — gives to his ambitious and equally respectable wife. She was willing to work without rest, to make any sacrifice demanded of her, to get the things she wanted, and she considered Ira's character ideal for her ambitious ends. His mind was good, she felt, but not so good that it would be conspicuous; he was gentle and kindly; he disliked untidiness and the raised voice, and he would not oppose her too much. She felt that she could shape him, that she could use his own desire to pull himself up in the world for her specific purposes, and on the whole she was well pleased with the course her life was taking.

She knew so clearly what it was she wanted. It was not very much, perhaps, but to her it seemed great indeed. Her ultimate wish was a home on Reedy Avenue — a home which, while not as imposing as the Palmiller house, or even the house the Kenworthys lived in, was yet solid, substantial, and certainly as good as any second-best. There were to be rich, colored rugs on all the floors, and lace curtains were to hang at the windows. In the parlor there were to be two pianos, one at each end of the room, for this seemed to her the ultimate in careless grandeur; but the one touch of magnificence which she added to her home from her own imagination was a fountain with three graduated basins for the lawn, a fountain which everybody who passed her house admired in a loud voice.

Fodie spoke after a moment, getting up from beside the stream and putting the books together exactly. "Papa's not a good man in a lot of ways," she said. "He don't accept responsibilities the way you do. When Papa has something on his mind he can't figure out, he just pretends it doesn't exist. . . . But maybe he's got you fooled the way he fools Mama. Maybe you'd rather not see him the way he really is."

Ira did not answer. He wanted to say that you didn't love people because they were worthy of love, but for other reasons, reasons so deep that more often than not you did not know them yourself. He now saw Wesley with complete clarity, far more clearly than Fodie was capable of seeing him, but that made no difference in his feelings. His affection had been given, and it could not now be taken back. In a way, he had created another and a more spiritualized portrait of Wesley during those days when they had worked together at the compress, a picture quite apart from reality, and one whose need was dictated not by the mind but by the heart. Then, since he had modeled his conscious being upon his own creation, he had made it a part of himself forever, so that now Wesley had become not alone his kindly father and his guiding spirit, but his son as well, thus creating between them a bond so complex, so deep and so selfless that it must last as long as the mind which held it lasted.

"I suppose you don't care anything about me at all," said Fodie after a silence. "I suppose that's what you're really trying to tell me now, after I've done so much for you from the beginning, and given up everything and everybody just to see that you get along in the world." Ira turned his head and looked steadily into her disappointed, unhappy face; then he laughed shyly and moved toward her across the grass, using his elbows to pull himself forward, as if they were little stilts. When he reached her, he put his arms about her and pulled her down to the grass beside him. Slowly he turned her unwilling head, and when her eyes looked directly into his, he bent above her and kissed her slowly. "The way I feel about you is something entirely different," he said. "Don't try to understand me, because that might just mix you up more. Just believe me when I tell you I love you better than anybody or anything in the whole world."

Fodie felt her old confidence returning to her and she laughed happily. She adjusted her body against the boy's with that characteristic, squirming motion which women in love understand so instinctively: a wriggling gesture of surrender, of intimacy to come and of furious, unswerving possessiveness of the things which, they believe, will also possess them. She looked up dreamily through the lacy umbrella of the willow tree, watching the sunlight fall downward through the varying shades of green, its power diminishing as it thinned out toward the lower branches, until, at last, there was only the indication of light: a mild, uncertain shimmer which seemed less a product of the distant sun, than an exhalation of the essence of leaves.

Far away, in the direction of the Negro quarters, two young babies screamed in shocked, angry repudiation of their existence on the earth. They cried shrilly, their wails sounding thin, yet entirely clear, in the silence. There were but two notes in each cry — a low, protesting note, and a high, sustained one; but although they were pitched in different keys, and although the wailing babies could not hear each other, their timing was so exact, that their alternating screams blended together and harmonized into a pretty, pathetic tune.

Ira, hearing the sustained cries, sighed and sat up against the tree. He had not worked at the compress for a long time now, for, when he was sixteen, he had found a better job at Milligan's Planer Mill. There was more chance for advancement there, and he was now a feeder, a young man making almost enough to take care of a wife and family of his own. He bent his head forward and said unexpectedly in his deep, hesitant voice: "I've never asked you to marry me, Fodie, but I've always meant to do it. I guess I've just taken it for granted that you would."

"I've taken it for granted, too," said Fodie, "but I always knew you'd ask me one of these days." She waited a moment and then said: "Are you asking me now? Is that what I'm to understand?"

"Yes," said Ira. "I'm asking you to marry me."

"I'll be your wife at the right time," said Fodie. "Don't worry about that any more." She hugged him with all her passion, all her concentrated desire to possess, to save, to acquire; then she kissed him on the lips with a gesture which was so grateful, so triumphant in its humility, that it somehow interrupted the flow of Ira's sentiment, and prevented his saying the other tender things which were in his mind.

"But you're too young yet," said Fodie. "You've got plenty of time to think about marriage later on, after you've made something out of yourself." She was all smiles again, all assertive tenderness. At her suggestion, Ira was taking a night course in bookkeeping and shorthand at the Reedyville Business College on Mason Street. She had felt that a knowledge of such things would be the surest means of enabling him to break away from manual labor and into the office-worker class, which was the first step upward for him in her plan for his success.

Fodie, remembering her ambitions once more, said: "Come on, Ira. Let's not waste any more time. Give me the book and I'll dictate to you some more. You've got to write at least a hundred words

of new matter a minute, if you expect to hold down a real good
position."

He picked up his notebook at her bidding, and, with his back
braced again against the willow tree, and the notebook resting on
his extended leg, he put down the symbols for the drowsy words
which Fodie read from the book with the uninspired precision of
a metronome. When he had finished the lesson, she examined his
notes, although she could not read them, a sense of triumph in her
thin, quivering breast. "I tell you what let's do," she began. "In
future, why don't you get up an hour earlier than you do now. I'll
get up at the same time and fix your breakfast before Mama and
the others are out of bed. In that way we can get in a whole extra
hour of practice."

Ira agreed at once, as he agreed with each proposal she made
for his success; and that is the reason why he was already awake
and dressed when The Goodwife came to the Boutwell door on
that May morning of 1904 to tell them that a boy lay drowned in
Sweethearts' Looking-Glass. Afterwards, he went to the mill as
usual, but all that day, as he fed boards into his machine with
exact, automatic timing, he could not banish Rance Palmiller's face
from his mind, nor could he understand the forces which had impelled the child to take his own life. Then, slowly, he began to
assemble each memory he had of the boy, each small circumstance
of his life, no matter how trivial it might seem to others. "There
must be a reason back of it," he thought. "There must be things
connected with it that I can't see yet." He arranged his facts over
and over in his mind, in different patterns, in varying combinations,
with that slow, deep thoroughness which was later to become so
characteristic of everything he did. His mind sifted, rejected and
combined with the patience of the born scientist, tirelessly, methodically. He had little hope of finding, so easily, the answer he sought,
and yet he knew that if, by chance, he should stumble upon the
peculiar combination of truth and emotion which had been valid
for Rance himself, something deep and primitive in his own mind
would respond with an instinctive certainty, reinforcing and con-
firming the paler, more tepid truth of intelligence.

He wiped his brow with his sleeve and leaned back for an instant
against his machine. Suicide seemed so unnecessary, so inexplicable,

for a child who, like Rance, had been so watched over, so protected all his life — a child who had never known the terrors of cold, hunger and brutality in his entire existence. It seemed an ending more appropriate for a person like himself, who had had so little to live for in childhood, so bleak a prospect facing him for a future; and yet, as he rested there listening to the whining, falling tune of the saws, he knew that self-destruction was an ending impossible for him, no matter how unbearable his life became, no matter what suffering he was called upon to endure.

He lifted a new board from the dolly at his elbow, and started it on its journey through the machine; and as the rollers engaged it, and moved it onward to the waiting saws, he realized that in the past he had always thought that if people possessed the things he lacked, they were happy. He knew, now, that this was not necessarily so. Then a startling thought came into his mind: Perhaps the unmodified violence he had known had, in a sense, been his salvation, since his guardians had never complicated their cruelty to him with affection. Suppose his grandmother had treated him not only with fury, but with tenderness too? Suppose his simple, unshaded hatred of her had been complicated with other emotions which tied him to her? That would have been horrible, indeed, and he knew it. He could never have broken away from her so easily in that event, never achieved any separate existence for himself at all. . . .

He watched while the saws planed the board into the pattern desired, the sawdust falling in a thin stream to the chute beneath the vibrating machine. He turned to reach for another board, but his hands trembled so much that he could hardly lift it. Involuntarily he stepped backwards and caught his breath, for at that moment he saw clearly how his grandmother might have destroyed him, as she had wanted to do. He laughed with relief and bent down to tie his shoes securely; then, standing upright again, he went back to work with a nervous, increasing vigor, thankful, all at once, that his guardian had been too lacking either in subtlety or imagination actually to accomplish the purpose she had set for herself.

The suicide of Rance Palmiller, although he did not know it at the time, was to have an effect on his own life, for it was to bring him in contact with the last, and perhaps the most important, of his father figures: the man who was to shape him into his final form, who was to finish what the drummer at the country store had commenced; what Wesley Boutwell had nourished and sustained. It came about in this way: A few days after the child's funeral, Ira received a note from Professor St. Joseph, whom he had never met, which read, in part, as follows: "I will be most grateful if you will call at your convenience and tell me all you know concerning the tragic death of the little Palmiller boy. His mother is prostrated with grief, and she has asked me to get this information for her. Any details that you can give, no matter how trivial they may seem to you, will be gratefully received."

Ira said: "I don't think I'll go. I'd only feel out of place with an educated man like Professor St. Joseph asking me questions. I'll write him a letter instead. I'll tell him everything I know that way."

"No," said Fodie decidedly. "No, Ira. You must go and see him like he asks. You can't tell what might come out of it. The Professor goes with the very best people in town. You could do a lot worse than to make a friend out of him. You can't tell how much you might be helped in future by just knowing him."

Ira, feeling self-conscious and out of place, made his call the following night. He was anxious to get away, and he told what he knew as quickly, as simply as he could; but the precision with which he spoke, the exactness with which he remembered each detail, impressed St. Joseph a great deal. Embarrassed, nineteen-year-old boys were nothing unusual in his life: There were many of them that age in high school, and in order to put Ira at his ease, he talked down to him, asking him questions concerning his work, his education and his early life. Ira answered warily. He spoke exclusively of his life in Reedyville, as if nothing had existed for him before that period of his existence. In the course of his talk, he mentioned the fact that he had first seen Rance on the day Wesley Boutwell enlisted, adding that since that time he had often seen both the Palmiller children at his home.

"I didn't realize you knew the boy personally," said St. Joseph. He deliberated a moment and then added fairly: "You have a remarkable memory, and you seem to be a close observer of things.

. . . Now, tell me this: From what you saw of the child, did you consider him mentally unbalanced, as so many people in town are saying now?"

Ira waited so long to answer, his face so set, so suspicious and stolid, that St. Joseph came to the conclusion that the question was beyond him. To save his guest further embarrassment, he added quickly: "I'll take that question back, Ira. It wasn't a fair one to ask, was it? I suppose it's something only a doctor would really be able to answer."

Ira said, in explanation of his long silence: "I was just thinking that everybody must seem crazy if you see deep enough into their minds." He stopped suddenly, as if already he had committed himself too greatly, and pressed his hands together, cracking his knuckles.

"Yes?" said St. Joseph. He waited expectantly, and then added: "There was something else you started to say, but decided not to. What was it, Ira?"

"It wasn't anything very much. It's something that might sound silly to a smart man like you. . . . But what I just said is only a part of the truth, and not even the important part, because it's not how deep you can see into another person's mind that determines what you really know about him: the important thing is what level of your own mind you are able to see him with."

St. Joseph lit a cigarette and looked strangely at the tall, gangling young man with the long, knobby nose, whose voice was so deep, so earnest. "That's a very interesting thought," he said. "You must tell me where you read it."

"I didn't read it anywhere. I didn't have to read it. It's the truth."

St. Joseph's attitude toward the boy changed at once. He wanted to know more about him, much more than Ira, himself, seemed willing to tell; and in order to gain his end, he first talked about himself, of his own individual experiences and thoughts, knowing this was the surest way to win the confidence of another. The boy had meant to leave quickly, but now he found that he could not. He spoke eagerly in his turn, and with no self-consciousness now, for he found St. Joseph so much easier to talk with than anybody he had ever known before. With him, he need explain nothing, apologize for nothing, no matter how odd it sounded. At last St.

Joseph said laughingly: "I think I understand something of your particular philosophy now. You believe that nothing in human behavior is left to chance, don't you? That every act, no matter how trivial, is predetermined in the mind?"

"Yes, sir," said Ira. "I do. What else could I possibly believe?" He felt an enormous confidence in the new friend he had made, and he continued quickly: "There's something else I want to tell you. I've never told it to anybody else, but I'll tell it to you because I know you'll understand it, and because I think you won't repeat it to anybody else." He paused anxiously, eager to make a complete confidant of the man, but doubtful, too, of the wisdom of such an action.

"You can tell me anything you care to, Ira. I won't betray you. That's one thing about me that you may be sure of always."

"I believe you," said Ira slowly. "I really do." He stopped again and then said rapidly: "This will illustrate some of the things I've been saying to you. . . . Nobody in this town knows it, because I've never told it before, but I'm a bastard, and I never knew who my father was. Well, for a long time I wouldn't look a man in the face. I wondered why I wouldn't do it, and then Wesley Boutwell did me a good turn one day, and after that I didn't hate men any more. I was surprised, but afterwards I found I could look straight at men, just as I can look at you right now."

"Yes," said St. Joseph. "What else?"

"You might think I didn't look at grown men because I was ashamed to," said Ira, "but if you do, you'll be wrong. I wouldn't look at men, when I was a little boy, because I was always afraid that if I did, I'd recognize my own father, and that if I did meet him, I'd have to kill because he'd wronged me so. . . . So you see? Not looking at men was sensible after all, although I didn't know why I acted that way. It saved me from getting myself in a lot of bad trouble."

It was time for the boy to go, and as he got up and went to the door, St. Joseph said: "Maybe I'm presumptuous to suggest it, but would you like to be a special pupil of mine? You can come at night, or whenever you're free. I can help you much. I can teach you a great deal."

Ira, who had no ability whatever to dissemble, stood quietly at the door, a distressed look on his face. "I don't know," he said. "I don't know whether that's possible or not."

"You'll learn everything you need to know by yourself," said St. Joseph. "All I can do is to make things a little easier for you." He wondered at the boy's frozen withdrawal, at the quality of cautious, almost animal suspicion which had taken possession of him so suddenly.

"I'm truly obliged to you," said Ira regretfully. "I sure appreciate your wanting to help me out." He sighed and shook his head. "I don't think I can right now," he continued. "I don't believe it's possible the way things are."

He wanted more than anything to see St. Joseph again, for never before had he met a man so stimulating, so full of ideas; but he knew that if he did, he would inevitably tell him about his mother and the revenge he planned to take on her, and as yet he could not bring himself to discuss these shameful things with another — not even a man as cool, as detached as his new friend. He started to speak again, but could not. He merely sighed and rested his hand on the doorknob.

"Don't make up your mind now," said St. Joseph. "Think it over first, and if you decide later to come, just let me know." Then, as Ira opened the door and started down the stairs, he added: "Anyway, I think I can get you a better job than the one you've got now. Your hours will be shorter and you'll have more time to study, if you want to do it alone."

"Yes?" said Ira.

"It's a good thing you know shorthand," said St. Joseph. "I think I can place you in Robert Porterfield's law office. He's always having trouble with his stenographers. He's particular and hard to suit, but maybe you can do the work. If you're interested, I'll speak to him in the next day or two."

"I'd like that very much," said Ira. "Very much indeed."

He went home thinking St. Joseph would forget the matter, since there were so many other things to occupy his mind. He did not even mention it to Fodie, as he did not want her to be disappointed too; but at the end of the week a letter came from Robert Porterfield, written in his own hand, suggesting that Ira call at once for an interview. He went that same day, and as a result of the visit, Robert agreed to take him on trial for a week or so; but long before the probationary period agreed upon was over, he knew that Ira was to become the perfect secretary he had been looking for so long.

It seemed strange that the people of Reedyville generally spoke of Robert as "that little Mr. Porterfield," for he was exactly six feet tall. His hair was thick, straight and dark red — almost the color of polished mahogany. His face was rather long, his nose delicately chiseled and curved. He was the town's outstanding bachelor, and he was considered by local mothers as the perfect mate for any daughter. He was always polite, always smiling, and nobody had ever known him to lose his temper. He had been very successful in his profession, and St. Joseph, his close friend, who admired him greatly, had once said of him: "Robert's mind is so fine, it's a pity it isn't better," which, in a sense, was a perfect summary of the man. There was something of the snob, a little of the prig, beneath his calm, courteous manner, although he would have repudiated such accusations with an amused, easy-going tolerance.

When Ira had been working at his position for some weeks, and was well-established there, Mrs. Palmiller came to the office one afternoon to consult Robert about a matter which troubled her greatly. She had never met Ira, but seeing him at his typewriter in the outer office, and realizing at once who he was, she came to him quickly. She was dressed entirely in black, and a long black veil shrouded her face. When she spoke, she raised her veil, as if this were a courtesy which even the suffering could not deny another.

"I want to thank you," she said. "I've wanted to thank you for some time, but this is the first chance I've had." She took the boy's hand and pressed it in her own. "I shall always be grateful to you," she said. "I shall always remember it was you who — " She broke off and turned, for she was on the verge of tears again. "You understand me, don't you? You understand what it is I'd like to say to you, but cannot?"

Robert, hearing her voice in the outer office, came to his door and spoke. She straightened her veil, pressed the boy's hand once more and moved toward him. They were about the same age, and they had known each other all their lives. "You should have telephoned and made an appointment," he said mildly. "It's just luck that you found me in." She went with him to his private office and sat facing him across the desk. "You don't know how sorry I was to hear about your boy," he continued. "I'd like to say something to you to make it easier, but I suppose there's nothing anybody can say."

"There is nothing," said Cindy. "Nothing."

He looked at her with sympathy in his eyes. They had been childhood sweethearts, and he had taken her to the school dances and parties as a matter of course in the days before she had known Hubert Palmiller. He had always loved her, and her sudden marriage when he was in law school had left him feeling weak and perplexed; but he had never mentioned his affection for her afterwards, preferring to let both her and the town consider it something which he had long since outgrown. He lowered his eyes self-consciously and fumbled at the onyx inkstand on his desk, thinking how attractive she still was, how little she had changed.

Cindy pressed her gloved hands together and spoke rapidly: "What I'm going to say may sound foolish to you, Robert, but it means a great deal to me. It's about the slab which my husband had put over the child's grave. He had carved on it the fact that Rance killed himself. '*By His Own Hand*,' is the precise wording . . . That was so cruel of him, Robert! So cruel, and so unnecessary!"

"Yes," said Robert. "It was cruel and needless."

"It's unjust, too," said Cindy. "I should have found some way to prevent my son's death. I blame myself for it. I really do. If he had put on it, '*By His Mother's Hand*,' I couldn't have objected. I could only have said, 'Yes, it's quite true! I can't deny it, even if the knowledge breaks my heart!' "

Robert moved toward her and sat on the arm of her chair. He took her hand and held it, stroking her black glove with his thumb. "Cindy! Cindy!" he said. "Please don't! Please don't say such things! I've heard all the things which have been said in this town, and nobody has blamed you. Not one. Everybody agrees that you were a fine mother to the boy."

"I was so stupid," she continued. "I should have known so much more than I did. I should have understood him better. . . . Is it fair for the pitiful little boy to be scorned now merely because his mother was too silly to understand him?" She got up and walked toward the bookshelves, speaking with her back to him. "This is what I want to consult you about," she began rapidly. "Has Mr. Palmiller the right to put such a thing on Rance's tombstone? If he has the right, then haven't I the same right to have the stone taken away — to have another put in its place?"

He stared at his hands for an instant, then resting against his desk, he said harshly: "Move it anyway! Put whatever you want in its place!"

She sat in one of his big, red leather chairs and pressed her handkerchief to her eyes, not daring to speak. He came to her at once, and stood beside her. "Poor Cindy!" he said gently. Then he added: "Don't tell anybody what you mean to do. Have the stone that you want lettered the way you want it. When it's ready, let me know, and I'll see that the substitution is made. If Hubert tries to have his slab put back, we'll get a court order preventing it. We'll put the burden on him." He sighed and walked to the window, looking down at the traffic in Court House Square. "You look so small and helpless in mourning," he said. "Really I can't stand to see you suffering so much."

When she had gone, he sat again at his desk, thinking of the past and of the life they might have had together. He sat there so quietly, so absorbed in his thoughts, that at last Ira knocked on his door to remind him that there were clients waiting to see him in the outer office. But he felt disturbed at the visit, and he wanted to be alone that evening, to see nobody. "Please call St. Joseph," he said. "Tell him I won't be able to see him this evening. Tell him I'm not feeling entirely well."

Ira saw St. Joseph often during the following weeks, and each time he saw him, he wondered if he had offended him by his refusal. He wanted deeply to take advantage of the professor's offer, but the idea alarmed him a little too, for he knew that with St. Joseph his last reticences would be broken down; that he would tell him those things which he had determined to tell nobody. Fodie had never understood the real goal of his ambition, but St. Joseph, he knew instinctively, would understand these things at once, and while he would make no effort to prevent the revenge which seemed so important to Ira, he would not approve of it.

The working-plan of his retaliation, which already had begun to shape itself on the day he arrived in Reedyville, had now taken its final form, its details worked out with precise attentiveness, each small contingency anticipated and provided for. Of late, as the time for its accomplishment came nearer, he thought of it almost constantly, and often he found it difficult to concentrate on those undramatic, everyday matters which had no place in the larger detail of his vengeance.

He had left his old quarters at the Boutwells, and Fodie, after a methodical search, had engaged a room for him at Mrs. Furness' boarding house, since she considered this establishment the most respectable, the most genteel in town. At first he had not wanted to move, seeing no need for it, but Fodie had insisted and he had acceded to her wishes, as he acceded, at length, to every demand she made upon him.

Her reasons for the move had been both precise and explicit: Now that they were to be married, she said, and could no longer be considered children by any stretch of the imagination, she felt that it was both unwise and immodest for a young man to live under the same roof with his prospective bride. The people of Reedyville had long memories, and she did not mean to have the solid respectability of her future endangered by some old bit of unresolved gossip. Then, too, he had to break away sometime from the Boutwell environment, if she was to follow him as she expected to do, and she took the move as a favorable sign, the first step forward in a procession of moves which was to lead them both to Reedy Avenue at last, to a life of solid worth in the house she planned for their comfort. Later on, Ira was glad, too, that the move had been made, for it gave him more freedom in the working out of his plan, solving automatically some of its more baffling factors.

His plan was quite simple, and it was this: Since his mother had not only been the instrument of his degradation, but had, by her abandonment of him, acknowledged to all that he meant nothing to her, he intended to visit her house on the day he was twenty-one years old, and a man in his own right: to see her for the first time in his remembered existence not as a son, but as a paying client, like any of the others she entertained so indiscriminately.

For a while he considered the possibility of revealing himself to her at the end of his visit — carelessly, at the moment he left her house; later, he knew that this would be a false note, a touch of the

theater at once sentimental and in bad taste. Whether she knew or
did not know his identity was a thing of no essential importance
insofar as his own purpose was concerned. He, at least, would know
well enough who he was, and that knowledge, he felt, would be
sufficient. His mere presence, his right to buy his way into her
house, would serve his need with no further elaboration, would say
to his spirit with as great an effectiveness whether his mother knew
his actual identity or did not know it: "See me now! You thought
of me as something too shameful to acknowledge, didn't you? You
wanted me to die quickly, just as the others did, so you wouldn't
have to face my existence. But I wasn't destroyed, after all, as you
can see for yourself! I've even pulled myself up in the world, and
what's more, I'm going a great deal higher — and with no thanks
to you!"

He felt that he must not confront his mother as one of the local
young sports of Reedyville, for that would be too simple somehow,
too obvious — but as some distinguished gentleman passing through
the town, whose whim dictated his visit: a foreign gentleman of great
distinction preferably, one far superior to the clients she was accustomed to seeing. This question of the identity he was to assume
before his mother was the first important problem which he had
had to work out, and in the beginning he had considered the possibility of being an Englishman for the occasion. He rejected the idea
almost immediately, considering it too trite, too lacking in a sense
of either the alien or the romantic. A Parisian was much better, but
since he did not speak French, an accomplishment which even the
dullest would expect a Frenchman to possess, and since Violet generally had at least one girl in her house from New Orleans, who
could catch him in his elaborate lie so easily, he gave up that idea
too. The solution to his problem came to him unexpectedly one
morning at the moment he woke from a long, troubled dream,
and instantly he wondered how it had been possible for him to
have considered anything else.

He knew, now, that he must visit his mother as a gentleman
from Prague — a young man who was finishing his education with
a tour of the United States. He would not say outright that he was
a nobleman, but if the question were to be asked him by Violet or
one of her girls, he would not deny it either. He would only smile,

raise his finger warningly, and change the conversation. Then, as he washed his face in Mrs. Furness' decorated, china basin, seeing the distorted pink roses imprinted on its bottom pull loose from their background and waver up at him through the water, he recalled the few facts he knew about Prague: that it was an ancient city in Bohemia — perhaps the capital; that its population was above the half million mark, and that it had been built on two sides of a river.

He pressed his head deeper into the flowered bowl, then, shaking the water from his eyes, he dried his face and hands carefully, thoughtfully. "But why Prague?" he thought. "There must be some other reason why that place is important for me! I wonder what it can be." He sat down to tie his shoes, and almost at once he remembered what it was he wanted: —

Years before, when he had been very young indeed, a lady from the village had come to his grandmother's house to buy eggs, and while Hannah was gathering them for her, the visitor had told Ira a story concerning a porcelain stove which existed somewhere in the famous city of Prague. It was a stove with magical qualities, and it had come by chance into the possession of a boy whose circumstances were so much like his own; and afterwards the little foreign boy had only to make a wish, and there waiting for him in the oven was the thing he had longed for. The stove was still somewhere in Prague, the lady said. It was lost again, but that was only for the time being. It would be found once more. Of that he could be sure.

He finished dressing and went down to breakfast with a sense of relief. The problem of who he was to be was now settled; but another problem, the problem of what a gentleman from Prague would wear on such an occasion as he planned, automatically took its place. This new dilemma of dress was to be solved only a few days afterwards, when he noticed for the first time an old, fly-specked chart which hung on the back wall of the Crown Barbershop.

The chart was composed of a series of gracefully arranged ovals, and in each of them there was a tinted picture of a most elegant gentleman, whose purpose was to model his preferred type of haircut, and who was dressed appropriately for the profession he represented. The first of the ovals was labeled "Conservative," and it showed rather a stern old man with white chin whiskers and a heavy gold chain stretched across his pearl-buttoned vest. The gentleman in the second oval resembled John Wilkes Booth a great deal and, appropriately enough, he was labeled "Artistic." His hair, which appeared to have been outside the province of barbers for many years, hung almost to his shoulders, but it had been curled and turned up at its ends by a professional hand, as anybody could see if he looked closely enough.

Ira gazed attentively at these first two figures, but finding them so different from anything which he himself could ever hope to be, he let his eyes drift downward, examining in slow succession "Capitalist," "Handsome," "Gentleman About Town" — who occupied the spot of honor, a larger oval in the center of ovals — "Athletic," "Dude," and "Ladies' Favorite." When he had seen them all, his eyes went back to "Gentleman About Town." He examined him again more thoughtfully, recording in his mind each detail of the man's costume. He was wearing full evening dress, with a cape lined in scarlet draped languidly over his shoulders. In one hand he held white gloves and a high hat; the other hand was stretched forward in welcome to somebody outside the picture. He ended abruptly above his ankles, the oval frame cutting off his feet, and as Ira stood there examining him with such minute care, he wondered what kind of shoes a gentleman of this sort wore. Then, practically, he came to the conclusion that shoes were probably optional, since otherwise the artist would have considered it necessary to show them too.

At the time he made these important decisions, he was a full year from his twenty-first birthday, but he assembled his clothes with care, in secret, and at last everything was in readiness. It was at this time that he added one final touch to his plans, a detail which made the purpose of his visit more explicit and more subtle, for he decided not only to call on his mother on the day when he became a man in his own right, but to enter her door at the precise moment of his birth as well. He knew both the hour and the minute of that event, for they had been impressed on his mind forever by a thing he had heard his grandmother say to Mr. Kingman while in his store one day. She had finished her shopping and Ira was obediently picking up the parcels when the afternoon train passed. At once she had put her fingers to her ears and had said: "There goes the 2:20, right on time, and whistling for the crossing like it was plumb crazy. I can't abide that train whistle, nohow! It sounded that-a-way on the day my daughter had her baby, and I don't know which of them was a-squealing the loudest, her or the locomotive! Then when the train passed the crossing and took out down the road toward Duncan, my daughter's bastard popped out, and for a second or so there was all three of them making a racket together!"

Ira's birthday came on a Wednesday that year, and long in advance of that day, he had asked Mr. Porterfield to give him the afternoon off. When the day arrived at length, he came to work earlier than usual, typing furiously all that morning in an effort to crush the nervousness from his hands and feet. He hoped nothing would happen to defeat his plans, and promptly at noon he got up, closed his desk and went to his room. He tried to eat something, but he could not; then, after he had waited awhile in an effort to compose himself, he took a cold bath and looked out of his window, watching Mrs. Furness' cook decapitating the chickens which she meant to cook for dinner that night; but when the clock on the courthouse struck for one o'clock, he began to dress; and at ten minutes before two he was hurrying down the back stairs, hoping that nobody was watching him. He had planned each move, and he went promptly to the corner at Millwall Street, where he had ordered a cab to wait for him. He got into the cab and said: "Drive in the direction of the depot. I'll tell you later where to go from there."

He sank back against the cushions, glad that everything had gone according to plan, and after he had passed the section of town where he was likely to be recognized easily, some of his nervousness disappeared; then he sat up again and leaned forward, for there, crossing the street ahead of the lumbering cab, was The Goodwife of Death herself. Seeing her there ahead of him, her lips moving, but without sound, her dark eyes half-veiled and fainting with passion, he recalled one of her more dramatic oddities, a singularity often discussed by the people of the town, and it was this: As she went about her task of preparing the dead for burial, she would, at some place in her work, stop and look searchingly into the waxen face below her. Then, furtively, she would bend lower, and when her lips were even with the ear of the dead, she would whisper some intense message into it, her eyes moving seductively at such times in their sockets, her hands making tiny, impassioned gestures of surrender.

Most of the people of Reedyville dismissed this small ritual as a thing of no importance. It was only something she did, they maintained — a habit like any other. Ada Boutwell belonged to this school of thought. "I guess everybody talks to theirself, sometime or another," she had said. "She's just acting the way all lonely old people act. There ain't nothing else to it, so far as I can see."

St. Joseph was of the opinion that she, understanding the plight of the dead, and wanting to make their strangeness less frightening, whispered words of encouragement to them. Minnie McInnis McMinn maintained that she gave the dead their first important instructions in the etiquette of death — instructing, advising and counseling her charges. Robert Porterfield, being a lawyer and more practical, was convinced that she rendered an account of her stewardship to her husband. . . . But as Ira Graley watched the demented old woman as she stepped onto the sidewalk and looked upward toward the sky, a sense of strange, nervous prescience came over him, and it seemed to him at that moment that all the guesses which others had made were wrong: That the things the Goodwife whispered into the ears of the dead were only her own erotic and babbling avowals of passion, and that she believed her words imprinted themselves on the spongy platen of the recipient brain she addressed, to remain there, secure and unblurred beneath the bony envelope of the protecting skull, until her husband took his victim at last, and then, at his bidding, the bloodless lips of the dead opened again to repeat voluptuously the hushed sentences of her love.

Ira shuddered at that moment and leaned forward to speak to the driver. "Forget about the depot," he said harshly. "Drive me straight to Mattress May's house."

Beyond the railroad station, not far from the place where the Nellohas had once had their store, was a short street, called inexplicably New April Avenue. It was lined with cheap stores, rooming houses and small factories, but at its end, in a gray house from which the sun had long since blistered most of the paint, a house which tried to hide its barrenness in a thicket of crape-myrtle trees, Violet Wynn lived surrounded by her girls.

The driver stopped at the door, and Ira, in the interval before he stepped down to the pavement, glanced once more at his shoes. He wondered again if they were quite right for his evening clothes. Not knowing what "Gentleman About Town" wore on his feet, he had bought a pair of expensive, lemon-yellow Oxfords, since they had been advertised in the *Courier* as the choice of fashionable gentlemen everywhere. . . . But there was nothing to be done about it now, and he sighed and looked at his watch. Everything had worked out perfectly, and he went up the steps at once and nervously rang his mother's bell.

It was precisely 2:19, and Violet, having just finished her breakfast, was yawning widely over Mrs. McMinn's society column in the *Courier,* when Lizzie, her maid, came in the back parlor to tell her that a peculiar young gentleman had asked for her personally, and was now waiting in the reception hall. "He talk funny," she continued. "Like a Frenchman maybe, but not exactly. He's a foreign gentleman I expect, but he ain't like nothing we ever had in the house before."

Violet put down the *Courier* petulantly, with regret. "What's he thinking of — coming so early?" she asked. "Why didn't he come at sunup and be done with it?" She was flabbily stout, and like all night workers, her skin was a dead, unshaded white. Her hair had been dyed so often that it had assumed the color and texture of straw which had been subjected to intense heat. She had had no chance to dress it that morning, and it was still piled high on her head from last night, while a fat, artificial curl, even yellower than the base to which it was pinned, hung half-detached above her crepy, blue-veined shoulder. She got up, went to one of her numerous peepholes, and stared out at her visitor.

There was one thing which Ira had not taken into consideration when making his plans, and that was his mother's experience. She placed his type at once, and with great accuracy, saying to herself: "He's never been in a place of this sort in his life. He hasn't even been with a woman yet." Such young men were usually ashamed of their innocence, and she knew that well, but rarely had she seen one who went to such pains to conceal it. "Hand me my boudoir cap," she said to Lizzie. "I won't bother to fix my hair." Then, smoothing out her negligee, and opening the top buttons so that her

breasts — which had always been considered her best features —
were only partly concealed, she parted the curtains and went out to
meet her son. "I'm Violet Wynn," she said. "You wanted to see me?"
She smiled ingratiatingly and rolled her eyes a little, but under-
neath she kept thinking: "I don't like him. There's something
about him that makes me sick. But then I never could stand the
little show-offs that come here."

Ira did not answer at once, for his mother, in reality, had been
so different from his expectations that the cynical words he had
meant to say to her seemed no longer appropriate. He had pictured
her as being younger and more attractive: more like the actresses
whose photographs he saw in magazines. He had expected to find a
quality of stimulating depravity in her, a sense of exciting sinful-
ness, but as the afternoon sun fell squarely upon her puffed, chalk-
like face and shoulders, picking out, and accentuating, the beer
stains on her shoddy, pink negligee, revealing its cheap, elaborate
lace, its soiled, ruffled train, in complete detail, she seemed not
sinister to him, but pathetic and rather repellent instead. When his
eyes had taken in each detail of her appearance, he turned his head
away, thinking: "I wouldn't want to touch her. Not even with my
hands."

He took off his scarlet-lined cloak and threw it over the back
of a chair, while she stood there in the sunlight facing him, yawning, in spite of herself, behind her bleached, ringed fingers: looking
even older than her years — frowsy and bedraggled and with the
sleep not yet out of her eyes. She was hardened to scrutiny, and she
stared back at her son with complete unconcern, noting the distaste
in his eyes, but not caring. Reactions of this sort were common-
places. You pleased some, she argued; some you did not please.
It was no importance one way or the other, but she felt, nevertheless,
a sense of resentment against her visitor for other reasons: "What
right has he got to come here cold-sober, and in broad daylight?"
she asked herself. Then, feeling that her personal feelings had no
place in her work, she smiled with professional exactness, moved
toward him, and said: "You looking for a girl? You come down
here to get your palm read?"

"Yiss," he said with the accent he had rehearsed so thoroughly.
"Yiss, *Madame*, I theenk zo."

She invited him into the back parlor, and when he had seated himself on the fringed, tapestry sofa, she came closer and sat opposite him on a straight-back chair, knowing that she was now too plump to sit on a sofa effectively. He had mastered his initial embarrassment, and with no encouragement whatever from his hostess, he talked volubly of his life in the capitals of Europe. "I come too soon, yiss?" he asked. "You must pardon me very much. In my country it is not thees way." He lit a cigarette in what he hoped was the manner of "Man About Town," but his hand still shook with nervousness, and Violet, pretending not to notice, went to the door, answering him over her shoulder as she walked: "Well, different countries, different ways of doing business — as the fellow says." Then, pulling her body together with determination, she called out shrilly: "Lizzie! Lizzie! What's keeping the young ladies? . . . And tell Miss Ella I want to see her, too."

She stood there expectantly at the door, her toe tapping the carpet, and in that interval, as he examined his mother more impersonally, Ira knew that no matter what else her life had been, it had not been happy and it had not been luxurious: that existence had been as hard, as bitterly won, for her as it had been for himself. Some of the certainty went out of him at that instant. He felt a sense of depression, knowing that his plans had somehow gone wrong. The resentment, the hatred which he had nourished all these years, seemed a little pointless after all, of no essential importance; and he wondered, at last, why he had considered this elaborate visit to his mother of any particular significance. He wanted to get up and leave, but he had committed himself too greatly to retreat now, and so he only sat farther back on the sofa, cracked his knuckles nervously and glanced about the room.

Violet spoke suddenly: "I don't know what's keeping my girls. It looks like they get lazier every day." With her head turned from her visitor, she need make no effort to hide the boredom in her face, and for that she was grateful. She had already made up her mind about her guest: If he had money, and was willing to spend it — well and good! She'd make the best of the situation. But if he didn't, she'd get rid of him quickly enough! She had a headache from last night, and her feet hurt her, as they always did so early in the morning, before she got settled down on them. At this moment she asked nothing more from life than to stretch out on

the tapestry sofa and finish reading Minnie McInnis McMinn's society news in that morning's copy of the *Courier;* but knowing it
was impossible with a guest to entertain, she came back to her chair,
sat down and said: "How about buying a drink? I think I could
stand something right now."

She spread her legs wide and let her body sag downward from
throat to ankles, and Ira, gazing at her critically, thought that there
was nothing so depressing as the shabby old age of things which
were shoddy to begin with; but he turned toward her with a false
animation and said: "I will gladly buy you drinks. It is a celebration
for me. My twenty-first birthday." He waited an instant, alert to
note any reaction to his words, for, after all, she too had participated
in the event which he considered memorable. But if she remembered
anything, her face did not show it. She merely reached up and
detached the fat, pressing curl which hung above her shoulder,
hiding it, self-consciously, under a sofa pillow, where it could not
be seen.

Hearing steps on the stairs outside, she said in exasperation:
"Lizzie! Lizzie! How many times do I have to call you? . . . The
gentleman is buying drinks for the whole house. Ask the ladies
what they'll take." She looked about her helplessly and added:
"Where's Miss Ella? Did you tell her I wanted to see her right
away?"

"Miss Ella'll be here directly," said Lizzie. "I had to wake her
up, but she 'bout ready now."

Violet breathed deeply, with relief. Perhaps this young man would
want to trade after his drinks had given him more courage, and
if he did, Ella was the perfect companion for him. She was patient,
co-operative and willing, and she expected nothing at all from life,
having been discouraged, years ago, not by a lack of love, but by
too great an abundance of it.

Three of the girls came in just then and Violet introduced them.
"This is Lottie," she said. "She's a fine, stately blonde, isn't she?
. . . And this is Jeannie, a little lady from New Orleans." She decided not to introduce the third girl, who seemed on the point of
going back to sleep at any moment; instead, she half-turned to the
door once more and repeated: "Where's Ella? Why don't Ella come
down?"

Ella came in at that moment, looking fresh and rested and ready for any emergency. She was dressed in a lacy, yellow kimono, and she said gaily: "Here I am! Who's calling me?" Violet sighed and pressed her friend's hand. Ella was one in a thousand, she thought. You could depend on her. She wasn't like these young girls who had neither pride in their profession nor faith in themselves. Violet called her "my utility infielder," and Ella, when they talked over their past together, after they had had a few warming drinks, would laugh good-naturedly and say: "That's me all right! An old utility infielder! Not quick enough for the regular nine, but carried along with the team anyway, because I can play any position in a pinch." Then she and Violet would go off into peals of laughter, remembering old jokes, old situations which they had shared.

They were about the same age, and they had known each other almost from the beginning of their public careers. They had met first in Pensacola, in Lily Sampson's house, and their names had been linked together in an oddly amusing way. At that time Ella was participating in a tableau of passion which one of Lily's clients arranged each week with clocklike precision — a little scene which, with no elaboration, fulfilled his deep, erotic desires. The blueprint of his pleasure was simple but precise, and Ella, who played the principal role, must be dressed for these occasions in a long black robe; then, with her face whitened with chalk, she was required to simulate death on a black-draped couch.

It seemed a part simple enough to cast, but Lily had not found this to be true in practice. The girls who had attempted it before Ella took it over had each brought an individual interpretation to the role, adding, as a bit of realism of their own, a staring eye or a suddenly relaxed and gaping jaw. But Ella, everybody had agreed, was ideal; and as soon as she met Violet she suggested her for the bit part, since the girl who had formerly played it had come down with an attack of screaming hysterics. "You're like me," she said. "You're not nervous. You'll be good. . . . Now, all you got to do is stand by the window dressed in black. But you mustn't speak and you mustn't move, no matter what happens."

On that first occasion, when the gentleman came into the dimly lighted, flower-decked room, Violet had examined him stealthily from the corners of her eyes, surprised somehow to find him young, powerfully built and handsome. At first he stood against the door for a full minute, then, making a moaning noise, he walked slowly

toward Ella's unmoving body. He stood above her for a time, weeping passionately, and then, taking a rosebud from her hand without
once touching her flesh, he left the room abruptly, without so
much as a backward glance.

"Is that all?" asked Violet in astonishment. "Is that all there is
to it?"

Ella moved over, and the two girls sat together on the couch,
laughing until they were weak. "My God!" said Ella. "My God!
If there's anything funnier than love, I don't want to know about
it!"

Violet, remembering these old things from the past, looked up
at Ella and shook her head, thinking: "In this business you got to
be prepared for surprises. You learn something new every day."
Then, hearing one of her girls speaking, she brought herself back
to reality again.

"I bet you got a funny name," said Lottie. "I bet it's something
an American can't even pronounce good."

Ira took a new ten-dollar bill from his wallet, crumpled it into a
ball and tossed it upon the floor. "My name is on ziss, maybe.
Would you like to see for yourself?" The girls stared at the money
with a hostile, suspicious look, as if they had all agreed to ignore the
insult; and then, when he thought nobody was going to touch it
after all, his mother, Ella and the three girls scrambled for it at
once. Violet got to it first, and tucked the bill safely under her garter.
She was beginning to like this young man, and she said more
cordially: "Hurry up and bring us another round of drinks, Lizzie!
The Duke here is flush and feeling his oats!"

He bought drinks three times for the house, and then his mother,
who was warming up into geniality, said: "Why don't you ask Ella
to take you upstairs and show you what makes a clock tick?" Ira
smiled and said in what he hoped would be a sophisticated voice:
"That is agreeable. I bow to *Madame's* choice."

Ella nudged Lizzie in the ribs and said in a whisper: "The old
infielder on the job again! I get the ones just out of the cradle that
don't know any better, and the ones stepping down to the grave,
who don't care no more what happens to them." Then, seductively,
she approached Ira and said: "Come on up with me now. You don't
have to worry about anything. We run a clean house here."

When he came down the stairs again, the girls had gone back to their rooms, but his mother was waiting in the back parlor, facing the door. She met him at the foot of the stairs and stood there, the *Chronicle* in her hand, looking up at her son. He had anticipated this final scene, and, taking a twenty-dollar bill from his pocket, he waved it insolently beneath her nose. Then before she knew what his intention was, he pulled her toward him and thrust the bill contemptuously down the back of her negligee. "Here's a little present for you," he said distinctly, making no effort, now, to keep up his foreign accent. "A souvenir of my visit to the Land of the Free."

His mother gasped and giggled with delight, wriggling with an exaggerated motion of her hips, so that the money would drop onto the floor, where she could pick it up. She was feeling well disposed indeed toward this young man. Peculiar or not peculiar; experienced or inexperienced in the ways of the world, he was certainly free with his money, and Violet found it difficult to harbor resentment against anybody who gave her good American cash.

"You come back and see me sometime soon," she said warmly. "I'm sorry things got off to a slow start, but we don't generally have early callers, except maybe on a Saturday. But you let me know in advance next time, and we'll be ready for you."

"I don't think so," said Ira. "I'm leaving tonight."

He turned at the door for one last look at his mother, knowing that he would never see her again. Now that he had met her and talked with her, she seemed even stranger, even more unreal than she had before. He knew, now, that none of the things which he had thought or imagined about her were of the slightest importance, and at that moment he wanted only to get away as quickly as possible. Later, he entered his room at Mrs. Furness' and took off his grotesque clothes, looking at them with distaste, wondering what series of events had prompted his incredible action. It seemed to him as he lay stretched on his bed, watching the patterns of sunlight on the wall before him, that he was ready, now, to enter a new land of reality, a place of substance rather than of reflected shadow: that everything he had thought or done in the past had been significant only as a preparation for this larger, richer life he anticipated — this new existence which lay so teasingly in the future, so tantalizingly beyond the grasp of his eager, outthrust hand.

He got up from the bed and dressed once more in his ordinary clothes, remembering there was much filing to be done at the office, work which, in his impatience to get away, he had neglected to do. Nobody expected him back, and the work could easily wait, but all at once he wanted to return to his desk, to complete all the things he had avoided.

When he arrived at the office, he saw at once that Robert had a client with him, and as he came into the small filing-room, he realized the visitor was Mrs. McMinn, hearing her voice plainly through the half-open door to the chamber beyond. She had just completed her novel, *Shattered Roses,* and she wanted to read certain parts of it aloud to Robert, ostensibly to determine whether or not they were libelous, but in reality — since nothing would have suited her more than a big damage suit — to see the mocking admiration in his eyes and to hear him say: "I think you're wonderful, Minnie! Absolutely wonderful!"

Ira sat down at the pine table and sorted the letters at the moment Minnie said: "Now listen to this part, Robert! Listen carefully! . . . It's my little heroine speaking to the committee who have her on trial." She cleared her throat, lowered the shade a trifle and read dramatically: "You may imprison me, you may heap every manner of shame upon me, but in my own eyes I have not sinned, for a woman's love is like a crystal stream. Flowing. Free. . . . It reflects in an opalescent glow the face of the worshiper who kneels in adoration above it, speechless before the eternal mystery of the feminine, as he bends in reverence and sips its honeyed sweetness. A woman's love flows limpid through the mire of daily living. Clean. Pure . . . And so I say to you who sit in judgment upon me, that my sin, if sin it be in your eyes, is only that my woman-heart was my undoing! . . . But has not a heart too gentle been the undoing of my sex since time began? . . ."

And Ira, listening there in the filing-room to the high-flown language of Mrs. McMinn's heroine, put down his pencil and rested his head anxiously against the table. The aftereffects of his visit to his mother, which he had hoped to escape through a concentration on tangible, ordinary matters, seemed very close to him now, and he got up hurriedly and began opening and shutting the drawers before him with no discernible purpose behind his nervous hands.

For a time, as he stood there making his senseless, disturbed gestures, he was aware, in the deep, hidden parts of his mind, of the unnumbered ones who had lived before him: those who, like himself, had believed their unique identities the precise core of the universe, who had desired so greatly to imprint their own images against the surface of the world on which they moved and breathed. They had longed greatly and they had struggled with desperation; and yet the sum of all their lives together was now of less importance than a dinosaur's foot on a river bottom, or a fern leaf imbedded in coal.

He came back to the table and sat down, thinking that if man could only feel the immensity of time, could accept the unimportance of his own small part in it, he might plan his life with less arrogance and shape it more intelligently. He picked up his pencil and went on with his work, endeavoring to banish these thoughts from his mind, but he could not. Mrs. McMinn's crisp voice came through the half-open door again. She was saying: —

"Now, listen to this part, Robert! Listen carefully and tell me exactly what you think about it." She centered her handbag in her lap, sat back in her chair, and read: "And now, gentlemen, since that is what you call yourselves, do with me what you will. No pain you can inflict upon me can match the pain of my broken faith; no humiliation can equal the humiliation I feel at this moment, knowing that the one I love, the one to whom I entrusted my innocence and my honor, has not proven worthy of the sacred trust."

Ira went to the door and closed it, shutting off the flow of Mrs. McMinn's romance. He walked up and down the small room, no longer making an effort to defeat his emotions; and then an inexplicable but encompassing moment of revelation came to him — one of those flashes of inner knowledge which were to prove of such value to him later in life, clarifying, as they did, and making easier his patient work among the perverted, the criminal and the insane. Later, he came to welcome these moments of deep disclosure; but now, not knowing what was happening to him, he caught his breath and pressed his hands together, feeling that man had drowned himself in a looking-glass which had neither softness nor depth; that he valued, in reality, only that image of himself which he projected so earnestly onto others: the image which, when he needed it, he rediscovered with ingenuous cries of pleasure. This ability to value himself alone had been at once the symbol of his power, and the measuring stick of his defeat, for he had tripped at last and had broken his neck in a senseless effort to embrace his shadow.

He put away the work he had meant to do and came into the outer office, knowing at that moment that he must see St. Joseph again. This was the best time to find him at home, this period of late afternoon, and Ira knew that well. St. Joseph had an apartment in the Porterfield house, with a separate entrance of his own, and when Ira reached the place and rang the bell, the professor answered after a moment. He was getting ready to take his bath, and the water could be heard running in the tub. He tied his bathrobe about him, smiled and said, with no surprise at all in his voice, as if he had always known the boy would come back one of these days: "Come in, Ira. Please sit down. I'm very glad to see you again."

Ira said: "Teach me! Teach me! I'm mean and ignorant!"

St. Joseph looked at the boy intently, wondering what had happened to him; then, casually, he nodded his head and said: "Of course. Of course I will." Then, seeing how disturbed the boy was, he went back into his bathroom, to give his guest a chance to calm himself. "Do you read German?" he asked after a moment. "There are some things being written in German which should interest you a great deal."

"I'll learn it, Professor. I'll do whatever you tell me to."

St. Joseph turned off the faucet, bent above the tub and tested the temperature of the water with his finger. "This is the second exceptional person I've had a chance to teach," he thought. "I mustn't make any mistakes this time, as I did with Rance Palmiller." He came back into the room, thinking: "But they are so different in temperament. Rance was all mind. This young man is all feeling."

After he left St. Joseph, Ira went to see Fodie Boutwell. He told her that she must marry him that night or never at all. She grumbled, saying that she was not prepared, that such an early marriage upset her plans; but feeling the new stubbornness in him, she gave in at last and they were married that night in Ada's cluttered parlor.

That had been in 1906, and from the beginning Fodie had been vaguely dissatisfied with her husband, for it seemed to her that he now had no ambition at all in the conventional, material sense of the word — the sense which she understood, and had hoped to encourage. She became more shrewish, more strident, as she saw her plans getting further and further from fulfillment. She nagged her husband a great deal, making his life miserable.

On the night when Wesley fell from the culvert, they were in the tenth year of their marriage, and when Dover approached their house, he saw that they were sitting on the front porch. As usual, they were quarreling. He came closer, hearing his sister say in her thin, bitter voice: —

"I can't understand a man like you, and I'll say it again and again. If you'd only apply yourself more, there's no telling what you might accomplish. You could have studied law and passed the State bar examinations, with all the pull Mr. Porterfield has got. . . . Or if you'd only listened to me, and gone to work in the bank for Mr. Palmiller six years ago, like you had a chance to do, you might have worked your way up to be a cashier by this time."

"I know," said Ira. "You've been over all that a thousand times."

"But oh, no!" continued Fodie. "You must always keep your long nose stuck in a book! But it's never the right book, I notice! . . . Why can't you forget all that foolishness you study? What are you aiming at, anyway? What do you hope to accomplish?"

"I'm trying to understand some of the complexities of the mind," said Ira patiently. "Do you consider that so foolish?"

"What's there to understand?" she asked. She was losing her temper again, and Dover, deciding that this was no time to make his presence known, stepped around the corner where he could not be seen. Fodie's voice rose a little and she demanded angrily: "What's there to understand about a person's mind that everybody don't know already?"

Ira laughed in spite of himself and said: "I find you incredibly stupid, my dear!"

His words angered her even more, and she said: "It ought to be the other way round: Somebody ought to be studying *your* mind!

Everybody in town says you're cracked. Even Mama thinks you're not quite right in the head. She said so just the other day!"

"She's an authority on such matters, too," said Ira. "That's what makes it so hard for me to bear."

"You're just a common loafer without any ambition to advance yourself," said Fodie. "That's what I think about you. . . . You waste your time on foolishness, instead of working and trying to make something out of yourself, like other men do."

Ira got up and walked to the door. He stood there a moment, as if making up his mind, and then he said distinctly: "I think we've reached the end of the road. It's time for us to break up. I intended to wait a few months longer, but it might as well be now as any other time."

Fodie, who had not anticipated this, stared at him in surprise. "What are you talking about?" she asked. "You must be out of your head completely." Then, understanding the import of his words, she began to cry; and Ira, watching her square face, her jutting, triangular teeth, knew, at last, what she had reminded him of all these years: That her face was like the cowcatcher on a locomotive, and that it came rushing at you, hurling everything from its path without discrimination. "You might as well stop," he said gently. "I've made up my mind, and it's not possible for you to exploit my gratitude or my sense of guilt any longer."

Fodie, without answering, got up and went into the house. Ira followed her slowly, pausing a moment in the door to look about him. Then, turning and speaking to her in the darkness, with no anger at all in his voice, he continued: "It will be better for us both this way. I intend to turn over everything I have to you. . . . You're only thirty. You still have time to meet the kind of man you want and to be happy with him." A little later he went into the house, turned on the light and began to assemble the things he meant to take away with him.

Dover waited a moment longer, watching the chair which his sister had quitted so abruptly rocking back and forth from the momentum of her vanished body. When it came completely to rest, he wiped his hot face with his sleeve, examined an abrasion on his heel, and then turned resolutely in the direction of Minnie McInnis McMinn's cottage on the west side of town.

Chapter 7

‖‖

‖‖‖MINNIE McINNIS
McMinn had been betrayed into an unpleasant marriage, not by
her good heart, as she maintained so aggressively, but by her bad
ear. That, at least, had been the joking opinion of St. Joseph, and
once, in elaboration of his theme, he had said: "When a literary
maiden named Minnie McInnis comes in contact with a gentleman
called Morgan McMinn, union is inevitable! It's merely alliteration
claiming another of its small victories: it's the trap into which the
stylist who prides herself on an avoidance of the mixed metaphor
invariably falls."

She had met her husband during her first year on the *Courier,*
and although they had lived together for three full, distressing years,
all she remembered of him after their divorce was that he had had
a triangular mole at the base of his spine, and that he shaped his
heavy, black eyebrows with a razor, in the way that some men shape
a mustache. He had been weak, lazy and rather dishonest, and,
although she would have denied it with indignation, he was the
only type of man it was possible for her to love.

Mr. McMinn, it seemed, had been as disillusioned by marriage
as his wife, and, standing before the bar at the Magnolia Hotel, he
told his side of the story with an engaging lack of reticence. "That
woman I had the bad luck to marry!" he would say. "I swear to
God I don't understand the first thing about her! She blames me
for everything that happens. She's always talking about woman's
humiliating role in marriage! . . . All right! All right! But am I
responsible for that? . . . The way that woman goes on, you'd
think physiology was something new, and that I'd thought it up
just to spite her!"

Minnie gave a big party in celebration of her divorce, and after her husband had left Reedyville the way he had entered it — with a hangover, and reciting quatrains from Omar Khayyam — she said that she was glad to be rid of him, glad to have her freedom back. In reality, she mourned for him a long time, and it was her secret wish that, without her, he would find himself unable to battle the world: that he would return to her at last crushed and repentant; but he never did.

Her father had been a man much like her husband in temperament, and the McInnis family had lived in an atmosphere of recriminations, tears and sickening reconciliations — just short of hunger, just at the edge of actual need. He had been a veterinarian, when he was sober enough, or interested enough, to work. On Sundays he was tenor soloist at the First Presbyterian Church on Reedy Avenue. During the day, when he should have been busy making a living for his family, he would often lock himself in his office and refuse to see his clients, being interested, at such times, in designing jewelry so elaborate and so expensive that only the favorite of a maharajah could have afforded it. He had a smattering of both Latin and Greek, and it was his boast that he could play any musical instrument by ear. He was the man of small, diversified talents of whom others mistakenly say so often: "What a pity he drinks! With his ability, he could be one of the outstanding men in this country, if he could just control himself!"

Her mother had been the real head of the McInnis household, the practical, dependable one to whom you came for advice and protection; and although Minnie as a child had rebelled angrily at the way her family lived, the pattern of weak-talented man, strong-reliant woman, became so deeply fixed in her growing emotions that, when she was a woman herself, she could neither understand nor accept any other relationship between a husband and wife. Thus she kept alive in her own being the situation which she had struggled so desperately to escape: prolonging, during the span of her own life, the unresolved drama of her parents' trivial and forgotten ashes.

But she was more intelligent than either of her parents, and if she never quite understood that her defeat lay in the simple fact that the only man she could love must be a man that she also despised, she had some disturbing inkling of her emotional impasse, and for a long time she tried to force herself to fall in love with St. Joseph, who suited her in so many ways, and who asked her to marry him at least twice a month. She could not. He was too strong, she felt vaguely; too self-assured. Then she would sigh with regret and say: "He'd make any woman a fine husband. But I can't. I can't be interested in him, and I needn't try any longer."

And so she rushed about Reedyville, participating in everything, seeking new outlets for her alarming energies. *Shattered Roses* was a great success from the beginning. With some of the money she earned, she bought a house at Montrose, on Mobile Bay; and in the early spring of 1908, she got a leave of absence from her paper and went there to work on a new novel. She had not blocked out her plot in detail, but already she was sure of two things: Her book was to be titled *A Belle of Old Mobile,* and its heroine was to be a girl like Clarry Palmiller, both in looks and in temperament.

She had seen much of Clarry during the Christmas holidays which had just passed. Since the suicide of her brother, she had gone to Miss Ainsley's School-on-the-Hudson, that being her father's wish. She was grown up now, and she had become a great beauty, as Hubert had so often predicted. She was to make her debut the next year, when she was eighteen, and he looked forward to the event with far more enthusiasm than she herself did. Her resemblance to her father was startling, and during the time that she was home, he was with her constantly. She was gracious, composed and she seemed more mature than her years.

"I don't see why people think me so beautiful," she said to her mother. "I'm five feet ten. I'm the tallest girl in the school." Her eyes had deepened, her hair had darkened a little, but she was still remarkably blond. Then she said: "I do wish you'd tell Father not to give me the sort of jewelry he delights in. It's not for me. I can't wear it at all. I've talked these things over with *Madame* at the school. She's an expert, and she says I must wear nothing fancy. She says I should really wear nothing except pearls."

Cindy was somewhat awed by her imposing, assured daughter who talked with such familiarity of the things which she had only read about. The bond between them had never been close, not because she, herself, wanted it that way, but because Clarry had a way of politely rejecting affection which was too intense. That

Christmas her daughter had said to her: "I know I seem un-friendly and not very articulate to you, Mother! I'm not very demonstrative, and I know that well. I seem so cool with others. The girls at Miss Ainsley's read silly novels about love and talk of nothing except the boys they know at home. They seem so strange to me, Mother. Sometimes I think I don't love anybody at all. It often worries me."

Cindy had wanted to say quickly: "But you love me, don't you my dear?" but she did not dare, for she knew her daughter would tell her the truth. Instead, she touched Clarry's hand affectionately and said: "I'm sure you must love your father a great deal. I hope so, because he worships you. You're his whole life, you know."

Clarry sighed and put her white, sculptured arm about her mother's waist. "Of course," she said slowly. "Of course I do, Mother. I'm very fond of him. I see his good points and his bad ones too." Then she laughed apologetically and turned away. "I haven't any illusions about myself," she added. "I'm a complete mess." She went toward her bedroom to dress for the dance her father was giving in her honor that night. At the door she paused, lowered her head, as if ashamed, and went on: "The girls at school call me 'Big Snow-White,' and they're much closer to the truth, in some ways, than they know."

She returned to Miss Ainsley's school early in January, and afterwards her mother missed her a great deal. Cindy had never entirely recovered from the shock of her son's death, and she still wore black for him. One day in early spring she got a long letter from Minnie McMinn describing her new surroundings in de-tail, and asking Cindy to come at once and visit her.

Never, in all your life, have you seen anything so beautiful, Cindy [she had written]. My house is on top of a high bluff, and I like to think that the spot I live on is the place where the last Appalachian hill falls into the sea. I'm only a few hundred feet away from the little, sandy beach below me; but between me and the beach there is a thicket of pines, red gums and magnolias, so that when I look down from the porch where I work, my lawn is the terraced tops of trees. In the morning I watch the sun rise below me in the east; in the afternoon I see it set in Mobile Bay. To the north of me is a network of rivers and bayous and lagoons; in front of me, shining through the trees, is the bay itself; to the south, on a clear day, I can see the Gulf of Mexico sparkling in the sunlight.

The place is beautiful, Cindy! It really is, and you must see it for yourself. Come quickly, while the yellow jasmine is everywhere. The azaleas are just coming into bloom. You see them all about you, growing among the pines and blossoming in whites, pinks and the most beautiful shades of watermelon red. The one growing beside my front gate is a delicate shade of coral. It is said to be twelve feet high and to have a circumference of thirty-five feet. If you can get away from Reedyville sometime this week, it should be in full bloom for you when you arrive.

Cindy came the following Friday morning, and Minnie met the early boat. She had hired a rig at the livery stable, and the two women drove slowly down the brick-red road, through an endless arch of new green. "Oh, I forgot to tell you," said Minnie. "I've got a little surprise for you. Robert Porterfield, of all people, called me up last night. He's in Mobile trying a case in the Federal Court. It's something about a salvage claim, I believe. Anyway, I asked him over for the week end. I really couldn't get out of it. I hope you don't mind." Then she added gaily: "I'm sure it will all be most proper and respectable, because you and I, my dear, are a little too battered to be the least bit enticing."

He came late that afternoon, and Cindy thought at once how well he was looking — how healthy and satisfied. Then she contrasted his dignified well-being with her own depressed sadness, seeing clearly at that moment the sickly failure she had made of her own life. Minnie's house was set in a grove of bay trees and young pines, and from its back yard, a path, cut into the side of the bluff, and terraced by some long-forgotten hand, led downward to the beach. Dogwood bloomed on either side of the path, and fell with it downward to the bay.

That afternoon, Cindy said: "There's nothing left to show you but the beach, Robert. Shall we go there while Minnie compromises her central character?"

"Show him the variegated bluff," said Minnie absently. "But don't get lost, and don't stay too long. My cook has pouting spells if supper isn't served exactly on time."

They went together down the steep, terraced path, holding on to the rail for support, but before they had reached the bottom, Robert stopped and said in surprise: "A spring, of all things! A clear spring running out of the bluff!"

"It makes a stream across the sand," said Cindy. "It's very effective."

They came to the beach and sat on a drift log; then, taking off their shoes and stockings, they put their feet into the cool water. To the left there was a piece of driftwood, roughly oval in shape and worn to satin smoothness through the action of the waves. Robert picked it up, smiled and threw it into the rank growth of shrubbery behind them. "I don't want Minnie to see that," he said. "It's sure to remind her of something about Life."

Cindy said, "This is really very nice, isn't it? I haven't been wading since I was a little girl." Then suddenly she added: "Do you remember when we were children, and how we used to wade in that brook out back of the canning factory?"

"I remember everything that you've ever said or done," said Robert. "It seems to be all I have." There was a silence between them, while Cindy looked at him with surprise, and then he went on: "I hadn't intended to come to Mobile at all. One of the other men in the office had planned to try the case." He picked up a twig and began making pictures in the sand. "Do you want to know why I really came?" he asked. "Or do you know that already?"

"I'm not sure," said Cindy. "It seems so unbelievable to me."

"I came to see you," he said. "I never have a chance to talk to you at home. I couldn't get your face out of my mind since you came to see me about your child. I kept seeing you and thinking — " He broke off suddenly and said: "What is your relationship with Hubert? Please tell me. I have a reason for asking."

"There isn't any," said Cindy. "There hasn't been for many years. We live in the same house, that's about all." She looked straight ahead, toward the gulf, avoiding his eyes. "Don't think me too imaginative, but are you trying to tell me that you are still in love with me?"

"Why do you think I've never married?" he asked angrily. "Why do you think I've denied myself everything that other men have?"

"My dear!" she said. "My dear! I treated you so badly, didn't I? But I thought all that was over and forgotten long ago."

"It wasn't," he said. "At least not as far as I'm concerned. I never got over you. I couldn't go on from that point. I got stuck at the point of adolescent courtship." He got up and said: "We'd better go back. I shouldn't have told you these things so bluntly, at such a late day. It wasn't a very appropriate moment, was it? I've kept quiet all these years, and now I blurt everything out before I even know how you feel about me."

Cindy waited a moment and then said: "I'm a little mixed up. You mustn't expect an answer from me too quickly." They put on their shoes and stockings, not daring to look at each other again. "I've already tried to forget you," said Robert. "So don't tell me to do that, for God's sake! I've always loved you, and it looks as if I always will, whether I want to or not. When I thought you were happy, it was a little easier for me; but seeing you so sad and beaten-down is more than I can stand."

They walked in silence up the steps, and when they reached the place where the spring was, Cindy said: "Have you really never been in love with anybody else?"

"I've tried to think I was," said Robert. "Once or twice I almost succeeded."

"Was one of them Constance Howard?"

"Yes," said Robert. "But after a while I knew why I was in love with her, and I said to myself: 'It's only because she's like Cindy Lankester. If it wasn't for that, I wouldn't even look at her!' "

"She's not a bit like me!" said Cindy indignantly. "What you ever saw in that silly little thing is beyond my understanding!" Then, looking into his grave, steady eyes, she threw back her head and laughed for the first time in months, the Lankester dimples appearing plainly in her cheeks. "You see?" she said. "You see what a mean disposition I really have?"

He put his arms about her and she leaned back against him, while they balanced themselves precariously on the narrow walk. "Nothing that you ever do can be wrong for me," he said slowly. "This may strike you as silly, but every woman in the world except you seems a little repulsive to me."

Suddenly she began to cry. "Don't!" she said. "Don't say those tender things to me! I can't stand them!" When she was quiet once more, she added: "What do you want me to do? Tell me what it is you expect from me?"

"I want you to divorce your husband and marry me."

It was then that Minnie called to them in her loud, cheerful voice, telling them that supper was ready. They separated guiltily and went up the steps toward her, not daring to look at each other again. She was smiling when she met them. Her book was shaping itself with unanticipated ease, and she was in high spirits. Later, she sat with them on the porch upstairs, watching the swaying tops of the trees below them, and the moonlight beyond, as it spread out evenly across the bay. She outlined, in her nervous, eager voice, the things she had already settled in her mind regarding her characters and her plot, but Robert and Cindy, thinking of other matters, heard little that she said. In a way, they were glad not to be alone, for they were going over and over the things which, already, they had said to each other; and they were adjusting themselves to a new relationship which, as they both knew in their hearts, was inevitable. Minnie, noticing their preoccupation at last, said: "What's the matter with you two, anyway? Aren't you on speaking terms any more?"

She yawned and went into the house, and when she was out of earshot, Cindy said in a small voice, as if her words were the ending of a long, silent conversation they had been having: "He'll never divorce me, Robert! I know that! He won't!"

The following day was Saturday, and at breakfast Robert suggested to Cindy that they go to Mobile together for the day. Minnie, coming out of the kitchen at that moment, heard him and said enthusiastically: "I think that's a fine idea! I'll go too. I've always wanted to go through the old Owen home — it's where The Goodwife lived as a child, and I've been curious about it ever since old Mrs. Wentworth described it to me."

To her surprise, Cindy caught her hand, looked earnestly into her eyes and said: "No, Minnie! You aren't to go! You aren't invited!" Mrs. McMinn stared with disbelief, astonished at such rudeness from Cindy, of all people. "Well!" she said bleakly. "Well, that's definite enough, isn't it?" Then almost immediately she understood the situation, since romance was, in a way, her special field. The hurt, half-angry look disappeared from her face, and impulsively she bent and kissed Cindy's cheek. "I'm so glad!" she said. "So glad for both of you!"

"There's nothing between us," said Cindy. "Don't jump at conclusions, as you always do, Minnie. There's nothing at all."

"It's all on my side, so far," said Robert. "I've been in love with her as long as I can remember. I blurted it all out this afternoon, down by your pretty spring."

Cindy said: "Please! Please, Robert!" She got up in embarrassment and went into the hall. She stood there irresolute, and then called softly: "Minnie! Minnie, please come here a minute, will you?" And when her friend joined her she said: "I'm tired of black and the things it stands for. I'm not going to wear it any longer. I'm through with that phase of my life forever." She glanced at her image in the hall mirror, turned away with distaste and continued passionately: "You and I can wear the same clothes. Lend me something pretty to wear for him. Something I can laugh in, and something bright that he can remember afterwards."

Minnie nodded vigorously and said: "Come into my bedroom with me. I've got a new dress that I've never even worn. You'll be crazy about it." She spread the dress on her bed and then asked in a casual voice: "What are your real feelings toward him? He's too fine a man to play with, you know. I won't have you making him unhappy."

"I don't know how I feel," said Cindy. "Yes, I do know: I feel gratitude. I feel as if I'd been called back from the grave. It's only gratitude, I suppose, but if he doesn't stop being so sweet and gentle and solemn, I really believe I'm lost." She sighed and pressed her cheek against Minnie's hand. Minnie said: "There's a big leghorn hat lined with pink silk which goes with the dress. It's very flattering. It'll make you look sixteen again. When I get through with you, you'll be so ravishing that people will turn around on Dauphin Street and point you out to others." She assembled the rest of the costume; and some deep-seated instinct for intrigue made her tiptoe, her index finger held cautiously to her lips, as she walked from bureau to wardrobe and back again.

She waved gaily to them as they went toward the morning boat, watching them with an approving, professional satisfaction, as if they were two of the more attractive characters she had created, and had given life to between-the-covers of one of her books; and she was waiting excitedly when they returned late that night.

They came silently through the gate and went at once to the summerhouse beneath the trees. They had talked through their entire lives that day, and they were tired.

Minnie waited as long as she could, and then, coughing significantly, she joined them. She had expected to find them locked in each other's arms; to hear them murmuring words of passion; to witness wild, unashamed gestures of endearment. Instead, it seemed to her as if they were the completest strangers who had met a moment before by the slenderest margin of chance. When she joined them, making her small clattering noises of warning, they were sitting well apart, discussing trivial matters with cautious politeness. They seemed to welcome Minnie's arrival, and when she sat down with them, they began to talk to her with animation, glancing furtively at each other from time to time.

Robert's case came to trial the following Monday morning, but he came to see them each night for almost a week. At the end of that time it was necessary for him to return to Reedyville. Long before that day arrived, Cindy was deeply in love with him. On that last night, when the three of them sat together, watching the lights on a freighter move slowly up the bay, Minnie said: "But what are you going to do about it? Have you reached any decision as yet?"

Robert spoke regretfully: "It seems to depend on Hubert. No matter what plans we make, we always come back to him. Cindy is going to talk to him when she goes back home and see if she can straighten things out."

Minnie, whose methods were always direct, said quickly: "Why wait, Cindy? He'll either give you a divorce or he won't. Why don't you telephone him and settle the matter. And if he says no, if he won't let you two marry respectably — well, there are more ways than one to skin a cat!" She brought her heels down solidly upon the floor, hoping, as a matter of principle, that Mr. Palmiller would refuse the divorce, and that Cindy and Robert would become converts to the new freedom she believed in so aggressively. She had nothing but contempt for the conventions of mankind. She was not content to ignore them where she, herself, was concerned: she sought earnestly to repeal them even where they did not impinge on her own life. Thus she affirmed an abiding belief through a fanatic wish to destroy. She got up and went into the hall, where the telephone was. "I'll put in the call for you now," she said. "And when he answers, don't give him any details. Just tell him you want a divorce."

When the operator rang back a few minutes later, Cindy went at once to the telephone. She finished her little set speech, and then Hubert's resonant, Eastern voice came strongly through the receiver. "You may as well get that idea out of your head, and at once!" he said distinctly. "I think you overestimate your importance to me, my dear. Personally, I don't care what you do, or how you lead your life! . . . But I have my daughter's future to consider, and I won't have her life complicated by you, or anybody else."

"But this is important to me," said Cindy. "It isn't just a whim. My future happiness depends on it."

"I've said all that I mean to say," said Hubert coldly. "Please don't bring up the subject again. I've made up my mind, and I'm not likely to change it, as you should know by this time." Then adding: "I hope you are having a pleasant vacation. Everything here is going along about as usual," he coughed, said good-by and hung up.

"You see?" said Cindy. "He's so unreasonable. You can't discuss anything with him. He doesn't even listen to what you say. All he does is to state his views over and over."

Later that night, after Robert had gone to bed, the two women sat on Mrs. McMinn's sofa talking together. "If it were me, I know very well what I'd do," said Minnie in a positive voice. "I wouldn't let him triumph that way. I'd take what I wanted, and I'd damn everything and everybody that got in my path."

"I've been over all that," said Cindy; "but Robert won't hear of it. He swears he'll never do anything to hurt me in the eyes of others. He only loves me a great deal: he doesn't understand me at all." She shook her head and laughed ruefully. "I don't want to change him in any way. I think he's perfect just as he is. But I do wish he wouldn't be so awfully romantic about womanhood."

"The whole thing should be settled between you tonight," said Minnie; "before he goes back to Reedyville. If it isn't, it might turn into one of those situations where you'll both sit back and watch your lives drift away in front of your eyes. You know. The way poor Ella Doremus and Joe Cantrell did."

Then, grimly, she stated the plan she had in mind for forcing the issue immediately; and Cindy, to her surprise, agreed with her at once. "If you can't have everything, then take what you can have and make the most of it," said Minnie sententiously. The advice we give others is usually advice that we would not take ourselves. Certainly Minnie was the last woman in the world personally to consider a halfway measure; but now that she had spoken her thought with such vigor, compromise seemed natural enough for Cindy. "I know a left-hand alliance has one serious drawback for poor Robert," she continued, "but that must be faced squarely and accepted."

"You mean about Hubert?" asked Cindy. "You think he'll try to protect his little home with a deadly weapon? If you do, you're wrong. He hasn't the faintest interest in me one way or the other, and if I don't make a scandal, he'll pretend that nothing is going on. If he says anything at all, it will be, 'I don't give a damn what you do, my dear. But keep Clarry's name out of it! I won't have her involved!' That's the way he'll react, Minnie. I know it. He won't be interested in Robert at all."

"I had something quite different in mind," said Minnie. She paused and wrinkled her brow, phrasing her thought delicately. "I happen to know that next to you, Robert wants a son more than anything else in the world. It's a tradition in the Porterfield family, you might say. I was talking to him yesterday coming up from the boat, and he's crazy for a child of his own. That's what I really meant when I said compromises would have to be made."

Cindy sat thoughtfully for a moment, in silence, and then she said: "Why isn't it possible? If he wants a son, he shall have a son, if I can possibly produce one for him. If he wants six sons, he shall have them all! And on each of their little pink behinds I'll have inscribed in colored inks the words: 'To Robert from Cindy, with all her love.'" Minnie threw back her head and laughed suddenly, her intricate, chapel-like throat plainly visible. "It's like Mama used to say," she gasped with delight: "Once you get a really good woman started on the downward path, she'll go the whole hog quicker than anybody in the world!"

An hour later, dressed in Minnie's laciest nightgown and perfumed as delicately as a bride, Cindy entered Robert's bedroom and stood with her back to the far wall. He had been sleeping lightly, and when he heard her, he sat up in bed, rubbed his eyes in astonishment, and said: "Cindy! Cindy, what's the matter? Have you lost your mind?"

"Be quiet, my dear," she said in a quivering voice. "Be quiet. You must not talk at all now." Then, moving into the room a little, standing with her knuckles resting against his night table, she added: "You see what I am now? . . . I have no shame at all. No reserve. Are you smiling now because you once thought it necessary to marry me?" Then she came closer and bent above him, and he took her in his arms. "We must never be parted again," she said. "Never. If this is all that there is to be for us, then we must take it and ask no questions." He moved, making room for her, and she added: "And never let your conscience trouble you about me, because you can bring me nothing but blessings."

They came down to breakfast next morning laughing softly and whispering together, their fingers interlocked. Minnie was waiting for them on the porch, and when Cindy saw her, she said: "I'm going to cook his breakfast for him. I think I should, don't you? I should do it better than most brides, too, being so much more experienced."

At breakfast the two women discussed Robert's departure. Minnie was of the opinion that he should telephone Ira Graley and tell him that he would be away a week longer, on the theory that every man was entitled to a honeymoon, and that a honeymoon took precedence over everything else. Robert turned toward Cindy and rubbed his cheek against her own. "You must be the judge," he said. "Shall I stay? Do you want me to, my darling?" Cindy's wishes were so plain that it was not even necessary for her to answer, and Minnie said in her loud, cheerful voice: "I think we should plan a little celebration for tonight. I'll go down to the village this morning and see what I can find in the way of rare food."

He stayed ten days longer, and after waiting a day or two, Cindy followed him to Reedyville. On the day she left, Minnie laughed and thrust a sheaf of typewritten pages under her nose. "Look!" she said tragically. "That's all I've done on my book since you came to visit me! I can't be expected to write a novel of the Old South while a real romance is going on right under my nose, can I?"

Cindy paused in her packing, put her arm about Minnie's waist and said: "I'm so sorry. I should have been more circumspect, I know."

"If I had the nerve," said Minnie, "I'd dedicate the damn book to you and Robert when it's finished — if it ever is. . . . Wouldn't that cause a local sensation though? Wouldn't *that* make old Mrs. Wentworth forget about her rheumatism?"

In her own mind, Cindy and Robert were to be associated forever afterwards with *A Belle of Old Mobile;* and later on, whenever the book was mentioned, she thought immediately of them. She finished it in Reedyville, the following November, and while she was working on the final chapter, Cindy called unexpectedly to see her one morning. "Do you remember our talk about conventional women, and how there's no stopping them, once they step on the path of easy virtue?" she began laughingly. "Well, it's happened, Minnie! I'm going to have a baby!" Minnie wanted all the details at once, and when Cindy had told her everything, she said: "Robert's birthday is about the middle of June, too, isn't it? Wouldn't it be a wonderful coincidence if his son were born on his birthday?"

"I thought of that, too," said Cindy. "It's entirely possible." Then she looked down thoughtfully, tapped the carpet with her toe, and added: "Robert doesn't know anything about it yet. I don't want him to know for a time — certainly not until after Clarry's debut is over. He'd only worry about me and get himself upset, and I need all my energies for the party, heaven knows!"

The date for Clarry's coming-out party had been set for late November, and everybody in town, with the possible exception of herself, seemed to take an enormous interest in it. When her father would discuss with her some new detail of magnificence, she would smile her sweet, vague smile and say: "Of course! Of course, Father! You're always right about such things!" She was approaching her nineteenth birthday, and everybody predicted that she would make a brilliant marriage. "With her looks and breeding," said old Mrs. Wentworth positively, "she can just sit back and make her choice. She'll make a good wife, too!" she added. "Clarry has repose and graciousness, and those characteristics are rare among the flighty young girls of today."

Afterwards, the people of Reedyville agreed that Clarry's debut had been the most impressive the town had ever seen. Hubert had gone the limit, and as he stood with his daughter to receive the guests, he knew definitely that this was the happiest moment of his life. A long mirror faced them, and often he would examine the images of himself and his daughter reflected together, thinking anew how greatly they resembled each other. Clarry was dressed in white satin. The gown was cut simply, and she wore no ornament at all except a necklace of pearls which her father had given her. He had wanted her to have her hair dressed elaborately for the party, but she had smiled, touched his cheek and refused. She wore it now precisely as she wore it every day: plaited in two long, silken braids and wound severely around her head. A classic plainness suited her type, and she knew that well. She greeted her guests, her voice low and correct, her manner gracious yet withdrawn. She was that type of woman whose charm seems a promise of mental and emotional richness lying just beyond the barriers of breeding. Actually, what Clarry showed to the world was what she was. There was nothing at all beyond. There was only a repetition of what one saw instantly and admired.

Minnie came to the party in a dual capacity: One, as Society Editress of the *Courier;* the other as Cindy's guest. She came late, after the receiving line had broken; and she went at once to the library, knowing that was where she would find her hostess. Cindy was sitting beside the window talking to St. Joseph and Robert Porterfield, and when Minnie approached, the two men got up and made a place for her.

"Have you told Robert about the birthday present you're going to give him?" she asked breathlessly. "He looks a little scared!"

"Oh, no! I don't expect to tell him for some weeks, Minnie!"

"I just had a birthday," said Robert quickly. "I don't expect another for a long time yet. Not until next June, to be accurate."

"We know," said Minnie. "We know that quite well. . . . But this present takes a certain time to get ready. It's something that simply can't be rushed." The two women glanced mysteriously at each other, raised their eyebrows and shook their heads, as if each cautioned the other to use more discretion.

"Why don't you girls quit being arch and significant?" asked St. Joseph. "Come on, Minnie! Tell us what it is! You know how I am. You said yourself that curiosity was my worst failing."

"Just leave them alone," said Robert. "You won't get anything out of them that way. . . . Anyway, I already know what it is. I'm still able to put two and two together."

"You *do?*" asked Cindy in mock surprise. "You do *really?* — That's interesting, isn't it, Minnie?"

"Yes, you do!" said Minnie. "If you really knew, you'd scream and fall back in a dead faint."

"It's a shotgun," said Robert in a bored voice. "I knew what you were after when you were asking me all those innocent questions the other day. You're having it made specially for me at the factory. You expected to give it to me for Christmas, but when you found out they couldn't deliver it so soon, you decided to put it off until my birthday, and to give me a copy of *Cream of the New England Poets* in burnt leather for Christmas!"

"Simple!" said St. Joseph. "Women give themselves away every time they try to be mysterious. Their dear little brains just aren't up to involved thought." He nudged Minnie gently with his thumb, but to his surprise, she merely smiled sweetly at him and said: "You're a long way off, Robert. Oh, a long way!"

"Is it animal, vegetable or mineral?" asked Robert. Cindy was about to speak when Minnie said quickly: "Don't answer that question, Cindy! You know the way he lays traps for people on the witness stand! Don't tell him anything!"

"Is it something you bought?" asked St. Joseph.

"Certainly not!" said Cindy. "I think that's terrible!"

"Is it something you made yourself?" asked Robert.

The two women looked slyly at each other, and to the amazement of St. Joseph and Robert, they went off immediately into peals of laughter.

"Not entirely," said Cindy after a moment. "Robert helped me a little bit."

"It was hardly worth mentioning," said Minnie. "So don't look so puffed up and important."

"Well, that rules out my guess," said St. Joseph. "I was going to say a new desk set for your office, but of course Cindy couldn't make anything as complicated as that."

"You don't know how talented I am when I put my mind to a thing," said Cindy. "He underestimates my ability, doesn't he Minnie?"

Robert shook his head and drew his brows together. "Are you sure I had anything to do with it?" he asked. "You want to stick to that?"

"I do," said Cindy. "I most assuredly do. My whole case hangs on that fact."

Robert shrugged his shoulders and said: "That's strange. I haven't the faintest recollection of it."

To his surprise, Minnie threw back her head instantly and laughed stridently. She turned red, coughed and fanned herself with her handkerchief in helpless mirth. "Lord knows I don't expect much from men," she gasped, "but that is really the most unchivalrous remark I ever heard a gentleman make!"

Clarry, hearing them laughing together, came up and said quietly: "Tell me the joke, won't you, Miss Minnie? I haven't heard anything amusing all evening." Instantly she knew that she had managed to spoil the talk, and she wondered what she had unwittingly done. After a moment's silence, Minnie got up briskly and said: "You're just the person I wanted to see, Clarry. Come along with me, won't you? I'm going to spread your debut all over the Society Page, and I want you to give me all the information. I particularly want to know the names of your out-of-town guests, and how prominent they are, and why."

Afterwards, she went from person to person, chatting for a moment, or stopping to make an occasional note in her book. She left early, in time to get her story done for her paper, and as she came down the walk and approached the iron gate, she was already shaping her opening sentences. "It is but fair," she repeated under her breath, "that when the loveliest bud of the Southland

opens her petals to the prosaic world about her, that the setting
be worthy of the jewel it shows to the world, and so it is that — "

Then, hearing voices on the other side of the hedge, she stood
still, the train of her thought broken. A group of seventeen-year-
old boys stood just beyond her, on the other side of the fence. They
were laughing disdainfully and making vulgar remarks concerning
the Palmillers and their pretensions.

"That big white heifer," said one of the boys. "What makes her
think she's so much better than anybody else in town?" He spat
on the pavement and swaggered up and down before his friends.
"From the way they act, you'd think they was God, or somebody."

Minnie had not been able to place the voice, but when she came
outside at the moment the speaker raised his hand and pushed back
his cap, his inverted thumb plain in the moonlight, she said: "Why,
Breck Boutwell! What are you doing here, using such language?"

He looked up, when she spoke, and grinned knowingly, and Minnie thought how quickly he had grown up. There was a restless,
half-angry humor about him, and he moved away from the fence,
not slouchingly, as the other boys did, but with an easy, defiant
grace, as if it were impossible for him to make a clumsy movement. He smiled, showing his white even teeth, and said: "Write
up a good story about 'em, Miss Minnie. Mama will sure enjoy
reading about it tomorrow."

When he had been younger, he would often stand where he was
standing now and stare angrily at the Palmiller house. "That's
where he lives!" he would say to himself. "He's the one that treated
Honey so dirty!" Then he would kick angrily at the iron fence, and
add: "He said my own sister wasn't fit to live in the same town
that his daughter lived in. That's what he said, because I heard
him. And he said it right out in front of other folks, too!"

But now, with approaching maturity, with the developing of
his mind, he had repressed these old memories as things too shameful to be faced, for their implications, he now realized, concerned
not only his sister, but himself, and the entire Boutwell family as
well. Thus the basis of his anger lay below the level of his consciousness, forgotten at last, but working still with an unabated
force. He found other reasons to justify his resentment, other
means of showing his contempt for the Palmillers. His delight,

at that period of his life, was to go about town whispering involved, bawdy scandals which concerned Hubert, Cindy and Clarine without discrimination; but in the end nobody believed the stories, for they were too ridiculous, too imaginative to be credited.

He started to move away with his companions, but Minnie stopped him with her most imperious gesture. "You really hate the Palmillers, don't you, Breck? But why? What have they ever done to you?"

For an instant he seemed at the point of answering her question, and then, cocking his head to one side with an anxious alertness, he spoke: "How did you manage to get chalk all over your back, Miss Minnie?" he asked. He gazed at her steadily, his eyes innocent and soft. "It looks to me like you been leaning up against a blackboard somewhere."

Minnie twisted her neck, trying to see over her shoulder. "What chalk?" she asked quickly. "What chalk are you talking about?"

"It's all over you," he said. "You can't go down the street that way, now can you? . . . Here, hand me your handkerchief and I'll see if I can get some of it off."

He took her handkerchief from her, turned her toward the light, and rubbed vigorously at her shoulders. "Hold still, Miss Minnie!" he said. "It'll take only a minute! It's coming off fine!" He winked at his companions, shoved his cap back at a rakish angle and began to rub Mrs. McMinn once more, whistling provocatively under his breath.

"Is it almost off?" asked Minnie. "I wonder how in the world I managed to get *chalk* on me!" Then, as his hands worked under her arms, and downward, toward her flanks, she twitched nervously, and said: "Hurry, Breck! Get it off before anybody comes!"

"I got most of it off your shoulders already," said Breck, "but the worst of it is farther down." Then, to her surprise, he circled her waist with his arm, and held her firmly while he massaged the small of her back with such an insinuating thoroughness that she gasped with a high, nervous sound. Breck stopped at once and said cheerfully: "Well, that part was easier to get done than the shoulders!" But at once he made a shocked sound with his lips and shook his head with disbelief, as if unable to credit the evidence of his eyes. "Lord God almighty, Miss Minnie!" he said.

"How did you manage to get it all over your *backside* this way?"

She turned quickly and looked at him; and fearing that she was becoming suspicious at last, Breck shrewdly restored her confidence in him through impersonal abuse: "You must have sat right down in a box of colored crayons — the way your dress looks in the back! You'd think a grown woman that can write books would have sense enough to look where she sits, wouldn't you?" he asked sternly. Then, with assumed exasperation, he added: "How you expect me to get *that* out, I don't know!"

He was silent for a time, as if he planned a campaign of the utmost importance, and then he said with hurt patience: "Bend over, Miss Minnie, and hold on to the fence. I'll try to pat it out easy. That's the only way to do it, it seems to me. If I try to rub it, it'll smear and ruin your new dress sure."

She seemed a little unwilling to accept his suggestion, but having already gone so far, it seemed a little silly to back down now. Then, too, there was a persuasiveness about Breck which was difficult to combat; and so she clutched the iron fence after a moment, bent over and said: "Well, I hope nobody passes by and sees me in this peculiar position!"

The position she had taken did not entirely suit Breck, and grasping her thighs daintily with his hands, he re-posed her with fussy insistence; then, when he had her arranged to his satisfaction, he patted her posterior gently to the rhythms of "*La Paloma*" which he whistled innocently through his white, gleaming teeth. After a moment, his friends, no longer able to control themselves, began to snicker audibly; and Minnie, realizing at last that there was no chalk on her dress, and that there never had been, made a muffled, screaming sound and pulled away indignantly from his musical, pattering hands.

"Just let me get my hands on you, Breck Boutwell!" she said angrily. "I'll break your neck with pleasure! . . . Of all the insolence! Of all the nerve!"

The other boys turned and ran away, snickering now without restraint; but Breck stood his ground, dodging her striking hand. He laughed good-naturedly and said: "You sure give up easy, don't you Miss Minnie? It ain't hard to talk you into anything, is it?"

Then, shrugging his shoulders and swaggering self-consciously, he walked away, turned the corner beyond the Chapman residence, and was lost to sight. After a time, Minnie's anger subsided, and she thought: "Just the same, he's a handsome boy. He ought to be horsewhipped, but he's got a certain dashing quality about him. There's no doubt of it."

A little later she dismissed Breck from her mind, and as she walked under the trees, she went on with her interrupted story of Clarry's debut. "A veritable galaxy of wit and beauty," she repeated under her breath, "gathered last evening at the palatial Palmiller home on Reedy Avenue, to pay tribute to the beauty and charm of Clarine, the radiant debutante daughter of the family. She was a vision of heavenly beauty — a walking dream designed to make even the most blasé masculine heart beat faster, and her lovely pale blond hair was arranged in . . ."

The story when she completed it was one of the most effective she had ever written. Afterwards, it seemed to her that her column was concerned constantly with Clarry and her social life: First, she was in New York for the season; then New Orleans, Atlanta and St. Louis. It was plain that her life had now settled down into an unending series of dances, parties and teas. She was visiting in Louisville when her mother's third child was born. It was a boy, as Cindy had wanted it to be, and he came into the world, not on his father's birthday, but two weeks later. "His name is Ralph Porterfield Palmiller," said Cindy, her words somehow having an unfinished sound, a defensive rising inflection, as if she had meant to add, in explanation, "He's named for Robert's father, you know," but had thought better of it. Then, more positively, she added: "That's the name we've decided on, and that's the name he's to have!" And she would stare challengingly at people, as if daring them to ask the clarifying question which, as she well knew, was in everybody's mind.

She had been correct in her predictions regarding her husband, for Mr. Palmiller did nothing at all when the child was born. He did not even show surprise. He merely ignored the new baby, as if its existence were no concern of his own. His conduct caused much talk in Reedyville, much laughter. Perhaps old Mrs. Wentworth put the town's amusement into a definitive form when she said:

"No matter how much Hubert Palmiller hates what he calls 'the unscientific legends of the Church,' he either believes in the doctrine of Immaculate Conception, or knows that his wife has a sweetheart."

As the months passed, and the boy outgrew the chubbiness of babyhood, his resemblance to Robert, noticeable from the beginning, became even more pronounced. Later, everybody saw that he had his father's long chin and mahogany-colored hair; that he had even inherited the thin, delicately chiseled nose so characteristic of the Porterfields. He was like his father's people in disposition too, being solemn, courteous and undemonstrative.

It was then that Hubert, who before had ignored the existence of the child, changed his attitude toward him; and patiently he began a campaign to win the boy's good will. It was one of the contradictions of his nature that he was able to give to the son of another man the devotion which he had denied his own son. Later, he took the little boy with him everywhere, exhibiting him proudly to his friends, as if he were a banner on which was inscribed both his humiliation and his triumph. It was a quiet affection, for Hubert and the boy rarely spoke, being content merely to be with each other.

Cindy was somewhat puzzled at her husband's conduct and she talked over the situation with Minnie McMinn one afternoon. The latter had been lying down with a headache, but she raised herself on her elbows and said: "Perhaps Hubert is trying to be a martyr — who knows? Perhaps he's trying to get even with you in some obscure way of his own."

Cindy shook her head. "No," she said. "No, there's a deeper reason. He's really very fond of Ralph. He isn't pretending." She began to speak in detail, to analyze the motives behind her husband's unexpected behavior. This was the kind of talk which, as a rule, would have interested Minnie the most, and ordinarily she would have explored with excitement each possibility which Cindy's words brought up — enlarging and elaborating the details which fell before her. She tried now to simulate an interest which she did not feel; but she could not, and she lay back wearily, her hands twitching nervously.

Of late she had been strangely preoccupied with her past, and at unexpected moments she found herself with tears in her eyes, her toes curled tightly in her shoes, while her lips, against her will, repeated phrases from her childhood, such as: "How poor we are! How we have to struggle! What makeshifts we endure!"

Cindy stopped talking suddenly and looked at her friend steadily. Minnie seemed so quiet, so unlike herself, that she was a little disturbed, and she said: "Do you feel all right Minnie? Shall I get you something?" Minnie sighed and shook her head, and Cindy went on: "I think you've been driving yourself too hard. Why don't you stop working for a while and take things easier?"

Minnie sat up at once and stared, as if Cindy had proposed something shocking and dangerous. "No! No!" she said quickly. "I couldn't do that! I'm behind as it is. They've called up three times from the *Courier* this afternoon to find out when I'll be back!"

"Why didn't you tell them that you're never coming back?" asked Cindy. "You don't need the job any more, do you?"

"I couldn't," said Minnie. "I simply couldn't." But when Cindy had gone, she turned over in her mind the unfamiliar idea of lessening, rather than increasing, her activities. Her second novel had done even better than the first, and her financial position, she felt, was now sound. But the money she had earned served her little. She regarded it with wary suspiciousness, for the pinched thriftiness of her early years was so deeply fixed in her emotions that she could not believe, except with her mind, that the dollars she had piled up so impressively in the Palmiller State Bank were actually hers; that they made her independent; that she could spend them and have what she wanted in return. The knowledge came to her now with a certain shock and she said to herself in surprise: "Cindy is right. There's no sense in my slaving on the *Courier* for next to nothing. That's a part of my life that's behind me. I've gone way beyond that now!"

She got up instantly and wrote her resignation — a long, rather flowery affair. She addressed and stamped the envelope, but when she was on the point of going outside to mail it, the thought came to her that others might think she took this indirect method because she was afraid to face the issue; that she dreaded the violent and dramatic scene with her editor which she knew was inevitable. She looked down at the envelope and struck it with the back of her fingers. "If you think that, you're greatly mistaken!" she said. "Anybody who knows me at all knows very well that's entirely silly!" With something of her old truculence, she tore up her letter and went at once to the editor's office. There she quit her job with stylized, dramatic thoroughness, her voice louder and more penetrant than the editor's; her wordiness more elaborate, more involved; her figures of speech more apt. Then, coming outside, she collected her pencils and dictionaries and erasers and stowed them away in a mesh shopping bag which she had brought with her for that express purpose.

Hazel Chester said sarcastically: "You'll be back with us before long, like he says. You'll go crazy without anything to do, Miss Minnie. You'll be back. People never know when they're well off."

"I'll find plenty to do, don't worry," said Minnie. Then, lifting her neck suddenly, in the manner of a harassed mare, she added: "I started work on another book last winter, but I haven't had a chance to do much with it. It's a little involved, and it requires quite a lot of research work."

Miss Chester, who was one of Minnie's truest admirers, said quickly: "Why, I didn't know you were working on something else. What's the new book about? Sit down a minute and tell me, Miss Minnie. You know I'm crazy about everything you write."

"It's a love story, of course," said Minnie in a bored voice, "but with a historical setting, this time. I'm calling it *Unending Quest,* and that fits in all right with the background, because so much of it has to do with De Soto's expedition of 1540. He'd been in Peru, previous to that, as you know; and he was convinced that there were Indians here in Alabama — right on this spot where Reedyville now stands — richer by far than the Incas ever dreamed of being." She broke off impatiently, and then added: "I'm sure you're familiar with these commonplace details. Why bore you any further?"

Miss Chester, whose knowledge of De Soto was limited to a belief that he had been involved, in an odd sort of way, with the Mississippi River, answered in a doubtful voice: "Well, no. I'm not. I never did learn much history in school."

"The expedition will be the background," continued Minnie. "But the principal characters will be a handsome Spanish captain serving with De Soto and an Indian princess — the daughter of the great chief Tuscaloosa, to be exact."

As she discussed her story, she became more enthusiastic, seeing possibilities in the material which had not occurred to her before.

"Do you mean that De Soto and his men were right here in *Reedyville* at one time?" asked Miss Chester with a new note of pride in her voice, as if this knowledge gave her native city a greater significance.

"Yes," said Minnie. "Yes, of course. What else have I been trying to tell you for the past ten minutes? Nobody can be sure, but Reedyville — or at least the spot where the town now stands — was probably the place where De Soto had his famous meeting with Tuscaloosa."

There was a document of great interest, bearing on this precise point, in the Wentworth library. Its authenticity was disputed, and most scholars considered it an out-and-out fake — perhaps the work of old Colonel Wentworth himself, who had been known both as a historian of some importance, and a forger of rare excellence. For a moment or two Minnie debated the idea of communicating the contents of this interesting document to Miss Chester; then, deciding against it, she went on with her packing, thinking: "Right or wrong, it doesn't really matter to me. After all, my book is fiction, too."

When she had all her articles assembled in her mesh bag, she went back home, and that afternoon she started work on her book once more. She wrote earnestly for a month. At the end of that time she felt even wearier than before, and often, in the middle of one of her overwrought sentences, she would pause and press her forehead against her desk; and, remembering old, irremediable scenes from her childhood, she wept until she was exhausted. Then, in despair, she would put down her pencil with a small, throwing motion, lift her eyes upward and address, in anguish, the voiceless dust of her dead mother: "Mama! Mama!" she would say. "If you had only lived, I could have made up for everything you had to suffer. I could have done so much for you!"

During this period, she shut herself away from her friends, and she would neither acknowledge their letters when they wrote, nor answer the telephone when they rang; but despite her wish of the moment to escape the outside world, one day, as she walked down Millwall Street, she saw St. Joseph approaching. It was not possible for her to escape, so she stood quietly under the trees until he came up to her.

He began speaking in a half-humorous, half-scolding voice: "What's got into you lately? Everybody has been worried about you. I saw Cindy the other day and she told me you even refused to see her."

"I've been busy. I'm trying to write a book, you know. I've just wanted to be by myself. Is that any crime?"

"Why don't you stop this foolishness?" he asked. "Why don't you marry me, Minnie?"

She tried to be gay and clever, as she had in the past, but this time she could not, and she only said: "I don't know. Really, I don't know. Don't ask me for an answer now."

"You've got to make up your mind soon, or it will be too late," he added. "You're forty years old. Neither of us has much time left."

To his surprise, her face twisted suddenly and she said harshly: "Let me alone! Let me alone, can't you? Why do you want to torture me this way?"

"You mean that you won't marry me," he continued in a quiet, steady voice. "Not now. Not ever. . . . That's what you really mean, isn't it Minnie?"

"I cannot," she said desperately. "I cannot!" Then she added: "I've tried hard enough, but it isn't possible. I like to be with you. I admire you a great deal. But to be your wife is something else entirely! I cannot! Please believe me when I say it's not possible!"

He stood there staring at her for a long time, thinking: "We are both such clever people. What little consolation there is in that." Then, turning stiffly, he added: "I know this time that it's final. I won't ask you again." He walked away in the direction from whence he had come, but she stood there longer under the trees, watching his retreating figure, dabbing at her eyes with her hand-kerchief.

It was then that she knew the thing she wanted most was to go away from Reedyville, as if thus she could outwit her childhood years; and as she walked home slowly, she pondered the means of escape open to her. She reached her house and inserted her key in the lock, thinking: "It doesn't matter whether I finish *Unending Quest* or not. I'm going away for a long time. I've never been anywhere in my whole life; I've never really seen anything. I think I'll take a long sea voyage. No, a tour of Europe would be better. Oh, much better. I'm going there at once, and I'm going to stay as long as I please."

She felt better now that she had made her decision, and immediately she began her preparations for departure. Later, Clarry Palmiller telephoned and asked if she could come along too. Minnie said that she could, and in the summer of 1912, the two women set out on their journey. When they came back to Reedyville, ten months later, Minnie seemed completely restored, completely her old self again. She had finished *Unending Quest* between her visits to museums and churches, and already it had been accepted and was being prepared for publication.

She had seen many things of interest, and she told of them all with vivacious concentration; but the one thing which had impressed her the most had been neither a painting, a ruin nor a cathedral: It had been Honey Boutwell herself, and she had talked with her in Paris one night. "You'd never believe it," said Minnie, "but she's famous over there. They call her *Madame Honey, la Négresse d'Alabama.* She's taken quite seriously. She's considered a very great artist, and people turn out in droves to hear her sing. At first I never connected the celebrity everybody was talking about with our own little Honey; but when I did, Clarry and I got tickets instantly, and went to see her."

"Honey Boutwell?" asked Miss Kate Ponders in a startled voice. "I taught her in the sixth grade. I can't believe she didn't end up in the gutter."

"There was a program note about her, too," continued Minnie. "It said that while Madame Honey, the celebrated Negro contralto, was not born in slavery herself, she was the child of slaves, who had instructed her in the old tribal customs."

"Old Ada Boutwell will enjoy hearing that," said Cindy. "I can see her face now."

Minnie nodded, smiled and went on with her report: "Madame Honey, as a little girl, worked long hours in the cotton fields —

or at least that's what the biographical note said. It was here that she perfected her art, singing the traditional songs of her race while her little brown hands flew industriously among the cotton bolls."

Miss Ponder laughed disdainfully. "Honey Boutwell picking cotton of all things! Why she wouldn't even make her own bed! She wouldn't even wash a dish for her poor mother."

There was a silence, and then Cindy said: "What kind of songs did she sing, Minnie?"

"Just the old ones," said Minnie. "But they sounded different in Paris. And I must say that she really sang them beautifully. The one I liked the best was the one called 'Sweet Lord, Hold Down the Rising Sun.' I'm sure you've heard it. It's about a Negro woman who's waiting for her sweetheart to be hanged. When she finished it, the people simply went crazy. They were applauding and crying at the same time. They kept calling her back, time after time." Minnie was silent a moment, pulling thoughtfully at a button on her coat, and then she said: "Her voice is much richer, much fuller, now that she's grown. If you closed your eyes, you could easily believe that you were listening to a dramatic tenor."

"Well," said Ella Doremus. "I've heard everything now."

"When the concert was over," Minnie went on, "Clarry returned to the hotel where we were staying. . . . But you know how I am: Nothing would satisfy me except to go backstage and see The Alabama Negress in person. And so I went. Honey was glad to see me again, and we had a long talk about the folks back home. I wanted to ask her about Paul Kenworthy, but just when I got up nerve enough to do it, in he came himself. He was looking very well, too. He started to back away, to pretend he didn't know me, but I said, 'Don't act silly, Paul! What you do is your own affair! It doesn't make the least difference to me!' . . . He's her manager. And so all three of us went out for a bite to eat later on. We had a very pleasant evening, I must say."

"I'm astounded!" said Miss Ponder. "Paul Kenworthy, too!"

Minnie continued: "Later on in the evening I said to her, 'What made you claim to be colored, Honey? What was the sense in that?' And so she told me, 'It's what they like here. If they thought I was white, they wouldn't pay any attention to me.' She seemed afraid that people would find out her secret, and the last thing she said to me when we parted was: 'Please don't tell anybody I'm really white, Miss Minnie! It would only ruin me!' And so I said of course I wouldn't tell."

After her long holiday, Mrs. McMinn felt all her old energy again. *Shattered Roses* was made into a moving picture that year, and it was most successful. *Unending Quest* was published in the following autumn. It had an unusual sale even from the beginning, and it began to look as if no product of Mrs. McMinn's pen could fail. Recently the studio which had produced her first novel proposed filming *A Belle of Old Mobile,* too. The story had to be changed in several particulars, and Minnie had suggested that she do the adaptation herself. "If I can deliver what they want," she confided to Robert Porterfield, "they've promised me a contract. That's where I'm going next. That's where the money is. Why should I waste my time in this place any longer?"

She was working on her adaptation when Dover came up her steps and rang her bell. She let him in, pushed up her eyeshade and listened absently to his story. "Why, of course! I'll let you have the money with pleasure," she said. "Your poor mother must be worried to death." She opened her pocketbook and said: "Here! Take five dollars. You may need something for medicine." Then, as if the implications behind his story had just occurred to her, she said: "You mean to tell me there's a doctor in this town who refused to see a sick man until he had his money in his hand?"

"Yes, ma'am. That's what he said."

Minnie took back her bill and returned it to her purse. "I will not tolerate such conduct!" she said indignantly. "You go right back to Dr. Snowfield and tell him that he's to go to see your father at once! Tell him I said so! Tell him that if he doesn't, I'll personally see that his license is revoked!" Then, noticing that the boy still hesitated, she added: "Would you like for me to go with you and tell him myself? Nothing would give me more pleasure, you know!"

"No, ma'am," said Dover in a shocked voice. He backed out of the room, his eyes fixed on Mrs. McMinn, as if watching her for unexpected violence. When he was on the street again, he sighed and stood still. There was nothing left for him to do except go to the poolroom and see if he could get the money from his brother Breck. He sat down a moment to rest; then, getting up regretfully, he turned and went once more in the direction of Court House Square.

Chapter 8

W HEN Breck Boutwell took over the management of Rowley's Pool Parlors, that meeting of aptitude and opportunity, the nagging ideal of the efficiency expert, occurred in marriage so appropriate that even his mother, who disapproved of almost everything he did, said to her clients: "I hope it all works out satisfactory in the long run. Anyhow, he couldn't have found a job that suited him better. I was saying to my husband just the other night, 'Breck's lucky, ain't he? He don't have to go to work, the way other men do. He spends all his time at the poolroom, anyway!'" Then she put down her sewing and continued. "The way he's been behaving is disgraceful, and I want to be the first to admit it! He worries me more than all my other children put together, now that Honey's done left us. I can't figure out where the two of them got their common way of behaving from!"

A few days later, Breck moved his belongings from the Boutwell residence to the big room above the pool tables; and that same week, as if there were actually an All-seeing Nature, as Mr. Palmiller believed: a personified force eager to keep the scales of the universe tipped on the side of wholesomeness, The Society for the Fostering of Temperance and the Eradication of Vice added a new member to its executive committee: a lady who had already made a name for herself locally as a free-lance crusader against evil.

She was the wife of Joe Cotton, a Reedyville man who traveled a line of cotton piece goods, and who made his headquarters in his home town. Nobody knew very much about her except that Joe had married her in Atlanta a few years before, and that she did not get along very well with her husband. She had been unaware, at first, that she could abate, in some measure, her own suppressed but still itching lewdness through a preoccupation with the bolder lechery of her fellows; but having once discovered this ideal means of release, which indulged the most voluptuous of her phantasies, and yet affirmed her moral superiority to others at the same time, it became a necessity that she could no longer do without, and it was plain from the beginning that she was destined to become the society's most efficient member. And so it happened that she went eagerly about Reedyville, to turn over the ordure of others, her lips firm, her brows shocked and virtuous — her breast hot with her blood, and fainting with erotic, infantile pleasure.

Breck Boutwell was, she considered, a particular problem in immorality for herself to solve alone; but this time she found a person quite capable of dealing with her on her own terms, and to her chagrin, she invariably emerged second best from their encounters. He made a book and took bets on horse racing, and she knew these things well, although she could prove nothing. Upstairs, above the poolroom, adjoining the room where Breck himself slept, a crowd of Reedyville's young men gathered nightly to drink, discuss their experiences with the girls they knew, and shoot dice. But again she discovered that she needed more than her individual disapproval to make a case which would hold up in court, and this knowledge made her clamp her jaws down and speak rather bitterly of the coddling silliness the law shows in maintaining the privileges of the immoral, forgetting, naturally enough, that only such jealous foolishness on the part of the law made her own activities possible.

She might have abandoned Breck entirely, and directed her good works into more productive channels of endeavor, had his erotic life been less public, less flamboyant: less a topic of amused conversation in the town. It seemed that he was constantly involved with one girl or another, and once at a meeting of the Executive Committee, Sister Cotton, at the end of one of her tirades against him, sighed and straightened her back slowly, lifting her bosom upward with such balanced precision that it almost seemed as if she placed a final sandbag delicately atop a threatened levee. "When I think how that young scoundrel takes advantage of the innocence of the young ladies of this town, I get so mad I see red!" she remarked. "And the strange thing is that not one of them will say a word against him! It's really shocking! I don't know what the world is coming to! Take that little Dunphy girl he used to run around with. I even took the trouble to go out to the canning factory to see her, and begged her to make me her confidante, but she just looked at me with a straight face and said she never heard of anybody named Breck Boutwell in her whole life!"

A lack of resentment among his sweethearts was not difficult to explain, for they regarded him less as a man who belonged permanently to any one of them than as a loving cup to be possessed, in turn, by the most deserving. He was everything that the public masculine figure — the actor, the orator, the bullfighter — should be, but rarely is. His was the supple maleness of the selective cat rather than the snorting maleness of the sweating bull. His forehead was low and broad, his eyes as dark and melting as his father's, but with a quality of sardonic amusement added to them: they gave you a feeling of impending laughter, even when his face was in complete repose. His skin was clear, light olive, with much color lying beneath, and his teeth were so white, and, somehow, so intimate, that when he smiled at you suddenly, you felt that he had also touched you with his hand.

To his catholic love life he brought not only imagination and grace, but a pleased amazement that so many found him irresistible, as well. Under his management Rowley's became the headquarters of a certain set of young men who had taken Breck for their hero, who tried, with little success, to simulate the qualities which, in him, were innate and uncalculated.

But even his love affairs, as varied as they were, and his sporting life, with its long hours of application in the interest of old Mr. Rowley, did not quiet all his emotional drives, and if St. Joseph was the town's wit, Breck Boutwell was assuredly its wag. Here, too, in even the most macabre of his pleasantries, was to be found a certain absolving charm, and like artists in other fields of endeavor, the development of his waggery fell into distinct imaginative periods. The first of these phases of joking was a period of the unfocused hoax: the jape directed at no one person, which involved only those people with a natural bent toward gullibility.

A product of this early stage of his development was the hoax involving a mermaid. Breck swore that he had seen her swimming about in James' Lake, obviously lost and in distress. He had been about fifteen at that time, and he had run down the street repeating his breathless story to all who would listen. Most jokers would have been satisfied with the story as it stood, but Breck had added other details from his imagination. He had got a good look at the mermaid, he said pantingly. She was wearing a sort of cotton wrapper, a dress shapeless enough to please the most exacting missionary. Then, after they had stared at each other a moment, she had spoken to him. He could not be sure of what she said, since she spoke in Spanish, but it was his impression that she had questioned him regarding directions: had asked, in his own words, "How the hell do you get out of this town, anyway?"

Since there is no limit to human credulity, many people believed the tale. It revived an older story to the effect that James' Lake was connected with the Gulf of Mexico through a series of subterranean rivers, rivers which the Indians had used as places of sanctuary years before. Old Mrs. Highnote said: "Don't tell me a boy could make up a story like that out of his own head! I believe he's telling the God's own truth! . . . Now, look here: Suppose the mermaid he seen was chased by something real bad while she was swimming out in the ocean, and then hid out in one of the underground rivers for a spell until everything quieted down! If she done that, and I don't see anything to prevent it, what could be more natural than for her to get lost, the way Breck says she was, and to wind up right here in James' Lake?"

A number of people went to the lake with cameras, fishing poles and nets. The Perez family, who spoke Spanish, arranged themselves at strategic points around the shore and called out at intervals in the mermaid's native tongue, telling her that if she would only show herself again, she had nothing at all to fear. Through all this excitement, Breck moved with indolent grace, telling his story over and over, but varying in no betraying essential.

This, then, was a sample of his early style. His second phase was more centered in its aim, and his jests during this period were directed chiefly at Mr. Palmiller and the members of his vice society. The Executive Committee of the association met in the directors' room of their leader's bank, as we have already seen.

When their duties were done, their host, as a gesture of courtesy, usually ordered ice-cream sodas and sandwiches in for their refreshment.

On one occasion Breck and an admirer of his, a boy about his own age named Charlie Bradley, were loitering in the soda fountain when Mr. Palmiller's order went out. Instantly Breck stopped talking, and, moving away from the counter, he caressed his cheeks with his inverted thumb. Charlie got up and followed him. "What are you thinking about now?" he asked. "What have you got in your mind this time?"

"I'd like to do it myself," said Breck, "only they know me too well. . . . Now, listen! You got to help me this time!" He showed his white, even teeth, pressed his forehead against a rack of tinted post cards, and laughed in anticipation of what he was about to do. Those who persecute others with a righteous composure, who can inflict the most unbearable agonies on their fellows with the clearest of consciences, are peculiarly shocked at the thought of the unpleasant or the painful happening to themselves. They are the true hypochondriacs. They feel alarm at the trivial scratch; they are thrown into panics of anxiety when faced with the unexplained ache in their backs or loins. Breck knew this quite well, and he meant to capitalize his knowledge.

He turned around, when he had control of his laughter once more, and said: "Come outside with me, Charlie, where we can talk. I don't want anybody else to hear this." He moved away with his body poised and centered, and as he walked languidly toward the pavement, you could almost hear his excited blood purring and crackling in his veins.

He outlined his plan in detail, and after they had waited long enough for Mr. Palmiller and his associates to eat their sandwiches and drink their sodas, Charlie, with his light hair disarranged, his eyes worried and his voice frightened, appeared at the side door of the bank and rapped desperately. The Negro porter opened the door cautiously, and at once Charlie said: "Were some sodas and sandwiches delivered here a little while ago?"

"Yassuh," said the porter. "Yassuh, they sure were. I took 'em in myself."

"But they haven't *eaten* them, have they?" asked Charlie, his palms pressed together in alarm. Then, since the porter did not answer him at once, he added: "Go in and take them away as quick as you can! Hurry, man, hurry! There's not a minute to lose!"

The porter, alarmed now at the young man's intensity, said: "I think it's too late. I think they done et 'em by now." He wiped his forehead and added nervously: "Fact is, I know they done et 'em. I seen 'em munching away when I come to open the door."

At this, Charlie clapped his hands to his forehead and swayed dizzily against the door. "So I was too late, in spite of all I could do!" he said. "I wasn't able to prevent it, after all!"

"What you talking about, white gentleman?" asked the porter. He was feeling distinctly uneasy, and he shifted his feet back and forth on the threshold. "If anything was wrong with that food, and you knows it, why don't you come out and say so?"

"Forget that ·you talked to me," said Charlie tragically. "It won't do any good now! You must never mention this talk to a living soul, do you understand?" Then, glancing nervously to right and left, he put his forefinger to his lips in warning and backed away into the darkness; and when he was outside the porter's range of vision, he turned down a side alley and joined Breck at the corner across the street.

As they both knew, the porter would not keep his secret long. He came into the directors' room wiping his forehead, apologizing for his intrusion; and standing there just inside the door, he told his story, his wild and rolling eyes fixed not on the people he addressed, but on the empty tray which had contained the sandwiches. When he had finished, there was, at first, the completest silence. Then Mr. Palmiller eased his collar with his trembling forefinger and remarked with a lightness he did not feel: "It was probably that young Boutwell boy that you talked to. Does he think he can frighten intelligent people with a silly story like that?"

"Nawsuh," said the porter positively. "It wasn't him. I knows him as well as I knows you all. It was a young gentleman I seen somewhere befo', but can't rightly place. He looked to me like one of them new young gentlemen that works at the soda fountain." He raised his eyes for an instant and added: "Maybe he really know something."

Again there was a dead silence in the room, while the committee turned soundlessly in their chairs, their faces suddenly pale. Mr. Palmiller regained his composure after a moment, wiped his forehead and said: "That will be all, Henry. Thank you very much for informing us."

"Iffen you want to know what I *really* think," said the porter as he moved away, "I think them sandwiches was poisoned. You know there's lots of people in this town that have got it in for you folks."

He had put into words the terrifying thought which had been in all their minds, and at once Mr. Baker Rice said sharply: "Nobody asked for your opinion! Mr. Palmiller told you that would be all!"

Shortly before the porter interrupted them, the committee had been concerned with a case which, they all conceded, was most distressing. It had to do with a Mrs. Roberta Handley, a bookkeeper at the canning factory, and it appeared that she had embezzled, over a period of many months, sums of money whose grand total was almost two hundred dollars. She was a woman with a bedridden husband and four small children to take care of, and she had made her timid, desperate thefts in sums so small that instinctively you closed your eyes and turned your head away before the heartbreaking pathos of her poverty. The money she had stolen had been the precise difference between not quite enough to eat and actual starvation; and the representative of the bonding company who had investigated the career and thefts of this shabby, terrified woman, had refused to take any action against her in the courts.

Mr. Palmiller's committee had other and sterner views on the matter. Regardless of the mitigating circumstances, which everybody admitted freely, the woman was a criminal by her own confession, and as an object lesson to others, she must be sent to prison. Sentiment, as Mr. Baker Rice pointed out, had no place in the administration of justice. A person was either honest, and lived respectably with his fellow creatures, or he was not, and was sent away to an institution of correction. Mrs. Daniel O'Leary, who had never missed a meal in her entire life, added in a shocked voice that she couldn't understand how anybody could be so depraved, so lost to God, as to value the comfort of his mortal stomach above the salvation of his immortal soul.

She had hardly finished saying these things when the porter appeared and told his story. When he had gone, she pressed anxiously against her own unimportant, material stomach, glancing about her fearfully. It seemed to her, at that moment, that already she could feel the poison gnawing without pity at her vitals, and she stood up in alarm, her throat dry and sanded, her body covered with an icy sweat. "Come, Daniel!" she said. "It's time for us to be going home! The children, you know!" She inclined her head significantly in the general direction of the Good Samaritan Hospital, and Mr. O'Leary understood at once the thought in his wife's quick, capable mind.

At that moment the ladies and gentlemen of the Executive Committee could no longer contain their anxieties. They got up from their chairs and came through the bank's corridor with a rush, almost upsetting the porter in their haste. He opened the door for them as quickly as he could, and instantly they headed for the hospital a few blocks away. At first they walked rapidly, trying to salvage what they could of their imperiled dignity, scorning a pace more appropriate to terror; and then old Miss Emmaline Maybanks, realizing that she was being outdistanced by her associates, broke from behind Mr. Howard Carraway and Miss Eulalie Prescott and sprinted desperately down the sidewalk, her old neck thrust forward, her skirts held high above her knees.

"Come back, Sister Maybanks!" said Baker Rice sternly. "There's nothing to get excited about! It was only a joke, like we all know!"

But Mr. Rice had hardly spoken his reassuring words before he, himself, began to run. "Why, I'm doing the same thing myself," he thought in surprise. "How peculiar. I'm even running faster than old Miss Maybanks herself!" He reached up and touched the tinted wen which eternally pouted his upper lip, and, thrown off his stride in that second, the O'Learys passed him easily. Mr. Carraway, since the others were running, ran too; and then the entire committee was running, faster and faster down the deserted street — running in desperation, as if their lives depended, now, on the soundness of their wind and the driving power of their leg muscles; and as they neared the hospital and stumbled up the steps, Miss Maybanks screamed hoarsely: "Get out the stomach pumps! Quick! The stomach pumps! The stomach pumps, you fools!"

It was the kind of story which could not be kept quiet, and for a long time afterwards Reedyville laughed whenever it remembered the Executive Committee of the Society for the Fostering of Temperance and the Eradication of Vice having its collective, godlike stomach pumped by the bored and bawdy interns at the Good Samaritan.

Not long afterwards, Breck went to work at the poolroom, and Sister Cotton affiliated herself with Mr. Palmiller's committee, as we have seen. She had heard the story of the sandwiches at once. She did not consider it amusing. "That Boutwell boy is mixed up in it somehow," she said. "He's cagey, and you can't pin anything on him, but I know he did it, just as well as I know my name's Alice Cotton!" Then, tightening her wide, patent leather belt, she added grimly: "I'll put him in his place quick enough! I know how to handle people like him!" At that instant she dedicated her mind and her spirit to his quick confusion, and with her resolve to overthrow him, Breck entered into the third, the rococo period of his waggery.

She had one distinct advantage over him, for in addition to her activities with the vice society, she was prominent in a religious sect called "The Christian Gladiators," and she had their organized power behind everything she did. There was a flourishing branch of the organization in Reedyville, and as an opening move in her fight on Breck, she got a permit from the city to hold open air meetings on the sidewalk in front of the poolroom, since blackmail, if done in the name of God, is legal everywhere. Thereafter she and her fellows sang hymns and prayed, distressing the quiet air with their street organ, horns and tambourines. But Breck was too shrewd to show openly his distaste for the shouting vulgarity of his visitors. He merely stood in the door and looked at them, his eyes filled with sardonic amusement, his white teeth flashing as he turned from side to side and smiled at the people he knew.

At that time there was a garrulous old man who slept on a cot at the poolroom, and who did odd jobs there for a living. He was called Zobby, a practical contraction of his impractical surname which was so crowded with diphthongs, so bristling with unexpected consonantal combinations, that no American mouth could ever aspire to speak it. He had come originally from a remote district in North Europe, which, from what he said, seemed to be somewhere in the vicinity of Esthonia. His countrymen were all lumbermen, he said, and a number of them had already emigrated to America, some of them ending up as loggers at the sawmill in Hodgetown, only a few miles from Reedyville itself. Zobby had worked there too until his career ended abruptly when a log rolled down a ramp and broke his legs. He was a lighthearted, gabby old man, and when nobody would listen to him, he talked excitedly to the pool tables, sometimes in his native tongue, sometimes in his grotesque but entirely fluid English.

He admired Breck Boutwell more than anybody in the world, and he was eager to do anything to please him; and so it happened, on the fourth consecutive night when the Christian Gladiators appeared on the sidewalk outside the poolroom, that Zobby, after having been exhaustively coached in his part, came out of the establishment where he worked and joined Sister Cotton's group, eager to confess the most shocking of his sins. He started talking at once, and to the dismay of Sister Cotton, there seemed to be no way of shutting him up: not even the tambourines and the horns could silence him, for his strong, woodsman's voice carried above them with ease.

He seemed to have but one desire, now, and that was to bare his soul to its final autobiographical detail, to describe, as a warning to others, the hollowness of the life he had led before the Christian Gladiators had brought him peace. He talked on and on, his voice loud and booming, and at last Sister Cotton, who didn't like to take a back seat for anybody, found herself being nudged out of her own meeting. In order to rid herself of her earnest and obnoxious convert, she cut her meeting short, deciding to come back a little earlier the next evening. She did as she had planned, but hardly had her group commenced its first militant hymn before Zobby came bouncing out of the poolroom, eager to confess all over again. She stared at him angrily, but there was little she

could do except tap the pavement with her foot, since the avowed
object of her organization was to save souls, and apparently a
tiresome soul with a voice like roaring surf was as precious in
the eyes of the Lord as one entirely mute. But she stuck it out
for another night, and then, feeling that there would be no end to
Zobby's penitence, she abandoned her campaign against Breck for
the moment, and held her meetings in another part of town.

She had other plans in mind for his annoyance, and a day or
two later, recalling the fact that it was illegal for a minor to
enter a poolroom, she had two of her Gladiators deputized as
sheriffs and stationed inside the building, to examine every patron
who entered. From the conversation of these two guardians, Breck
soon discovered that the Gladiators were planning a present for
Sister Cotton on the anniversary of her leadership of their sect
in Reedyville. Their gift was to be a surprise and it was to be
tendered her on the twelfth of the month, which was only a few
days distant.

And so it happened, on the twelfth of the month, that Mrs.
Cotton received a package from a special messenger, just as she
knew that she would. She turned back toward her door, but seeing
her neighbor Mrs. Wadley craning her neck, and consumed with
curiosity, she generously held up the the package and said: "It's
supposed to be a surprise from the Gladiators. I pretended to be
dumb, but I knew about it long ago."

"Well," said Mrs. Wadley, "it's sure nice to be appreciated,
isn't it?"

The package was elaborately wrapped and sealed, and Sister
Cotton examined it from every angle, wondering where to start
untying; but noting that Mrs. Wadley had stopped her sweeping
and had come to the fence where she could see better, she tore off
the wrappings quickly; and there in her hands was a velvet box
of unusual depth, obviously the rich container of expensive jewelry.
Had she looked closely, she would have seen that the box was
secondhand, that its blue velvet had worn away at the edges, but
in her excitement she was not concerned with such things.

"What ever in the world is it?" asked Mrs. Wadley. "Do you
suppose it's a gold cross and chain to match?"

Sister Cotton laughed modestly and said: "They really shouldn't have done a thing like this for me. It's too much. Everybody knows I don't care anything about jewelry and trinkets." Then, as she solved the combination of the catch at last, the box jumped open suddenly, and there, pinned to the lining of the upper lid, was a card containing the single word "Boo!" . . . And in the circular well of the box, a depression which had once held an expensive bracelet, were the two dead, filmy eyes of a sheep.

Mrs. Cotton read the word and saw her gift at the same instant. For a time she could not draw her own eyes away from the horrible, dead eyes which looked up at her with such a clammy, knowing intimacy; then, to the astonishment of Mrs. Wadley, she flung the box and its contents from her in horror, screamed and sat down heavily on her front steps. "Breck Boutwell had a hand in this!" she shouted furiously. "I'll prove it this time, too! I'll have him jailed, see if I don't!" Then, when she had quieted down a little, this incredible woman turned to Mrs. Wadley, raised her arms outward, as if evoking the spirit of fair play, and added: "Who does he think he is — interfering in the lives of other people? I've got a right to privacy, like everybody else has, and I'm going to see that he understands that fact in future!"

Mrs. McMinn and Clarry Palmiller returned to Reedyville at a time when the town was still laughing over Sister Cotton's gift from her admiring fellow Gladiators. The two women had become close friends, as a result of their long trip together, and they were now in each other's company a great deal. "I hope Sister Cotton makes her next move quickly," said Mrs. McMinn. "I can't stand this waiting. It's really getting me down, Clarry." She parked her new automobile in front of Shepherd's Department Store, and added: "I won't be gone a minute. Why don't you wait here for me?"

Clarry laughed mildly, touched her pale hair with her finger tips and said: "Breck grew up to be quite a handsome man, didn't he? I caught a glimpse of him the other day when I passed the poolroom, and, would you believe it, he had the nerve to whistle at me!" She laughed again, with tolerant disbelief this time, and continued: "Of course I ignored him, but I kept thinking: 'What a pity he has no respect for anything or anybody. He could be so attractive, if he just made the effort.'"

Minnie, who had got down to the sidewalk, said: "Well, speaking of the Devil! . . . There's Breck now! There, right across the street! He's with that Bradley boy." She called to him loudly, regardless of the opinions of the people who passed. "Breck! Breck Boutwell!" she said. "Come here a minute, if you're not too busy! I want to talk to you!"

He came at once and stood with his foot on the fender of the car, surveying the two women with his soft, derisive eyes. Clarry said, "This is quite a coincidence. We were just talking about you when Miss Minnie looked up and saw you there across the street." Then, since she was two years his elder, and many grades his social superior, she added with just the slightest touch of patronage in her voice: "I was just saying that you'd turned out to be rather a good-looking boy."

Breck lowered his dark eyes with exaggerated humility. "God," he said softly. "God, you don't know what that means to me, Little Missy!"

His humor seemed wasted on Clarry, for she nodded, smiled graciously and added: "Why don't you leave Father and that eccentric Mrs. Cotton alone? Why don't you interest yourself in other things?"

"Oh, so you're on that side too!" said Breck. He raised his brows and smiled his white, dazzling smile. "I should have known that. It's natural for you to side with them against me."

"You're wrong," said Clarry calmly. "I'm entirely neutral. I can see both sides, I hope. I'm only advising you for your own good."

Minnie, who had waited for this pause, broke in vigorously: "What do you think Sister Cotton will try next? Have you any idea? And have you planned any more jokes on her and the Gladiators?"

Breck shook his head mockingly. "Now, Miss Minnie!" he said reprovingly. "You know I got too much sense than to answer a question like that!"

Mrs. McMinn was to find out quickly enough what revenge Sister Cotton intended to take for the gift of the sheep eyes, for a few weeks later, she and her organization of Gladiators decided to force the poolroom out of business through a public disapproval

of it. Petitions were prepared demanding that its license be revoked, and the Gladiators meant to get the signatures of so many
voting citizens that the Mayor of the town would be forced to
close the place on the grounds of political expediency. There seemed
to be no flaw in the plan, and no doubt it would have succeeded,
but on the morning her corps of workers started out on their quest,
washed and shining with goodness, determined to thwart evil at
last, an electrifying rumor concerning Sister Cotton's somewhat
misty past was started.

Later, when that indignant victim of her neighbor's gossip determined to trace the rumor to its source, she got as far as the
telegraph office, and no farther. The story had started, it seemed,
when a Mrs. Anna Wheat, a woman of unimpeachable character,
had gone into the place to send a telegram of congratulation to her
daughter and son-in-law, who had that morning become the parents
of their first child. As Mrs. Wheat was composing her message, her
eyes fell idly on another message which had been written on the
first blank of the pad she had meant to use. It was unfinished, and
Mrs. Wheat had started to tear it off and throw it into the waste-
basket, but seeing that it was addressed to the Chief of Police of a
Western city, she read it through twice before she understood
its meaning. Excitedly she got up and showed it to the clerk at
the counter and he read it slowly: "Mrs. Ruth Opal residing here
under alias Mrs. Alice Cotton. Suggest send detectives for purpose
of — "

The message broke off at that point, and naturally there was
no signature. The telegraph clerk shook his head, as if baffled,
and Mrs. Wheat said: "Maybe the person sending the message
got scared at the last minute. Maybe he decided to telephone instead,
figuring that would be quicker."

The clerk, as if answering his own unuttered question, said: "I
don't know who could have written it. The place has been full
of people all morning."

"Do you suppose it's true?" asked Mrs. Wheat. "Do you think
she's really Ruth Opal, like the message says?"

At that time, Ruth Opal's name was known to everybody in the
United States literate enough to read a newspaper. She had lived
quietly in a town in the Midwest, and, as it later developed, her

only social contacts with her neighbors had been their unhurried dismemberment, after she had first struck them with a hatchet. She had lived undetected for some years, committing one murder after another, and then, somehow, the trivial things which people had discovered about her fitted together so convincingly that a plain-clothes man had come out to her farm to question her. She had offered the detective a cup of hot coffee. He had accepted, and that had been a mistake, for not long afterwards he had toppled over on Mrs. Opal's parlor rug, thus becoming the last and the most naïve of all her victims. Then, stripping the clothes from his dead body, she had escaped her townsmen disguised as a man. She had never been caught, but at regular intervals there were news stories reporting her active again in places as remote from each other as Vermont and Mexico.

Mrs. Wheat put the message she had found in her bag; and when she had sent her own telegram, she went to Shepherd's, as she had intended, to do some shopping on behalf of her first grandchild. There she showed the message to the saleswoman who served her, and for a few minutes they leaned over the counter, talking excitedly together.

At first there were only a few people who knew the story, and then everybody in Reedyville was discussing Sister Alice Cotton and her crimes, for they had instantly accepted the fact that she and Mrs. Opal were the same person. Thinking back, they remembered a great many things to justify the wildest of their statements; and suddenly everybody was whispering that police officers from out of town had already arrested Mrs. Cotton, and had taken her back to the scene of her old crimes; that her husband, who was supposed to be out of town on one of his selling trips, had actually been murdered too, and that his body had been spaded up, a few minutes before, from its shallow grave back of his own chicken house.

And so Sister Cotton, who had striven so earnestly to marshal the prejudices of the unthinking against Breck Boutwell, found, to her dismay, that prejudice directed not against him, but against herself; and when her battery of Christian Gladiators called that morning with their petitions, they found the doors of Reedyville slammed rudely in their faces. "Go away!" people said. "Go back and tell that murderess we don't want anything to do with her sort!"

The story, once started, could not be stopped until it had run its full course, and at last the local chief of police, hoping to claim the big reward for Mrs. Opal's capture, took Sister Cotton into custody until her fingerprints and her past could be checked. She spent two nights in the jail to which she had sent so many of her townsmen, and when she was released with apologies, she was consumed with a rage so intense that she would easily have duplicated all the crimes of which she had been suspected. "He did it!" she muttered to herself. "Breck Boutwell did it! You can't tell me! Nobody but him could have thought up such a nasty little trick! He did it all right, even if nobody can prove it on him!"

She waited a long time, brooding over the injustice done her, thinking almost constantly of Breck, and planning ways to trap him at last, and bring him to justice. Much of her power in Reedyville had been lost with her arrest, although she had been completely vindicated, and even the most loyal of her Gladiators, seeing that their leader could be rendered as vulnerable as one of her own victims, treated her now with a clucking sympathy which she detested, a hushed, head-shaking patronage which almost drove her out of her mind, for she realized that even those who defend the victimized and the defrauded with the greatest vigor, season their spoken compassion with a mild, unspoken contempt.

Later, she considered it likely that Breck sold bootleg whisky at the poolroom, but if he did, she could never find anybody willing to testify that they had bought it from him. She took up the question with some of her Gladiators a few days later. "We all know what he's doing, right here under our noses," she said, raising her formidable bosom upward; "and we all admit he's as clever as a fox when it comes to sidestepping trouble. So why waste time trying to catch him red-handed? What's the sense in going to all that unnecessary trouble over a technicality? . . . Now, I know my suggestion may seem a little underhanded to people who can't think straight about an issue, but why don't some of you gentlemen swear that you bought whisky from him *anyway*? If several of you do that, the Grand Jury is obliged to indict him. The result will be the same, any way you look at it!"

There was a silence, with coughing and an elaborate shuffling of feet later on; and then Sister Cotton continued patiently, as if she addressed children: "You got to fight fire with fire, I say; and that's a truth we all got to learn, if we hope to accomplish any real good in this town. Now, I ask you in all fairness: Do you consider that a little untruth, when told with a clean conscience, is as bad as letting him go on selling whisky to your friends and relatives, like I'm sure he's really doing at this minute?"

She paused and stared triumphantly about her, waiting for her first volunteers. To her disgust, she found nobody willing to co-operate with her, although she was never to know whether their unwillingness was grounded in their moral scruples, or in their enormous respect for Breck Boutwell himself, their entirely justifiable fear of his quick and deadly reprisals. Seeing that her proposal was not popular, she dropped it regretfully. Later, she decided to have a warrant issued calling for a surprise search of the poolroom. This, she concluded, was probably the most effective plan after all, and it was the one she determined to put into operation.

But this time she felt that she needed the support of Mr. Palmiller and his powerful associates, and she went to see him at his bank, to discuss the working details of her plan with him. He promised his support at once, and on the day fixed for the raid, the police made a surprise descent upon the poolroom, flanked on the left by Sister Cotton and six of her most muscular Gladiators, on the right by Mr. Palmiller and his entire executive committee.

Breck let them in and stood with bored amusement, flashing his smile at everybody indiscriminately. He opened closets and unlocked doors at the bidding of the police, and when they found nothing at all in the poolroom itself, he accompanied them upstairs, where they meant to continue their search; but this time, Mr. Palmiller, Sister Cotton and all six of the Gladiators remained below, and Breck turned and looked at them thoughtfully, wondering what their motive was. He was to find out quickly enough, for hardly had the policemen begun their search when he heard a breaking of furniture and a smashing of mirrors in the poolroom beneath. He shrugged his shoulders, smiled and ignored the obvious destruction; and when the policemen came downstairs once more, having found nothing incriminating, not even an obscene post card, the poolroom was a wreck: Chairs had been broken, mirrors shattered. The cloth on the overturned tables had been ripped methodically with knives. The pool cues had been snapped in two and piled triumphantly in the center of the room. Even parts of the floor had been angrily ripped up.

Breck, examining all this destruction, smiled his white, ingratiating smile and said: "It's all insured, so why should I care one way or the other? I won't even say anything to you, because it's out of my hands now. But you people better be thinking what you're going to say to the underwriters when they ask you why you did it, in court! They're not good-tempered, like me, and that's something you're going to find out. They'll soak you plenty for what you've done, because they've got fifty million dollars behind them to do it with!"

He moved toward his friend Charlie Bradley, his lips drawn down with distaste, his eyes bright and disdainful. "I hope you got a lot of fun out of your little party," he added, "because it's going to cost you plenty to replace everything you've broken! And if there's any way for the insurance underwriters to add a jail sentence too, they'll do that with a lot of real pleasure!"

Mr. Palmiller looked reproachfully at Sister Cotton. Neither had anticipated this precise development, and it left them fearful and consumed with baffled fury. Mr. Palmiller tried to speak twice, but he could not, and then, in a voice hoarse with desperation, he said: "You are a disgrace to this community! You aren't fit to live with civilized people!"

"I know! I know!" said Breck. "It all sounds familiar. Don't you people ever put on a new record?"

At that moment Mr. Palmiller lost control of himself and began to shout. "Your whole family is an eyesore, and the sooner Reedyville is rid of the lot of you, the better off the town will be!" he said furiously. "There's no decency in any of you! I thought we'd taught you a lesson when we ran your filthy sister out of town, but it seems we didn't!"

At that instant all the sick hatred which Breck had once felt for Mr. Palmiller, and which he thought he had forgotten years before, came back to him in a rush so powerful that unknowingly he took a step forward. He closed his eyes and breathed slowly, trying to keep control of himself; but again, in all its shameful detail, he remembered the meeting of the executive committee so many years before, when he, as a boy of twelve, had hidden in the courtyard behind the bank and had listened to the deliberations which were to seal his sister's destiny; again with the most limpid, the most sickening clarity, he saw Mr. Palmiller nod his blond, handsome head in approval, and heard him repeat in his nasal, Northern voice: "We must make an example of her! A depraved girl of that sort isn't fit to breathe in the same air that a pure girl like my own daughter breathes!"

All the good-natured contempt had gone out of his face. He closed his jaw with a sudden snap and narrowed his eyes. He stared fixedly at Mr. Palmiller, his glance cold and full of hate. He lifted his arm and ran his hand roughly over his white face. "This has to do with you and me!" he said. "You better keep my sister's name out of it!"

"Why should I keep her name out of it?" asked Mr. Palmiller in an angry, artificial voice. "She did nothing in this town to deserve the respect of people! Why should I show consideration for a common little prostitute who ran off with a decent woman's husband?"

A wild, insane look had come into Breck's face, an expression which Charlie Bradley and his other friends had never seen before. Slowly, with the calm, deliberate grace of a dancer, he bent down and picked up the heavy end of one of the broken pool cues; but instantly Charlie Bradley had him by the arm. "You fool!" he whispered. "You crazy fool, you! Do you want to play right into their hands? Do you want them to have something they can really pin on you?"

Breck, being unable to speak at that moment, shook his head and sighed; then he looked about him, frowned and closed his eyes in concentration, and with his face lifted upward a little, his hands moving nervously across the buttons of his coat, you could almost see his quick, shrewd brain working out his revenge. Charlie was right. Violence was always stupid. It got you nowhere, and that was a thing he knew well. It was unnecessary, too, for there must be other and more subtle ways of revenging himself on Hubert Palmiller for this unforgivable insult. The thing to do was to find your enemy's unprotected side and strike at him there; and the weak point in Mr. Palmiller's almost impregnable defenses was his blond daughter whom he adored so blindly, whom he considered so much better than Honey, or anyone else in the world. "That big, white heifer!" he thought contemptuously. "We'll see what she's made out of! We'll see what sort of special air it is that she breathes!"

Then suddenly he straightened up, and with an almost tender concern he replaced the broken cue on its pile of debris. The sardonic light came back to his eyes and he smiled his brilliant, triumphant smile at his enemies, for already he knew what his revenge was going to be. It was a thing so simple that he wondered why he had not thought of it instantly. He would begin a courtship of Clarry Palmiller at once; and on the success of that courtship would hang the fulfillment or the failure of his bitterest joke. He would see if she were made out of some pure, incorruptible material as her father seemed to consider, or if she were merely flesh and blood, like other people. If he failed, there would be other plans to consider. If he did not, his triumph would be enormous indeed. It would mean the defeat of Mr. Palmiller forever. It would pay him back neatly, in his own cruel, unique coin.

He stood there a moment longer, stroking his cheek with his thumb, his eyes hard and shining with excitement. Then, unexpectedly, he turned directly to Hubert and bowed mockingly. "You'll be sorry that you said what you did about my sister," he remarked gently. "The day will come when you'll wish you'd cut your tongue out first!"

As if he had lost interest in the entire affair, he turned to Zobby and said: "Clean up the mess these ladies and gentlemen have made, as best you can"; and quickly, without a backward glance, he went upstairs to his own quarters. "That stupid white heifer!" he said aloud. . . . "We'll see! We'll see in time!" Then, standing there beside his own door, he began to laugh, for already he knew what he meant to do. If he succeeded with Clarry, as he thought possible, then, when he had gained her complete confidence, he would induce her to go with him to one of the places on New April Avenue which rented rooms to couples like themselves. And while they were there together, Charlie Bradley would

telephone Sister Cotton or Mr. Palmiller and tell them how they
could trap him, Breck Boutwell, with one of his depraved sweethearts! The idea of Clarry Palmiller turning up as a victim of
one of her father's vice raids appealed to him at that angry moment. He went into his room and stood by his window, thinking: "Before I'm through with him, he'll wish a thousand times
he never said those things about my sister!"

But this time he knew that he must proceed with the utmost
caution, that he must keep his wits constantly about him, prepared
to adjust himself instantly to her wishes, to take advantage of each
small circumstance. He waited for chance to bring them together,
in a meeting which would appear unplanned. This accidental nature
of their first contact seemed important to him, for he felt that
thus his pride would be saved if his charm and his technical
facility failed this time; and not long afterwards, observing her
go into Parker's Soda Fountain, he waited precisely two minutes
and then followed her. She had taken a table at the back of the
shop, behind one of the dusty, artificial palms, and he approached
her from the rear, seating himself beside her.

He pretended to be surprised when she looked up and turned
her face to him. He smiled his white, brilliant smile and said
rapidly: "I got only a glimpse of you through the palms. I thought
you were that big blond Evans girl. You know, I've had my eye on
her a long time now, but I haven't got very far, and so I said to myself: 'This is your big chance, Son! Go over and give her a sales
talk!'" Then, lifting his eyebrows and sighing audibly, he added:
"But it turned out to be you instead. The drinks are on me this
time, and no two ways about it."

"You're disappointed, I take it?"

"Naturally," said Breck. "A little, anyway. That stands to reason,
don't you think?"

Clarry smiled with amusement and moved her soda farther from
his elbow. "I really don't know," she said. "I have my following,
too. There are those who find me attractive, no matter how odd
that may sound to you."

"Of course you have!" said Breck cheerfully. "I'm not denying
that! Somebody finds everybody attractive. Sure, there are lots of
people that admire you. Lord knows you go around enough."

"But you aren't one of them? Is that the point of your story?"

He felt it wise to give her this small, initial advantage over him, and so he said with false ingenuousness: "Now, Clarry! Don't try to get me all mixed up! Of course I admire you! But you see, I never think of you as a woman, like other people. You remind me of one of those statues they dig up in Greece — you remember, don't you? The ones Miss Blackfoot used to tell us about in grammar school. Just something pretty to look at, but too cold to put your arms around and kiss." He moved back his chair, pretending that he was going, but Clarry said in a distressed voice: "Wait, Breck! Don't hurry off. You know we haven't really seen each other in years — since we were children, in fact."

There was a silence, while she turned over in her mind the things he had said about her. She spoke after a moment: "I hear you and Father have been at it again!" And when he merely smiled and shrugged his shoulders, she added: "Why do you hate Father so? It's a thing I've often wondered about. Why do you try to irritate him as you do?"

"Why not?" asked Breck. "You got to hate somebody, haven't you?" Then, in a voice so soft, so different from the voice he had been using, that she was thrown completely off her guard, he continued: "Anyway, I don't hate you, my dear, although I admit I've tried to hard enough. I wish to God I could hate you; but you see you've always meant something very beautiful and pure to me."

Had she laughed, as he expected her to, he was prepared to laugh with her, to drop his hushed, cathedral manner; but to his astonishment, she seemed to see nothing absurd in his words. This was the kind of thing she had heard all her life, and being on familiar ground now, she leaned back in her chair, waiting for him to tell her that every man needed an angel of goodness and purity in his life, expecting him to implore her to play that role in his own existence. Had he been stupid enough to do so, she would have got up at once and left him, feeling that there was nothing further in him for her to discover; but as she sat there waiting for the familiar, reassuring words, her eyes fixed on the marble surface of the table before her, half in triumph, half in boredom, she heard him laughing at her instead. The change in his manner was so unexpected that she looked up quickly in mild confusion, and opened her purse without purpose. "Breck!" she said reprovingly. "Breck, you're the most peculiar man I've ever met! What do you find so amusing all of a sudden?"

He would not answer her at first, but he had followed her shallow thoughts with ease, and to himself he said: "You're even simpler than I thought. You think you've got me right where you want me now, right where you got all the others, don't you, you big white heifer? But you'll find out different pretty soon! You'll see your mistake in time!" He laughed again, and Clarry, her brows drawn together in a patient exasperation, her blue, unwavering eyes a little hurt, a little puzzled, continued: "You're really being rude, you know."

"I'll tell you what I was laughing at," said Breck. "After all, you and I grew up together. If we can't tell each other the truth, then nobody can. All right, here's what it was: Watching you sitting there so stiff and cold and unwrinkled made me say to myself, 'She's actually like one of those pretty wax bouquets which old ladies put under a glass bell and keep in the darkest part of their parlors.'"

He glanced at the wall decorations above her head, as if her limitations were plain to the world, and they exhausted him. "That's all there was to it," he added. "Now, are you satisfied?" Again he moved his chair backward a little, and with the movement of his body, his hand fell from the edge of the table and rested, spread out and languid, against her warm, plump thigh. It was the sort of thing which people who have lived together for years, who know the contour and texture of their partner's body even better than their own, do without conscious thought. The hand rested there without interest, and without pressure other than its own weight. There was no greater attempt at intimacy, there was only the relaxed hand lying there, as if that were the position it had taken as a matter of custom, of convenience.

Clarry, with one palm flat against her cheek, glanced uneasily from side to side, suffering, at that moment, a kind of minor, self-conscious anguish. She was very aware of the impertinent, intimate hand, although its possessor seemed not to be, and she wondered what she should do about it; but she waited too long, and even in her moment of deliberation, the gesture took on the quality of those nervous, prolonged handshakes, which, having lost their spontaneity before they terminate, pass strangely from the conventional act to the embarrassing situation, becoming, thus, almost impossible to end.

If she moved the hand with one of her own, she opened herself to further charges of prudishness, further ridicule; and if she permitted it to rest there unchallenged, she admitted an understanding between them which, at this instant at least, she found distasteful. Breck rested his chin in his other hand and looked squarely at her, his eyes bright with amusement, understanding so well the way her mind was working; and at the moment when she decided to shove her handbag from the table with her elbow, to shift her position in order to pick it up, he moved his hand of his own accord. He stood up to go, and again she saw his sardonic eyes staring knowingly into her own, as if already there were a relationship between them so subtle and so binding that she could not hope to escape it.

"I've got to go back to work," he said. "Maybe I'll see you here again. I come in often about this time."

Clarry lifted her heavy, classic face, and, attempting a lightness of manner which she could not quite carry off, she said: "Perhaps you'll even see your friend Miss Evans again, and that will be even nicer for you, won't it?"

He moved away, turning unexpectedly at the door to look back, knowing that she would follow his figure with her eyes. Their glances met, as he expected them to, for a final time, her eyes steady and puzzled, his own, hard, glittering and derisive. Then, as if dismissing her from his thoughts, he shrugged, passed through the doorway and came out on the street, well pleased, on the whole, with this first meeting between them. In his campaign to defeat her, he had expected her to be indignant at first, hoping that her anger, her hurt pride, if nothing more, would impel her to see him again; but now, as he cut diagonally across the square, he knew that she was incapable of feeling resentment against himself or anyone else; that somewhere in her, and lying close to the surface of her consciousness, was a quality which would welcome, not repudiate, suffering, and that while she would do nothing to arrange the defeat of others, she would willingly arrange her own; that some deep, hidden guilt would make her accept any punishment, any revenge against her, as both just and appropriate — a thing desirable and right. It was a quality which he had often experienced in the women he had known, and it invariably left him puzzled and angry. Perhaps the same trait existed in some men too, but of that he had no definite knowledge: at any rate, he knew that Clarry would want to see him again, not to defeat him, as he had anticipated, but to have him defeat her. "We'll see!" he thought in triumph. "We'll see what makes her better than others! We'll see what sort of special air it is she breathes!"

Later that afternoon, Clarry came into her room and sat down at her desk, her mind still busy with her meeting with Breck. "It isn't that I want to be made out of marble," she said. "It isn't that I want to be something locked under glass. I've only been what others expected me to be." Then, disquieted at her preoccupation with Breck, and his opinion of her, she added defensively: "Why should I pay any attention to what he thinks? Really, he's quite illiterate, quite common! Very much the cheap, small-town sport!"

Then, even as she reassured herself, she felt the imprint of his hand again. She kept touching the place, and thinking that it must be inflamed, she turned to her mirror in a sudden panic and exposed her smooth, milky thigh. There was nothing — no reddened spot, no imprint of a vulgar hand; but the feeling that his hand still rested against her flesh persisted, and making a gesture of distaste with her lips, she said: "Anyway, I hope he has nothing contagious! I'd hate to be infected by him, of all people!"

After a time, she dismissed him from her mind, but that night she dreamed of him. It seemed that he and her father struggled for her possession, and although she opened her mouth gaspingly and tried to cry out, she could not, for her throat was made, not of flesh, but of marble. Then she saw her breast and her limbs become marble too, and she thought: "If I am stone, I should not feel at all. And yet I do feel. I suffer unbearable pain at this moment." . . . And now Breck was not himself at all, but her brother who had died so many years before, and somehow she managed to say: "Stop it! Stop this struggle over me! I'm not

worth fighting for! Save Rance, not me! He's the important one!"
And turning at last on her pillow, she woke up crying.

The dream had had a deep effect on her, and she tried not to
think of Breck Boutwell again, but against her will, she found
herself returning to Parker's at the hour when she had first met
him there, hoping that she would see him again. She took a table
by the window this time, so that she could see him at once. He
passed at the moment when she had given him up, but this time
he merely smiled mockingly and lifted his hat. The next day,
seeing her there, he joined her, and said: "Let's move to the back
of the store. You don't want your father to see us, do you?" A
few days before, she would have said: "What does it matter whether
he sees us or not? I have nothing to hide." But now, as if she concurred in subterfuge, she got up nervously and followed him to
their original seat beneath the palm, and Breck, feeling the change
in her, knew that this was the first small concession which would
lead to her inevitable capture.

"It's odd how Father has changed toward you," she said after
a moment. "He used to like you so much, when you were a little
boy. I remember once, years ago, when he was teaching Rance to
play baseball. You were at our house that day too, and when
Rance wouldn't act the way Father wanted him to, you stepped into
the breach. You two had such a good time together that day.
Afterwards he said that he wished Rance were more like you in
disposition."

"I go to a little shack on the far side of James' Lake on Monday
afternoons," said Breck. "It's my day off. Charlie Bradley owns the
place, but he's never there when I am, because he's working for
me that day at the poolroom. It's not much to look at, but nobody
could ever find a person there. Not even Sister Cotton. Not even
your father."

Clarry, as if she had heard nothing he said, continued gaily:
"Do you remember the wonderful party I had on my tenth birthday? You came dressed as a Roman emperor, I remember. You
were mad the whole time, for some reason or another, and wouldn't
enjoy yourself."

"I remember it," said Breck. "I remember it well. I was mad

because Mama made me wear pants under my toga, and I knew an emperor didn't."

"We've changed so greatly since then," said Clarry. "Everything is so different now. So much more complex, and difficult."

"I'll show you how to get to the shack," said Breck. "It'll be easy for you, in your new roadster." He took a menu card from its rack and sketched rapidly, drawing both the lake and the roads that led to it, indicating the exact location of the shack with a cross surrounded by a circle.

"I came to the party as an Easter lily," said Clarry. "I was incredibly silly to take myself so seriously. I wonder who selected such a costume. I'm sure I didn't. Possibly it was Father's idea."

"You were a big hit just the same," said Breck, "particularly with the old ladies." Then, stretching himself languidly, without so much as moving his arms from his sides, he continued: "Here's the map. Take it. But be sure to turn off the highway at Cowan's farm." He bent forward and touched her cheek with his spread hand, his eyes soft and drawn upward a little. "I'll drive out early — about two o'clock. Nobody'll know anything about it, so you needn't be afraid to come."

He shoved the map toward her, and without turning again, he walked out of the store. She sighed and shook her head in astonishment. "Of all the conceit!" she said. "Of all the vain, cheap little Don Juans I ever met, he's the champion!" Her instinct was to tear up the map and throw it away, but she did not. She held it in her hands, staring at it with disbelief; and then, as if resigning herself to the inevitable, she put it away carefully in her handbag.

She did not see him again that week, although she thought of him a great deal. There was one imaginary scene between them which she rehearsed over and over. In it, he came to her, stripped of his arrogance, repentant and affirming her purity, her goodness, as all the others had done in time. During these days she thought a great deal about sexual love, wondering again, as she had wondered so often in the past, but now with a new, a more personal interest, why it seemed so important a factor in the lives of the people she knew. She had not loved any man thus far, certainly not in the accepted, physical sense of the word, and for that reason she had not married, although she had had many chances to do so;

but she meant to marry some day, feeling that the loneliness of old age would be less desirable, even, than the sharing intimacy of marriage.

Her coolness troubled her at times, and in her own defense, she told herself that it mattered little whether or not she lacked the capacity to bring passion to her union with a man; that those marriages in which the physical bond was negligible on the part of the wife were the ones most likely to be happy and untroubled. There would be children from her marriage, she hoped, and that, she felt, would compensate her for those sacrifices of privacy which seemed so shocking to her, in such bad taste.

But now, in her more specialized feeling for Breck, she felt her old definitions, her old reticences, slipping from her. Her new vulnerability frightened her, and she wondered what fascination he held for her, aside from his obvious, excited good looks which seemed to appeal to so many other women too. Often she was irritated with herself for not clearly seeing the causation of her growing bondage. She need not have taken herself so strictly to task, for to understand the thing that was happening to her would have been to understand almost the total content of her mind, to face once more many of the old, terrifying emotions which she had experienced long ago, and had forgotten.

Even the simplest minds are so complex upon examination that one is astounded at the elaborateness of their involutions; and so it was that Clarry's emotion carried not only a positive feeling for Breck as a man in his own right, but a repudiation of her father, his enemy, as well — a cold denial of his coldness, his eccentricities, which she never suspected herself of possessing, and which, under no conditions, would she have permitted herself to express to others. Thus it was that many of the things which she had hated and found shameful in her grotesque father found a permissible release, through indirection, in her admiration of the man he disapproved of the most.

Then, too, Breck and her brother Rance had been the same age, and they were tied together in her mind in countless small, inescapable ways. She had been fourteen when Rance drowned himself; and afterwards her guilts had been almost too great to bear. "If Father had loved Rance more, and me less," she would say weepingly to herself in those days, "my brother wouldn't have killed himself! I'm responsible for his death as much as anybody, because I took my share and his too!" Now, these old, forgotten guilts found expression through her brother's surrogate, and it was almost as if she believed, somewhere in the depths of her mind, that by loving the man who stood for him, she could bring her dead brother back from his grave, could undo, at last, his lonely, pitiful end.

But despite the still living power of these old, forgotten things, the factor which influenced her the most in her increasing bondage to Breck was the fact that he, unlike the other men she had known, demanded no special qualities of goodness from her — did not think of her as a bloodless badge to cover a sterile heart. Those others had asked the right to worship her, to protect her from reality and pain; but Breck would make her suffer, as living people suffered, and oddly she found that possibility both stimulating and desirable.

Realizing some of these things, not as thought, but as vague, almost terrifying feeling, she said to herself that Monday morning, still undecided whether or not to meet him, "He has no respect for me at all. Perhaps that's why I have so much respect for him, because, you see, I have no respect for myself either!"

She found the shack with ease, and as she approached it, she saw him waiting for her at the crossroad. He got into the car beside her, and instantly she moved aside, giving him the wheel, as if it were his right. He drove the car into a thicket of blackjacks and left it there, where it could not be seen; and then he put his arm about her, drew her to him, and kissed her, his leg pressing intimately against her own. "You big white heifer!" he said laughingly. "You great big white heifer!"

"Please, Breck!" she said. "Please don't. If I'd known you meant to act this way, I wouldn't have come."

She glanced up at him helplessly, for although she had been taught all the things which are calculated to arouse a man's interest, she knew none of the defenses against him, once his passion is put in motion. She lived in a false and artificial world which pretended that all men were to be trusted, that an intangible halo of virtue was enough to protect the most alluring woman from harm.

He opened the door after a moment, laughed once more and helped her to the ground. "If you'd thought I was going to act any *other* way, you wouldn't have come! Isn't that what you really mean?"

They walked together to the lake and sat there, looking out at the water. To her surprise, he made no further effort to touch her. They talked mostly of the past which they had shared, of the things they remembered from their childhood, laughing as each drew up from his memory things which the other had forgotten. Later, toward the early, April sunset, he drove her car to the road for her, and told her good-by; and as she turned to wave, she knew that she was tied to him forever, no matter what a future with him might bring. She considered, now, the possibility of becoming his wife, and as she drove home that afternoon, she made her trustful, ingenuous plans. Marriage with him would be hard to arrange, although it would not be impossible. Her mother, no doubt, would give her consent easily enough; her father would oppose it with all the strength of his fanatical fury. She put her car in the old carriage house and paused at the door to arrange her hair. There would be many difficulties to be overcome, many factors to be considered, but she would solve these interfering things later, when they came up to bother her. She went into her bedroom, and hardly had she got there when, even before she had taken off her hat and coat, she sat down and began a long letter to Breck, to say all over again the things which had already been said.

She saw him again at Parker's a few days later, but as if there were a deeper, a more secret, understanding between them now, he did not go to her table; but catching her eye, he shaped his lips to form the words, "Next Monday, sure!" She came promptly to the meeting place, and as he concealed her car among the blackjacks, she said: "Is it necessary for us to be so furtive? I don't like intrigue! I don't like underhand methods at all!"

They went first to the lake and walked arm in arm under the new, spring green of the trees; but when a cold wind came up from the East, rippling the water and making their eyes and their faces smart, they laughed and ran back to the shack. Kneeling there on the hearth, Breck built a fire; and afterwards they sat before it, thinking their thoughts. Suddenly Clarry laughed and said: "I'm still a little cold, Breck! That wind off the lake goes right through you, doesn't it?" Instantly he put his arm about her and drew her to him. Then, lifting her chin, he looked quickly into her eyes, his own eyes dark and excited; and although she knew nothing at all about love, was incapable even of feeling physical desire, her body seemed to lift upward under the force of its own desperation and flow forward to meet his own, in that graceful, unchanging motion so characteristic of surrender. She put her hand back of his head and whispered: "Don't! Don't! You must not!"

Then he bent slowly and kissed her, surprised at the easiness of his triumph, contemptuous, even at that moment, of the abjectness of her need for him. She resisted him in no way. She made no effort at all to protect herself. She merely said helplessly, over and over, not even listening to her own trembling words: "Don't! Don't, Breck! You must not! Really, you must not!"

Afterwards, it almost seemed as if she were the pursuer, the one who patiently asked favors, for there is no woman so insatiable, so jealous of her privileges, as the one who loves without passion. It is almost as if, realizing that they have relinquished so much, such women demand, as compensation, a wider application of the courtesies of affection, the accent of their desire falling not upon the consummation of love, but upon the fulfillment of its small, precious preliminaries. She telephoned him a dozen times a day, although he would not telephone her; she wrote him tender, pleading notes which he did not answer. She fell at once into any plan he suggested, as if she had given up all right to make a choice for herself, and for a time he met her almost nightly in the room above the old carriage house in her own yard.

It had once been a playroom for Rance and herself, and now, professing a sudden affection for it, she fitted it up again as a place of sanctuary for her lover. When the house was asleep, she would go there furtively, and sitting in the dark on the couch, her mind occupied with its unending, shadowy dream of a future with Breck Boutwell, she eagerly waited his coming.

It was now late June, and although Breck could have taken his revenge many times over, he did not; he would not. At first, he had thought that this affair would be like the others he had known, except that it would be more brilliant, more difficult of arrangement, since the level of society in which Clarry moved was so far above the level in which the others he had known had moved. He said to himself that she would prove more intelligent, more un-predictable than the others, since her education and her experience had been so much wider than theirs; and that while things would be essentially the same at last, they would be more sharpened, more sophisticated in tone. At no time had he considered a triumph more conclusive than that of the superficial flesh, and the unexpected depth of her love for him, her selfless surrender to his slightest desire, were things entirely outside his plans.

The fact that she had neither the desire nor the capacity to resist him left him feeling tricked and uncertain, and often he found himself angry at her for reasons which he could not have explained. He had abandoned his original plan long ago, but one night as he lay beside her on the couch, he suggested, in order to test his power over her, that she meet him at the house on New April Avenue. She merely smiled her sweet, shallow smile and touched his forehead with her finger tips. "Yes," she said. "Yes, of course, if you think best, my dear!"

He sat up angrily and said: "You fool! Haven't you got more common sense than that? Suppose the place happened to be raided, and Sister Cotton, or one of the others, caught you there with me? A fine fix you'd be in then, wouldn't you?"

She merely smiled at his anger, as if he were a little boy. "I wouldn't be frightened if you were there to protect me. Your mind works so quickly. You'd be sure to think of something, and I know that very well." She pulled his head down and kissed him gently. "I trust you completely, my darling," she said. "I know that you'd never ask me to do anything, if you thought it would hurt me in any way."

He could not sleep that night, and at last he sat on the side of his bed, his head held in his hands, thinking: "How could I have done such a mean thing to her? My God! My God, I must have been crazy! . . . No matter what her father is, she's not responsible!" He got up nervously and went to his window. Then, lighting a cigarette after a moment, he nodded his head, knowing that the first thing he must do was to end the relationship between them at once. He wanted, now, to undo some of the damage he had done her, and since the limitations of our own minds must determine our understanding of the minds of others, it seemed to him that if he could make her hate him dramatically, in the way that he hated her father, for example, that her deep, emotional dependence upon him would be quickly broken. For this reason, he determined to tell her the exact truth, no matter how humiliating he found it.

He met her that next night as they had planned, and sitting there with her in the moonlight, listening to one of the little Harrison girls practising her scales on the piano, he told why he had striven so earnestly to seduce her; how he had planned to have her father find them together at last. When he had finished, he got up and stood by the door, hoping that she would turn upon him in fury; but she did not. She did not even cry, but a moment later as she sat there staring at him with a look so crushed, so terrible that he was never to forget it, she shook her head slowly from side to side and said: "No! No! It's not possible for you to have done such a thing! I know you too well!"

"I did it just the same," he said. He moved closer to the stairs which led downward to the alley, adding, with a carelessness which he did not feel: "Now you know the kind of man I really am! Maybe you'll get over your craziness! Maybe you'll know better next time!"

She sat there shaking her head from side to side, and at last she got up and came to him. "You must not try to see me again," she said quietly. "You must not even speak to me again if we meet by accident." Then, as he stood there with his hand on the knob, not able to think of anything to say for the first time in his life, she took his head in her hands, as if he were dead, and she told him good-by, and kissed him on the lips. "You must not let this trouble you," she said softly. "You must remember that I don't blame you at all. I can see your side, too. You must not feel guilty over me, because I'm to blame as much as you are."

He opened the door and stood outside on the top step, and instantly he heard her shove the bolt, so that he could not enter again. "Clarry!" he said. "Clarry! Maybe we can work things out, after all!" She would not answer him, and as he stood there with his face pressed against the door, he could hear her walking up and down the room, whispering over and over to herself, her voice soft and anguished: "I'm so ashamed! I'm so ashamed!"

The days that followed seemed so terrible to her that often she wondered how it was possible for her to live through them. Later, she was to look back at them with regret even, for toward the end of July she knew definitely that she was pregnant. A period of anxiety and anguish and self-loathing set in, and as she lay sleepless night after night, she wondered what she was to do, what solution there was for her. There was no one she could speak to, no one to confide in, and as she went through her deaths of doubt and remorse, she saw clearly the hand of divine providence in her plight.

At last, in her desperation, she went to see Dr. Snowfield, hoping that he would help her; and thus it happened that the defeat which Breck had planned for her, and had begun, was to be brought to its conclusion by another man — a man to whom she was also of the utmost importance, not as a human being, but as a symbol.

When she left him after that first visit, Dr. Snowfield lay on his bed a long time staring up at the ceiling above him, his eyes hard, intense and unmoving. He thought not of her desperation but of his own, for he had so completely identified himself with her, that it was impossible for her to have significance for him except as a mirror in which his sick mind could see a part of itself reflected. Thus his need, now, to destroy her had more in common with a desire for suicide than a desire for murder.

And so he lay there, his cold mind moving coldly through the maze of its doubts with a lost, terrifying intensity. Then, gradually the world of reality left him, and he stood again on the top of a hill and watched the world being covered with pure and uncorrupted snow once more. The flakes fell quietly, steadily, and soon the unbearable earth was lost under a pure, rounded coverlet: those sharp things which wounded the hand that would touch them, those smells which sickened the nose that approached them too closely, those sights which shocked the eye which beheld them . . . And now there was nothing left in all the world but sound, and that was the beautiful, pure sound of the silver bell which tinkled a tune as small and sad as the tune of a music box — but always out of sight, always beyond the reach of the upthrust hand, its thin music shaking mechanically, and falling to earth as remotely, as coldly, as the cleansing snow itself.

That night he lay quietly without sleep, but not moving from his original position on the bed. At last, toward daybreak, he thought: "She was the one thing I believed in, and she betrayed me. She was the thing that made my life bearable, and now I no longer have that."

But again, even in this, the overwhelming crisis of his life, his doubts were so paralyzing that he was unable to act, just as he had been unable to ask his parents, before they died, the important question which had once so occupied his mind. Then, turning on his side, and pressing his hands against his thin, birdlike face, he said: "I must leave things to chance. I'll do what I can to help her, but I won't sterilize the instruments I use."

The more he considered this compromise, the fairer it seemed to him. He was being more than just to her, he thought; he was giving her more than an even chance. The possibilities of infection, under the conditions he planned, were not nearly so great as people thought, and if she came safely through the operation, as she probably would, he would consider it a sign from some mysterious power, telling him that he was free of her at last. If she died, then he died with her; and one could hardly blame a man for taking his own life when suffering made life intolerable for him.

She came early the next morning as she had agreed, bringing the letter with her, and even in that moment of his anguish, even though he thought of himself as a man already doomed, the untouched, logical side of his mind made him examine the letter with an intense care, to see that everything was in order, that he was protected from the results of his act. She went into his office, as he told her to; and a moment later he followed her, and did the thing she had asked.

Two days later she telephoned him, telling him that she was feverish and disturbed, that things had not gone as they had expected. He listened to her to the end, and then, without having said a word, he hung up the receiver. That night she was worse, and the next morning, knowing she was now desperately sick, she asked her mother to call in Dr. Kent.

But Breck Boutwell knew none of these things. He had not seen Clarry for a long time, and he thought it better not to ask others about her. He no longer found pleasure in his particular manner of life, and recently he planned to leave Reedyville. And so it hap-

pened, when Dover came into his brother's room, he found him
packing a suitcase. He had burned all his letters, all his amorous
keepsakes, in the fireplace an hour or so before, and those things
which he did not intend taking with him were tossed into one
corner of the room.

Dover delivered his message, and Breck said: "You know how
excited Mama gets. There is nothing the matter with him, except
he's drunk as a coot. He tried to borrow some money off me,
after Mattress May put him out, but I told him I couldn't spare it."

"Where you going, Breck?"

"I'm going to New Orleans, first. When I get there, I'm going to
join up with the Marines, if they want me. After that, I don't
know." Then passionately he turned and said: "I'm sick of this
town! I never want to set foot in it again!"

He finished his packing, and turning to his younger brother, he
said: "Come with me to the depot. We just got time to catch the
9:45." They reached the station a little before the train pulled in,
and Breck said: "I'd give you the money any other time, and you
know it. But the way things are now, I've got just enough to see me
through."

A little later the train pulled into the station and Breck got
aboard. He walked at once to the vestibule of the last coach, and
standing there, he stared earnestly at his native town, as if he meant
to fix it in his mind forever. It is well that he did so, for he was
never to see it again. In 1917 he was to be sent with his regiment
to France; and in September of the following year, it was his destiny
to die in the fighting at St. Mihiel.

The train pulled out of the station, and Breck straightened up
and waved to his brother; and looking up once more at the soft,
purple sky which stretched like a starry, pastoral cloak above the
town, he turned, went into the coach and found himself a seat.

||||||||||||||||||||||||||||||||||||||||||||||||||||||||||||||||||||||||||||||||||||||

||||||||||||||||||||||||||||||||||||||||||||||||||||||||||||||D OVER stood on the platform beside the station and watched while the 9:45 disappeared around the bend below the water tank with an impetuous, rushing noise. At the crossing the whistle sounded shrill and tragic, just as he knew it would — a vibrating, wailing sound which echoed among the low hills to the west and returned to the town softened by distance, thinned out by the wind. He had exhausted the sources his mother had suggested for getting the money, and now he did not know what to do next.

Beside him was a fenced plot of lawn and shrubs, the pride of the local baggage master, who tended it with patient hope. He had left the sprinkler going, and Dover, from where he stood, could hear the soft, breathing sound the water made as it lifted upward in exact arcs from the rotating hose, gleamed in the light from the baggage room window, and fell inaudibly to the parched, yellowing grass.

The water had wet the trunk of an ornamental holly tree which grew close to the iron fence, and its bole gleamed in the light with a dull, steady polish. Dover, who liked to touch things, who believed in the existence of nothing that he could not put his hands on, bent forward and rubbed his finger tips against the glistening bark. The sensation was delightful, and it seemed to him that this must be the way the wet hide of an elephant felt. He raised his hands higher on the bole, but he took them away at once, for his thumb had come in contact with some sticky, gum-like substance, put there, no doubt, by the unresting mouths of insects. He turned and went away from the station, and as he walked, he kept separating and joining his sticky thumb and his sticky forefinger, as if he sought to make shadow pictures on a wall.

He stood still again at the edge of the platform, frowned and shook his head in perplexity, wondering what he was to do next; then, with no definite plan in his mind, he crossed the tracks and walked slowly down New April Avenue, in the direction of Violet Wynn's establishment. He was familiar with the exterior of this fascinating house; its inside, he was not yet old enough to see. Her place was the last house on the short street; beyond, there was only a vacant lot, a lot outlined in small oaks and grown over thickly with weeds which were as sharp and as sickening to the nose as the sugary, sweating smell of horses.

When he came to this place, Dover sat down and stared with curiosity at the drawn, red shades of Violet's parlor. This was the room where his father spent his Saturday afternoons, and he knew that well. That knowledge made him think once more of Wesley, and sharply he saw him again lying beside the culvert, his breath coming from him in slow gasps, the dried blood flaking his cheeks. Perhaps at this moment his father was breathing his last; perhaps he had died long ago and his mother and Lula had already washed him and laid him out in the front room. The thought terrified him, and he leaned forward and rested his face in his palms. "I done the best I could," he said. "I done everything Mama told me to do."

At that moment Violet came into her darkened bedroom above him, drew back her curtains and put her head out to get a little fresh air. Her afternoon and early evening trade, which consisted mostly of young sports who came to buy beer and show off in front of the girls, was over. It was still too early for the paying, substantial customers — those who meant business and wanted secrecy. They would not start coming for an hour yet, and Violet was always grateful for this breathing spell between.

She was calculating in her mind the amount she could reasonably expect to take in that night, and was already moving away from her window, when she lowered her eyes and caught sight of Dover on the curb across the street. Something in the lost, dejected line of his body moved her to pity, and at once she stepped back a few paces and spoke to her maid, who was fumbling without purpose in the room. "Lizzie!" she whispered. "Lizzie, come here a minute!" The two women watched in silence, and then Violet continued: "That boy's in trouble, just as sure as you're born!" She waited a time, making up her mind, and then said: "Go down and see what's the matter with him. Take him through the back yard into the kitchen. Maybe he's hungry. I'll be downstairs just as quick as I can."

Lizzie said: "That's a good way to get into even more trouble than you already in most of the time. If it was me, I wouldn't have nothing to do with that boy."

"Go do what I tell you!" said Violet petulantly. "Don't waste valuable time sassing me!"

She had a soft spot in her heart for abandoned boys, and she thought often of her own little son; but, so completely had she repudiated the passage of time, she invariably thought of him as being exactly six years old, for he had, of necessity, stopped growing when she ceased aging. She came excitedly down the back stairs, a sense of well-being fluttering her breast. Of late she had entered into a literary phase of development, and she now read all the popular fiction of her day, crying convulsively over the histories of outcast girls, with whom it was so easy for her to identify herself.

Hers was the day of sentimentalized vice, when the fallen woman was the heroine of romance, the idealized brothel her background; and, so great is the influence of the printed word, Violet was content to regard her own extensive experience as not entirely typical; to draw her knowledge of her profession not from what she knew, but from what she read in books or saw on the screen: the imaginary and more convincing products of artists who had never, in their entire lives, encountered a prostitute outside their own rich phantasies.

When she came into her kitchen, Dover sat there on one of the cane-bottom chairs, surrounded by her girls. He told his story, and when he had finished, Violet turned her head away to hide her distress. "Can you picture people being that mean and hardhearted?" she asked. "It's like I always say — it takes good people to act nasty, don't it?" She raised her eyes helplessly and then added more practically: "I never trusted that Dr. Snowfield anyway! There's something funny about him as sure as you're born! . . . There he is, a healthy young single man that lives all by himself. He never goes out with girls, and never once has he set foot in this house!" She sighed and looked at her girls, and they nodded their heads indignantly with her.

Recently she had seen a moving picture which had moved her a great deal. It was called *Shattered Roses,* and it was, she thought, even finer than the novel from which it had been taken. The situation which now confronted her was not unlike one of Mrs. McMinn's own dramatic moments, and as a tribute to that lady for the pleasure she had given her, Violet felt now that she could hardly act less generously than the fictional landlady of her favorite author, who had instantly befriended the little heroine when she was about to have her baby, and had given her love and sympathy after her respectable friends had condemned her and turned away. Remembering the scene once more, she touched her eyes with her handkerchief and lifted her skirts so high that her white-lard-like flesh could be seen bulging above her red satin garters, whose buckles were two miniatures on ivory — one showing Venus coming out of her bath, the other showing the same lady corrupting Adonis with a wealth of explicit, biological detail.

From beneath the Adonis garter she extracted three one-dollar bills and handed them to the boy. "Here, my child!" she said. "Take this money for your father. It's a free-will offering. It's not a loan. . . . And remember that when the respectable people of this town refused to help you, old Mattress May, that everybody laughs at and scorns to associate with, did!"

The girls had watched this scene with some astonishment, and they stood in silence, not knowing what to say. Violet straightened her stockings, turned to them and continued: "You think what I just did was bad business, don't you?" She glanced at each of them searchingly and then went on: "You're wrong if you do think that, because a kind deed is never wasted. I'll get the money back some day. You watch and see if I don't. Nobody ever lost anything yet through doing a kind deed for somebody less fortunate than theirself."

Audrey, one of the new girls, said: "Just the same, if it had been my three dollars, I'd a-held onto them. Money's too hard to get these days to throw it away. Nobody else is going to look out for you, I've always found. Look out for yourself, I say. You won't ever see those three dollars again, and you can bet on that."

"Oh, I don't expect to see those *particular* dollars again," said Violet, laughing with amusement. "I'd have to be very simple to believe that, my dear. But I do maintain that the good Lord on high will see that I get paid back in one way or another, if not in this world, then in the next. That's what I meant when I said what I did."

At that moment the doorbell rang, and Lizzie went at once to open it. Violet and her girls peered with boredom into the kitchen mirror, regretting that their interesting talk was over, patting their hair into place and powdering their noses and throats. "It's probably nobody but that old Mr. Hardesty," said Violet. "I've been expecting him any night. I saw by the *Courier* that his wife's visiting her people in Pascagoula again."

She remembered the boy who had been standing behind her only a moment before, but when she turned to look for him, to tell him to run home at once, she saw that he had already gone. At that moment he was sprinting in the direction of Dr. Snowfield's office, and when he reached Court House Square, he looked up and saw the light still burning in the doctor's office. He went up the stairs two at a time, and, fortified by the knowledge that this time he had the doctor's fee clutched safely in his fist, he was not concerned with the minor courtesies. He pushed open the door without knocking and went in boldly, and there, sitting as if he had not moved since he saw him last, sat Dr. Albert Snowfield. The muscles in his face twitched spasmodically, and his lips were pressed tightly together, as if he suppressed some unendurable pain. He seemed hardly to notice the boy at all, but when Dover went over to him and spoke, he lifted his head a little and said: "Who are you? What do you want with me?"

"I'm one of Wesley Boutwell's boys. Don't you remember me? I was in here a while back to tell you that Papa fell and hurt himself. It was off a culvert. You said you wouldn't come treat him till I brought you your three dollars. Well, I got it now. It's right here in my hand." He started to give the money to the doctor, but changed his mind. "I'll pay you off after you done seen Papa," he said cautiously. "You didn't trust me. I don't trust you, either."

Dr. Snowfield pressed his fingers into the hollows behind his ears and shook his head, as if he were both grieved and perplexed. "Did I do that?" he asked. "Did I refuse to see a patient?" He got up stiffly and reached for his medicine case. He put on his hat clumsily, not bothering to shape it to his head, adding: "That was wrong of me. I ask your pardon." He seemed suddenly filled with energy, and he called out: "Hurry! Hurry, now! We've no time to waste!"

They reached the curb and the doctor opened the door of his automobile, indicating that the boy was to get in beside him. "I've been disturbed," he continued in his tense, nervous voice. "You mustn't judge me too harshly." He felt the need of justifying himself to the boy, and after a moment he continued: "When she told me what she did, the end of my world came very quietly. I can truthfully say, 'My life stopped when the hands of the clock were in such a position; and what's more, I know precisely the reason why it ended as it did.' It's strange for a man to die and yet be able to witness his own dissolution, isn't it? It's cruel! It's too cruel to be endured!" He broke off suddenly, his eyes narrowed in caution, and said harshly: "Do you understand me? Do you know what I'm referring to?"

Dover stretched out his foot, exploring with his toe the delicate graining in the leather upholstery. He was more interested in the feeling of the leather against his foot, a sensation he had not before known, than in the words the doctor was saying. Grown people were always talking, he felt, and most of it was not worth listening to; but he looked up when the doctor addressed him directly and said, "No, sir. I haven't got any idea at all." Something in the doctor's glassy, feverish eyes startled him and he pulled away from him, crowding against the door of the car. There was something tense and terrifying about Dr. Snowfield, a quality which seemed to communicate itself to the air about him, and as Dover examined him cautiously from the corners of his eyes, he thought that while he had never before felt this diffused uneasiness, this almost tangible anxiety, hovering like shivering mist about the body of a human being, it was a commonplace among animals waiting to be slaughtered; animals which — with nervous terror rippling like water beneath their wrinkling hides — while having no conception of death, could yet roll their eyes upward, low with a desperate anguish and paw at the earth with their protesting, futile hooves, knowing that death was at hand.

"But I didn't harm her," said Dr. Snowfield sighing and raising his thin, birdlike face upward a little. "You must believe that. I couldn't have harmed her myself. She was a part of me, you see."

"Yes, sir," said Dover. "Yes, sir." But his words carried no assurance, and they ended with an uncertain, falling inflection, as if he were prepared to withdraw them and substitute others at the first sign of disapproval from the doctor.

Throughout that hot September night, small, indecisive breezes had blown for a moment or two and then vanished, as if the effort of movement in all that world of hot, sweating stillness was too enormous to be sustained for long. Now, there was no breeze at all, and the leaves of the trees were limp, bitten and lifeless, drooping from their stems under the weight of their incrusted dust.

In the unmoving air, the enduring smell of Reedyville, dissipated, unremarked, when wind blew, came perceptibly to the senses. Now, there were the rich odors of eaten food still living, but as dim as ghosts, in the quiet world above the town; there was the moldy, gunpowder scent of decaying flesh which died relentlessly while its host still talked, spat, and regarded with neither amazement nor concern the world in which he was imprisoned. There was the smell of the town's massed bed linen, saturated with the odors of those who had slept so intimately upon it; the tang of liniments rubbed on a thousand aching backs; the sad smell of mown grass dying on yellowing lawns; of wet, rotting woodwork, and of old dresses put away forever. Then, too, there was the smell of horse dung from the town's stables, and of scented, late-blooming flowers: petunias, phlox and larkspur, which, blending first with themselves, blended again with wood smoke, and with the seasoned, ammoniac odor of urine.

Dover said: "You know where to go to? You know how to get to our house?"

"Yes," said the doctor. "I know that very well."

He turned into the Reedyville road and approached the culvert. Lula came to the gate to meet him. Having carried her half of Wesley's solid bulk down the dusty road, and having held him upright while Ada sponged him off with warm water and laundry soap, in order that he might be respectable when the doctor arrived, she now felt a deep, personal interest in his welfare. "Maybe I'm nothing but a sassy nigger overstepping her place," she began angrily. "Maybe that's all I really is, but I'm gwiner tell you right to your face that you're the stingiest, skinflintingest man ever I heerd of, and I've knowed some sorry white folks in my time! Folks gwiner know what you done, too, 'less God seals my black mouth with fire!"

Dr. Snowfield turned to the woman and said wearily: "You could say a lot of things about me, and they'd all be true; but I'm not stingy, and I'm not avaricious." He approached the bed where Wesley was lying and went on: "I've been under a strain. I'm not myself tonight, and if I've done anything I shouldn't have, I apologize."

He felt his patient's pulse, bent above him and listened to his slow, steady heartbeat; he examined the man's superficial wound, painted it with iodine, sighed and turned away, his face twisted suddenly with pain. Ada could endure the silence no longer. "Tell me the truth," she begged. "Is Wesley hurt serious? I'd rather know the truth, no matter how bad it is, than wait this way any longer."

Dr. Snowfield waited so long before replying that it seemed as if already he had forgotten his patient. "There's nothing at all the matter with your husband," he said at last. "He's had too much to drink, but he's coming out of it now." He picked up his instruments and began putting them away. "I wish to God I was that healthy," he said passionately. "I only wish I could get drunk like that and forget everything."

At that moment Wesley belched and turned on his side, his lids fluttering coquettishly, his lips framing words which could not be understood. He pressed his cheek deeper into his pillow, lowered his chin and laughed his high, schoolgirl laugh, raising his mutilated arm at the same instant and waving it back and forth in the air. Dimly he was aware of people about him, people who discussed his person and his conduct with the completest candor; and gradually these calculable things merged with the sensuous, dimensionless dream he was having, and the dream itself, finding in its fluid framework a place for the movement and sound of the world beyond its own limits, reversed its pleasant direction, and turned, not into reality, but into memory, so that now his brain took up again at the precise point where it had ceased functioning some hours ago.

He was in Mattress May's establishment once more, and she was urging him to go home, telling him that he was drunk, that he could not even walk straight, and adding over and over that it was people like himself who gave her house a bad name. At that moment he had caught hold of her arm and pulled her down into his lap, hugging the poor woman until she thought her bones would snap under the strain, rubbing his chin against her own and whispering that he'd go home willingly if she'd first take him upstairs and show him the new curtains in her bedroom.

Violet pulled herself free, straightened her hair and said with considerable acerbity: "I don't run a charity home. I'm not in business for my health. You show me three dollars, and I'll be as sweet to you as any woman can be." Then she added, her patience gone: "But you haven't got a cent of money on you. I know that. You never come to see me when you got money on you. You haven't got any consideration at all for a working woman like me that tries so hard to make both ends meet. . . . Oh, no. You'd rather waste your money buying whisky for those loafers at Moore's Livery Stable." She fixed the strap on her low-cut, purple evening gown and added: "If you like them so much, why don't you ask one of them to show you the curtains in *his* bedroom!"

The ridiculous picture which her words had evoked was too much for her to endure and she hugged herself, shook her head and laughed until she was weak, her plump, white back resting against the door. Wesley said: "Now, Miss Violet! Now, Miss Violet! Don't talk that-a-way!" He laughed good-naturedly, got up and lunged for her, but she kept beyond his reach. "If you was even good *company,* I wouldn't mind so much," she said, "but what do you talk about all the time? Do you talk about the things ladies are interested in? . . . Oh, no! Not you! All you can talk about is the block houses on San Juan Hill, and how they blew up the *Maine!*" Then, losing patience with him, since the afternoon business was beginning to pick up, she nodded significantly to Lizzie, and the latter, knowing so well what was expected of her, took her place in the hall, beside the wide front door. When she was stationed there, her hand waiting on the knob, Violet pretended to be convinced against her will. She sighed, winked at her girls and said: "All right. I give in. It looks like I can't get rid of you any other way."

She took Wesley's arm and guided him into the hall, maneuvering him into the precise position she wanted. Then Lizzie, well versed in these tactics, opened the door at the instant Violet gave her guest a vigorous push, and shut it again before he could recover himself. "Go away!" said Violet through her peephole. "Go away, before I call the sheriff and tell him you're making a commotion!" The surprised, baffled expression on his face made her laugh again. "Well, that's the end of him!" she said triumphantly. "You won't hear anything more out of him tonight!"

Now, in his returning consciousness, Wesley relived this undignified but amusing incident. He smiled to himself and stroked his pillow. Violet was a cute one. She was nobody's fool, and you had to give her credit for handling a difficult situation with tact. She was a sweet woman, he thought, but high-spirited, and a little hard to manage at times. At that instant he raised his head from his pillow and said in a hurt voice: "Is that the way you treat your good customers, Miss Violet? . . . Many's the dollar I've spent in this house on a Saturday afternoon, and now you throw me out because I'm a little short." He sat up and shook his head ponderously from side to side. "If this is the way you want to act, it's all right with me, but don't expect to see me back, that's all I can say."

He sighed deeply twice, from the depths of his being, and ran his hands roughly over his face. "All right, Miss Violet!" he said in a hurt voice. "All right, have it your own way!" He yawned, shook himself all over and returned to consciousness; but this time he looked not into the eyes of Violet Wynn, as he had expected, but into the eyes of his lawful wife.

The implications behind his muttering entered her mind slowly. She stared at him with disbelief, her mouth opening automatically, as if her brain were occupied at that instant with things more important than the management of a muscle. She recovered quickly from her surprise and began to shout: "So that's where you been going every Saturday after dinner? So that's where you spend your time? I might of knowed it! I might of knowed there was something funny going on under my nose!"

Dover had watched anxiously from his post at the foot of the bed while the doctor examined Wesley. As long as the boy believed his father hurt, helpless and dependent upon him for his safety, he had successfully stifled his own grief, his own fears; but now, seeing him so miraculously restored, his emotions came to the surface in a flood which he no longer sought to control. He was fourteen, and he was approaching the final, decisive step toward maturity. His was the age when the uncertainties of childhood face the great, implacable changes; when the mind debates nervously with itself the wisdom of trading the indentured security it knows for the more doubtful blessings of freedom. Already he had gone far on the inevitable journey, but at that moment his new, wavering maturity slipped from him, and without thought he ran toward his father and put his arms about him. "Papa! Papa!" he said. He held his father tightly, as if his own security depended upon Wesley's continued existence. "Papa!" he said again. "Papa!"

"I ought to have figured out for myself what you been up to!" said Ada. "I ought to have had that much sense, at least! But, oh no! I trusted you! I knew you wasn't above a lot of things, but running after strumpets was the one thing I didn't calculate on."

Wesley lifted his son and held him in his arms. "Now, Dover!" he said gently. "Now, son! What you so scared of all of a sudden?" He seemed impervious to his wife's denunciations. He sat down on the bed again and rocked the child back and forth. "They can't kill your Papa as easy as all that!" he said reassuringly. "It's going to take more than that to kill me!" He reached up with his remaining hand and tried to smooth back the boy's hair, but at that exact instant Dover passed out of his infancy forever. Never again would it be possible for him to cry publicly without shame as if he were a baby with no standards of conduct to maintain; never again would he show his love for his father so nakedly, for the last shreds of his lingering babyhood had fallen from him with his tears.

Ada, seeing herself ignored, was now working up into a fine rage. She walked up and down the room, throwing her arms about dramatically. "I believed you was above such things!" she screamed. "I even defended you to others! . . . And here we been worried to death about you; and little Dover running his po' legs off all night to get you a doctor!"

Lula, from the door where she was making herself as inconspicu-
ous as possible, spoke quietly: "Yassuh, Mr. Wesley! That's the truth.
What Miss Ada says is God's own truth." She was glad, now, that
she had not gone on to the singing with Jesse. Her evening at the
Boutwells' had been one of the most enjoyable in her life, and as she
stood quietly in observation, she stored up many interesting things
to tell Jesse and Amos about the fascinating home life of white folks.
Dover pulled away from his father and went to the table where
Dr. Snowfield was. He looked at his father with new interest, as if
he were seeing him for the first time in his life. To himself he kept
thinking: "Why, I don't need him so much, after all! I can look
out for myself, if I have to, as good as anybody." His mother had
exhausted her first wrath, and in that interval of silence, while she
was thinking up more wounding things to say, he took the three
dollars from his pocket and gave them to the doctor. "Here's your
money," he said with his new dignity. "Take it and put it in your
pocket quick."

"Keep it yourself," said Dr. Snowfield. "I don't want it."

Dover was insistent. "We promised to pay you for coming," he
said. "We aim to do it, too." His voice dropped sullenly, as if he had
meant to add: "Even if you didn't do nothing at all to earn it."

"It's scandalous!" said Ada. "That's what it is — scandalous!"
Then, overcome with emotion, she ran out of the room and across
the breezeway, steadying her globular belly with her hands. She
went into the bedroom which the boys had once used and lay down
on Breck's old bed. Lula made a clucking, sympathetic sound and
followed her. At the sight of the woman standing beside her, Ada's
rage broke forth again and she shouted: "A man of his age! A man
fifty-four years old with grown children acting that-a-way! You'd
expect a man of that age to have some sense, wouldn't you Lula?"

Lula, as if trying to be fair, deliberated and then said frankly:
"No, ma'am. No, ma'm, I wouldn't."

Dr. Snowfield held the three dollars in his hand, not knowing
what to do with it. He spoke cautiously to Wesley. "Would you
like to finish your afternoon the way you planned it? Does that idea
appeal to you, even after what's happened?"

From across the breezeway, Ada's voice rose shrill and tragic.
"It looks like you'd have a little respect for your family, even if you

ain't got none for yourself!" she said. "I don't see what made you come home at all! Why didn't you just stay right there with Mattress May?"

"Yes, sir," said Wesley. "I sure would, Doctor." He rolled his dark, innocent eyes appealingly and said: "I don't guess it would make any difference one way or the other now. Ada couldn't be more riled than she is, no matter what I do!" Then he sighed, took out the stub of a toothpick and chewed it slowly. "But what's the use of thinking about that?" he asked. "I haven't got one cent of money on me."

Dr. Snowfield came to him at that moment and stuffed the money in the pocket of his clean, blue shirt. "Go get what you want!" he said. And seeing the conventional protests which were already forming on Wesley's reluctant lips, he added with sudden harshness, as if the past, which he had forgotten for a time, had now come back to him in all its terror: "Go take what you want! And thank God you know what it is! Thank God it's simple enough to be bought and sold!"

From across the breezeway, Ada's voice came petulantly, but tempered now with sarcasm. "If old Mattress May is what you like, why don't you go back and *see* her?" she asked, not realizing how well her suggestion fitted into the conversation going on in the room beyond where she was lying. "Go on back to her, I say! She can have you from now on, for all of me! Personally, I don't want no further part or parcel of you!"

Wesley got up with an excited alacrity and moved toward the door. He stopped and winked knowingly at the doctor. "You stay here and watch until I get as far as the bend in the road," he whispered, shaking his shoulders and moving his mutilated arm back and forth in the air for emphasis. "If she comes out and asks where I've gone to, you tell her I left my pocketknife in Moore's back room and went there to get it before — " His wife's voice interrupted his instructions. "What are you waiting for?" she said with heavy sarcasm. "Why don't you go on back to her like you want to? But don't come crawling back to me on your hands and knees when she gets tired of you!"

The tone of his wife's voice was now so familiar that Wesley, from the door, turned and said automatically, from sheer force of

habit: "All right! All right, sugar! I'm going now!" He went down
the steps shaping his battered old hat jauntily. He leaped the fence
like a young boy, not bothering, in his eagerness, to open the gate,
and cut through the weeds which grew along the banks of Sweethearts' Looking-Glass, that route being shorter. As he hurried along,
he turned over in his mind some of the complex problems of marriage. The trouble with women was, that when they got to really
like you, it was all or nothing. They were always telling a man he
had to choose between one thing or another! Now, that wasn't what
a man wanted to do at all, and the idea of him having to make
a choice between Ada and Mattress May was too foolish even to
contemplate. He wanted them both, but not at the same time, and
that was the great lesson women couldn't get through their heads.
Women, somehow, were not able to understand how a man could
love his wife and family and yet want a little romance, a little glamor
in his stodgy existence!

He was still concerned with these problems when he reached
Violet's house and rang her doorbell triumphantly. Lizzie opened
the peephole and said with exasperated disbelief: "Miss Violet!
Miss Violet! That military man's done got sober again. Here he is
back!"

Violet nudged her maid aside and looked for herself. "Now, you
listen to me, Wesley Boutwell!" she began. "I told you we don't want
you around here! Can't you take a hint?"

Wesley said: "Don't make up your mind too quick. Wait till you
see what I got for you." He unfolded the bills and waved them in
triumph under her nose. "How about it now?" he asked. "What you
going to say now?"

Violet turned to her maid. "Let the gentleman in, like he says,"
she said chidingly. "Don't keep a good customer standing on the
porch." For a moment she wondered where he had got the three
dollars, and then dismissed the matter from her mind as no concern
of hers. The important thing was that he had them, and she was
willing to let the matter rest there. She was never to know where the
money came from, never to know that her belief in a benign, re-
warding force was dramatically justified, and that was a pity, for
faith is the rarest virtue of all in the suspicious, yapping world we
live in.

When the girls in the back parlor, hearing voices outside, came into the hall and looked about inquiringly, Violet raised her eyes toward the ceiling and sighed patiently. "It's only The Sergeant back again!" she said. "It looks like we're going to have to sink the *Merrimac* after all!" Then, seeing that her guest was approaching her, his gentle brown eyes now loving and luminous with his simple desires, she murmured, more to herself than anyone else: "The things I go through with to make a living! The things I have to put up with every day!" She took a deep breath and braced herself at the moment Wesley encircled her unstable, white flesh with his arms, wondering if her ribs would this time prove stronger than his grunting tenderness.

He had forgotten his wife entirely, but at that moment Ada, having worked through her first anger, came into the room where she thought her husband was, to continue the quarrel at closer range. Dr. Snowfield was getting ready to leave, and he gave her Wesley's message. Ada said: "Go back to town with the doctor, Dover, and see if you can find your father. He still ain't entirely sober, and he might fall and hurt himself again. Tell him I said for him to come home right now! Tell him I haven't said half of what's on my mind! Tell him he's going to hear me out, even if I have to hog-tie him first!"

She walked back to the room where Lula was, and Dr. Snowfield and the boy went down the steps. The doctor stopped at the gate, sighed and looked about in puzzlement, as if he were not entirely sure where he was at that moment. In the church to the right of Sweethearts' Looking-Glass, the congregation was singing a new song — a Mississippi favorite which they had not before heard, and one which Amos was teaching them patiently. Just then his voice rose rich and powerful in the solo part: —

> "Oh, Moses, Moses, you couldn't ben' low,
> And so you never entered in the Promised Land.
> Yo' head was high and yo' heart was proud:
> And so you never entered in the Promised Land."

Dr. Snowfield said: "You know that Miss Clarry Palmiller is sick, I suppose? You know about that, I imagine."

Amos' voice rose suddenly in tragedy and in power. It floated like

the threatening notes of an organ across the dried-out pond, through
the still, oppressive air, as if it carried a passionate warning for the
sick of the world: —

> "Ben' me, Jesus, ever'-which-a-way!
> Ben' me, ben' me, ever'-which-a-way!
> Ben' me, ben' me, ever'-which-a-way,
> And break my prideful heart!"

"Yes, sir," said Dover. "Seems like I haven't heard much of anything else tonight."

Dr. Snowfield went through the weighted gate, in the direction
of his car. When he reached it, he paused again to speak aloud the
thoughts which had been passing endlessly through his brain that
night. "I see one of my mistakes, now that it's too late. . . . You see,
I never thought of her as having a right to an existence apart from
mine. I thought of her always as a part of myself: the most important
part of all, more necessary to me than eyes or hands."

The congregation blended their voices with that of their leader.
Together they sang: —

> "Bigetty brother, you can't cross Jordan,
> Bigetty brother, you can't cross Jordan,
> Bigetty brother, you can't cross Jordan,
> No, you can't cross Jordan 'less you ben' down low!
> Low, so low! Low, so low!
> No, you can't cross Jordan 'less you ben' down low!"

Dr. Snowfield closed his eyes and then looked upward, making a
lost, hopeless gesture with his spread hands. Now the moon was high
up in the sky, shrunk to the size of a man's head. It was bloodless
and wasted, and it drifted without purpose, wizened with all the days
that time has known. It had passed its zenith long ago, and already
it was approaching a horizon of low hills, its surface frosted over and
blurred into a halo of shallow, uncertain light beneath the rain clouds
which pushed forward so gently, so imperceptibly from the south.

"That was wrong of me," said Dr. Snowfield. "It was quite wrong.
She had a right to an existence of her own, an existence apart from
me." He turned to the boy and said: "What shall I do now? What
must I do?" Before the boy could speak, Amos' voice rose again from
the church, pleading and passionate, as if his words carried a message

for all who live in despair on the parched, yellowing surface of the
world: —

> "Bigetty brother, you better 'umble yo' pride;
> Bigetty brother, you better 'umble yo' pride;
> Bigetty brother, you better 'umble yo' pride;
> You can't cross Jordan 'less you 'umble yo' pride
> Low, so low! Low, so low!
> No, you can't cross Jordan 'less you ben' down low!"

Dr. Snowfield started his car with a jerk. "Why do I tell you
these things?" he asked. "Nobody in the world can understand
me. . . . Why should I expect you to?" He drove slowly, and in
silence, for a time, past the bend in the road, past the culvert where
Wesley had fallen. Then he spoke again: "There's a favor I want to
ask of you. It will be easy to grant. Will you do it?"

"Yes, sir," said Dover. "I guess so."

"I want you to watch the Palmiller house for me," said Dr.
Snowfield, "and if anything happens to her, you must come at once
and tell me. I'll be waiting for you in my office." He lifted his hands
from the steering wheel and passed them roughly across his face.
"You will do it?" he asked eagerly. "I can depend on you?"

He stopped his car a block from the imposing residence, and Dover
got out and went to the alley at the rear of the house. He saw immediately that The Goodwife had preceded him; that she was standing close against the carriage house, her draperies blending into the
gray shadows cast by the moon. A moment later she walked into
the alley and stood in the moonlight, where she could be plainly
seen. She walked up and down, her lips moving with her limping yet
gliding stride. She smiled to herself, nodding her head occasionally
for emphasis. She looked upward at last and spoke in confidence
to the moon, her wrinkled old face content and a little sly: —

"I was very lucky to make the marriage I did," she said distinctly.
"It was a most farsighted move. . . . I've given up some things,
naturally, and I've worked hard; but then I've escaped all the
sorrows, all the tragedies, which mortals know. Others will suffer
and die, but I shall go free. The thing that happens to others will
not happen to me. The work that I do is too important. I've served
my master too long, and too well, for him to permit that." She lifted
her black draperies and covered her face, as if overcome with a

sudden modesty which she had not foreseen. "I don't know how my husband will arrange it at the end," she said softly, "but he will think of something. He will know how to save me when the time comes." Then, hearing some slight sound from the Chapman house, she dropped her pose and stepped back into the shadows, composing her face into its habitual lines once more, arranging her draperies primly about her ankles.

The moment her eyes were turned, Dover went back to the front of the house. The gate was open and he went in, hiding himself behind the hedge at a place where he could watch both the house and the street. He crouched there for what seemed an interminable time, watching while the blurred, milky moon dropped to the horizon and disappeared from sight; then, hearing voices approaching, he looked through the hedge and saw Angus McKinnon and his brother Fergus coming toward him. They were business associates of Mr. Palmiller, and, like him, they had been famous athletes in their day. They lived with their wives, their children and their surviving relatives in the huge old McKinnon home in a kind of patriarchal splendor, with Angus, since he was the eldest, the acknowledged head of the clan. As they crossed the street and came closer, Dover could hear them plainly. Angus was saying in a worried voice: —

"What complaint is Miss Clarine suffering from, Brother Fergus? Has anybody been told?"

"It's some sort of fever. Some tropical fever, I understand."

"Perhaps we'd better not stay long," said Angus. "I think if we just ask how she is, offer to do what we can, and leave our cards, it will be enough. I think — "

He broke off and turned at the same moment his brother turned, and lifted his hat courteously. Mrs. Kenworthy was rounding the corner, and the McKinnon brothers, seeing the difficulty she was having, went to her assistance. She was forty-six years old, in full, pink bloom, for she weighed at least three hundred pounds. Her arms above her elbows were as large as hams; her hams, themselves, one could only estimate with awe. She found it difficult to walk, to support her weight, and on the way from her house she had stopped every few minutes to brace herself against the fence of one of her neighbors and pant painfully.

"I was almost asleep once tonight," she said. "I had a sick head-ache, and went to bed early; but just when I was dozing off, that young Boutwell boy had to come clattering up the steps. He got me so wide awake, I thought I might as well get up and see if I could help Cindy in any way." She turned to Angus and continued: "How is Clarry? Has she passed the crisis?"

Angus said: "She's worse, Milly. She's very low."

The brothers deployed themselves on either side of Mrs. Kenworthy, and with their assistance she walked more rapidly. A little later the three of them proceeded up the long, brick walk and entered the house; but hardly had their voices died away before others took their places in the hot, oppressive air. This time it was Jesse and Lula with their house guest Amos. Lula was talking with muted eagerness of the amusing things she had experienced at the Boutwell house that night. Apparently she had told most of her long story on the road, for she was now concerned with things which had taken place after Dover had left with Dr. Snowfield.

"Well, sir," she was saying in an eager, guarded voice, "you know what Miss Ada done after I told her that? She didn't do nothing for a while 'cept rock back and forth and look down the road. Then she got up and said, 'Lula, you been a good friend to me tonight, and I want you to do me one more favor before you go meet Jesse at the church. I want you to cut my hair,' she said; 'short, in that fashionable way Violet and her girls wear theirs! I want you to cut my hair short,' she said, 'and then I want you to get that old pair of curling tongs out of the top bureau drawer and curl it too!' I done what she told me to do — I cut it and curled it too. Then she said to me, 'Lula, there's a make-up box that my daughter Honey used to use in the house somewhere. Look in the bottom of that leather trunk in the boys' old room. If it's not there, let me know and I'll come help you hunt.' I found it where she said it was, and then she painted her face and mouth just like them low-down women on New April Avenue do."

Jesse scratched his red, kinky hair. "How come she do that?" he asked. "What make that white woman act such a funny way?"

Lula giggled and slapped her leg. "Lissen to him, Amos!" she said. "Lissen to that ladies' man talk!" They had reached the place in the hedge where Dover was hiding, and they stopped before turning down the side alley which led to the servants' quarters.

"Here's why she done what she done," continued Lula. "She figgered that iffen Mr. Wesley liked the way a strumpet looked, then that was the way she was gwiner look too!"

"I figgered that one out," said Amos ponderously. "That ain't hard to understand if you know women real good."

"Then Miss Ada say to me: 'Lula, I can't rightly blame him for acting that-a-way. You know yourself how good-looking and fascinating he is! . . . It ain't like I was married to an everyday man that nobody else wanted. It ain't like other women didn't have their eye on him all the time and throw theirselves at his po' head until he didn't know what he was doing half the time!' " Lula reached over and broke a twig from the hedge, chewing it thoughtfully. "So I just sat there on the front gallery and rocked," she went on. "And kept saying, 'Yassum! Yassum, that's the truth, ain't it?' just like she wanted me to; and when I had to get up and leave, knowing that you two was waiting for me on the road, she said to me: 'Lula, where do folks buy that stuff they put on hair to make it turn yellow?' "

"That the way you gwiner do when you find out I been back-tracking on you?" asked Jesse coyly. "You gwiner act sweet and pretty like Miss Ada done?"

Lula, forgetting where she was, snorted noisily and then clapped her hand over her mouth, raising her forefinger in warning, as if the others, and not herself, had disturbed the quiet night air. "Not me!" she said laughingly. "I ain't white! I don't have to act pretty!"

"Lula's telling that for a joke," said Amos, "but it's the truth just the same. Mama used to be always sayin': 'It gwiner take a strong, mean man to quiet that gal down!' "

"Here's what I'd do, iffen I caught you back-tracking," said Lula in delight. "I'd say, 'Why don't you come back in the house where you belongs, sugar pie? Lula's done fixed you up a mess of cowpeas cooked with a ham bone. *Um-m-m!* Don't that smell nice! *Um-m-m!* Don't that taste good! But don't fill yo'self up too full, 'cause I got a nice little smothered chicken, cooked the way you likes it, and a panful of hot biscuits just running over with melting butter!' "

"Lissen to that sweet-talkin' woman talk sweet!" said Amos laughingly. "It don't soun' like old Mississippi Lula to me!"

Jesse elbowed her off the sidewalk and said affectionately: "That the way she talk now, though. I started working on that gal right away. Done whittled her down to a sweet woman now."

"And all the time you eatin' yo' cowpeas and chicken," said Lula, "there's something going on that you don't know about, 'cause I'm heating me up a kittle of water while I'm talkin' so nice."

"That's Lula coming out now!" said Amos explosively. "I knowed we'd get around to Lula sooner or later!"

"And I'm gwiner start pourin' when the last mouthful of chicken and biscuit goes bouncin' down yo' gullet," continued Lula. "Gwiner hold my kittle high up, too! Gwiner pour careful! Gwiner pour where it'll make yo' lady friend the most put-out!"

All three of them laughed together, and Lula added gaspingly: "I ain't white folks, like I said! People don't expect nothin' from me, nohow! I don't have to act pretty lessen I want to!"

Cassie, the Palmiller cook, came around the side of the house and spoke in a hurt voice: "Ain't you ashamed to frolic and cavort in the presence of death! It ain't enough for you to go to the singing and leave ever'thing here at home for me to take care of! Oh, no! That ain't near enough! You got to stand out on the street too, laughing and making a ruckus to trouble the dying with!" She covered her face with her hands, turned away and said: "She's gwiner die! I knows it! The Goodwife standin' in our alley already!"

At that moment Mrs. McMinn came rapidly down the street, her heels beating a nervous tune on the pavement. She approached the group of Negroes, now silent and subdued, and said sternly: "Cassie, go back to the house at once! Your mistress may need something from the kitchen." To the others she added: "You go straight to your quarters, and stay there. You may be needed too, later on." The Negroes answered in chorus. "Yassum!" they said. "Yassum!"

When they had gone, Minnie went up the front steps and entered the house. Cindy met her inside. "I'm glad you came so quickly," she said. "I hope you'll forgive me for telephoning, but I didn't know anybody else to turn to. I'm at the end of my rope. I really am this time. I kept saying to myself: 'Minnie is so strong and capable in an emergency! Minnie will surely know what to do! Minnie will — ' "

Mrs. McMinn said: "Cindy! Cindy! You mustn't let yourself give way. You must not, no matter how bad things seem!"

"She's dying," said Cindy. "I can't fool myself any longer with senseless hope. Even Dr. Kent admits it in a roundabout way. He said to me just before I came down to let you in, 'I've done everything a man can do to save her, and I want you to know that, Cindy.' But I said to him, 'Please don't apologize, because really I can't stand it now. Nobody is to blame but myself, and I see it so clearly. I'm responsible. I failed her, just as I failed Rance. I'm a fool, and everybody must have known it all along except myself. I'm a self-centered fool who never understood the least need of others.'" Her face had a stretched, desperate look, but she spoke with smiling carelessness, as if what she said was of no importance.

"I want to talk to you frankly," she went on; "to tell you everything. You've always defended me. You've always kept my sickening little secrets, and I know you'll keep this one too." Seeing that Minnie was about to interrupt her, she touched her friend's lips lightly with her finger tips and continued tensely: "Oh, I know you gossip a little, like everybody else in this town; but you've never really betrayed a confidence in your life. I'm entirely sure of that." They had reached the landing at the second floor, and Cindy said: "Come into my bedroom. We'll be alone there. We can talk with nobody to interrupt us."

When they were in the bedroom, and Cindy had bolted the door, Minnie spoke in a worried voice. "I didn't realize she was so desperately sick. I've hardly been out of the house for the past two or three days. I thought it was only some mild kind of food poisoning. Mrs. Boutwell told me that yesterday when she came to clean up for me."

"That's what I want to talk to you about," said Cindy. "Only Dr. Kent, Hubert and myself know the truth. I didn't want Hubert to know, but Dr. Kent thought he must be told. . . . In a minute, you'll know the truth, too." She closed her eyes and talked rapidly for a few minutes, telling in detail the things which Dr. Kent had told her. When she had finished, Minnie said: "Cindy! Cindy! Do you know what you're saying?"

"I know quite well. There's no doubt of it. Her father is almost out of his mind. He won't leave her alone. He keeps nagging at her, trying to make her say who performed the operation, but she only says, 'That's of no importance now. What difference can it possibly make? The person who did it, did it out of sympathy and kindness for me. I knew there would be some risk. I was warned of that in advance. I was not misled in any way.' Then she closes her eyes and turns away. She's so exhausted! So completely exhausted, Minnie! . . . Then Hubert tries to make her say who the man was — who her sweetheart was, I mean; but she won't reveal that either. You know how stubborn gentle people like Clarry can be, once they make up their minds. She keeps saying: 'I will not tell you! You must not ask me that, Father! I will not tell you!' "

Cindy began walking up and down the room nervously. "When I saw you coming down the street, and went to meet you at the door," she said, "Hubert was still pleading with her. He was saying: 'You must tell me who the man is. You must think carefully now, and tell me his name, where you met him and how he betrayed and seduced you. Think carefully, my darling! Think carefully, and tell me everything! The man must be punished! He must not escape the consequences of his crime!' But she only sighed so wearily that my heart broke for her. 'Nobody is to blame,' she said. 'I want nobody punished. I will not drag others down with me.' "

Cindy went to the door and unbolted it. "Now you know everything," she said; "and I want you to come with me to her room for a moment. She was always so fond of you. She often spoke of how much she admired you." She opened the door and beckoned peremptorily, as if every moment were important now. Together the two women ran up the remaining flight of stairs, but when they reached the third floor, and turned into the long, wide hall which led to Clarry's bedroom, Miss Bigelow, the nurse, came toward them rapidly. "You'd better come in now," she said to Mrs. Palmiller. "She's sinking fast. You must hurry if you want to see her alive again."

Minnie had moved forward with her friend, but Miss Bigelow barred her way firmly and said in her whining country voice, which she, herself, considered both professional and soothing: "This is something for the family alone. . . . Why don't you go down to the library and wait with the others? I'll tell you just as soon as the end comes." She turned and hurried down the hall, her starched uniform cracking against her thighs like small, efficient whips. She reached the door to the sickroom at the instant Cindy reached it, their hands touching and pressing each other around the knob. Cindy glanced desperately at the nurse, as if there might be some final hope left in her face, and then said: "I'm so frightened! I'm so frightened, Miss Bigelow!"

"You'd better go in," said the nurse. "You'd better go in now."

They entered the room together and the nurse went at once and took her place beside Dr. Kent, waiting his orders. Clarry lay without movement in her wide, brass bed, the blue silk coverlet which she used shoved back and hanging to the floor. Her long hair had been plaited in two thick, yellow braids, which lay, now, like silken ropes beside her body. Her blue eyes were wide open and staring, but there was no meaning, no understanding in them. She looked steadily before her, at a fixed point on the pink-sprigged wallpaper of her room, a curious, subtle smile, which was at once anguished and thankful, fixed, as if with paint, to her whispering, unresting lips.

Cindy came toward her. "Clarry!" she said. "Clarry, you must not! You must not leave us!" She lifted her child's dying hand, held it against the warmth of her own breast, and said hoarsely: "Try, my darling! Try for the sake of your father, if not for your own. Think of him now. Think how much he has always loved you." She waited, as if she expected an answer; then the nurse came up and whispered: "The patient is unconscious, Mrs. Palmiller. She can't hear what you're saying."

But, to their surprise, Clarry moved a little, trembled and leaned forward toward her mother, as if Cindy's words had touched the small bit of her mind which was yet a part of the living world. She parted her lips and tried desperately to speak, but she could not; and then, falling back against her pillow, she sighed with a shallow sound, touched her breasts, and her golden braids, and died.

Hubert kept watch from the far side of the bed, staring without comprehension at his daughter. The knowledge that she was dead, that she was lost to him forever, was too great for him to take in immediately, and so he stood beside her as if stunned, hearing the lost weeping of his wife as if her grief were grounded in some intimate emotion which concerned women alone; and when Dr. Kent drew up the sheet and covered Clarry's face with it, he merely sighed, leaned forward and followed precisely the movement of the doctor's hand.

Then the inevitable acknowledgement of the power of death came with its inevitable repudiation, and, as if the control of his body was a thing now entirely beyond his will, his knees sagged slowly beneath his weight, and he sank down to the carpet. For a moment he looked about him, shaking his head from side to side in puzzlement; then suddenly he cried with a noise so harsh, so terrible and so tearing, that the sound of his grief could be heard throughout the house, in the servants' quarters, and even in the alley beyond, where the Goodwife waited.

"No!" he said. "I don't believe it! . . . No! No!"

Cindy came to him, touching his forehead with her fingers, but he did not heed her; he only lifted his weeping face and looked at the people before him, uncaring, now, who saw the stripped, undignified nakedness of his despair, his pride resolved at last into the components which had composed it, his self-assurance, his arrogance, no longer enough to sustain him. He had broken greatly in the past few years, and the athletic perfection of his body, of which he had once been so proud, had been lost long ago under a covering of soft, encroaching fat. His eyes were pouched and had a veined, swollen look, and nothing remained of his yellow curls except a fringe of graying hair which stretched from ear to ear and gave the back of his head a faded, unwashed appearance.

Cindy spoke quietly. "Hubert!" she said. "Hubert!"

But he pulled away from her and pressed his face into the blue coverlet on the bed. "No! No!" he said. "I don't accept it!"

Dr. Kent and the nurse came forward and tried to lift him up, but he would not move from his post beside his dead daughter. "It's the first time he's ever known sorrow," said Cindy. "That's why it's so unbearable for him now." She went to the window and stood there, thinking not of herself, but of her husband. "It must be terrible to know grief for the first time at his age," she said, but quietly, as if speaking only to herself. "I don't see how he stands it. I don't see how he stands it as well as he does."

Hubert lifted his head from the coverlet and pressed his hands harshly against his face, as if this lesser pain to his flesh could somehow assuage him; then, as if the words were torn by force from the depths of his being, he expressed, without thought, the ultimate level of a grief too deep to be endured. "Oh, my God!" he cried, his face twisted in agony. "Oh, my God! Why couldn't it have been me, instead?"

Then, as if no longer understanding what was happening to him, he permitted Dr. Kent and the nurse to take his elbows and guide him toward the door; but realizing, when he reached it, that their intention was only to separate him from his child, he turned stubbornly and shouted: "What are you people doing here? Get out, all of you! What concern is this of yours?"

"You're close to a nervous collapse," said Dr. Kent. "You must let me put you to bed and give you something that will make you sleep." He approached his patient gently, placatingly, but Hubert shoved the doctor from him, and when Miss Bigelow came to his assistance, he stepped toward her so menacingly that she was alarmed; but she was familiar with these emergencies of grief, and, remembering the powerful McKinnon brothers waiting in the library, she went out of the room to summon them. When they entered with her, a few minutes later, Hubert was again on his knees beside his daughter. His eyes had a fixed, dull look, and he stared about him with a lost, suffering expression.

The McKinnons approached, and took hold of his shoulders. "You must do what the doctor tells you," said the elder of the brothers. "What he suggests is for your own good."

Hubert said: "I will not have it! I will not accept it!"

Then, locking their arms about him, the McKinnon brothers lifted him up and carried him bodily from the room. "You haven't had any sleep in a long time," said Fergus. "You must sleep a little now. You'll feel better for it afterwards."

Hubert struggled, but he was powerless in their grasp, and when he realized this, he began to cry again with a frenzied, horrible sound. "Why should this thing happen to me?" he asked. "Why should I be asked to bear this?"

"Please take him to his bedroom," said Dr. Kent. "I'll be there at once."

"This is most regrettable, Hubert," said the elder McKinnon. "Most regrettable for everybody concerned." His voice was uncertain and a little apologetic, as if he announced to the stockholders of the bank that a dividend must be passed up.

"I've never done a mean or an unkind thing in my whole life,"

said Hubert to the astonished people who had known him so intimately. "Why should this happen to me? Why should I be singled
out?" Then, as if pleading a case which he had already lost, he continued: "I have always done my duty in the past. I have harmed
nobody. I have wronged no one. I have always lived an honorable
and an upright life. . . ."

Dr. Kent turned down the bed and the McKinnons lay Hubert
upon it; then, as if realizing his complete helplessness, he cried more
softly. He continued to cry even after Dr. Kent had given him a
hypodermic, and then gradually his weeping subsided, his eyes
closed in weariness and he slept; but even in sleep he could not
banish his child from his mind, for as he lay there, he dreamed that
she had died, and he kept turning his head on his pillow and repeating in an anguished voice: "Why couldn't it have been me
instead? Oh, my God! Why wasn't it me instead?"

After they had undressed him, Cindy came into the room, a place
where she had not been for many years. She had wanted to say:
"Now you understand at last some of the things that others feel,"
but seeing him lying there, his lips shaping the name of his daughter
over and over, she could not. She felt no anger against him any more.
Revenge and hatred seemed such small, such unimportant things
to her at that moment. Unconsciously she spoke aloud: "I forgive
everyone for the wrongs they have done me," she said. "I want others
to forgive me the wrongs I have done them, too."

Feeling more composed, she left her husband and went in search
of Mrs. McMinn. When she found her, she said: "People must be
told at once. She had so many friends. There were so many who
loved her. Will you telephone the ones who should be notified?"

"I'll take care of everything, Cindy. Please don't worry so."

"I want to get in touch with Robert, too," said Cindy. "I want
him with me now. He's with St. Joseph, at that shack on the north
side of James' Lake where they go fishing. Jesse knows where the
place is. Will you tell him to take the car and go for him as quickly
as he can?"

Minnie nodded her head. "Yes," she said. "Yes."

Hearing voices in the hall outside, Cindy paused and went to the
door. "Lula?" she called softly. "Lula, is that you?" And when the
woman answered her, she continued: "I want you to take little

Ralph to my mother. Ask her to keep him for a few days. He's too young to be faced with these things. You'd better go upstairs and start getting him ready at once. I'll come up as soon as I can."

She pressed her hands against her eyes, wondering if she had overlooked any of the necessary, immediate things which must be attended to; then, since she could remember nothing else, she turned and walked blindly toward Minnie McMinn, her arms outstretched. Minnie said: "I'll stay with you through this. I'll come back as quickly as I can manage. You may depend on it."

The two women parted in the hall, and Minnie opened the front door and went quickly down the steps. Dover Boutwell, seeing her approach, came from his hiding place and met her beside the big, iron gate. She told him at once what he wanted to know, and when she had disappeared around the corner, he turned and ran in the opposite direction, toward Court House Square, where Dr. Snowfield waited for him. There was a new, a clinging freshness in the air, a knowledge of approaching dampness. The Gulf wind had commenced again, bringing closer the saturated, lethargic clouds which rested lower, now, above the horizon to the south. It blew neither steadily nor in any consistent direction, but unpredictably, with those clowning, kittenish puffs which precede rain in dry September. Its bustling, erratic gusts dipped downward at intervals and bellied out the lace curtains of the town, bringing them suddenly to life and giving them, for a moment, a fluid and ghostly shape; it sucked out the stiff, half-drawn window shades, flapping them up and down above their sills with an excited, cracking noise, like tough applauding hands; it upset brooms and mops which rested neatly in their angles on back porches, and it rattled the town's washbasins, which hung dry and scoured on their separate, rusting nails, with a clanging, tinny sound.

Dover, as he moved along toward the doctor's office, could feel the teasing wind against his back. He hesitated when he reached the Palmiller State Bank once more, then turned and cut straight across the square. There was a light still burning in the doctor's office, and he went at once to the steps and started to ascend them; but immediately he saw that that was not necessary, for Dr. Snowfield was standing in the shadows of the court waiting for him. Neither spoke for a time, and then the doctor said timidly, as if he feared the boy's inevitable answer: "It's all over? She's dead?"

"Yes, sir," said Dover.

The doctor half-turned and waited again, his eyes closed with resignation, as if he expected something overpowering and enormous to happen to him.

"What time did she die? Do you know that too?"

"It was a little after twelve," said Dover. "I heard the clock on the courthouse strike a little before Mr. Palmiller started to cry and take on so bad."

Dr. Snowfield waited a little longer for the shock which he was convinced must come, and to which he had resigned himself, his muscles tense, his spine rigid and braced. He had taken it for granted that he must die, too, when Clarry died; and he had accepted it willingly enough, feeling that his life would be without a point, without a goal, if she should be taken from him. And yet, nothing at all had happened to him: he still breathed, still spoke, still moved his long, thin hands at will.

Then, as he gazed searchingly at the boy, he had an unexpected sense of well-being, of contentment: a deep feeling of happiness such as he had never before known. In his astonishment, he turned and walked up and down in the paved, echoing court, thinking: "I'm free of her now! I'm free of her and her whiteness forever!" Then, as he walked more rapidly, a feeling of jubilation came over him, a relief so enormous, so clarifying, that he could hardly contain himself, as he knew that he must in the presence of others; and in a winning voice which was almost coy, almost coquettish, he took a silver dollar from his pocket and offered it to Dover. To his surprise, the boy shook his head sullenly and refused it.

"I thought boys your age always wanted a little extra money," said the doctor, his face covered with an elated smile. "But maybe times have changed since I was young."

He tried desperately, at that moment, to see once more both the image of Clarry which he had built up in himself for his own destruction, and the image of her which others saw; but he could see neither of them, and since he could not, he laughed with nervous relief, thinking: "How close I came! How close I came to being destroyed forever."

"Keep it yourself," said Dover. There was something strange

about the doctor, he thought. Something odd and unwholesome, something outside his own experience. He did not know what it was, nor could he have described it to another: He knew only that he did not approve of it. "I don't want no part of your dollar!" he said angrily. "No part of it at all!" He pulled his cap down and eyed the doctor suspiciously, his legs planted stubbornly and wide apart.

The wetness in the air had increased, and the boisterous, nudging wind came at quicker intervals now. Then, without speaking again, Dover walked away, not looking back to see Dr. Snowfield with his head leaning against the wall of the courtyard, nor listening to hear him laugh with thankful, passionate relief. There was only one thought in his mind, and that was to get home before the rain came; and as he went along the silent, deserted streets, he stopped only to touch each gatepost that he passed, in the magic ritual of childhood. Then he passed the last house of the town and turned into the Reedyville Road, but at that instant he stood completely still and listened, for already he could hear the rain hissing and rushing toward him. Almost at once he saw the rain too. It moved slowly down the streets of the town like a gray unwavering wall — calm and unhurried, as if knowing that all things are accomplished in time.

Then he turned and ran down the red, clay road, his feet kicking up puffs of dust as he moved along. He had a feeling of excitement, hearing the rain coming over the rooftops, through the streets of Reedyville, closer and closer toward him, with a soothing, yet stimulating, sound. All at once he had a wild desire to outrun the rain, and as if somebody had flicked him with a whip, he leaped forward, lowered his head and sprinted furiously, his elbows held close to his sides, his brown legs thrown back and pumping wildly.

It was almost as if Time itself pursued him, and that it would catch up with him inevitably, and pass him on the road when it chose to do so. . . . But Dover was too young as yet to be concerned with such possibilities. He did not even believe in them, for the testimony of his strong, slowly beating heart, of his vigorous racing legs, was too overpowering to disregard; then, at that instant, the rain struck the road and moved down it, closer and closer to his flying heels. It was almost as if somebody beat a carpet behind him with a keen, swishing stick, and when he heard the sound he laughed and leaped forward, shouting excitedly: "Not me! Not me! . . . You're not fast enough to catch me!"

He summoned the last ounce of his energy, running faster and faster, but try as he would, he could not outdistance the rain, and a moment later he felt the drops against his tough, back-flung heels. Then the rain came up to him and held a course evenly with his moving body, as if it gathered momentum for a greater effort; and slowly, imperceptibly it pulled away from him easily, swishing and sighing and rushing down the road ahead. He stood there in the middle of the roadbed, wet to his skin and laughing with delight, hearing the rain as it struck Sweethearts' Looking-Glass with a spread, shallow sound, as if it were only an old, outworn drum which could summon nothing. He was exhausted from his long run and he sat down at the roadside, hugging himself with delight, laughing with a senseless, animal pleasure. "We needed rain," he said to the vacant air. "We needed rain bad. Everybody will be glad it came."

Chapter 10

‖‖‖

‖‖I N late January of 1942, I was
in Reedyville gathering material for the book I was writing. As
we have already seen, I called immediately on Professor St. Joseph,
my old teacher. That was the afternoon when I read Dover Boutwell's composition on the things he saw from his window, and after
I had finished, St. Joseph said: "Take it along with you, Richard.
It may come in handy." He tightened the knot in his tie, smiled and
added: "I seem to have underestimated Dover's abilities. He's
certainly done well in this town in the past few years. . . . No
doubt you've already seen his new place of business; but putting
a garage on Reedy Avenue was a shock to some of the older citizens.
They seemed to think the dust there was sacred, like the ashes of
a saint."

The Boutwell Garage was on the site of the old Palmiller home.
After the death of his daughter in 1916, Hubert had offered the
place for sale; but already the residential part of town was moving
westward, and for a long time nobody wanted it. Then Dover Boutwell, who was doing so well for himself in business, bought the
property and tore the house down. The hedges were uprooted; the
lawns were destroyed with a coating of solid cement; the magnificent
iron fences were dismantled and sold for scrap. Above the driveway,
an enormous electric sign flashed first the words, "Boutwell Garage,"
and then, a second or two later, "Cars Washed And Parked." I had
driven in that morning to get gas, and instantly a squad of agile
young men, each wearing a coverall cut to his individual figure,
rushed up to me, anxious to know my pleasure and to make it come
true. On the back of each uniform, in crimson braid, were the
words: —

Boutwell Garage
Best in the City
At Your Service

St. Joseph seemed restless that afternoon, for he got up and straightened the magazines on his library table. "In a way, I was sorry, myself, to see the Palmiller place go. I'm sure it was an emblem of something or other which can never exist again." He shrugged his thin shoulders and went on: "I consider Dover a truly happy man. He married young, you know — one of the little McKinnon girls. I don't remember which one she was, but it's not important, for they all looked exactly alike. Their eldest daughter graduated from high school last year, and that'll give you a rough idea of how time gets away from us all."

He sighed and took off his glasses. They seemed to grow thicker and more complicated with the years, so that it seemed now as if they were composed of superimposed layers of the finest and most transparent piecrust. They were like those magnifying lenses with which boys focus the rays of the sun, and behind them his eyes appeared fixed, artificial and reduced in size — like the tiny, desperate eyes of eels.

"I keep my car at Dover's place," said St. Joseph after a moment; "so I often see him. There's only one thing that disturbs his peace of mind: He has eight children now, and all of them are girls! The last time I saw him, he mentioned the subject again. I gathered from what he said that he feels such a mass production of females is a reflection on his masculine vigor. Biology was never my specialty, but I told him what I knew about such matters, hoping it would reassure him."

St. Joseph laughed in memory of the scene and raised his hands outward, his glasses swinging between his thumb and forefinger. With his glasses off, the change in his appearance was remarkable. His face gave up its intensity at once, and his eyes themselves lost their alert focus and became merely the eyes of an old man, watery and vague and inclined to bulge. He touched his eyes with his handkerchief and set his glasses firmly upon his jutting, eagle-like nose.

"I thought I was being very scientific and detached," he continued, "but when I'd finished my little discourse, Dover looked at me in a shocked way and said, 'Professor St. Joseph, you're the last man in this town I expected to hear talk dirty!' " St. Joseph laughed again, and added: "You see, Richard? You see the penalty of talking too much, of trying to air your knowledge?"

After his retirement by the school board, St. Joseph had gone to live at the Reedyville Arms, a modern apartment house which had been erected upon the old Cameron property. It was there that I saw him, surrounded by those things from the past which he had prized, and had brought with him. There was a nip in the air that afternoon, and we drew our chairs closer to the fire. As we sat there, he told me many of the things I wanted to know, his face alert and expressive, his manner animated.

In the autumn of 1916, Ira Graley, with his assistance, had gone to New York to continue his studies, to prepare further for what he considered was his life work. He had lived there ever since, and he was now famous in an obscure way. The professor considered him to be a man whose effect on his own times, whose wonderful contributions to the science of the mind, would be fully understood only after he had died and had been interred along with the confused generation which had produced him. Then, leaning a little toward me, he added: "Do you know him personally, Richard? If you don't, you must let me give you a letter of introduction to him. Call on him by all means when you go back to New York! You'll like him. He's really a great man! One of the truly great people of our day!" He talked of his protégé, and the things he had accomplished, a little longer, and then his mind turned to other matters: —

Fodie Boutwell was married again — this time quite happily. Her second husband was a Mr. Owen Witherspoon, and he was conventional, thrifty, cautious and respectable. They lived in Dothan, and she had acquired everything she wanted from life except, perhaps, the fountain with its three basins for her lawn. She still had that to look forward to, and St. Joseph was convinced that it would be a reality for her yet.

Ada, her mother, had died not long after the Armistice in 1918. "Do you remember the way her stomach used to push forward?" he asked. "It was one of the springboards for conversation at the livery stable. The boys there used to joke Wesley about it. They said his wife was going to present him with an elephant, since it took so long to bring her to bed." St. Joseph sighed and shook his head. "As it turned out, it wasn't an elephant, after all. It was a tumor, and when Dr. Kent took it out, it weighed something like thirty-six pounds." He remained perfectly silent for a moment, staring down at the carpet. "Poor old woman!" he said pityingly. "Poor old work mare! How she struggled to get along! How hard she tried to make something out of her children!"

He bent forward and stirred the fire with a heavy brass and copper poker which he had brought with him from his old quarters. "Do you remember Jesse, the Palmillers' old servant, at all?" he asked. "He takes care of me now. His wife Lula is thriving too. She's sassier than ever. She comes in every now and then to do a bit of cleaning which Jesse considers beneath his dignity as a man."

I said that I remembered them both, and St. Joseph added: "Before we start going through the old records, suppose we have a drink — if such things interest you. I generally have one at this hour of the afternoon." He rang the bell beside his chair, and almost instantly Jesse appeared carrying a silver tray which contained everything needed for highballs. His reddish hair had thinned out, and it had receded high up on his polished, butcher-paper skull. The scattered freckles across his flat nose give him a rakish, unregenerate expression. He glanced at me with a polite eagerness, wondering who I was. While he mixed the drinks, he followed everything the professor said, making small nods of confirmation, or shaking his head in disapproval if a certain thing was not precisely the way he remembered it too.

"I hope you noticed how punctual Jesse is," said the professor jokingly. "That's because he's still a young man."

"I ain't so young," said Jesse. "I'm sixty-six years old. They didn't call that young when I was a boy."

"This is Mr. Richard Mellen," said St. Joseph. "He used to live here in Reedyville some years ago. He was one of my pupils. He's writing a book about all of us, so you'd better mind your manners, or he might put you in it too."

"Yassuh," said Jesse. He went to the window and raised the shade so that the late rays of sun came into the room and made a shallow pool of light on the hearth; then, with an expression which was almost flirtatious, he lowered his eyes, smiled ingratiatingly and said: "I don't mind being put in a book. Fact is, I speck I'd like it."

"Mr. Mellen will be in town for a week or ten days," said the professor. "I've given him permission to go through my papers. If he calls when I'm out, give him anything he needs."

"Yassuh," said Jesse. "I'll see that he gits ever'thing he wants." He straightened the table, pulled it back from the fire and went out. When he had gone, St. Joseph continued: "You should find something of interest among my old school papers. My record books are there showing the school grades of half the people in town. At least you'll learn what marks Breck Boutwell made in arithmetic and physiology during any given month, or how long his sister Honey stayed in the sixth grade, and why." We talked for a long time, and then, when it was growing dusky in the room, we were conscious of Jesse standing beside us once more. "Excuse me, Professor," he said softly, "but why don't you tell Mr. Richard about the ruckus Mrs. Kenworthy caused when she died? Maybe that's something that might look well in a book."

St. Joseph leaned back in his chair and laughed suddenly. "You tell him, Jesse!" he said. "It's your story, not mine. You tell it better than I do, anyway!" Jesse seemed a little doubtful, wondering if it was entirely in good taste for a servant to entertain his master's guests. The professor seemed to have no understanding at all of the social barriers which separated people, and Jesse was often shocked, not only at the unconventional things he did as a matter of course, but at the people he entertained in his apartment, apparently on the assumption that they were his equals, as well. He solved his problem after a moment by pretending to work as he told his story, and as he talked, he fiddled about the room, cleaning an ash tray, straightening a book, or stooping occasionally to pick an imaginary thread from the rug. Thus he created the impression that he was merely talking to himself; that if white people listened to him, it was a thing which did not concern him in any personal manner.

"I speck you remember how big and fat Miz Kenworthy always was," he began, "even when she was a young lady just mar-

ried. . . . Well sir, it looked like she got bigger and bigger ever'
year; and at last it got so she couldn't go nowheres at all because she
wasn't able to walk down her steps to the carriage. Ever'body kept
telling her she was gwiner die one of these days if she didn't stop
getting so big, and sho' enough she did; but it wasn't the fat on
her that done it, 'cause she passed on of an upsot stomach. Folks
said it was caused from eating peach pie and cucumbers, but as to
that, I don't rightly know. Anyway, she wasn't exactly young,
either. It happened only a few years back, and she must have been
close to seventy at the time."

"Come to the point, Jesse," said the professor. "You're getting
to be as bad as I am. It comes from being around me so much,
I suppose."

"Yassuh!" said Jesse meekly. "Yassuh!" And added: "Anyway,
the po' lady died, like we already know, and the professor, when
he heard about it, told me to go over there and he'p out in any
way I could. Her nephew, Mr. Lucius Reedy, took charge of
ever'thing, and he ordered her a casket made extra big — a pretty
one with big silver handles on it. It looked roomy enough when it
come, but when we tried to put her in it, just before the services
started, she wouldn't fit. Nawsuh! She wouldn't fit in that coffin,
no matter how hard we tried!"

"It was like trying to squeeze a number twelve foot into a number nine shoe," said Jesse, "and after a little bit the undertaker's man
told me to hurry down to the sto' and see if they had anything bigger in stock. The gentleman there acted sort of uppity. He said
to me: 'Naw, we ain't got nothing bigger. That's the biggest coffin
ever been in this town! That coffin big enough to bury anybody
in!' He sure seemed put out, and then he said to me: 'Go on back
to the house, and tell 'em to try some more! Tell 'em they ain't tried
near hard enough!' "

"Well, sir, I come back and I told 'em what the gentleman said
to me, and so the undertaker and his boys kept sweating and grunting and trying to make her go in it. The preacher already come
long ago, and the music been playing almost an hour by then.
Ever'body outside was waiting for the services to start, so Mr.
Lucius said he better go out and tell 'em there'd been a little delay.
He come back acting nervous-like, and say to the man: 'God damn

it! Quit fooling around! Get Aunt Milly in that casket, and do it quick!"

St. Joseph said: "I was there for the services. It was really amusing, in a ghoulish sort of way."

"So then we all tried some mo'," continued Jesse. "Then the undertaker's gentleman said to me: 'Jesse, you anchor her feet firm while Mr. Kenshaw here holds her shoulders fast. Iffen we get that done, I'll see iffen I can get her behind worked down.' It look for a minute like he done hit on the way to do it, like she was all bedded down at last, but while we stood resting and wiping our faces, her shoulders sort of sunk down lower and her stomach riz up a foot higher than the coffin top. And so Mr. Kenshaw said: 'Come on boys. Look like we got to try it once mo'!' Well, sir, we kept it up I don't know how long, but we just couldn't manage nohow, because ever'time we was sho' we had her settled at last, one end of her would rise up. Iffen it wasn't her stomach, it was her shoulders; and iffen it wasn't her shoulders, it was her feet. Ever'body wondered what the matter was, and the minister kept coming into the parlor to see how we was getting along, and then leaving sudden with a curious look on his face. And at last word got around about what was going on in the back parlor, and then ever'body started laughing."

"It was disgraceful," said St. Joseph. "It really was."

At that moment Jesse abandoned all effort to maintain his dignity. He leaned against the bookshelves and laughed without restraint. St. Joseph, who had heard the story many times, laughed too; and when I could control my voice again I asked weakly: "What happened finally, Jesse? What did they do at last?"

"What did they *do?*" repeated Jesse gaspingly. "There wasn't nothing to do except bury her temporary in the wood box the coffin come in. So they done that and then sont to New Orleans and had a big casket tailormade to fit."

Jesse, with an instinctive sense of timing, turned and went back to the kitchen. St. Joseph said: "I remember that Minnie McMinn was at the funeral. It was the last time she was in Reedyville. She's been living in New York for the past few years, you know." He went on to tell me a little more of her personal history. She had gone to Hollywood in 1917, as nearly as he could remember: Anyway,

it was right after the successful adaptation she had made of her
novel, *A Belle of Old Mobile,* for the movies. She had stayed there
a long time, and she was now repulsively rich. Later, tiring of
California, she had moved to New York, to write radio serials. She
had been successful at that, too, and the audience she reached seemed
almost unbelievable to St. Joseph.

"You can hear one of her transcribed serials on our local station
every morning at half-past ten," he said. "She does several, I understand, but this particular one is called 'Janie Richmond, M.D.,' and
it's about the adventures of a woman doctor. She's a lady suffering
from most of the anxiety hysterias, it seems, but she has paranoid
character traits, too. Jesse and I listen to it every day. This morning a stranger turned up and offered Dr. Richmond ten thousand
dollars if she'd come at once and treat a little girl, but she must agree
to make the call with her eyes bandaged — the 'Ali Baba and the
Forty Thieves' touch, isn't it? — and she must promise further not
to look once at her patient's face, after the bandages are removed,
presumably. Anybody else would have called the police, but apparently Minnie's heroine sees nothing out of the way in the situation. Poor Jesse has been worried about her all day, and while we
were listening this morning, he kept whispering back into the
radio, so that the stranger couldn't hear him too, 'Don't you do it,
Dr. Janie! You know you got out of a peck of trouble just *yesterday!*
Remember your luck ain't gwiner last always!' "

He seemed very gay that afternoon, very happy to see me again,
and he told me much; but after a time he looked regretfully at his
watch and said: "Why don't you come in tomorrow afternoon,
Richard? I've got to leave you now. I promised to go to a cocktail
party this afternoon at six, and I've just time to dress." The party
was being given by Robert and Cindy Porterfield, and he was dining
with them later. "Hubert Palmiller lost everything he had in 1929,
when his bank failed," said St. Joseph. "He went back to New
York about that time too. But long before then, he gave Cindy
the divorce she had wanted so long. She and Robert Porterfield
were married immediately. It seems unbelievable, but their wedding
took place almost a quarter of a century ago."

"What became of their son?"

"You mean Ralph? Why, Ralph is on one of the New York papers.

They say he's doing well, too." He laughed and added: "It looks as if most of Reedyville's old citizens are living in New York now, doesn't it? Maybe that's where your book should end too. Maybe that's where all books about the South eventually end."

He walked with me to the door, still talking with animation. "Oh, yes," he said. "There's another thing I forgot to tell you: You're the second person I've seen recently who's writing a book. The other was a young gentleman from the Library of Congress gathering material on African rhythms in American folk tunes, or something of that sort. He was digging up data on Honey Bout-well. She was the first something-or-other, and she's important. She's become a historical character right before our eyes."

Jesse came into the reception hall and said, "You better hurry, Professor. You know how long it take you to get fixed up nice."

"So I told the young man that Honey wasn't a Negress. I said I'd taught her in school, that I knew the family well, and all that sort of thing. I'm sure he didn't believe a word of it. She's a legend now, like Washington's cherry tree, or the old bloodstains of a king." Then, shaking my hand once more, he smiled, bowed and went back into his living room. When he had gone, Jesse held the door open for me and said hopefully: "My wife Lula would sho' like to be in a book by a white gentleman. I keep a-wonderin' iffen you can't squeeze Lula in somewhere."

"You and Lula will both be in it," I said. "Don't worry about that any more."

I came into the street and looked up at the sky. There was perhaps an hour of daylight left, and I walked about the town revisiting places which I had not seen for many years. I went first to Court House Square. The Howard Block, once the town's standard of opulence, had been demolished long ago. In its place, there was a modern office building which towered above the square, dwarfing the oaks and the sycamores below. There was a new post office too; and, what was more unexpected, a new railroad station. I went there after a while to watch the evening train from the West pull in. There was nobody I knew at the station, nobody I had ever seen before. There were only masses of soldiers in winter khaki from the near-by training camps: soldiers looking undecided and unhappy, not knowing what to do with themselves.

When the crowd at the station had dispersed, I turned and walked away in the direction of New April Avenue. If Court House Square had prospered with the years, this part of town was even shabbier than I remembered it. I stopped at length before Violet Wynn's old sporting house. The place had given up at last, and its floors sagged downward to the earth in a plump arc, like the dragging belly of a lazy cat. Fire had destroyed a part of the building, and its charred west wing, rising upward from the withered weeds, seemed twice desolate against the hard, January sky. A For Sale sign had been fixed to the doorpost, but it had turned, as if in shame, upon its nail, and the wording was now upside down. The windows had been broken years before, and as I watched, a flock of querulous swallows flew up, ruffling out their feathers and chirping piteously as they found their chilly, familiar nests beneath the eaves.

Already I knew what Violet's individual fate had been, for that had been one of the first questions I asked St. Joseph. He had told me in detail, for he was in a special position to know the facts. She had died from the delayed effects of what might be called one of the occupational diseases. It was a thing she had contracted early in her career, and of which she had been cured; but in her old age, something dreadful had happened to her arteries, and something dreadful had happened to her kidneys, and that was the end of her. She was penniless when she died, and Ira Graley had paid for her funeral, although St. Joseph had arranged its details. She was buried in Magnolia Cemetery, and over her grave, her son had put a marble slab which gave her true name and the dates of her birth and death.

There had been a religious service in the dingy chapel of the undertaker's establishment, and St. Joseph had put a funeral notice in the paper, although he did not believe that anybody would come. Probably a dozen people had been there. Cindy Porterfield and Wesley Boutwell were two of them. Ella Doremus, oddly enough, was another. Then there was a man named Mc-Dermott, from the south part of town, and several other men and women whom nobody could identify. Ella the utility infielder had been there too. She had nursed Violet in her last sickness, and she was the repository of her friend's last wishes. "Violet was a real good woman, no matter what people said about her," she told St. Joseph. "There was an old hymn that she loved real well, and sometimes when we were sick and down-and-out, not knowing where our next meal would come from, we used to sit in the dark and sing it together. Before she died, she asked me to sing it again at her funeral."

It was arranged as Violet had wished it, and before the service began, Ella got up and sang in a thin, tremulous soprano: —

> "Now, Saviour, take this crimson hand:
> O, pitying Jesus, pity me!
> And lead me safe through hateful land:
> O, pitying Jesus, pity me!
> Little pitying Jesus, pity me!"

It was at this point that the most unexpected thing of all occurred, for old Mrs. Wentworth herself came to the funeral. Her rheumatism seemed bad that day, for she hobbled down the aisle on her silver-headed canes, her pearl choker high, stern and uncompromising. She seated herself and stared straight ahead, her face grim and determined, as if she were alone in the chapel. Then one of the strange women began to cry into her handkerchief, and Ella, after hesitating a moment, went on with her song: —

> "Now, Saviour, make me sweet again:
> O, pitying Jesus, pity me!
> Wash from my flesh each horrid stain:
> O, pitying Jesus, pity me!
> Little pitying Jesus, pity me!"

The service began immediately afterwards, and Mrs. Wentworth sat through it as if made of stone. Later, having spoken to nobody, having looked at no one, she hobbled again to her carriage and was driven away. St. Joseph had wondered what impulse made her come to the funeral of this dead, notorious old prostitute, and then one day he asked her the question outright. She stared at him in astonishment, surprised at his lack of discernment, and her answer, when she gave it, embraced both the best and the worst of her generation. "I came because it was my *duty* to come," she said. "Don't think I wanted to be mixed up with such people! I thought nobody else would dare come, that's all; and when I read the funeral notice in the *Courier,* I said to myself, 'They shall not bury the old creature alone. Someone must be there, in common decency. I'm going, if I have to crawl there on my hands and knees.' So I went."

Remembering these things, I circled the west part of town, coming out at length on the Reedyville Road. It had been paved long ago, and with its improvement, all its individuality seemed to have disappeared. The Boutwell house, and the Negro shacks near by, had been torn down. Where they had once stood, there was now a municipal park, planted with trees and shrubs. Sweethearts' Looking-Glass, where lovers had once walked, and admired their trailing images in the water, had been filled in and sodded, so it was possible, now, only to guess where it had been. I stood there for a time looking about me, and then, since night was coming on, I turned and went toward the hotel where I was staying.

In all that walk, I had seen nobody that I remembered from my past until I came to the building which had once housed Rowley's Pool Parlors, and there, sitting on a bench, was Wesley Boutwell talking to a group of young soldiers. He was eighty years old, and his once magnificent body was now bent and twisted with arthritis. His thin hair was long and white, his face incredibly old and wrinkled.

"I'm telling you," he was saying in his patient, trembling voice. "I'm telling you again I seen fighting in the Philippines. I could prove it easy enough, if I was a mind to prove it."

The young soldiers nudged one another and laughed loudly. One of them said: "Guhw-a-a-n, Grampaw! You could'na' seen fightin' deh! You too old! Anyway, if you was deh in December, what you doin' back heh in January?"

Wesley sighed and moved his mutilated arm back and forth, but he did not answer. There was little use in speaking to these young men of things which had happened so long before they were born. They thought he was concerned with the present war in the Philippines, and he made no effort to correct that impression, for he dwelt, now, in that timeless land in which the very young, who have just come from infinity, and the very old, who, with no regret, will soon return to it, live their remote, unscheduled lives. The young soldiers believed his mind to be muddled with age; he, in turn, thought that they concerned themselves too greatly with distinctions of no importance. He could have told them, had he cared to, that time completes its circle over and over, and that when you have lived through it once, as he had, you know there is no essential difference in anything. He raised his dark, imploring eyes, still bright, still undimmed by time, and said: "I'm telling you! I'm telling you what I seen!"

As I stood there listening, I remembered a thing St. Joseph had said before we parted: "It's lucky I have Jesse to keep me straight, because I never know what time it is any more. I maintain that clocks were invented for the pleasure of the vain, that they are the concern of the ardent and the proud — those who believe that what they accomplish, and who they are, is of any importance to others."

The following afternoon I went back to see him; and I called regularly thereafter for a week. Sister Cotton, he said, had died, appropriately enough, of a ruptured blood vessel. Her old enemy, Breck Boutwell, was dead too, but his ending had been more dramatic, more unexpected.

In the fighting at St. Mihiel, it seemed that his squad was surrounded by the enemy, and they were in danger of being taken prisoners. The corporal had considered that capture was the only escape open to them, but Breck, to whom the idea of being a prisoner was unbearable, preferred to fight his way through to freedom or to die where he stood. He crawled out of the shallow trench where the others were, and armed with his rifle and all the hand grenades which remained in the possession of the squad, he walked calmly forward toward the machine guns which had trapped them, a doomed figure of defiance in all that world of hate. He was hit four times, but he continued to throw his grenades with a self-conscious, studied precision; and those of the gunners who were still alive, alarmed at last by his invincibility, turned and ran into the woods. He reached the nest and fell forward on his face, his hand, with its inverted thumb, touching the gun which had killed him.

When I was returning to New York, St. Joseph said: "Before you put your book into a final draft, I think you should have a look at Minnie McMinn's old ledgers. She has everything you need in them. She'll never use the material herself, and she must realize that by now."

"Do you think she'd let me see them?"

St. Joseph thought a moment, pulling absently at his ear. "I don't know," he said. "Really, I don't know. Minnie was always a little unpredictable." Then he added: "Of course I could give you a letter to her, but that might hit her the wrong way, and get her neck feathers up. Now, here's what I suggest: I expect to come to New York when the weather gets a little warmer. I usually go up in April. Why don't you wait until then? If you do, I'll take you to see her personally."

We parted with that plan in mind, and true to his promise, he wrote me early in April saying that he expected to see me in about a week. Robert and Cindy Porterfield were coming with him this time. Their son Ralph was enlisting, and they wanted to see him before he went away to a training camp. "I wrote Minnie after I talked with you," he concluded, "and hinted tactfully at what you were doing. She's enthusiastic over the idea of a book about Reedyville, and she suggested the ledgers of her own accord. So everything is now arranged. I'll get in touch with you as soon as I arrive in town."

A few days later he telephoned from his hotel and said: "Look here, Richard! Minnie had planned a little party in your honor. It's for this afternoon, and she's going to have in several of the Reedyville New Yorkers to meet you — people she thinks you'd be interested in seeing again. She's invited them for five o'clock, I believe. Later on, she's having a good many other people in — celebrities and that sort of thing. Can you make it on such short notice? Why don't you meet me at her place a little early? About half-past four would be about right. That'll give us time to get settled down before the others start arriving."

I said that I could easily arrange it, and he added: "Do you know about Minnie's fabulous establishment? Where to find her? She lives on Central Park South, in great magnificence, my boy! Her living room is papered — if that's the right word — with zebra skins and mirrors. She's thirty stories above street level. Possibly it's fifty. I'm not sure which. Anyway, her view of New York is staggering. You're sure to like that, even if you find your fellow townsmen a little too dull, and the other guests a little too successful."

That morning had begun with a snowstorm, although the weeks before had been mild and springlike. The dense, whirling snow seemed inappropriate at that time of the year, for already the willows had turned green; already the meadows and the sheep pastures of the park were showing an intense new carpet of grass. The snow had swirled all day, excitedly in its own patterns; or it had drifted to earth languidly when the lifting wind, which gave it life, died away for a time; and as I walked through Central Park some hours later, on my way to keep my appointment, the wet, ghostly snow still fell, swirling, now, in great sweeps beneath the wind, lifting and falling like tidal water, pausing, floating and drifting outward; filling the air completely; obliterating old paths, old landmarks.

St. Joseph met me at the door and the butler took my hat and coat. Instantly Mrs. McMinn came toward me too, her hand outstretched in welcome, her mouth stretched wide in its old gesture, the pink cave of her throat exposed. She guided me at once to her terrace, and making a sweeping gesture, one which included her plants, her trees and her fishpond, she said: "Isn't it disheartening? . . . This snow, I mean! Just when my shrubs were turning green again! I hope my moss roses aren't killed. I had a terrible time finding them. You don't seem to see old-fashioned moss roses any more, do you?" Then, smoothing down her brilliant, almost tomato-colored hair, she went on: "Well, anything can happen, can't it? And so often *does,* too!"

She was perhaps seventy years old; and she was so smoothed-out, so lacquered, so ingeniously tinted, that she seemed, now, less a woman than a work of art. Her face had that bland, ominous smoothness which is the hallmark of renovated and redistributed flesh. There was not a line in it, not even the lines which children have in their faces. Her lips and hair were the same shade of crimson, and her long, tapering nails were incrusted with a metallic substance which was far redder, far more costly than blood. She somehow gave the impression of an old ruin which had miraculously erected itself again, this time on the most modern of lines, and painted with the shrillest, the brightest of colors. Obviously she had spent large sums of money to keep her youth. In a grotesque sort of way she had been successful, for people, when meeting her, thought instantly: "How *young* she looks! She must be seventy, at least!"

I sat on the couch close to the long windows which faced Central Park, and after a little Mrs. McMinn came and sat beside me. "St. Joseph has been telling me about you. I remember you quite well as a little boy. Do you remember me too? Your mother was one of the Ralston girls, wasn't she?" Before I could answer, she went on: "And now about those old ledgers of mine. You're welcome to take anything in them that you need. My secretary will fix you up a place where you can work comfortably. Telephone him, won't you, and make the arrangements that suit you both."

She got up and straightened the magnificent Cézanne above her mantel. In the silence, I said: "Do you mind telling me which of the Reedyville people you've invited? If you will, I can be thinking of what to say to them, before they get here."

"There won't be many," said Minnie. "Cindy and Robert Porterfield, of course. Their son Ralph is coming too. Then I've asked Ira Graley and Honey Boutwell. I think that's all." She sat beside me once more and continued: "When I finished my list, I thought to myself: 'But they're all so old and battered! With the exception of Ralph, Honey Boutwell is the youngest in the lot, and she's fifty-two.' "

"It isn't possible," said St. Joseph quickly. "Not really that old, Minnie!"

"She's fifty-two, all right!" said Mrs. McMinn. "She was born in 1890. I looked it up in one of my ledgers the other day. When her father went away to the Spanish–American War, I called on her mother as a representative of the *Courier,* and that day she gave me the names and birthdays of all her children for my record. I put it down just as she told it to me, so I can't be wrong." Then, turning to me, she added: "Don't you simply *hate* old people, Mr. Mellen? Heaven knows, I do. They seem so helpless and apologetic and pitiful to me! Why, old people actually *smell* old! That's the reason I surround myself with the young. People with life and energy and blood still in them. People who accomplish things!"

St. Joseph laughed, took her hand and drew her toward him affectionately. "You see, Richard?" he said. "Didn't I tell you that

Minnie was too unbelievable for your book? Didn't I tell you there
was nobody in the whole world just like her?"

"I started to ask Hubert Palmiller too," said Minnie. "I didn't,
for several reasons, all of them good. In the first place, I'm sure he
wouldn't have accepted. Then, too, his wife and her second husband
will be here, although I hardly think that would embarrass anybody. . . . But the main reason I didn't ask him was the fact that
Honey Boutwell is coming. Now Honey Boutwell rich and famous
and married respectably to a real prince is hardly the helpless little
girl that Mr. Palmiller ran out of Reedyville that night so long
ago. I didn't think it tactful to bring the persecutor and his victim
together, particular since *La Négresse d'Alabama* is quite capable
of bouncing one of my nice chairs off his head."

Somewhere, in the distance, a telephone rang faintly. A moment
later Minnie's secretary came in to announce that her agent was
on the wire and wanted to speak to her. "What does he want?" asked
Minnie suspiciously. "Did he tell you? Do you know?" The secretary bent forward a little and whispered something in his employer's ear. At once Minnie threw out her arms desperately and
said: "Tell him no! Tell him I will not consider doing another
serial for anybody! No amount of money will tempt me! I work
my fingers to the bone as it is, and what do I really get out of it?
. . . No! No more serials. Five is enough for any one person to
keep moving."

When the secretary had gone, Minnie went on in her natural
voice: "Hubert Palmiller hasn't a cent to his name any more,
but I'm sure you already knew that. He lives on the allowance
which Ralph Porterfield makes him, and Ralph is probably the
only person in the world he talks to. He lives in a cheap flat somewhere in the West Sixties, not too far from Central Park, and sometimes when I take my walk there, I bump into him. He's become
very eccentric indeed. He thinks everybody is down on him — that
everybody is plotting to steal the little he has left. Ralph once told
me that he has six different locks on his door, and that even in
summer he keeps his windows closed and bolted. I often wonder
what he thinks about — there in that cheap, dark little place."

The butler entered with a tray of cocktails, and when we had
each taken one, Minnie continued: "I tried to speak to Hubert one

day. I stopped him, and said: 'Hubert! Hubert Palmiller! You remember me, don't you? I'm Minnie McMinnis McMinn.' He backed away from me, muttering something and shaking his head, while I stood there in the path, thinking: 'How soiled and bent he is! How incredibly old!' I followed him, trying to make him understand that I meant him no harm, but he only said: 'Keep away from me! I'm warning you! You'd better keep away from me! I don't know who you are! I don't know who anybody is!' And so I stood there until he passed out of sight. He spends much of his time in the Park feeding the birds. I've often seen him at the lake bending over the water, his hand stretched out to the swans. But he never looks at the birds he feeds: he looks at his own reflection in the water instead; and as he kneels there, you can see his lips moving. I think that it isn't really himself he sees, but Clarry, who looked so much like him. I think the words he repeats over and over are the ones he kept saying the night she died: 'My God! Oh, my God! Why wasn't it me, instead!' "

Outside the snow swirled excitedly about, or drifted outward in long, thinning streamers, and settled down, whitening the frail, toy-like roofs so far below us. Occasionally, when the wind blew in a certain way, it herded the nervous snow and trapped it in the angle of Minnie's terrace, so that the effect at such times was that of white, lacy surf lifting upward and breaking above a ledge. For a time we watched the snow, sitting in silence, thinking our own thoughts, and then Minnie said: "Is there anything in particular you wanted to ask me? We haven't much time. The others should be coming before long."

"I was wondering what became of Dr. Snowfield. Do you know?"

"I can tell you a little something about him," said Minnie. "Not much, perhaps, but at least something. After he left Reedyville, he gave up the practice of medicine, and dedicated himself to the radical labor movement, as I'm sure you know already. He went about the country making the most astounding speeches, but nobody paid very much attention to him. Then war came along — the one in 1917, my child — and it was then that he really denounced the Government in earnest! It was something about Negro soldiers being denied their right to be shot in the trenches as freely as their white comrades. I may be a naïve type, but it seems to me that the Negro soldiers should have been pleased at such discrimination, rather than offended. Anyway, that wasn't the way Dr. Snowfield's mind worked. He went about, finally, urging people to defy the law and resist the draft, so they had to take him into custody for the duration. When they let him out, he made a little speech which was widely copied at the time. He said it was impossible for him, or any other civilized person, to live in the United States with its stupid, cruel and oppressive Government of harsh, unfeeling capitalists. He said he was going to Russia where the rights of men were held sacred; where people enjoyed freedom and lived without fear. He did so. They shot him."

Minnie laughed her wide, panting laugh; and leaning backward a little, she pressed a concealed button behind her couch. A maid came in promptly, and she said: "I think we need more ash trays for the party, Lena. Get out the new crystal ones."

"How did you get in touch with Honey Boutwell?" asked St. Joseph. "Who told you she was back in America?"

"My dear!" said Minnie. "Don't you even read the newspapers any more? It was in all of them. Thousands and thousands of her fans were at the airfield to welcome her home. Oh, she got every ounce of publicity, you may be sure of that! Her agent is no fool! I telephoned her at once about a spot on one of my programs. Since then, we've had lunch several times together. She had intended coming home sooner, right after Paris fell, but she had so much trouble getting a visa for her husband, the Prince."

"Is her husband coming this afternoon?" I asked.

"I don't know," said Minnie. "It's anybody's guess. I invited him, but Honey didn't seem too enthusiastic. I don't know why. It certainly isn't because she's *ashamed* of him. I've met him once or twice, and really he's quite delightful." She readjusted one of the long, jade earrings which had been designed exclusively for herself, and continued: "One day Honey said to me, apropos of nothing: 'You know, Miss Minnie, when I went to school in Reedyville, all the little girls used to brag about how they were going to marry a prince when they grew up. It's funny, isn't it, because I never said anything at the time, and yet I was really the one that done it.'"

The bell rang, and Minnie, glancing at her watch, got up and went toward the door. "It's sure to be Cindy and Robert," she said. "They are always exactly on the dot." She came back with them a little later, and Cindy said, glancing at everybody, smiling at everybody: "Ralph is coming a little later on. I hope you don't really mind. He has so many things to attend to before he's ready for training camp."

She was dressed in that anonymous elegance of rich old ladies who have no faith in the new or the unusual. Her hair was now completely white. It had never been cut, and it was arranged in a knot at the nape of her neck. A wide, black velvet ribbon supported her disintegrating throat, and an enormous, old-fashioned sunburst of diamonds was pinned in the precise center of her breast. She seemed very frail, very tired as she stood there with her husband, and the knotted, lavender veins showed clearly beneath her transparent, papery flesh. She stood there in the center of the room and glanced about her with uncertainty, as if Minnie's bizarre opulence confused her a little; then, as if the gesture had now become reflexive, she extended her arm desperately and fumbled the air until she felt her husband's fingers locking about her own. She moved closer to him, looking into his face with an eagerness which she did not try to conceal, as if she realized the days that remained to them were not many, and she meant to waste no precious minute away from his side.

His back had become even straighter with the years, his gait, his gestures, more brittle. His long, distinguished face had a look of resignation above the high, starched collars which he wore. His mahogany-colored hair had hardly faded at all, and it seemed too young, too thick and vigorous, for his aged and mottled flesh. He bowed with a well-bred preciseness and sat beside his wife, lifting his arm a little so that she could press her body closer to his own.

"I'm so anxious to see Honey Boutwell again," said Cindy. "Is she really coming?"

"Yes," said Minnie. "Oh, yes. She should be here any minute."

For a time we talked of Reedyville, of the things which had happened there so many years before, but Mrs. McMinn seemed a little abstracted, and she kept glancing at her watch from time to time. Then, at last, the bell rang once more. Not long afterwards Honey Boutwell came into the room, and although she was worn and gaunt, and her dark hair was streaked through with gray, she was very beautiful still. She entered with perfect ease, perfect assurance, hardly noticing Minnie's magnificence, as if she took these theatrical settings for granted. There was about her that air of slovenly unconcern which only actresses, accustomed to appearing before large, applauding audiences, achieve in their private lives, as if, having known the hammering admiration of the many so long, they are unconcerned, now, with the effect they create upon the few, feeling themselves, perhaps, entirely alone in a group of people whose total does not exceed a hundred.

"Why, you didn't bring the Prince!" said Minnie chidingly. "We are all so disappointed."

"I started to," said Honey. "But you see, he don't speak English real good."

"What a *pity,*" said St. Joseph. He raised his eyebrows high above his thick, intricate lenses. "You must find that embarrassing!"

"Yes," said Honey. "I do."

She took a cocktail and sat down, stretching her beautiful legs toward the fire; then, with perfect good nature, she said: "You people want to ask me what happened to Mr. Paul Kenworthy, don't you? I know Miss Minnie has been dying to do that ever since I came back to America, but didn't have the nerve. All right. I'll tell you without your asking. That way you can save your manners, and find out too."

She went on to explain that Mr. Kenworthy had died some years before. It had started as an ordinary cold in the chest, but he had not rallied, as he should, and pneumonia had set in later. She described each step of his last illness, each detail of the treatment he had received. He had had the best doctors, the finest attention that money could buy, but he had died just the same, quite conventionally in his own bed. But if his death had been average enough, his funeral had been something quite outstanding. Everybody had turned out for it, even cabinet ministers. They had buried him in Paris, and that's where he still was. She rubbed her knees a little and drew back from the fire. "He was never sorry about leaving Reedyville," she added. "He never wanted to go back home, the way old men do in plays."

She tucked a strand of her graying, straggling hair more securely beneath the edge of her shabby, expensive hat; and stretching herself delicately, she added: "Now that I've told *you* something you wanted to know, Miss Minnie, I want you to tell me something I always wanted to know."

"Yes, of course," said Mrs. McMinn. "What is it?"

Honey said: "When I was going to school in Reedyville, the girls in my class used to say that you and Professor St. Joseph were sure to marry some day. But you never did. Now, why?"

"I tried hard enough to get her," said St. Joseph, "but I wasn't her type."

"Wait!" said Mrs. McMinn peremptorily. "Wait a minute!" Again she pressed a button, this time for her secretary, and when he entered, she said: "Let me have that little parable I clipped the other day. You know: the one I told you to file in the 'Material for Possible Use' folder." The young man found it almost at once, and when he returned, Minnie said: "This is my secretary, Mr. John Fielding." The young man bowed to us all, and Minnie went on: "I want you to read the story out loud, John!" adding instantly: "He's an actor. He reads beautifully. So much better than I do." Then the elegant young man, who seemed to have no capacity whatever for astonishment, moved gracefully to the long windows which faced the Park, and there, against the background of the falling snow, he read: —

"The End of the Farmer's Daughter

"The daughter of a certain rich farmer had been told that Love would surely ride up to her father's house one day and claim her for his bride. Afterwards, she thought constantly of the prediction, dreaming of the happy time when she was destined to ride away with Love to the lifetime of admiration for which she longed. Thus it happened that she thought of nothing but Love, spoke of nothing but Love; and as the mornings advanced, she would wash herself all over and change her clothes; then she would paint her lips and her cheeks, or spend hours on end examining herself in a looking-glass.

"On a certain day as she sat beside a spring, engaged at her unending task of making herself more worthy of Love when he came, one of the new hired men, just back from the fields, rode up to her and stopped. He had never seen her before, but at once he dismounted and told her how beautiful she was, how greatly he loved her. He could not live without her, he said, and he implored her to leave her father and ride away with him to his own country.

" 'Don't distract my attention, please!' she said. 'I've got work to do. Love might come for me today, and I want to be ready.'

"Later, when she had sent the hired man away, she went on with the arrangement of her hair; and when she had made herself as seductive as it was possible for any woman to be, she came back to her father's house and sat on the porch to wait, every hair in its proper place, every ruffle and flounce arranged effectively about her chair. Toward sunset, a group of girls came down the road, laughing and talking as they walked along. When they saw the farmer's daughter still sitting, still waiting, they said: 'Are you still here? We thought you had gone away.'

" 'I'm waiting for Love,' said the farmer's daughter. 'He should pass by any moment now.'

"The farm girls looked at one another in surprise, and then one of them spoke for all: 'But Love came to your house hours ago. From the fields where we were working we saw him ride up in all his glory and speak to you as you sat there dreaming at the spring.' At this, the other girls nodded their heads in unison and said: 'How was it you failed to see him too? How was it possible that you missed him?' "

When the secretary had finished, he took a step backward and lifted his head in expectation. Everybody applauded self-consciously, and as the sound died away, the young man bowed gravely and went back to his office in the rear of the apartment. Ralph Porterfield had come in during the reading of the fable, but he had stopped beside Mrs. McMinn's iron grillwork, at the steps which led downward to the sunken living room. He was tall, phlegmatic and pleasant, and when he had been introduced to everybody, he went at once and sat on the sofa with his mother and father.

"I don't know what's keeping Ira Graley," said Minnie. "I hope nothing has happened to prevent his coming." She fitted a cigarette into her holder, accepted another cocktail and shook her head mildly from side to side, as if she said to herself: "I don't like to be kept waiting. Surely he must *know* that."

Then, at last, the bell rang and Ira entered. He went quickly to Mrs. McMinn and took her hand. He was getting quite bald, and on each side of his head, just above his ears, there was an untidy tuft of white hair which barely escaped being comic, and which gave him an odd, owlish look. His serene face was old, lined and expectant. He bent forward a little as he walked, achieving, somehow, that intense, listening effect so characteristic of those who concern themselves all day with the minds and the emotions of others. "I can't stay very long, after all," he said. "I have a patient coming in at half-past six. But I was determined not to miss this opportunity of seeing you all together again."

"You know," said Honey thoughtfully, "I wouldn't have known you if I'd passed you on the street, Ira. My God! My God, how you've changed!" At once she added: "I don't blame you for getting rid of Fodie. She was awful, wasn't she? Did you marry again afterwards?"

"Yes," said Ira. "Quite happily. I have three children now. They're all grown-up."

Mrs. McMinn who thought it wiser to keep the talk away from these personal matters, said quickly: "I understand you're about ready to bring out your new book, Ira. I was talking with a most distinguished doctor at a dinner party the other evening. A refugee. I didn't quite catch his name, but he talked about you all evening. He said you were the greatest living man in your field."

Ira sighed and looked down at the carpet. Slowly he pulled at his nose with its thin bridge and its fleshy, arrow-shaped tip. When he looked up and smiled, you had to modify everything you had thought of him before. There was a quality about him so humble, so gentle and so selfless that you wondered how it was possible for him to have accomplished the things he had, working as he did, with no protection at all, among the savage, dangerously insane. Had you asked him the question outright, he would have shaken his rather comic head and answered that he did not know. Perhaps the basis of his success was his gentle, unconquerable courage, a thing which his patients recognized and understood even before he had spoken; perhaps the furious and the animal-like who, having no faith in men, had gone at last into the terrible country of their own minds, could yet find something to hold on to in the simple humility which they felt so quickly in him.

For a time he talked of his work, of the things he hoped to accomplish in the future, and then, as if understanding my own thoughts, he turned, put his hand on my arm and said so softly that nobody else heard him: "Don't be taken in by Mrs. McMinn's outward display. A more compassionate creature never lived. You

might be surprised if you knew all the kind things she manages
to do for others."

Mrs. McMinn's secretary entered the room once more. Since
he had now been introduced, he said to us all without discrimination: "I'm making a perfect nuisance of myself, but it can't be helped
this time." Then, bending above his employer, he whispered a long,
intricate message in her ear. When he had finished, he moved backward and took up his post beside the radio. Minnie said: "I'm sorry,
but it seems that I must listen to one of my own serials at five-
forty-five. The girl who plays the lead is sick in bed, and they're
using a substitute — an unknown. She's so promising that my agents
think she'll be ideal for a part in 'Castle-on-the-Hudson,' the soap
serial I do. They want me to listen to her, and give them my
opinion of her ability. Do you mind?"

Everybody looked at his watch, seeing that the appointed time
had almost come, and said he did not. Ira got up and joined me
at the window, and for a time we stood there in silence. The snow
had stopped at last, and the air was clearing. Below us, the Park
was covered with cold, impersonal white, and the buildings on its
western side cast delicate shadows across it — shadows tinted blue
and pink and lavender which moved forward implacably as the
light died out of the sky. Then, as we watched there, the strung,
elaborate lights of the Park came on, shining pale and timid on
that stretching waste of snow.

St. Joseph came to the window and stood beside us. "What is your
new book about, Ira?" he asked. "Are you satisfied with it?"

"It's about the death instincts," said Ira. "No, I'm not satisfied
at all. It brings up so many problems, and solves so few of them.
I've put into it everything I've learned in a lifetime of work, and
yet I know it only scratches the surface a little."

Honey Boutwell, seeing us talking so earnestly together, got
up from her chair beside the fire and came to us. "There's so much
to learn," said Ira. "So much work still to be done."

The young secretary, who had been staring hypnotically at the
dial of his watch, turned on the radio at that second; and Mrs.
McMinn, putting on her Harlequin spectacles, drew her chair closer
to listen, a notebook and pencil lying in readiness beside her. Ira
looked up, caught her eye and smiled; then, seeing that Robert

and Cindy were moving toward our group, he stretched out his hand and went quickly to meet them.

From the radio there came the artful voice of a man announcing the station to which we were about to listen, its wave length, and the broadcasting company which controlled it. "At the signal," he said, "the time will be exactly five–forty-five." The gong came with the ending of his words, and hardly had its vibrations died away before another voice, a lighter, more excited one this time, spoke triumphantly: "Myra and *Jim!*" As he spoke, the theme music swelled and then faded into nothingness. Then the excited, tenor voice went on: "And now for Myra and *Jim!* That exciting, heart-warming story of a modern young couple in their fight to achieve a place for themselves in the world. . . . But first a word from Douglass Weinkopf regarding Elsa Fletcher's remarkable, vitamin-fortified beauty preparations."

Ralph Porterfield had now joined the group gathered about Ira Graley. He listened quietly, smiling his remote, impersonal smile. Feeling that he was embarrassed, Ira slipped an arm about his waist and drew him forward with a simplicity, a friendliness which nobody else in the room could have possibly carried off.

And then a new voice came from the depths of the radio, a deep self-conscious voice which was a little stern, a little menacing: "Ladies, are you doing *your* share to preserve our democratic way of life? Are you making an effort to be as attractive as nature intended you to be? Now, as never before, you must struggle to keep that beauty of face and figure which is the particular heritage of American womanhood — that feminine loveliness which men desire so greatly, for which they are willing to fight and die, there on the great battlefields of the world."

"There is an instinct toward love and an instinct toward hate," continued Ira Graley, "and the instinct toward hate is the stronger. There is an instinct toward life and an instinct toward death, and the instinct toward death is the stronger, being so much older."

"Now ladies," continued the radio voice accusingly, "when your soldier boy comes home does he find a lovely, radiant woman who has preserved or enhanced her natural beauty through an application of Elsa Fletcher's remarkable, vitamin-fortified beauty preparations, or does he find one tired, listless and unattractive?" There seemed to be no one willing to answer, and so the voice went on: "This is my message to the womanhood of America: You, too, can be radiant and irresistible, if you will use Elsa Fletcher's remarkable vitamin-fortified beauty preparations. You, too, can defeat the Axis, can help win the great fight for democracy, if you will only . . ."

Unknowingly we had raised our voices a little, and Mrs. McMinn, making a protesting sound, shook her elaborate, crimson head in humorous warning. Afterwards, we moved closer to the window and looked steadily at the frozen Park so far below us, seeing, somehow, beneath the soft, muted fury of the snow, the new foliage of the incrusted trees, the green, eager grass of the meadows. And as I stood there, remembering the things which Ira Graley had been saying to us all, I thought once more of The Goodwife of Death.

St. Joseph had taken me to see her one afternoon, and it had been a shocking experience, as he had predicted it would be. She was ninety-six years old, and she still lived in the outdoor kitchen behind the Dunwoody place, the place which the Reedys had purchased for their daughter when she married Paul Kenworthy. St. Joseph bought the food, the fuel and the medicine which the old woman required: Lula, Jesse's wife, cooked for her, dressed her, and kept the place clean. It was fortunate that St. Joseph remembered so well, for everybody else in Reedyville had forgotten her, taking it for granted that she had died long ago. She had not died, although a thing far more terrible had happened to her.

When she was very old indeed, her remarkable health broke at last. She was forced to take to her bed, racked with unending pain. She lost the use of her arms and legs, and afterwards she could only lie helplessly on her bed, her breath coming in uneven gasps, adjusting itself to the rhythm of her agony. And so she lay there at last and watched the decay of her own body, feeling all the terrible pangs of dissolution without first knowing the mercifulness of death.

But she was destined to endure pain more terrible than the pain her flesh knew, for later, when her suffering became greater than her dread of death, she came back from the mad, individual world where she had dwelt so long, to the everyday world of reality which others knew. Thus, when it was too late to retrieve what she had lost, she was given the final bitterness, the knowledge that she had wasted her breath and her days on an illusion; that she had sacrificed herself needlessly, and had escaped nothing at the end.

On the day I went to see her, her mind was entirely normal, entirely clear, and as I bent above her wrinkled, pain-ridden old body, she said in her beautiful, great-lady voice: "I was never the Bride of Death. I was never a great queen. I was nothing. Nothing at all. Only a frightened, insane old woman. No more." New hair had grown upon the skull which she had kept shaved so long. It was now shoulder length, and it hung in white, silken ringlets about her face. The curls gave her an oddly inappropriate appearance, as if a wig meant for a young girl had been placed upon the head of a mummy. She was quiet for a moment, and then, as new spasms of agony passed over her, she looked at me imploringly, as if I could bring her release, and said: "Let me die! Be merciful to me! I'm old and sick and I've suffered too long! Be merciful! Merciful!"

I stretched out my arm, knowing that I could do nothing, and touched her white curls with my hand; then she closed her eyes with desperation, knowing that she would not die, that she would live there a little longer in her cluttered room, thinking, regretting, and watching her own decay. Lula came up then and bathed her face and hands with a cool rag. "Peace," she said softly. "Peace, sister!"

As I remembered this scene, I was conscious of the voice from the radio saying: "And now for Myra and *Jim!* . . . As you will remember from yesterday, Myra, returning from a shopping trip in town, saw Jim, her husband, who is running for the office of district attorney, talking with a young woman on a street corner. It seems to Myra that he is acting furtively, and investigation on her part reveals the fact that the woman in question is none other than Carrie Winslow, a gunman's moll. . . . But now listen to today's installment of this fascinating, true-to-life drama of a young couple in love."

The serial went on and on. Myra was warned over the telephone by a stranger that she'd better watch her husband, see? Then another character, a Negro cook named Mamie Logan, had paused in her dusting to deliver the comedy lines which Mrs. McMinn had written for her. . . . And now Myra, consumed with jealousy and hurt pride, completely disillusioned, is determined to leave Jim forever! And with no explanation. Is she justified in doing so? Are Jim's relations with Carrie Winslow entirely honorable? . . .

"A world is ending before our eyes," said Ira Graley in his soft, deep voice. "What will life be like afterwards? Will the change be a small one, so reasonable that we will hardly notice the difference? Will it be something overpowering and dramatic? . . . But it is ending. A whole world is ending as we sit here talking together. I wouldn't try to hold it back, even if I had the power to do so."

At that moment Mrs. McMinn, who was now making notes on the performance of the substitute player, raised her pencil and said: "Sh-h-h! Don't talk, please!" Then, indicating the radio with her head, she added: "This is *important!*"

It was six o'clock at last, and with a final plea to the womanhood of America, the program came to an end. The secretary shut off the radio, and after conferring with Mrs. McMinn, he took the notes she had made and hurried back to his office.

Afterwards, we stood quietly beside the window, waiting for Mrs. McMinn's new, celebrated guests to arrive, watching the lights along Fifth Avenue shine upward, against the buildings there, with a gentle, steady glow: renewing the soft, inherent sheen of the individual stone, accenting, anew, the luster in each weathered and shimmering brick. With the approach of darkness, the frozen Park seemed wasted and shrunken in size. Lights threaded it through with an involved, elaborate preciseness, but they were too small, too distant, for any human need — too pale for service, against the paler expanse of the snow. The whitened trees and the rocks were like toys, and even the roads themselves, with the tiny, desperate automobiles upon them, were things from remembered childhood, as if what stretched before us were not really a park, where people walked, but a consoling toy, a distracting thing designed for the pleasure of a pampered child.

Honey Boutwell was the first to speak. "You know, Ira," she said, "what you been talking about makes me think of a song they sang in Reedyville when we were children. You know the one I

mean, don't you? . . . The one about how the world's going to
end. First, it was to be with water, and then it was to be with
dryness; then fire, and maybe one or two other ways. But the last
way was the worst of all, and that way was with ice."

"Sing it, won't you?" asked Ira. "I haven't heard you sing since
you were a little girl, when you used to upset Fodie so much."

"I won't have the time," said Honey doubtfully. "Miss Minnie's
six-o'clock guests ought to be coming along any minute now."

"Oh, go on and sing it," said Minnie. "They won't be exactly
on time. I'm sure of it."

"I'll sing the last verse, anyway," said Honey. And standing
beside the steps, with no accompaniment, as the song had been
sung originally, she began, her low notes as deep, as resonant as
those of an operatic tenor: —

> "The world gwiner end with cold ice upon the land,
> With cold ice upon the land, a cold freezing on the land,
> Oh, the world gwiner end with cold ice upon the land,
> Prideful brother, you better trimble and hide.
>   Trimble, trimble, trimble and hide.
>   Trimble, trimble, trimble and hide."

When she had finished, there was another silence, longer than
the first had been. Then, at last, we heard the first contingent of
Mrs. McMinn's late guests in the hall outside, their voices vibrating with a nervous, feverish exuberance. The noise increased in
volume, and the doorbell rang, not once, but in a series of impa-
tient, staccato sounds. Then the butler opened the door, and all
those young, successful people, the ones with so much blood and
energy in them, came into the room with a rush, filling it completely with movement and bulk and sound.

THE END